Defend
The Valley

By Kenneth W. Jewett

NEW YORK

Defend
The Valley

Ithaca Press
3 Kimberly Drive, Suite B
Dryden, New York 13053 USA
www.IthacaPress.com

Cover Design   Gary Hoffman
Cover Art   Original Oil Painting ***Defend the Valley*** Paul McMillan
Book Design   Gary Hoffman

Editor   Erika Cooper

Manufactured in the United States of America

9 8 7 6 5 4 3 2 1

Library of Congress Cataloging-in-Data Available

Jewett/Kenneth
Historical Fiction/American Fiction/Biographical

ISBN 978-0-9815116-1-0

www.KennethJewett.com

❧ Author's Note ❧

Every attempt has been made to depict events accurately using original historical documentation and reference books. In many cases, the documentations varied in the retelling of the same event. Often, individual accounts were vastly different and, in those cases, the author chose the description most useful for this story. The fictional characters contain additional information that may not be verifiable. Actual historical figures grace the pages of this book. These characters were developed using information gleaned about their individual personalities from the writings they left behind and the observations written about them by their contemporaries.

In addition, the author is grateful to the Rockbridge Regional Library, the Rockbridge Historical Society, The Colonial Williamsburg Foundation, and the Jewett Family of America.

∽ Dedication ∾

This book is dedicated to Ronald Jewett ("Ronald Samuel") and Margaret Samuel Jewett ("Margaret Samuel").

☙ Preface ☙

Each time I visit Colonial Williamsburg, I send my nephew, who shares my love of history, particularly colonial history, a letter written as if I were visiting this city at some momentous point during our struggle for independence. This resulted in growing pressure from my family to expand this into a novel featuring family members and set in the Valley of Virginia, where I had property. My brother even went so far as to provide a list of characters as a way of encouraging me to move ahead with the writing. After retiring from the Air Force following thirty years of service, I ran out of excuses and sat down to write this novel.

Like with the letters my nephew received, I have placed family members in and around real events occurring during the years immediately prior to the opening of the French and Indian War. I have stayed very close to the personalities of several of my family members in writing this work, particularly those of my father, R. Wayne Jewett; my cousin, Esther Jewett; brother, Gregory L. Jewett; his son, my nephew, Philip G. Jewett; my uncle, Ronald Jewett; and my aunt, Margaret Jewett. For the other family members, I stayed close to their personalities when possible, but took more liberties when it would better fit the circumstances of the storyline. I am sure all of my family I have chosen to include will find things about their characters that do, in fact, match their personalities.

Where I have inserted a real historical character, I have tried to remain as close as possible to events they were known to have participated in. The main difference is the insertion of members of the family into the scenes. Edward Jewett, for example, is not based on any historical person though the events swirling around him are as accurate as I was able to make them.

Place names have changed over the years and I have strived to use those correct for the period by referring to the Frye/Jefferson Map of Virginia from 1751. So Rockbridge County, the site of the Jewett family settlement and Bordon's Grant, reverted to being a part of Augusta County; the Maury River reverted to its original name of North River; Washington and Lee University at Lexington reverted to Augusta Academy located at Greenville; and Natural Bridge reverted back to being called simply the rock bridge.

☙ Prologue ❧

Robert Jewett had been born and raised in Rowley, Massachusetts Bay Colony. A descendent of one of the founding families of the town, he had become a successful merchant and Elder and Trustee of the Congregational Church. After giving him three sons and a daughter, his wife Sarah had passed away while the children were still quite young. His spinster aunt, Elizabeth by name but called Bess, moved in and helped him raise his children and keep his household.

Edward was Robert's eldest son and Robert, though reluctant to part with any of his children, sent him off to England to receive a proper education. While there, he met and impressed the Fourth Duke of Bedford, the father of his school friend, James Russell. The Duke secured a Royal Commission for Edward and he spent the next thirty years working his way up through the ranks until he made Colonel. A diplomatic mission to the Dey of Algiers on the North African coast had attracted the attention of King George II so that when he requested retirement, his influential associates arranged for a Royal Grant of 10,000 acres on the frontier of the Virginia Colony, positioning him where they thought he could help in the growing crisis with France. He is a widower, his wife having taken her own life, and without children, so many a young widow and mother with a marrying age daughter in Rowley were anxiously awaiting his return home.

Edward's brother and closest friend Lewis had remained in Rowley, first taking up the trade of wheelwright before opening his own carriage works where he specialized in riding chairs. He married Marie and they had one son, Philip, and adopted another, Joseph, when his parents died of the pox. Marie was an accomplished equestrian and Philip was a bright boy, if more than a little spoiled by his father and grandfather.

Robert's third son was Henry, who had worked for Lewis for a time before chaffing at working for his brother, moved to Boston and worked for his father-in-law as a journeyman carpenter. He and his wife Mary had two children, a daughter, Sarah, and son, Charles. Life in Boston had not been kind to them and they had not prospered as they had hoped.

Robert's daughter, Esther, had remained unmarried and lived with her father and everyone's favorite, Aunt Bess. A handsome woman, there was no real reason for her to have remained unmarried, except perhaps that her older brothers could be intimidating to any suitor. So she contented herself by taking care of her father and Aunt Bess, who would only admit her growing frailty to Esther.

On receiving the land grant, Edward proposed sharing his good fortune with his family, all removing from their comfortable lives in town to the frontier of Virginia. Robert, Lewis, and Henry, after careful consideration, accepted the offer and prepared to remove first to Williamsburg to meet Edward, and then to the frontier. Sending his children ahead to meet their brother, Robert saw to the sale of Edward and Lewis's property in and around Rowley before following with Aunt Bess, Marie, Mary, and his grandchildren.

Tragedy struck soon after departing when Aunt Bess took gravely ill on the voyage, passing away shortly after their arrival in Williamsburg. She had held on just long enough to have her fondest wish fulfilled, to have all "her children" together and with her again. They buried her in the Presbyterian cemetery and sadly prepared to move to the frontier without her.

It was while in Williamsburg that the Governor began calling Robert "Sir Robert," after seeing the family Crest displayed during the funeral services. While this made Robert very uncomfortable, Edward advised them not to correct the Governor as it was harmless enough and could be to their advantage. Robert reluctantly agreed to say no more, but more and more people began applying "Sir" to his name and it was becoming a sore subject with him.

Making their way up the James River and over the Blue Ridge at Indian Trail Gap had not been without difficulty. They had run into both highwaymen and a large, determined force of river pirates before finally getting safely to their land. Their little group had also grown with the addition of two couples indentured to Edward and ten slaves Edward purchased and freed on condition of their signing indentures of seven years labor in return.

By the time they arrived, the Governor had the grant surveyed by the surveyor to the prominent Fairfax family and major in the militia, George Washington, so the family could immediately begin the task of settling in. Their first order of business was building a blockhouse for defense and to serve as a storehouse for their belongings. This was followed by cabins that were later linked by pickets until a little fort existed. The neighbors flocked to this fort during Indian scares and on a few occasions there was open conflict between the two major tribes who used this portion of the Valley of Virginia, the Cherokees to the south and southwest and the more aggressive Shawnee to the west and northwest.

The Cherokee made peace with the Jewett family but the Shawnee had to be dealt with more harshly. It was in one of these clashes that young Joseph died from acting brashly, as young boys will do, and not following Edward's instructions. The drubbing the Jewetts and their neighbors dealt the Shawnee resulted in a form of truce, where the Shawnee agreed not to molest the Jewett women or livestock while they remained in the vicinity of the Jewett fort. They even affixed a name on Edward, "Great Bear," as a result of their combat experience against him.

The frontier experience proved too much for Henry's wife, Mary, and she slowly allowed her fears to take control of her. Following a visit by the Cherokee where they conversed with Lewis, and he earned the name "Wise Owl," she became so agitated that she fled on horseback, with Henry and Charles in tow. Crossing the Blue Ridge in a winter storm was difficult enough when one went prepared, but, in her haste to get away, she was unprepared and perished in the snow. Henry and Charles just avoided a similar fate when Robert and Edward came upon them as they returned from a trip to Williamsburg. Frontier reality caused Henry not to remain a widower for long before he married the young widow, Jenny Thompson, whose husband and sons were killed during the same Indian fight that cost Joseph his life.

Edward, as a result of his Royal Commission, held the responsibility of military advisor to the Colony's Governor, Robert Dinwiddie. With the growing threat posed by the French incursion into the Ohio Country, claimed by both nations, Edward found himself increasingly called away from his lands to Williamsburg. In his absence, Robert proved to be an able garrison commander while Lewis took to running operations outside the little fort. Following the defeat of George Washington's small militia force at Fort Necessity, militia from neighboring counties was called out to help defend the frontier. A sergeant and six militiamen were added to the garrison at the Jewett fort, which was a point of refuge for all the settlers in the immediate vicinity.

Governor Dinwiddie sent Edward along with Major General Edward Braddock as he marched west from Alexandria to expel the French from the Ohio County. Together with George Washington, along as an aide to the General, they were present at his defeat, where Edward was wounded and originally counted among the missing before making his way home with the help of a young man employed as a teamster with the army named Daniel Boone.

❧ Chapter 1 ❧

Alone figure stood on the rise in the pre-dawn light facing toward the Blue Ridge where the morning sun would soon make its appearance. Tall and straight with squared shoulders, his frontier dress could not mask the military bearing.

"Edward," came Robert's soft voice just off his right shoulder. "You wouldn't allow anyone else to be out of the stockade alone at this hour, yet here you are, alone."

"But I'm not alone, father. You're here," came the quiet reply.

To that comeback all Robert could do was smile and nod. Edward had him there and, at the same time, had dodged the real issue of why he had ventured out beyond the walls, exposing himself needlessly should the Shawnee have picked that morning to raid their little fort.

"And then there's Philip as well," added Edward. "Are we speaking loud enough for you, Philip, or do you need to stand a bit closer so you don't miss anything?"

Robert was completely taken by surprise and snapped his head around. Sure enough, standing there about five paces back was his grandson, now looking a bit guilty for having been caught.

"Philip, you're supposed to be on watch in the block-house with your cousin, Charles. You know he can't possibly cover all four directions by himself. Now, off with you."

As Philip turned and walked back toward the block-house shaking his head, the two men heard him talking to himself. "I don't understand how Uncle Edward does that. It's like he has eyes in the back of his head."

Chuckling over his nephew, Edward observed, "You know, there are militiamen on watch with Charles. It's hardly like he's alone up there."

"I know, and Philip does, also. Yet he could hardly argue against the logic, now could he?"

Laughing now, Edward turned toward his father. "That grandson of yours can't stand to miss out on any-thing that involves you."

"Or you," Robert added. "But," now with a bit of sadness in his voice, "after tomorrow he'll be missing out on a lot of what goes on around here."

"True, true." The two men stood in silence for sev-eral minutes, watching the clouds over the mountains re-flect back the first rays of the sun and the mist start to form over the river, out of sight at the base of the moun-tains, until only the upper portions of the Blue Ridge were still visible, clear against the morning sky.

"Are you still having the headaches, son?" asked Robert, breaking the silence.

"Not as often now. Old Black Fish gave me a good bashing with that war club of his."

"I thought I lost you..." his words were choked off. Edward put his arm around his father's shoulders while Robert regained his composure. "Good thing you have such a hard head," he finally was able to get out.

"No, I think Black Fish meant to let me live, probably wouldn't have even bashed me if I wasn't the last of the army still shooting at them. But that's me, too prudent to charge, too stubborn to retreat, though they had us on the run that day."

"Was it as bad as the reports we've heard, a real massacre?"

"It was bad, alright, although I've actually been in tougher scrapes. Had we deployed in open order with the road as our center, I'm convinced we'd have overlapped them, kept them off our flanks, and forced them to come straight at us, like they had to do after the Regulars passed through the Virginians. That's what slowed them, even then, after they knew they'd won and their blood was up. Instead we stayed in the roadway we'd cleared, two ranks facing left, two ranks facing right, and every shot fired at us hit someone. If it missed hitting who they aimed at, it hit another in the back. I'm not even sure they needed to aim, just point and it'd hit one of us. Some were aiming, or maybe it was the French, because a lot of the officers and sergeants went down early."

"In Europe we form squares and fight that way, but because both armies are doing the same thing, it evens things out a bit. That's what General Braddock never understood. Fighting Indians in the deep woods is different, more intense. You hear their yells, see their muzzle blasts and smoke, but rarely see them. Mostly all you see is movement, that is, until they have you on the run."

"How well I remember…" Robert said, letting his voice trail off as he became lost in his own thoughts.

Edward turned and studied his father's face for a few moments. "But you know all this, don't you, father? Yet you never talk about it."

Choosing his words carefully, Robert began his story in a low, hushed voice, "I know and remember too well how it is. You were just four that winter when they called out the militia from the eastern towns to help guard the villages on what was then the frontier. Still is, if truth be told. And it was my misfortune to be sent to the aid of Deerfield. What a peaceful sounding name for a place filled with such horror."

"Were you there the night the Iroquois raided the settlement, father?"

"Luckily, no. We were on our way, trudging through deep snow and very cold temperatures, when we came upon a farm a couple of miles from town. The sergeant wanted to keep going, even though it was dark, but the captain said no. He didn't want to alarm the guard if we approached the stockade after dark, so he quartered himself in the farmhouse with the Dutch farmer's family while the rest of us made do in the barn. It was three or four in the morning. I was the sentry, trying to stay warm, when I saw light on the horizon toward where we knew Deerfield to be. Thought I heard a few shots, too, but that could have just been tree limbs breaking off in the cold. I roused the sergeant, pointed out what I saw, and he had us prepared to march even before getting the captain up. Off we went at the quick step, only we got there too late…" His voice trailed off and Edward saw the horror in his father's eyes, still there after all these many years.

Composing himself once again, Robert continued, "There wasn't much we could do in the village, so we set off after the Indians, leaving a corporal and three men to bury the dead as best they could in the frozen ground. The captain, he was intent on catching up to them and giving them a good thrashing. That's what he said we'd do, 'Give them a good thrashing.' Led us straight into an ambuscade, he did. If it wasn't for that sergeant, I wouldn't be here today. He didn't think much of the captain's ways, so he had us in the rear squad deploy in open order on both sides of the trail. When the Iroquois sprang their trap, those that survived fell back through us. We managed to slow the Iroquois down and then became the rear guard, holding them off for hours as we slowly retreated back toward Deerfield."

Pausing and looking up at Edward, he finished his narrative, "You know, that captain didn't save one of those poor people the Iroquois had carried off, only managed to get himself and a lot of other young men killed." He stood there for a few moments, shaking his head.

"Those of us that lived through it never spoke about it again and this is more than I've ever said about it. Yet even though that was over fifty years ago, I can still see it as if it were yesterday." Now putting his arm around Edward's shoulders, he looked his son in the eyes, "So, now you know that if you want to talk about it, I'm here and I'll understand because I've seen it, also."

They stood there, arm in arm, watching now as the sun cleared the tops of the Blue Ridge and the mist rose even higher until it finally blotted out the sun. As they turned to walk slowly back through the fog to the fort, Robert asked, "So, what do you think of that new long rifle you're carrying these days?"

"Oh, it's pretty good. I assume it was Black Fish who took my short rifle. All I do know is when young Boone found me, it was gone. Once his cousins had me well enough to get around some, I bought this from their local gunsmith and then we headed home. They've started making them long like this in Pennsylvania, a full foot longer than my short rifle, but it is well balanced and will serve the purpose."

They now entered the little fortified settlement, for it was hardly a fort. It was really just a street with three houses on a side, a blockhouse on one end of the street and a large cabin for the laborers on the other, with ten foot pickets between the houses to ward off attacks. It was September and they were still taking their meals together under a tent awning erected near the large laborers' cabin.

"It would be nice to build some regular houses instead of remaining in these log cabins. There are some real houses being built now, mostly of stone though some frame and even I hear a few brick further north," Edward observed.

"Now, let's not forget we're at war right now, son. We're far safer and better able to defend ourselves and this Valley just as we are. It may not be much, certainly nothing in keeping with your wealth, but we're all together and it's safer," cautioned Robert.

"Yes, but I'd like to see the day…" Edward and Robert joined the others already gathered for breakfast, just waiting on them to take their places as no one ate before Robert said grace.

The tables were simply planks set atop barrels and for seating they used three-legged stools Lewis and Henry had made just for this purpose. In addition to the extended Jewett family, their indentured servants, black and white, were also gathered, along with the miller, Mister Agner, and the soldiers not then on guard in the blockhouse, against surprise attack. Under Robert's influence, they had become a contented group with seldom a serious disagreement between them.

Robert and his sons, Edward, Lewis, and Henry, used the time over breakfast to discuss the agenda for the day, agreeing on the tasks to be done and who would do what. Joining them for these discussions were Miles, who acted as their farm manager, and Sam, the former slave who was now serving as foreman for the other former slaves who provided the bulk of the labor necessary to run such a large landholding. There was much to be done to be ready for the winter they all knew was coming, even if today was starting off rather warm.

Once the day's activities were all assigned, Edward moved over to where his sister Esther was chatting with Jenny, Henry's new wife, and Marie, Lewis's wife. "So tell me, sister, our Mister Agner seems to have grown fond of good castile soap more than I remember him to have been, and he's even combing and tying his hair into a neat queue these days. What do you suppose has gotten into him?"

"Oh, has he? I'm sure I haven't noticed."

"I think I know," interjected Marie, playfully. "I think he's trying to catch someone's eye."

"You know, I think you could be right," Jenny added, scarcely able to control her giggles. "But which one of us do you suppose he's trying for?" With that, neither could control themselves any longer and both laughed outright.

"Now stop that, both of you. Isn't it bad enough I have to put up with teasing from my three brothers? I certainly don't need the two of you joining them!"

"There, there, dear sister, let the ladies have their fun. After all, they're laughing at Mister Agner, not you. Though I must say, cleaned up and wearing decent clothes, he does make a fine figure of a man," said Edward teasingly.

"Well, now that the three of you have attracted the attention of everyone in the fort, I guess I'll just go and start cleaning up the dishes." As Esther rose, she turned so as not to look in Mister Agner's direction, hoping he didn't notice the color she felt in her cheeks.

Through all of the commotion, Philip sat in his usual place, across from his grandfather and uncle, quiet, thoughtful, not his normal talkative self. The combination of having been caught this morning and contemplating what was in store for him tomorrow had him lost in his own thoughts.

☙ Chapter 2 ❧

With breakfast over, Edward and Robert walked to Edward's cabin where they had arranged to meet with their white indentured servants, Aaron and his wife Betty, Miles and his wife Mattie. Aaron had effectively become Edward's manservant and traveled with him, seeing to his needs. Betty kept Edward's house and cooked for him, such as in the winter when they had to dispense with the communal meals. Miles had become a good farm manager and also drilled the laborers at arms. Since he was a Gunner in the Royal Navy, he was well suited to this and had overcome his initial aversion to arming the former slaves. Mattie was more the scullery maid and took care of Edward's laundry. All had become like members of the family, so Edward and Robert found what they were about to do difficult, or, rather, the potential outcome of what they were about to do.

With everyone assembled in Edward's cabin, Edward looked to Robert before beginning, "As you know, Aaron's term of indenture expired several months ago and Miles, yours expires here next month. Aaron, I signed your papers and gave them over to you before I left with the army's advance. Miles, here are your papers."

"But, sir, my term won't expire for several weeks yet," protested Miles.

Edward had never heard of an indentured servant arguing with his master over an early release. He signaled his surprise to Robert, "I am well aware of that, but as far as we are concerned," Edward motioned toward Robert who nodded his agreement, "you have fulfilled your obligation to us. Here, too, are bills of sale I've signed transferring fifty acres of the former Thompson homestead to each of you. These still need to be filed with the County Clerk before you'll receive full title to the property, but you are free to sell them or do with them as you will. Also, here are documents showing you each own the horse provided you by Colonel Byrd, should anyone question you about them."

Robert interrupted at this point, stating, "As for the suit of clothes my son owes you, I have them for you in the blockhouse, which I believe completes his obligation under the terms of the indenture."

The four servants sat in stunned silence for several moments before Aaron spoke up, "Sir, does this mean you are asking us to leave? And what's to become of our wives? I had planned on remaining here until her term was up, even though that's not for another nine months."

Miles nodded in agreement, adding, "Six more months for my Mattie."

Robert nodded to Edward who, after a pause, began to explain, "Here are Betty and Mattie's papers as well, and their new sets of clothes are at my father's cabin in the care of Esther. With this, you are all free to go as you will."

As stunned as they had been before, this shocked all four of them. When they had entered the cabin just a few minutes ago, they had all been bonded into service. Now they were all free of those bonds of indenture. It was Betty who regained her composure first.

"Sir, are you telling us you want us to leave? We've nothing prepared and winter will be on us soon."

"Let me explain, as I'm afraid my son has left too much unsaid," interrupted Robert. "Since General Braddock's defeat, we've known the Indians would be let loose on these frontier outposts. Thus far we've escaped attack, but they've already begun further north and west. Edward and I decided that, in fairness to you who have done so much and been so faithful to us, we would give you the opportunity to go back east, back where it will be safer, should you choose to do so. Nothing more sinister than that."

"Does that also mean we'd be welcome to remain here?" asked Aaron, tentatively. "We've come to think of this as our home. There's nothing back east for us."

"Of course, Aaron, and you too, Miles, but that needs to be of your choosing. I could not in good conscience force you to remain with the danger being what it has become," replied Edward. "And by giving you your papers now, you can be safely east of the Blue Ridge before Betty has her child. As for the others, they are at the beginning of their terms of indenture and I cannot afford to free them of their obligations at this time. You four are another matter, being at the end of your terms."

Robert and Edward then saw Betty nudge Aaron and, when he demurred, she whispered, "If you don't ask him, I will!"

"What Betty is wondering, sirs, is, well that is, if you don't have any objections, we'd like to stay on with you as we have been, only paid for our services, of course."

First looking to Robert and seeing his assent, Edward responded, "I'll pay £12 per year for the two of you and include thirty extra acres, deeding you eighty acres total. The same offer applies to you, Miles and Mattie. And Aaron, I owe you £3 for these past three months." He handed three coins to the astonished Aaron.

To own eighty acres, retain their current comfortable cabin, and have a paying position as well was more temptation than Miles could resist so he and Mattie quickly agreed to the terms offered. The four thanked the two Jewett men as they left to go about their business.

As Robert and Edward sat talking about how well the meeting had gone, they heard Charles's voice as he ran from the blockhouse, already calling for Edward before reaching the door.

"Uncle Edward, Uncle Edward, come quickly. There are riders coming and they look like soldiers," he panted as his uncle opened the cabin door.

Robert and Edward reached the gate in time to see a squad of mounted soldiers descend from the ridge, losing sight of them behind the wooded creek bed.

"Now, what do you suppose this is all about?" Robert asked of no one in particular as the rest of the family gathered behind him.

"Well, father," replied Edward. "I know of only one man who rides as effortlessly as that big man out in front. I'd say it looks like I'm about to be engaged in more military business for the Colony."

Robert looked at his eldest son, some concern showing on his face. He didn't think Edward sufficiently recovered from his head injury, but he held his tongue.

Edward could be stubborn, after all. No, he'd just have to watch and try to gently persuade Edward to continue on light duty.

By now, the group of riders, nine in all, had crossed the creek and were riding up to the gate, the big man far in front of the others.

"Colonel Jewett, I am so glad to see you. We thought you lost on the Monongahela and were very much relieved when we received your letter."

"Colonel Washington, welcome! This is a pleasant surprise! I had supposed you too busy in Williamsburg, reforming your regiment, to visit us on the frontier."

Tossing his reins to his orderly, Colonel Washington dismounted and the two tall men clasped hands and slapped shoulders in a warm welcome. By now most of the family had gathered at the gate and Edward waited while George greeted first Robert, then his brothers. When he came to Sarah, Edward had to smile. George first paused as he recognized her, but she was no longer the pretty fifteen-year-old, rather a beautiful young woman of eighteen. He bowed deeply, putting his best foot forward, while she feigned indifference.

"Miss Sarah, what a pleasure to see you again."

"Oh? I wouldn't have thought you cared after having avoided us for so long."

The rebuke left George a bit tongue tied and, after an awkward pause, he went on to greet Esther and Marie before walking with Robert and his sons to Edward's cabin.

"So, George," began Edward. "What news have you from Williamsburg? I assume the blame for our loss on the Monongahela is being heaped upon my shoulders, there, in Philadelphia, and in London. I should think you've brought a letter announcing I'm to stand before a Board of Inquiry."

Robert's face turned to concern for he had been so relieved his son had survived he had not even considered what the consequences could be for a senior Regular officer following such a defeat as General Braddock's, especially as the General did not live to take the blame himself.

George looked surprised, then, turning to Robert, asked, "Has he not recovered from the blow to his head?" He continued now to Edward, "Just the opposite. Your coolness under fire and handling of the rear guard has been touted. Your reputation is not only unsullied, it has been greatly enhanced, as has my own. And as soon as you're able and up to traveling, Governor Dinwiddie asks that you call upon him in Williamsburg."

Edward was both pleased and relieved, but now a little confused. "If you did not come to take me away in irons, what does bring you so far from Williamsburg and your new responsibilities, not that we aren't glad for your visit, mind you?"

George's face, which had been smiling, turned serious, "I need your help, Colonel. I am to organize and command the Virginia Regiment and then to defend the Valley from French and Indian incursions." Looking a little embarrassedly toward Robert, Lewis, and Henry, he continued, "I know so little about how to run such a large military organization. I'm afraid I've been entrusted with too much responsibility."

"Yes, and placed in a situation with no hope of being successful. You can no more stop the Shawnee and Iroquois from raiding the Valley than the King and Parliament can bring General Braddock back from the dead. But that's for later. First, let's talk organization, administration, and discipline. I daresay you already have the confidence and demeanor necessary to command."

As the two military men settled into their deep discussion, Robert, Lewis, and Henry politely excused themselves, having nothing to contribute to that conversation. They had barely closed the door behind them when Philip appeared. He spent the rest of the day with his father and grandfather. It didn't matter what they were doing. He just wanted to be near them and they understood, keeping him close and including him in their conversations.

Betty brought the two Colonels dinner and later supper, lighting the candles as the early fall evening fell, while Aaron kept them supplied with paper, ink, and sharp quills. Edward drew diagrams or pointed out passages from one or another of his books and George made copious notes.

After Betty cleared supper from the table, Edward suggested they stretch their legs, "We've been at this for hours now. What say we pick it back up in the morning, assuming you can stay another day, and take a walk around our little settlement?"

As they strolled, George continued to ask questions from their earlier discussions, though at a more relaxed pace. From the blockhouse, they could see Sarah and her stepsister Rebecca standing with one of the militiamen in front of Henry's cabin.

"Your niece is a very beautiful woman, Colonel. Is she really as angry with me as her greeting this morning would indicate?"

"Oh, probably not, and then again, maybe more so. It's so hard to tell with young women and it can change so quickly. I do know she was quite smitten with you when you first helped us locate this grant. Then she was quite upset that you never came courting her afterward."

"I was too distracted, what with my late brother's affairs to set in order, dealing with his widow, and then there were my duties in the militia. You know, I haven't had much time to think of my own life or of marriage..." His voice trailed off and a blush rose in his cheeks as he watched Sarah, taking in her graceful movements and trying to discern her expressions from this distance. After several minutes, he continued, "Do you suppose, or, rather, do you have any objections, to me courting your niece?"

"Are you sure, what with all those rich widows back east, that you'd be happy to take a frontier girl for a wife? Why even after the blow to my head I can still recall you talking rather fondly of a Miss Sally Fairfax."

Now embarrassed, George struggled for words, "Yes, well, that is, I do know Miss Sally, have for years..."

Edward could no longer stand George's discomfort, "George, you fall in and out of love too easily. Now, if you would like to spend some time getting to know Sarah, you'll have to ask her father, though I see no reason for him to object and I certainly have no objections. In the meantime, we have more work to do tomorrow, so what do you say we get a good night's sleep and start fresh in the morning?"

As they walked back to Edward's cabin, Jenny came out to usher Sarah and Rebecca into the cabin and shoo the militiaman away from her door. That was when George noticed Esther rise from where she had been sitting talking to Mattie, directly across the little street from where Sarah and Rebecca had been, say goodnight to Mattie, and walk toward the cabin she kept with her father. He was impressed, if not a little intimidated, with how well the whole family looked out for the children, even if Sarah was hardly a child anymore.

Reaching the door, George's orderly appeared out of the shadows. "Excuse me, Colonels, but," turning to George, "the Captain wanted his orders for tomorrow."

Turning to Edward, "Do you suppose we should take care of it in the morning?"

"I'd say so. Then you'll be free to leave whenever you need to knowing it has been taken care of properly."

"Yes, quite." Turning to the orderly, "Tell the Captain to have the Sergeant and guard assigned to this post assembled at dawn," looking quickly around for a suitable location, "here, in front of Colonel Jewett's cabin. The Captain will need to post my escort in their places. Understood?"

"Yes, sir, I'll tell him, sir. Good night, sirs."

❧ Chapter 3 ❧

Philip had slept poorly, rolling and tossing most of the night and getting up twice. He was excited, yet nervous; filled with anticipation, yet dread; happy yet sad. He had been able to spend time with his father and grandfather yesterday. He was really going to miss them. He also had hoped to spend time with Uncle Edward, only the arrival of Colonel Washington had spoiled those plans. Instead, Uncle Edward had spent most of the day and the night locked in his cabin with the Colonel, going over things Philip could only imagine. He had tried to interrupt once, but Aaron had answered the door with instructions the two Colonels were not to be disturbed.

It was half an hour before first light when his father had come to wake him for his normal watch, only to find Philip already awake and dressed. Grandfather and Charles were waiting for him at the blockhouse door just like every morning and both greeted him like today was nothing special. As he took his place inside one of the shooting loops and tried to see through the darkness, he wondered if it was his imagination or had his grandfather's hug this morning been longer, firmer than most mornings?

And was it really sadness he saw in his grandfather's eyes when the hug was over and they were turning to enter the blockhouse?

Time moved slowly as the pre-dawn light finally allowed them to see. That's when the real watching began. Just like they did every morning, Charles and Philip each took a wall while two of the militiamen took the other two walls and their grandfather moved around from one to the other, all looking for any sign there might be hostilities that day. Today was like so many others, nothing moving out beyond the little fort except the birds and deer.

At sunrise, with no activity to report from the watch, they were relieved by four of the soldiers who were part of Colonel Washington's escort. When they left the blockhouse, the two militiamen quickly formed with the other four behind the sergeant while Philip followed his grandfather and Charles to where the rest of the family had gathered. Philip moved closer to where his Uncle Edward was in serious discussion with Sam and Miles.

"Now, Sam, if you're sure that's what you all want to do, it will be fine by me," Edward was saying, although Philip had no idea what it was Sam wanted to do.

"Yes, sir, Colonel, sir, and it wasn't Mister Miles's idea, either. The others came to me and asked if I'd take it up with Mister Miles and yourself."

"Miles, are you alright with this?"

"Yes, sir, Colonel. I think it would be kind of fun. And these fellows have worked very hard. They deserve to be able to show off a little bit in front of our guest."

"Alright, but not until Colonel Washington is done addressing the militiamen. We don't want to interfere with his official duties. Well, don't just stand there grinning, go and get ready!"

As Edward turned around, Philip asked, "What is it Sam and Miles want to do, Uncle Edward?"

"My, my, you do manage to hear about anything worth hearing within the Valley, now don't you?" Then, patting Philip on the shoulder, "You'll see soon enough. Now, let's watch Colonel Washington, shall we?"

Philip was more disappointed by his uncle's response than he normally would have been. While he was curious about what they were talking about, he really only asked as a way to try and get his uncle to talk to him. After all, there wasn't to be many more opportunities.

His thoughts were interrupted as the militia sergeant called his detail to attention and put them through their morning drill for Colonel Washington. They had improved while being at the Jewett fort, and not just because of the critical eye of a Colonel with thirty years in the Royal Army. There had been a healthy amount of competition that had contributed to their improvement as well.

Colonel Washington was pleased, and said so, then looked to Edward and nodded, indicating his pleasure with what he saw. Not only were they proficient in their drill, but they were uniformly dressed, clean, well-equipped, and generally looked every inch like soldiers. He then invited them to stand at their ease while he addressed them.

Philip was only half listening to Colonel Washington, hearing something about reforming the Virginia Regiment; how they were to be absorbed into the regiment and would only be dismissed from service if they could show they owned more than fifty acres of property or were married, sergeants excepted; and how they would remain here as the duty he had been given was to defend the Valley and frontier of Virginia from incursions by the French and their allied Indians. Mostly Philip was lost to his own thoughts, at least until he caught sight of Miles moving forward with their laborers, the former slaves, all under arms and dressed in their finest clothes.

When Colonel Washington finished his address, he turned the task of enrolling these militiamen into the Virginia Regiment to the Captain, whose company they would join. That was when Edward walked up to him and, in a voice meant for all to hear, "Colonel, would you be so kind as to review our own little band of defenders as they do their morning drill?"

Colonel Washington concurred but the look on his face when he saw Miles acting as sergeant for eight armed black men was one of surprise touched with confusion. That look turned to amazement and admiration as he watched them perform the drill flawlessly, somewhat better than the impressive performance he had just seen from the militiamen. When they finished, he congratulated them on their performance and shook Miles by the hand as a show of how impressed he was with them.

Waiting for just this moment, Esther announced breakfast was ready, causing all to start moving toward the awning at the other end of the little street. As they moved, Philip found himself, quite by accident for a change, walking next to his uncle and Colonel Washington. Edward was explaining how these were former slaves, now bonded men for a seven year indenture, and that he had no problem with them being under arms, something that concerned George and the eastern planters a great deal. He then put his hand on Philip's shoulder and Philip braced for what he thought would be his uncle asking him to move out of hearing. Instead, what he heard was:

"Philip, be so good as to join me in my cabin immediately after breakfast this morning. I want to speak with you in private before you go."

Philip felt his spirits soar as he quickly responded, "Yes, sir." He would have the chance he wanted to talk with his uncle, alone, before he had to leave.

Breakfast was a blur to him as he ate almost automatically while focusing on all the things he wanted to say to his uncle. He tried to put them into some logical order, but the harder he tried, the more things he thought of that he wanted to say and they all became just a jumble again. Then people started getting up from the tables and he heard his uncle speaking to Colonel Washington.

"Colonel, if you would excuse me. We can resume our discussions later. Right now I have important business with my nephew that can't wait."

Colonel Washington nodded in the affirmative and Philip thought he saw him catching up to Uncle Henry, though he couldn't be sure as he matched Uncle Edward's brisk, purposeful strides toward his cabin. By putting him before Colonel Washington, Philip felt very special indeed. Before he was ready with his thoughts, they were out of the bright early autumn sunshine and into the dim cabin and Uncle Edward was offering him a seat.

"Philip, I understand what you must be feeling right now. I know what it feels like to leave your home and family while still so young, probably better than anyone else here. I was only two years older than you are now when I left for England, not to return home to live for thirty-five years."

Philip found his voice very consoling, comforting. It no longer mattered that he couldn't think of how to tell his uncle all those things, he knew now that Uncle Edward already understood.

They sat for nearly an hour, Edward doing most of the talking, before a light knock at the door interrupted them. Lewis had come to tell Philip it was time. They

stood and again Philip felt the awkwardness of not knowing just what to say next. And again, Uncle Edward rescued him by reaching for something in his desk before
turning to Philip.

"Philip, I want you to look after something for me,"
Edward said as he handed the object to his nephew.

Philip turned the silver case over to see the family
crest engraved between the initials "P" and "J." The top
slid off the case to reveal a small ink bottle in the center
flanked by two holes, each filled with a short quill pen. It
was a traveling writing set and it had his initials on it, not
Uncle Edward's. He looked up to see both his father and
uncle smiling at him. Overcome, he gave his uncle a hug.
Although he tried to turn away to compose himself, his
uncle held him close until he once again gained his voice
and could thank his uncle. Then he followed his father out
to the little street, leaving his uncle to his thoughts.

Philip said his goodbyes to everyone, saving his
mother for last. Then he climbed into the riding chair next
to his grandfather and they, accompanied by his father,
left the little fort he knew as home.

At first they rode in silence, which was fine with
Philip as to speak would have been very hard and would
have revealed his deep feelings about leaving home. It
wasn't long, though, before his grandfather started telling
him of the family he would be boarding with and Philip
began to feel better.

"They are an interesting older couple and their son
is to be your teacher. The father is an Elder in the Greenville Presbyterian Church. Lewis, I did tell you they were
building a stone church to serve both as a place of wor-
ship and sanctuary in case of attack, right? Yes, where was
I, oh, yes, he's a wonderful man, if a bit forgetful. He absolutely delights in gaming. Don't make such a face, Lewis. I

didn't mean gambling, but diversions, like chess only less thoughtful, more to draw a laugh. And his wife, poor woman, has her hands full reminding him of almost everything as he is quite forgetful, or did I say that already? Anyway, she is quite educated herself and reads quite a lot. We are really lucky to have them agree to put you up."

They chatted as they rode toward Greenville where the Augusta Academy would prepare Philip for enrollment at the College of William and Mary in a couple of years. It wasn't long before Robert even had Philip laughing at the antics of his new host. Robert had taken finding a good situation for Philip very seriously and had spent several weeks in Greenville getting to know the Samuels, which was their name, until he was comfortable entrusting them with his grandson. In the process, Robert had become great friends with Ronald Samuel, it helping that they were near the same age. Their newfound friendship was why the Samuels had agreed to take in a student boarder, not having done so in the past.

They had covered nearly two-thirds the distance when they stopped and ate the dinner Marie had packed for them, sitting in the shade of a chestnut tree by a brook of fresh, clean water.

"You know," said Lewis. "Your cousin Charles will join you at the Academy next year, and you will be home for visits regularly, so you shouldn't be too lonely for us, at least not for long. And…"

"Isn't that Charles now, and Henry, riding hard toward us?" interrupted Robert just as the sounds of hoof beats reached them.

Henry and Charles reined up by Robert's riding chair and Charles started things off by blurting out, "Indians were spotted and we've been sent to ride the rest of the way with you, to protect you."

"Henry, what's this?" demanded Robert.

"Melinda and Caitlyn Rice arrived at the fort after you'd gone. Four men had come to their cabin and told them Indians had been spotted in the vicinity. Edward sent us to ride with you the rest of the way to Greenville and then back again, just in case, while he investigates the report."

"She didn't know these four men?" asked Lewis.

"That's just it. They were strangers and Jim Rice was off on the patrol with Tom McCrary. Melinda did right coming to the fort the way she did, only Edward isn't so sure of the report of Indians. If there are Indians, what's happened to Jim and Tom?"

❧ Chapter 4 ❧

When Edward left to have his private talk with Philip, George caught up with Henry who was walking with Robert and Lewis. While his shyness had improved over the past three years, he still found this conversation to be awkward, even more so with Robert standing there, listening.

"Mister Henry, I was wondering if, well, would you have any objections to, I mean would it be alright…"

Henry reveled in the moment of having the young and now celebrated Colonel Washington finding it so difficult to ask him a question. His good nature, however, just couldn't let the young man's difficulty go on any longer than a moment or two, "I think what you're asking, Colonel, is if I would grant my permission for you to court my daughter. Is that the general idea?"

"Yes, sir, it is. She is quite the young lady now and I have, I think you'll agree, established my character. I have some property and stand to inherit more…"

"Yes, yes, enough of your qualifications, we know them all too well. I see no harm in you courting my daughter, though I must warn you, she may be of another mind altogether. She's said some harsh things about you when you failed to visit or write her and now you show up here asking permission to court her. Good luck to you, for I think you'll need it"

Thanking Henry, George nodded to Robert and Lewis before retracing his steps to the awning. There he found Sarah clearing the breakfast dishes with her back to him. He came up behind her and softly called her name. When she spun around, she was right against him and fairly trapped between the large young man and the table. The closeness caused her to blush in the awkward silence that followed.

"Ah, Sarah, there you are. Mattie is looking for those dishes to wash, so best get them to her." Esther's unexpected interruption gave both young people a start.

"Yes, Aunt Esther, right away," said Sarah as she quickly turned back to the table, picked up the dishes, and moved to take them around the back of the cabin. George took half a step back to permit her to pass.

As she passed the corner of the cabin, out of sight of George, Jenny was waiting for her and sat her down on the bench by the cabin's back door for a chat while Esther took care of matters with George.

"Colonel Washington, I assume you received my brother's permission to court Sarah as I saw you talking to him, nearly as red faced as you are right now. All of that aside, if he or my other brothers saw you place Sarah at such a disadvantage as I just witnessed, I daresay you would be more than just embarrassed. No, just let me finish," Esther said, shaking her finger at him. "We're not some poor, frontier family you can impress with your fancy title into handing over our young women's reputations without so much as a second thought. No, sir," she held up her hand to silence his protests. "You may not have meant anything by it, but I'm here to tell you that if you wish to remain welcome here, you will conduct yourself as a gentleman should. Now, sit down there and, assuming Sarah still wants to talk with you, she'll sit here, across the table as is proper. And don't think for a moment that I'm not watching!"

Having delivered her rebuke, she spun around and disappeared around the corner of the cabin before George was able to say a word in his defense. He stood looking down at his boot as it made circles in the dirt, wondering if he should go now or wait. A soft voice resolved his dilemma.

"Colonel, I believe you wanted to talk to me?" asked Sarah as she approached and took her place across the table from George.

"Why, yes, I do, miss," stammered George as he sat opposite her, just as Esther had instructed. He also knew that, while he couldn't see her, she was nearby keeping a close eye on him, and his face reddened again.

They sat talking for nearly an hour, her blond hair, blue eyes, and bright smile captivating him. Then Henry and Jenny came to the awning to tell them it was time to say their goodbyes to Philip as he left for the Academy. The four of them walked together, George walking with his hands clasped behind his back so as not to even give the appearance of impropriety in front of Sarah's parents.

After saying their goodbyes, George returned to Edward's cabin to continue their discussions from the day before while Sarah went with Esther and Jenny to the cabin Esther kept for her father. Jenny could hardly contain herself until the door was firmly closed behind them.

"Well, how did it go? He is quite tall and handsome and I hear he's got a fine estate back east," said Jenny, fairly bubbling.

"Yes, and I think he's been a bit too used to young women coming after him, if you ask me. So, Sarah, did you forgive him for ignoring you these past three years?"

"Well, not exactly. He was really quite charming and not nearly as painfully shy as before, though he is still a little shy. I just don't know what I would say if he were to propose marriage. I still haven't completely forgiven him slighting me like that."

Esther and Jenny looked at each other before Jenny took Sarah's hand, "Just remember, Sarah, marriage is different for a woman. You should be looking for someone who can provide for you, and that is something Colonel Washington can certainly do. What you don't want is someone looking for you to provide for them, what with your family's good fortune to be of more than comfortable means. Should it get that far with Colonel Washington, you must rely on your father and grandfather's judgment as to whether this would be a good marriage for you or not. It will be a little different for Rebecca when the young men start to court her as she will have no estate for them to covet."

Esther sat nodding as Jenny explained these things to her stepdaughter. They remained locked in discussion, later joined by Jenny's daughter, Rebecca, until it was time to prepare dinner. The older women tried to explain to the younger women the ways of men, courting, and marriage.

Edward and George joined the settlement for the communal dinner, George carefully choosing his seat opposite Sarah. Charles, taking his normal place next to Sarah, thought this was a grand thing, to have the Colonel's undivided attention, or so it was in his mind. He repeatedly interrupted the young couple's conversation with questions about being a soldier and the Braddock campaign that his Uncle Edward refused to discuss, before finding a shared experience in sea voyages, his from Boston to Williamsburg and George's to the Bahamas and back when he took his ailing brother there in hopes of improving his health. Esther and Jenny couldn't help but share a chuckle as they watched the animated Charles intrude on the young couple.

Just as dinner was ending, the blockhouse sent word of two women approaching the fort, unaccompanied. The soldiers immediately rushed to their posts in the blockhouse, the laborers to theirs manning the shooting loops in their cabin, while the others followed the two Colonels to the gate.

Arriving within earshot of the fort and seeing people gathered at the gate, Melinda Rice raised the Indian alarm, which sent most everyone else to their defensive positions. Robert, Edward and George, along with Esther and Jenny, remained at the gate to receive Melinda and her daughter, Caitlyn.

"Four men came by the cabin and warned us of an Indian raid, saying we'd better head for safety as quick as we could. Jim is out on the afternoon patrol with Tom Mc-Crary so, not knowing what to do, we came here as fast as we could."

"You did the right thing, Melinda," Edward assured her. "Now, tell me, did you know these men?"

"No, they were strangers. Each was well armed and well mounted and they had several packhorses with them. I didn't stop to count how many but there were at least four. I just took them to be hunters heading down the Virginia Road for the fall hunt."

Edward had heard enough. Calling for Aaron, Henry, and Charles, he sent Aaron to saddle his horse while Esther and Jenny took Melinda and Caitlyn to Robert's cabin. Turning to Henry, he said, "I need you and Charles to ride after father and Lewis. This may turn out to be nothing, but it'll be better if there are five of you instead of three. You'll need to ride hard, both to catch them and to avoid being caught yourselves in case there are Shawnee about. Go on to Greenville and ride back with them after they've seen Philip settled in."

"And what do you intend to do?" asked George as Henry and Charles ran to saddle their horses.

"I'm going to ride over to the Rice homestead and try to find out what's going on. I'd like to find Jim and Tom, too, if I can. If there are Shawnee about, they could be in trouble."

"Alone, I suppose?"

"Well, Colonel Washington, normally I would take one or both of my brothers along, but both are otherwise employed. I suppose this is one where a lone rider will just have to be enough."

"Nonsense, the Governor has given me the mission to defend the Valley. I'll leave the Captain and my orderly here and accompany you with my escort. That increases our response from one to eight and I like those odds better." Turning to his orderly, he barked, "Order the escort to horse."

The eight horsemen quickly covered the clearing to the creek, splashed through it and up the taller rise beyond before disappearing over its rounded summit, heading west toward the Rice homestead. The Rice cabin sat between the ridge beyond, forming the boundary of the Jewett Grant, and the Virginia Road. It was a fair distance of a couple of miles, but the horses were fresh so they were at the cabin in short order. Approaching cautiously, they saw Tom helping Jim onto a stool in the cabin yard, their horses loose and in Jim's cornfield.

"Colonel, am I ever glad to see you," Tom hailed them as they approached.

"What happened here, Tom? Is Jim hurt badly?" Edward dismounted and moved toward his neighbors to assess the situation, his eyes taking in the Rice's belongings scattered about the cabin yard.

"We were coming back from our patrol after not seeing anything unusual when we saw horses around the cabin here and men carrying things out from the cabin to packhorses. We let out a shout and spurred our horses when two of them took shots at us. Jim's horse threw him and he landed flat on his back…"

"And it hurts something awful, but I can move my legs so I'll be alright," interrupted Jim, with some irritation apparent in his voice. It was like they were talking about the dead. "Who's that you have with you, not that I mind seeing soldiers at a time like this?"

"This is Colonel Washington and his escort. So tell us, what happened to the intruders?"

"They headed southwest, I suspect to make for the Virginia Road. They haven't been gone ten minutes."

"Tom, can you get Jim to the blockhouse? Good, we'll go after those men. Move easy, Jim. If you are hurting like that you may be injured worse than you think."

With that, Edward nodded to George and the little cavalcade rode off quickly toward the southwest, following a fairly clear trail made by nearly a dozen horses. When they reached the Virginia Road, they halted.

"There's been just enough traffic on this road that I can't tell if they headed toward the Carolinas or toward Maryland," observed George to Edward.

"Melinda thought they were heading south, but there's no assurance of that. With packhorses, they can't be too far ahead of us, whichever way they went. Loan me one of your horse pistols. If you take three men and go toward Maryland, I'll take the other three toward the Carolinas. The first to spot them fires one shot to bring the others. Agreed?"

"Agreed." Handing Edward one of his pistols, George signaled to three of his escort to follow him and off they went to the northeast.

Riding hard, Edward led the other three soldiers to the southwest. They had only gone a few hundred yards when, clearing a rise, Edward saw the four mounted men with six packhorses in the road ahead. He halted and fired the pistol into the air, which drew an immediate response from the four men as they turned and fired on Edward.

ᖇᖇ Chapter 5 ᖇᖇ

"**W**e should go back," Philip said emphatically on hearing there was a report of Indians in the Valley. "Uncle Edward will need us."

"Not so fast, young man," Henry got the words out before Robert or Lewis even had a chance to protest. "Your Uncle Edward was very clear when he told Charles and me to make sure you got to Greenville and your father and grandfather made it home safely. I'll not have you showing up back home and getting me in trouble with your Uncle Edward. I'm not that stupid!"

Everyone laughed at this, everyone except Philip who, while he wanted to go to school, didn't necessarily want to leave home to do it. The issue settled as quickly as it was brought up, the five of them mounted and continued on their way down the Virginia Road toward Greenville, now just six or so miles to the northeast.

Once there, Robert led them right to the Samuel cabin. It was a double cabin, a story–and-a-half cabin to the left and a smaller single story cabin to the right, joined by a covered passage. The doors led off this passage into the two cabins, immediately opposite each other. A woman about Robert's age was standing in the passage to greet them, a large, warm smile on her face.

"Good afternoon, Margaret, how good it is to see you again," called Robert as they dismounted and moved toward her.

"Robert, I've been expecting you most of the afternoon and so hoped nothing had happened on the way. But, oh my, I wasn't expecting so many of you." Despite the surprise at the size of the Jewett party, the broad smile never left her face. "And which of these two fine young lads is Philip?"

"I am," volunteered Philip as Robert and Lewis gently moved him to the front.

"Well, you just call me Aunt Margaret. We're going to get along just fine, I can sense it already." She then gave Philip a big hug that he shyly returned. Turning, she shouted toward the door of the larger cabin, "Ronald, they're here."

A thin man, slightly stooped, with grey hair, came out of the cabin asking, "Who's here, mother?" Then, with a look of surprise, "Robert, we weren't expecting you today, and you brought your whole family with you, how nice!"

"Now, Ronald, we were so expecting them today. They brought Philip here up to start at the Academy tomorrow, remember?"

"Oh, that was today?" Chuckling and looking back toward the Jewetts, "I forgot."

Margaret just rolled her eyes before introducing Ronald to Philip, followed by Robert introducing his two sons and other grandson, explaining to the Samuels the reason so many Jewetts had shown up on their doorstep.

"Now don't worry about putting us all up. We'll take a room at the tavern and let you and Philip get better acquainted."

After some back and forth, Margaret finally agreed to those arrangements but insisted they all stay for supper. Henry went to make the arrangements at the tavern while Robert, Lewis, and Charles moved Philip's things into the loft.

"Now, Philip," Margaret told him. "The loft will be all yours. I can't climb the ladder any more and Ronald shouldn't, although I did catch him doing it to get it ready for you, so you'll have to keep it neat yourself. Meals will be here with us and occasionally our son, Elam, who lives in the adjoining cabin, joins us. I saw that face, but don't you worry, I won't let him harangue you about school during meals, not at my table he won't. If you need anything, just ask for it, but remember, if you ask Uncle Ronald he'll likely forget before he tells me and you'll end up doing without."

They sat around the comfortable cabin for a little while, talking and getting to know one another, until Margaret went to busy herself putting supper on the table. Robert had joined her to help set the table when they heard Ronald and Philip laughing.

"See, Robert, you won't have to worry about Philip at all. He and Ronald are getting along famously and I'll look after the both of them. After all, there's more of the boy in Ronald than I daresay there is in Philip, just from listening to him."

Robert patted Margaret on the arm, "Thank you." Then, looking back toward where Philip, Ronald, and Charles were sitting, laughing, "I'm going to miss him terribly, I'm afraid." Looking back to Margaret and smiling slightly, "Maybe it'll just give me more reason to come for visits. Or maybe I'll just come to visit with you and Ronald, challenge him to some of his diversions, and Philip won't suspect my real purpose."

The simple meal soon on the table, they all chatted and became better acquainted as the meal progressed. Just as they were finishing and beginning to help Margaret clear the table, the door burst open and in came a man in a simple red frock held closed by a sash. Like Ronald, he was thin and slightly stooped, though taller and with jet black hair. The glasses he wore perched on the end of his nose, coupled with the stoop, gave an illusion that he was walking around with his head thrust forward. Instead of the more common felt hat, he wore a knit hat, the tassel of which hung below his chin on the left side.

"Mother, father, I just heard a report of possible Indians to the southwest of here…Oh, hello, you have company?"

"Elam, let me introduce you, this is Robert Jewett, his sons, Lewis and Henry, and grandsons, Philip and Charles. Philip is to be your student and will be boarding with us. You remember, I told you about this last month. They came in from just south of Bordon's Grant this evening. Gentlemen, this is our son, Elam."

"Hello. Bordon's Grant? Then you must have heard about the Indians. Oh, if only school wasn't starting tomorrow I'd go up the Valley and lend a hand. I'm pretty fair with a fowler, you know."

"Actually, I think my other son, Colonel Edward Jewett, late of His Majesty's Army, has things well in hand. Why, when we left, Colonel Washington and his escort were also there."

"Oh, so you're the Jewetts they're talking about up at Staunton."

"Staunton?"

"You probably know it as Beverly's Mill Place. Their charter reads Staunton but there are still those, notably Mister Beverly himself, who are slow to change with the times. I of course meant 'down' at Staunton. Curious how north is down and south is up, all backward from the rest of the Colony and all on account of the flow of the Shenandoah River. Downstream is north, upstream is south..."

Any significance to the talk about the Jewetts in Staunton was now lost as Elam started talking geography quirks he was familiar with. He impressed Robert as being extremely intelligent and well read but, like many intelligent men, a bit eccentric and prone to jump from topic to topic in a conversation. Yet as he moved around, there was always a thread, no matter how thin, that linked the new topic back to the original subject matter.

It had grown late when Robert, his sons, and Charles said their goodnights to ride the short distance to the tavern. Philip looked lost for a moment as they left, but Margaret put her arm around the boy, who was actually a full head taller than her, and ushered him back into her cabin. Before leaving the yard, they all heard the peals of laughter coming from Ronald and Philip in the cabin, convincing Robert and Lewis that the boy would be fine.

Early the next morning, Robert and Lewis picked Philip up at the Samuel cabin and took him over to Augusta Academy where they were ushered in to see Mister Robert Alexander, President of the Academy. They presented Philip to Mister Alexander who, after a brief introduction to satisfy himself that the boy's education had been all Robert had told him it was, sent the boy into the classroom where Elam was about to start the first day's lesson.

Robert then satisfied Philip's tuition and Lewis asked probing questions on the course of instruction

Philip would receive at the Academy. Almost as an after-thought, Robert mentioned that Charles was in town and they would like to reserve a spot for him and Philip next year.

"Splendid. Tell you what, why don't you bring the boy by after dinner today? My duties will be concluded by then and we can show him around, get him excited about joining his cousin next year."

Late that afternoon, Robert returned with Henry and Charles in tow while Lewis observed some of Elam's class with Philip. They all then retired to the Samuel cabin where Margaret had insisted they have supper again, this time with Elam in attendance.

"Well, Sir Robert, you've neglected Philip's education. He's not well read in Bacon and Locke, though he seems familiar with his Newton. I daresay if more here in the Colonies knew their Locke, we'd throw off the yoke of the King. Why, you said your other son, the Colonel, was with Braddock. He knows firsthand of what I speak. Those people can no more govern these Colonies from London than we can control the Indians beyond the mountains."

Robert looked uncomfortable as yet another called him "Sir" when he had no claim or pretensions to hold that title. Seeing their grandfather's discomfort, Philip and Charles chuckled.

"Now, Elam, don't bother our guests with your crazy talk," Ronald interrupted, probably misinterpreting what was causing Robert discomfort. "You'll upset our guests and give me one of my headaches."

"But you know I'm right, father, and I would think our guests know it, also. Am I right?"

Robert gave a noncommittal answer while Lewis and Henry remained quiet, also now looking a bit uncom-fortable. Margaret rescued them by asking how they found the Academy. This got both Philip and Charles talking, shifting the conversation away from the English philosopher Francis Bacon and political philosopher John Locke.

Philip actually enjoyed his first day and thought studying new subjects with new boys near his own age would be exciting. Charles was bubbly over the prospect of joining Philip next year. Both boys had always been very bright and eager learners, excelling at reading and mathematics in their grandfather's classes.

"Yes, and you'll learn Latin and French as well," interjected Elam. "Making you the better able to read for yourself instead of being told what others want you to know."

"So, Elam," interrupted Robert, trying to steer the conversation away from subjects that might border on sedition. "You mentioned you were a fair shot with a fowler. Do you have much call to shoot, as the boys here are quite good shots in their own right?"

This worked well as the conversation turned toward shooting and weapons. Robert was not all that interested in the subject himself, but the two boys were. Of course, his own abilities and knowledge of shooting and weapons had increased under Edward's tutelage over the past three years. Now he easily held his own with Elam in the discussion. Ronald, on the other hand, had no interest in or knowledge of guns, but he did enjoy lively conversation so he sat listening intently.

"Perhaps I can bring Philip home for one of his visits. It would give me a chance to meet Colonel Jewett, Edward as you say I should call him, and perhaps we could do some hunting together. Few at the Academy have any interest in hunting or guns in general, preferring to purchase their meat and spend their time in their books. I, however, believe taking to the field to be good for the mind by providing exercise for the body and a chance to think clearly, without the influence of authors or editors."

The evening ended sadly as Robert and Lewis bid farewell to Philip. They would be heading home in the morning as he returned to class. Robert left Lewis and Philip in the passage to say their goodbyes alone after he had finished. It was some time before Lewis joined Robert, Henry, and Charles and he said nothing as they mounted and started toward the tavern.

As they neared the tavern, Robert asked, in a soft, soothing voice, "Is Philip having a tough time with our leaving?"

Lewis had to clear his throat a couple of times before he could get the words out, "Yes, and his father is also."

The next morning, as they rode along, Robert and Lewis were more subdued while Charles chatted away with his father. The conversation soon turned to the regular houses they'd seen in Greenville.

"When are we going to build our houses, grandfather?" asked Charles, putting his grandfather a bit on the spot. "From what I've been told, we're better off than most of the people around and yet we still live in cabins while they have real glass windows."

"Charles, mind your manners," Henry snapped.

"No harm done, Henry. Now, Charles, if we built our houses, all spread out around the Grant, wouldn't that make us more vulnerable to the Shawnee? We're at war, you know, and our first concern right now must be our own and our neighbors' safety."

"I suppose…" Charles's voice trailed off as he thought about what his grandfather said.

Eventually, Lewis found his voice, "Father, are you not concerned with Elam's brand of teaching? I mean, what might Edward say if Philip returned as full of sedition as Elam?"

"Ah, 'The Idols," said Robert, thoughtfully.

"The Idols? What do you mean, father?"

"Bacon wrote of four Idols that had a negative impact on the mind, and I believe your concern would fall under the 'Idol of the Cave.' Don't look so shocked. I've read Bacon, and I'd wager your brother Edward has, also. No, let Philip be exposed to Bacon, Locke, and even Elam. I think he is strong minded enough to make his own decisions on what to follow and what to discard."

Robert reined up and placed his hand on his gun as he saw three riders approaching them, relaxing when he recognized Tom McCrary and the two McNultys, father and son.

"Sir Robert, are we glad to see you four. We were to keep an eye out for you as we made our patrol. There's been trouble."

⊘ Chapter 6 ⊘

Edward felt his horse quiver but otherwise it remained calm as the bullets whizzed past from the four supposed hunters up the road. His horse had become accustomed to battle conditions after being in the thick of the fight along the Monongahela. It was a real war horse. Not true of the hunters, as their horses and packhorses milled excitedly about in response to the gun discharges.

Taking careful aim, Edward dropped one of the four before signaling the three soldiers to follow him as he charged up the road. The hunters found themselves entangled with their packhorses, their own horses unmanageable. Escape was impossible as was reloading their guns while mounted. Dismounting was not easy as well. One of them trying it ended up under the horses' hooves. And, at that moment, the soldiers were with them and deploying around them while they were still struggling to reload.

The two unhurt and mounted hunters dropped their lead lines and attempted to make their escape without the encumbrance of the packhorses carrying their booty. The first was able to break free and started on down the Virginia Road at a rapid pace. His partner, however, found his way blocked by a big soldier who showed no intention of giving up the road. Swinging his unloaded gun at the soldier, it was knocked from his hand as the soldier parried the strike with a heavy saber. Now, without a weapon of any kind and his way still blocked, he put his hands up in submission.

Thinking he was now in the clear, though heading back in the direction the soldiers had come, the remaining hunter spurred his horse on. As he neared the rise where the soldiers had first appeared, he reigned up sharply seeing soldiers now blocking his way. With more soldiers coming over the same rise these had appeared from, he looked back at his companions and saw them tossing down their guns and giving themselves up.

Looking back down the road after the fleeing hunter, Edward saw George riding hard toward him as his escort surrounded the hunter and started him back toward his companions. George was an accomplished horseman on a fine horse so he was well ahead of his escort, reining up on Edward's left he looked concerned.

"Colonel, your leg, you're hit."

Edward looked down at his leg and was surprised to see it covered in blood from his knee down with blood dripping from the toe of his boot onto the ground, forming a puddle between his horse's hooves. He had not felt a thing other than the recurring headache now building after his exertion. Reaching down to feel for the wound, he found it, but not in his leg. His horse had been hit, evidently in the initial volley, and was bleeding down Edward's leg. They both dismounted to see to the horse while the soldiers saw to gathering up and disarming their captives.

No sooner had Edward's feet hit the road when his horse collapsed with a wounded cry. The location of the wound and the blood coming from the horse's nostrils told the story plain enough.

"I'm afraid it's mortal, Edward."

"Would you loan me your other pistol, George? This one is empty," asked Edward, sadly. "He's too fine an animal to let suffer like this."

The pistol shot marking the end of his sad duty, Edward and George turned their attention back to their captives. A quick check showed they only needed to worry about three of the four, Edward's shot having been true. Searching the packhorses, they found belongings and valuables from what looked to be several different families, far more than what they could have stolen just from the Rice homestead.

Turning closer attention now to the three supposed hunters, they found before them three ruffians of the lowest sort. None were sorry for their crimes, only for being caught, and none showed any remorse at the loss of their companion. The soldiers had tied their hands and then tied them together so they could be led by just one soldier. The body they placed over the back of one of the saddle horses while Edward transferred his saddle to the best of the sorry lot of horseflesh belonging to the supposed hunters. Although the one ruffian had been stomped fairly badly, the soldiers showed him no compassion, simply tying him at the end of the rope so his falling wouldn't bring down the others, or at least not immediately.

Starting back toward the Jewett's little fort, Edward observed to George, "I'm afraid we can look forward to more of this. There will be more like these who will take advantage of the situation to steal from friends, neighbors, or anyone else they can."

"Yes, further adding to a difficult situation here in the valley and all along the frontier," agreed George. "Defending against Indian raids is impossible enough without having these thieves to deal with. I'll take these three up to the County gaol on my way back to Winchester. You can deal with them when the County Court convenes next month."

"On your way, could you ask into the owners of the other plunder so that we might return it to the rightful owners?"

"If you'll hold onto the property, I'll send the owners to you with a note signed either by me or the Captain, so you know we've determined they have rightful claims to property we've recovered. Would you mind doing that? I think it'd be better than having them crowd around the packhorses on the road, claiming this and that whether it's theirs or not. And as you sit as Justice on the County Court, no one could object to your serving thus in this matter."

"Done. I suppose that also means you'll be leaving right away."

"Oh, I'll say my goodbyes and not leave until morning, but yes. I should be getting back to my command. I must thank you, though, for all of your help. Could I continue to call on you for advice and assistance?"

"Absolutely! And even if it wasn't part of what I thought included in my duties as military advisor to the Colony, I'd do it for a friend," he paused and flashed George a large grin. "Though I will refrain from calling you an 'old' friend, young man."

Returning home, they quickly told the nervous inhabitants of the little fort that the Indian scare amounted to nothing more than an excuse to rob and plunder. A concerned Esther then took Edward to see Jim. She had put him in Robert's cabin where she and Melinda were keeping hot stones wrapped in wet cloths on Jim's very sore back.

"How are you, Jim?"

"Between my back aching as bad as it is and these vultures forcing me to lie here on my stomach, never a comfortable position for me, I'm miserable."

"Yes, but can you still move your legs?"

"Not as well as I could at first. It's not so much that they're stiff as they just don't seem to do what I want them to do."

"You just lie still and listen to the, what did you call them, 'vultures'?" Edward moved to one side of the cabin with Melinda and Esther.

"I don't think his back is broken," said Esther in a concerned voice. "But I can't explain him losing command of his legs. He is bruised badly, from his shoulders to his…" Her blush finished her sentence for her.

"Melinda, is he normally more comfortable lying on his side?" She nodded. "Then let's put some chairs together so that he might lie on his side and the chair backs will serve to hold the stones in place. I don't know what more to do than what you're doing. He's very lucky if he in fact didn't break his back. You and Caitlyn can stay here until Jim is back on his feet. Esther will see you're comfortable."

Edward was going to ride with Tom and spread the word for their neighbors to beware of strangers when George insisted two of his escorts go along in place of Edward, returning to the fort after seeing Tom safely home. Before leaving, Tom insisted on taking responsibility for organizing the morning and evening patrols to be done by their neighbors, now that the other Jewett men were on their errand to Greenville.

Returning to his cabin, Betty immediately saw how Edward was suffering from another headache, so she shooed George out, fixed Edward some tea, and forced him to lie quietly in the dark until supper was ready. Edward hated how these headaches left him weak, although he was thankful they were occurring with less and less frequency as time passed.

When Edward left his cabin to join the others for supper, Marie and Jenny anxiously met him right outside his door.

"So, you think the four ruffians were the cause of the Indian scare? Is there any reason to think Lewis, Philip, and the others in any danger?" asked Marie anxiously.

Although only partially recovered from his headache, Edward put on his most reassuring face. "Tom assured me there were no signs of Indians as he made his patrol all around the area. I'm quite sure they're fine. And," looking to Jenny, "with Henry and Charles now with them, I have no doubt all will return without incident. Less Philip, of course," he said with a little laugh.

Marie was relieved but didn't share Edward's humor. She was missing Philip already and hated that he had to be away at school. Jenny, also, was relieved as she hurried off to see to the final supper preparations.

"Maybe it would be easier if we'd had more children. With just Philip, I'm finding it very hard to let go," Marie confided in Edward. "Especially after Joseph..." her voice trailed off.

"I didn't mean to cause you any pain by my comment, Marie. I'm quite fond of the boy myself and, for as much as I teased him for always being underfoot, I do miss him as well. I think it will be especially hard on Lewis and father as those three are quite close."

Marie found his soothing voice a comfort even more than the words and gave Edward a small hug before moving to take her place at the tables. Edward had thought George would sit with him but found him seated opposite Sarah and, without Charles to interrupt their conversation, seemed totally absorbed in the object of his attention. Instead Edward sat next to a very tired looking Esther, patting her gently on the back as he sat down.

After supper, George again joined Edward in his cabin and they talked more of the things George needed to know now that he had been elevated to command a regiment. George was a quick study and asked probing questions. Some of his questions were the result of what he had witnessed while serving as an Aide to General Braddock, pertaining to proper application in the field of the theories Edward had been sharing.

George left the next morning feeling much more confident in his readiness to command. He took the three ruffians with him, the fourth having been buried, and promised Sarah he'd be back soon. As much as she hoped for the better, she looked a bit skeptical at his promise.

"So, my beautiful niece, how did your visit with the good Colonel Washington go?"

"Oh, Uncle Edward, stop teasing." Then, thoughtfully, "Are all men deceivers? I mean, do they all lie?"

"Why, what a question from one so young!" Putting his arm around her shoulder as he led her to the bench outside his cabin door, he continued, "When a beautiful young lady is involved, I'd have to say that, yes, all men are likely to engage in a little deception if they think it will help them win the young lady's affection. That doesn't mean they intend any malice or mischief, though some do. No, it is more what I'd call 'human nature.'"

"So, if all men are liars, how is a girl to know the truth?"

"Well, Sarah, if all men are liars, as you say, how can you trust anything I tell you? I am a man, after all."

Sarah thought for a moment, furrowing her brow in the process. "I think I see what you mean. All men lie, but they don't necessarily lie all the time. Is that it?"

"Yes, but I think there's more to it. I think your definition of a lie may be a bit all encompassing. If a man keeps something from you so as not to worry you, for example, would you call that a lie?"

"I would, wouldn't you?"

"Not a lie, as such, but perhaps a deception depending on the circumstances. I think it would be wise for you to be a bit suspicious when men tell you things, as long as you don't become overly suspicious. And I could ask if everything you said to George was truthful and complete." Her blush was the only answer he needed. "Then perhaps it isn't only men who use deception when it suits their interests."

They continued their chat for more than an hour. Sarah seemed satisfied with his answers, but Edward found himself wishing Robert were there to give Sarah better guidance than he could. He had spent his life motivating men to do things that were unnatural, to go willingly into harm's way even with the certainty of their death. What did he know about women, particularly young women, he thought to himself? He did know to what lengths some men would go to gain the favor of a woman, especially one as attractive as his niece.

He also thought of how easily George seemed to fall into love. True, he was a young man, now wealthy, well formed and becoming well known. It was natural for women to notice him and Edward guessed it was also natural for George to be attracted to them. Perhaps, Edward thought, George falls in love so easily because he hasn't found the right woman. That would explain it. He just hoped Sarah didn't get hurt in the process.

As he was freshening up for dinner, Esther came to his cabin.

"Edward, could you come look after Mister Rice? He seems to have completely lost the use of his legs and I don't know what more to do for him."

↶ Chapter 7 ↷

Tom McCrary and the McNultys escorted Robert, Lewis, Henry, and Charles back to the little Jewett fort. On the way, Tom told the Jewetts what had happened at the Rice homestead and of Jim Rice's injury. They hadn't gone far when they met Colonel Washington and his escort leading their prisoners toward the Virginia Road. It was going to be a slow march for them, dragging the prisoners like they were. They paused and exchanged pleasantries with George and he told them in more detail than Tom had of the capture of the ruffians posing as hunters. They then parted and continued on their own separate ways. Upon arriving home, Robert went straight to see Jim and found he had been moved to the blockhouse with Edward and Melinda attending him.

"I hear he's in a bad way," Robert said to Edward in a low voice. "Has there been any improvement?"

"Well, some. We moved him in here this morning when he lost use of his legs altogether and switched from warm stones to cold spring water. That seems to have brought some movement back in his legs. I'm still convinced the back's not broken but can't explain why he can't use his legs."

"If the cold compresses are giving him some relief, all I can recommend is to continue them. How are you holding up, Melinda?"

"I'm tired, but Esther has been a big help. I couldn't have done this without her, and Edward, of course. We sent Esther home to lie down for a while, she is so worn out she could hardly stand, poor girl. Jim seems to be resting more comfortably now…"

"I wish people would stop talking about me like I'm dead or something. I'm right here, why don't you just ask me?"

"I'm sorry, Jim, that was rude of me. I thought you might be sleeping," Robert said in a comforting voice.

"Oh, don't mind me. I'm just tired of being down like this. Colonel, if those ruffians didn't get it all, do you suppose a few sips of my 'medicine' would help?"

With that Melinda just rolled her eyes while the two men laughed, "Oh, he's feeling better, alright!"

Jenny arrived to help Melinda, knowing Robert would want to talk to all three of his sons. The men went to Edward's cabin for discussions on the situation at the fort and Philip's enrollment in to school.

"You should have seen how quickly he proposed to ride back here to help you fight the Shawnee," Henry laughed. "At that moment he would have done anything not to go to that school."

"He has an odd teacher in Elam Samuel. Elam is full of Bacon and Locke, Latin and German. He must also know French as he told Philip he would be learning French this year," added Lewis, looking to see how Edward reacted to the mention of Locke in particular. Edward just brushed it off, seeming to pay it no mind as he spoke to the three in French.

"What was that?" asked Henry, chuckling.

"Oh, I just said perhaps I should brush up on my French, now that I'll have someone to speak French with," responded Edward.

After finishing their discussion, Robert went back to the blockhouse to check on Jim and to inventory the stolen goods so as to be ready when their rightful owners came to claim them. He would also set aside those things taken from the Rice homestead for Melinda to take back with her. Edward watched as Sarah followed her grandfather into the blockhouse. He wondered how much of the inventory Robert would actually get done as Sarah asked him her questions.

The little fort settled into its winter routine. Mister Agner moved up from the mill to stay in the fort as soon as all the milling was done. He was paying close attention to his dress and cleanliness these days and Edward was unable to detect the smell of liquor on him, day or night. The reasons for this transformation continued to be the subject of lighthearted speculation, and not just between the Jewett men. It was the women of the compound, black and white, who did the most speculating.

Charles was missing Philip more than he expected, being the only boy now at the fort other than the infant Joseph, Sam and Rachael's toddler. Robert sensed his grandson's loneliness and restarted his winter classes for all of the neighborhood children. This helped Charles adjust as there were now several other boys around his age in the little fort nearly every day. In learning, however, Charles was in a class of his own, being a much more advanced and accomplished reader than any of the others, boy or girl, as Robert insisted on teaching both, not only the boys as was more customary. Robert gave Charles his reading assignments then would spend most of the time helping the others just learn basic reading skills. Outside of Robert's class, the other children had never learned reading or mathematics.

Jim Rice steadily improved to where he was able to walk and sit on a horse, though neither for long periods of time before his back began to ache. He and Edward began doing a little hunting together and, as his stamina improved, to take patrols together. Still, Jim preferred a chair by a warm fire to a chilly hunt any day, so much so Edward joked that for Jim to get a deer, it would have to come up on his porch and knock on the door. Before the Rices moved back to their homestead, Edward, Miles, and Sam rode down and cut a winter's supply of firewood for them, convinced the chopping would only serve to aggravate Jim's back just as it was showing signs of healing.

Five families did come to claim their property over the course of several weeks. Robert had the inventory and asked them to tell him what they were missing as a means of identifying what was truly theirs before showing them the items or the list. In this way, all the items found their way back to their rightful owners without any disputes.

George Washington returned in mid-December, leading a big, beautiful, black horse, which he presented to Edward to replace the one lost during his last visit.

"George, this is too much for me to accept."

"Nonsense, you lost your horse while on Colony business as you were assisting me in maintaining the peace of this County. The Colony owes you a replacement. I just happened to have this old nag of a horse eating up all my grain supplies so I thought bringing him here would help everyone concerned. The Colony fulfills its obligation, my grain will now last the winter, and you have a replacement for the horse you lost. Now feeding him becomes your problem."

"Yes, but this is hardly a nag. He's magnificent and worth far more than the horse I lost." George would have none of it and Edward finally relented.

"There is another matter I would like to discuss with you, Edward, if you have the time for me. There's a Royal Army Captain in Maryland, John Dagworthy, who has the audacity to issue me orders, claiming his Royal Commission from the last war makes him superior to any provincial officers who hold their commissions from their Governors. I'm sure you're familiar with the Royal Proclamation from late last year that set up this situation. What can you advise me?"

"I know of the Proclamation although I didn't think John Dagworthy retained his Captaincy at the end of that war. More importantly, I know Major General Shirley from the Louisbourg campaign ten years ago. Let me write an appeal asking him to intervene in this matter, in our favor, of course. Whether he wants it or not, he has now succeeded Major General Braddock as Commander in the Americas."

They worked on the appeal through the early afternoon until they were ready to turn their draft into final form. Wording was important because not only was William Shirley the Acting Commander of all His Majesty's Forces in America, he was also the Governor of Massachusetts Bay Colony and had been for fourteen years. A protégé of the Duke of Newcastle, he was a man who had to be courted gently.

As Edward sat to write the final letter, George went in search of Sarah, who he found in Robert's cabin visiting with her grandfather. George joined them, returning with Robert, Sarah, and Esther to eat dinner in Edward's cabin, the weather having turned too cold for the communal meals taken under the awning. From all appearances, Edward thought his niece and George were getting along quite well. George then proposed joining Edward for the afternoon patrol, which gave Edward the opportunity to try out the horse George had brought him.

George was the much more accomplished horseman, but Edward was able to keep up with him and found his new mount as magnificent to ride as he was to look at. They took the morning patrol the next day before George had to depart back to Winchester. He left with the letter to Major General Shirley safely tucked in his dispatch case to be posted as soon as he returned to his headquarters.

"George, if it helps to hold Captain Dagworthy at bay, you may tell him you are taking orders from me, and, as I hold an active Royal Army Commission as a Colonel, he should take the matter up with me. It's not the solution we need, but it might buy us time until we hear back from the Major General."

Late December brought a visit from Philip. Elam brought him home just before the Twelve Night celebrations so prevalent in Virginia but rare in Massachusetts. Ronald came along for a visit with Robert, but Margaret didn't favor traveling in the winter and remained in Greenville, snug in her warm cabin.

While Ronald entertained Robert and Charles with his diversions, Elam sat with Edward where the two got into some lively discussions on Locke's two Treatises of Government. Lewis retired to his own cabin with Marie and Philip so the three could catch up on the news of their son and enjoy his company, even if the visit would be necessarily short. Besides, Philip had endured enough of Locke and wanted nothing to do with the conversation going on in his uncle's cabin.

Listening to Ronald, Robert, and Charles playing their diversions, Esther couldn't help but laugh. Ronald would forget one of the rules, Charles would remind him of it, and he'd always respond with "Oh, you're right. I completely forgot." And she liked how relaxed Robert seemed around Ronald as they played their diversions or just sat and talked.

Finding Elam relished time in the woods, Edward took him out for some late season deer and turkey hunting. In his red frock, Elam rather stood out and they were unable to get the turkeys to approach within range. With deer they were more successful. Edward had to chuckle to himself how, when retelling the day's hunting experience for Philip and Charles, Elam would become very animated and for those sections he found humorous, his eyebrows would raise up and his eyes fairly protruded from his head as he made sweeping gestures with his long arms. He seemed to revel in having an audience.

"Can you imagine him in the classroom with a dozen teenage boys?" chuckled Lewis to Edward one evening after Elam had delivered one of his more impressive performances.

"That's the scary part, I can! I had an instructor at King's College very much like him. It's a wonder any of us got any of our readings done, we were always laughing so hard as one then another would do an impression of something he had done in class that particular day." Edward's eyes fairly danced at the fond memory of those long ago days.

Soon the too short visit was over and Elam gathered up Philip and Ronald for their journey home. At Edward's suggestion, Lewis, Henry, and Charles joined them to ensure a safe passage, which was actually Edward's way of giving Lewis more time with Philip. He knew Lewis missed his son terribly when he was away.

By the end of January, things had turned bitter cold and there was snow on the ground with more coming regularly. While many settlements had experienced Shawnee raids throughout the fall, these seemed to halt as the weather turned. None, thus far, had approached the Jewett lands or interfered with their neighbors.

The last day of January, a rider approached the fort with a message from Williamsburg for Edward. After giving Edward a chance to read it, Robert, Lewis, and Henry came to Edward's cabin to learn the news.

"George continues to have problems with his commission and Governor Dinwiddie is sending him to Boston to appeal in person to Major General Shirley. Because I know the General, the Governor has asked me to go along. George has added a note saying he will leave from his home at Mount Vernon, near Alexandria, on the 10th and if I'm going, to meet him there before that."

"But, Edward," observed Robert. "That is barely enough time for you to get there, and in this weather. Are you sure you should?" Concern for his son's still fragile health remained paramount in Robert's mind.

"Yes, I should. I'll leave in the morning. Aaron is already packing my Regimentals for the trip. I'll take him along, plus one packhorse. I think we can make Alexandria in time. George says there is no shipping heading toward Boston so we're to make the whole journey on horseback."

"That's easy for George to say, he's a young man. I shouldn't have to remind you, son, that you are more than twice his age. This journey will be very taxing on you so soon after you've recovered from your injuries."

Edward put a comforting arm around Robert and said, "I'll be fine, father. Don't worry. I should be back in six weeks time, just in time to make sure you get the spring planting started."

After his father and brothers left him alone, Edward began sorting through his papers for those he felt would help make the case to the General when a knock came at the door.

"Marie, what are you doing out on such a cold evening?"

"Edward, is it true you're going to Boston tomorrow?"

"Yes, it's true."

"If I write a letter to Hannah tonight, would you take it and make sure she gets it? I haven't heard from her and I'm starting to worry."

"Are you sure we have enough paper left in Virginia for another letter? I swear they are as long as books, both yours to her and hers to you! But in answer to your question, yes, I'll deliver it for you if you get it written. Where should I take it?"

"Start at her parents, they'll know how you can find her. I'll write down where they're living. Oh, thank you so much. Things have not been going well for her, what with her husband regularly out of work and all."

"You two have been friends a long time, haven't you?"

"Yes, ever since we were little girls. You remember her from our wedding, don't you? I think that was the first time you met her…"

"I remember, but if you spend all your time reminiscing with me, when will you write your letter?"

It was cold and snowing the next morning when Edward said his goodbyes, mounted, and, with Aaron, rode off into the deepening snow. This was not going to be an easy trip.

❧ Chapter 8 ❧

Philip was sitting at the Samuel's table near the fireplace writing for one of his school assignments when he heard horses in the yard followed by someone calling his name. Jumping to his feet, he announced to Ronald and Margaret that it was his Uncle Edward before grabbing his coat and rushing out the door with the Samuels not far behind.

"Uncle Edward, is something the matter with grandfather?" asked Philip, concern showing on his face.

"No, your grandfather is fine…"

"Father, then?"

"I see all this schooling hasn't taught you to wait and let a man finish his sentence before asking him the next question," Edward said, smiling broadly. "Everyone at home is fine. Your father just asked me to deliver a note to you as I passed. It's as simple as that."

"Passed? Where are you going?"

"First we go to Alexandria and then on to Boston on an errand for the Governor."

"That's a long way to go in the middle of winter, Colonel," Margaret observed. "I'm Margaret Samuel and this is Ronald. You both look cold. Come in and stay for dinner. It'll be ready soon."

Dismounting stiffly, Edward came up the steps and gave his nephew a big hug. "I'm afraid we can't stay. We have just ten days to make Alexandria so time is precious."

"Well, then, I'm going back in where it's warm. Let me know before you leave so I can say goodbye. Come, Ronald, let's give them some privacy." Ronald said something Edward couldn't hear and he and Margaret then returned to the warm cabin, leaving Edward and Philip alone in the passage.

"Are you really going all the way to Boston, in the winter?" asked Philip, unable to hide his surprise.

"Yes, and to make matters worse, there's no shipping that will get us there so we're riding the whole way." Looking closely into his nephew's face, he added, "Ah, finally, for once you're not jumping at the chance to go along with me! You're showing uncommon good sense. This school must be working," he chuckled.

They talked briefly and Edward handed Philip the note his father had written that morning. "Your father misses you, more than he will admit. He mopes around and it is really becoming quite annoying. I have been sending him out on most of the patrols just to relieve all of us from having to hear one more time how much he wishes Philip was here to see this or that, or do this or that. It's pitiful." The little levity helped but the melancholy he saw in Philip's eyes when he handed him Lewis's note didn't completely leave the boy. "Now, run and tell Mrs. Samuel we must be off."

"That's Aunt Margaret to you, dear, and we were just now coming. Here, I've made you both some ham biscuits and this jug is sweet cider pressed this fall so it hasn't turned hard," handing a sack and jug to Edward. "It was nice meeting you and, while I wish you'd stay and warm yourself, Philip has told me enough about you to know that nothing comes between you and your duty."

Aaron now mounted the steps and took the bag and jug from Edward, thanking Margaret quietly before returning to his horse. One more hug to Philip and quick goodbyes to Ronald and Margaret and the two riders were off again, quickly lost from view as the snow fell around them.

They pushed on hard, not stopping until well after full dark when they started having trouble discerning the path of the Virginia Road. An abandoned homestead well north of Staunton provided welcome shelter for them and their horses that night.

"Maybe some of last year's cider would have warmed us better than the sweet cider," Aaron observed as he refilled Edward's cup.

"Perhaps, but it would have made starting tomorrow before first light all the more difficult," Edward chuckled in response.

Starting early the next morning, Aaron's horse and the packhorse seemed to have recovered from the previous day's exertion and were better able to keep up with Edward's great black steed. That black horse never seemed to tire. While keeping up a steady pace, Edward was careful not to set a fast pace as they had a terribly long trip ahead of them.

They stuck to the Virginia Road instead of taking the shorter route up the Luray Valley, thinking they could make better time in these weather conditions on the better road. Aaron was also hoping for a tavern where he could get a hot meal and warm bed as he had found their night on the hard-packed dirt floor less than restful.

They found a tavern that night alright, abandoned like most of the homesteads they had been passing throughout the day. A few hearty souls were holding out, most of them living near the hastily constructed block-houses or small stockade posts that offered some little measure of security against an Indian raid. The Jewett's little stockade and blockhouse were better constructed and, with their laborers and the small contingent of soldiers, more defendable, but even so they knew it could not withstand an attack from a determined raid of even medium size.

The snow finally stopped the third day, though the further north they traveled the deeper it had piled up. Edward was not discouraged by their progress, only knowing they had little time to spare. Some of that time was eaten up forcing their way through the pass in the Blue Ridge where the recent snows had piled drifts in their path. Also here they had to spend a cold night under a stand of cedars, no other shelter being readily available.

That cold night being hard on both men and horses, they had to slow their pace the next day as they came down the eastern slope of the Blue Ridge. Much to Aaron's delight, however, east of the ridge they found an occupied tavern that had plenty of room. Who else would be foolish enough to be traveling at this unseasonable time of the year? Good grain and a warm barn worked wonders on the horses just as a hot meal and comfortable bed did the men. They still had nearly sixty miles to cover and were running out of time, so they didn't linger at the tavern, taking a cold breakfast and their leave before the tavern keeper was fairly up.

It took them two more days to cover the distance. Edward had thought they could do it in just over one but had not accounted for the icy roads, snows melting some during the day and refreezing at night. Still they arrived in Alexandria with a day to spare so they found comfortable accommodations and sent one of the tavern's slaves to Mount Vernon with a message announcing their arrival and that they would make the last eight miles after a leisurely breakfast the next day.

Good to his word, Edward let Aaron sleep a bit later and they both had a good, hot breakfast before making the relatively easy trip to Mount Vernon. Once there, they found a neat, story-and-a-half manor house, four rooms on a floor, and the necessary outbuildings of a good sized farm. Wood built, it was not the impressive brick manor house so common to the eastern portions of the Colony but it was also much better formed and larger than one would find a middling farmer to own, most of theirs being but two rooms on a floor.

"Colonel, I am very glad to see you. I was quite surprised to receive your note last evening, having already assuaged myself to making the trip alone," was their warm greeting. "My people will see to your horses and make you as comfortable as my humble home will allow."

"Yes, but 'humble home' seems a bit understated, don't you think, having visited us many times these past few months to know we have much less to offer our guests?" Both Colonels laughed at this rejoinder.

"I've been meaning to ask why you all don't construct proper houses. Why, except for the wood floors, you choose to live as your poorer neighbors," George continued.

"It remains a matter of security. Father has insisted we'll have ample time to build our estates after the French and Shawnee have been dealt with. Though, as our population continues to grow with the addition of your soldiers and more children, it does seem a lot smaller than it did when we first built it."

They dined rather lavishly and Edward had a chance to meet George's widowed sister-in-law, who still occupied a portion of the house as was her right. They tarried the next day as well and Edward explained how he proposed to address the issue of the commission with General Shirley.

George suggested, after seeing to Edward's horses, that they take fresh mounts from his stables for the next leg of their journey. Yes, the big black was still in fine shape, but the other two were showing their fatigue and there was no sense risking wearing out the black horse unless necessary. Besides, George had an uncommonly fine stable of horses, so Edward agreed.

Mounted on fresh horses, they departed the next morning, now four in number with two packhorses. They found a packet willing to take them across the Potomac at Alexandria. As they traveled north, conditions steadily declined. The snow was deeper, the cold more penetrating. At first, rivers were major obstacles, the ferries having ceased operation due to ice flows. Shifting further west, behind the fall line, they found the rivers sufficiently frozen to hold them, though treacherous to cross.

By time they were in New Jersey Colony, Edward was glad they had taken fresh mounts. Even these were tiring quickly as they set their moderate pace through the cold and snow.

"You grew up in this region, Edward, so, tell me, is it always cold like this in the winter?" asked George as they neared Boston.

"Oh, no, this is an unusual year," Edward responded with a grin. "Usually it's much colder and there's more snow."

Although George was anxious to go straight to the General and resolve the issue, he listened to Edward's advice and they found lodging first. Sending a note to the Governor's Mansion announcing their arrival and requesting an audience, they then set about refreshing themselves after their arduous journey. Both men looked haggard and gaunt and would not have made a very impressive appearance before General Shirley had they gone straight there, nor would their welcome likely be as warm had they arrived unannounced.

Edward received a prompt response from the General with an invitation to join him for dinner the next day, expressed warmly and with an obviously fond recollection of their time together before the French works at Louisbourg ten years earlier.

"I take this to be a good sign, George. Discussing the situation over a friendly dinner among old wartime friends will make it a lot easier to convince him than in a formal audience."

George was encouraged, but remained skeptical. He was staking a lot on this trip and was afraid he might come off too vain or desperate to the Major General and he would decide against him. That was why he was so glad Edward had agreed to accompany him on this mission.

They had a good dinner and Edward then sent a note to the Faircloths, Hannah's parents, stating his business with Hannah and asking her whereabouts so he could deliver the letter from Marie. As he and George were having their breakfast the next morning, a note came back from Captain Faircloth advising him Hannah was not in Boston but offering to explain more fully over dinner the following day. Edward found this a bit curious, but sent a note back accepting their kind invitation.

Captain Faircloth owned a number of merchant ships. He had retired from actively commanding himself, but had captains and crews in his employ who carried a good deal of the cargo shipped between the Bahamas, Bermuda, and West Indies and the northern Colonies. A good man and fair master, he was nonetheless called "The Admiral" by his captains, behind his back of course, for how he barked orders at them and kept his affairs under close scrutiny, unlike many of his competitors who mostly just looked to their account books.

George and Edward dressed carefully for their meeting with Major General and Governor William Shirley. They hired a coach to take them from their lodgings to the Governor's Mansion and arrived at the appointed time. A doorman answered and showed them into the parlor to await the General.

"Colonel Jewett, how good to see you again."

"And I you, General. Let me introduce Colonel George Washington, Commander of the Virginia Regiment. Colonel Washington, General Shirley."

"It's nice to make your acquaintance, young man." Turning almost immediately back to Edward, "Well, I am so glad to see you, Edward. You are just the man I need and have shown up at the most opportune time. I want you to command at Fort Oswego. I plan to launch a spring campaign against the Canadas and can use a good leader to keep things moving. We lost a grand opportunity this year when I couldn't get my forces organized."

George looked to Edward, just now realizing how Edward's mere presence before the Commanding General might tear Edward away from his family and Virginia. Yet Edward's calm demeanor told George this was not such an unexpected twist to the conversation. No, George thought,

Edward knew what he risked and he came with me any-way. Now that was a grand testament to friendship.

∞ Chapter 9 ∞

Robert so preferred the Virginia winters over those in Rowley. Here, just four days after the snowstorm and it was almost gone, lingering only in the north shadows of the cedars and on the northern slopes of the ridges. They had wisely placed their little settlement on the southern slope so, except close to the north side of their cabins and the blockhouse, they were free of the snow.

Rowley, close to the ocean, had relatively mild winters when compared to those further inland. Even so, they were cold and snow fell heavily and stayed long. No, his old bones preferred the warmer climate. Ever since that winter of 1704 when, out chasing the Iroquois, he had been the coldest in his life, he could not sleep if chilled. On the warmest days of summer, he still slept with a wool blanket pulled tight under his chin. Aunt Bess used to tease him about it.

Ah, Aunt Bess, how he missed her. Not a day passed when Esther didn't do something or say something that brought memories of that dear woman flooding back. He knew Esther missed her also, could see it in her eyes when he occasionally slipped and called her "Aunt Bess." That was happening to him more and more these days to where now he'd even called Sarah "Esther" a time or two. He remembered how his mother used to do that all the time, call him one of her brothers' names or call Edward "Robert." Yes, he definitely got that from his mother's side as Aunt Bess never did that, not once.

Looking out across the open field to the Blue Ridge with its line of mountains in front, he wished Aunt Bess had made it there to see it and to see how "her boys" were all pulling together to carve lives for all of them out of this frontier. They hadn't built their estates, he didn't think it prudent just yet with all this trouble with the Shawnee, but they were comfortably situated and lacked for nothing. Yet, in his heart, he knew her passing in Williamsburg was probably better than suffering along the trail at her advanced age.

"Grandfather, are you remembering Aunt Bess again?" came Sarah's soft voice as she slipped up beside him.

Putting his arm around her shoulder and pulling her close, he said not a word but somehow Sarah just knew. She leaned her head back against his chest and they both stood for several minutes watching the sun rise over the Blue Ridge. To Robert, family was the most important thing in life. It was everything to him, and moments like these were what he cherished most.

After the sun's brightness replaced the soft colors of sunrise, they turned and returned to the little fort they called home. Lewis and Henry met them near the gate.

"Father, we're about ready to head out. We won't be too far, just over the rise, there, to the southwest. If there's trouble, fire the wall gun, we're sure to hear that monster," Lewis said, all business this morning.

They had decided to take advantage of the mild winter weather to cut and clear more of their land for eventual planting. The timber would eventually be hewn for use in building regular houses for each of them, once the hostilities with the French and their Indian allies subsided and they could safely live outside the little fort.

Robert would be left with just the Sergeant and six soldiers, plus the women, within the immediate vicinity of their blockhouse and fort. Oh, Mister Agner would be there also, but he wasn't counted on much if there was fighting to do. Lewis and Henry would take Charles, Miles and the eight laborers with them, the laborers working under Sam's direction while the others rode patrol around them, watching for any signs of Shawnee. It wasn't too likely in the winter, but in these unsettled times one could never let anything go to chance.

"That's fine, for today. Just remember, I'm sending a note around with the patrol telling our neighbors that school will start again tomorrow, now that the snow is gone. You can take Charles with you today but he stays here tomorrow and does his lessons."

Charles feigned a groan that brought a chuckle from everyone. He actually enjoyed school, especially with his grandfather as his teacher. Even so, after four days cooped up in the fort, he was looking forward to getting out that day.

As they left the stockade, all twelve were well armed, their tools carried by two packhorses. They hadn't gotten very far when Marie came riding up to Lewis.

"And where do you think you're going?" Lewis asked with not a little sarcasm in his voice.

"You know how much I've wanted to get out and ride. There hasn't been much chance of that lately so I thought I could ride along with you. I'll even help by looking for Indian sign as I ride."

"And I know how much help that will be," Lewis said, bringing a burst of laughter from Charles who couldn't hold it in like his father was doing. "Well, come ahead, then. It wouldn't do me any good to send you back as you'd only follow along later."

They rode a ways in silence, Lewis and Marie moving out in front, Henry and Miles to each side, and Charles bringing up the rear, just as Edward taught them to do, when Marie started talking very excitedly.

"You know what I was just thinking? When Edward delivers my letter to Hannah, he can wait until she writes a response, but then he can also tell me how things are with her and I won't have to only rely on what she says in her letter. Isn't that exciting?"

"If you say so, but I thought you were helping me look for Indian sign. Big help you've turned out to be."

"Oh, stop. So, do you think Edward has gotten there yet?"

With that, Lewis reined in to a complete stop in mocked shock. "Woman, it's been four days! They haven't even made it to Alexandria yet, let alone all the way to Boston!"

"I hadn't thought about that. Did he say how long he expected to be gone?"

"Six weeks, he said, provided they didn't run into any trouble."

"Six weeks! That's going to seem a terribly long time to wait."

As they started forward again, Lewis observed, "It can't be helped. Boston is a long ways off, as you well know, and it's the middle of winter.

Reaching their destination, the laborers set to work with Sam overseeing while Lewis set up a ring patrol around them. He and Miles would travel clockwise starting on opposite sides while Henry and Charles would ride counterclockwise starting opposite each other. Marie would ride with Charles. This constant motion ringing the laborers would provide the most security and least opportunity for a hostile to make it through to the laborers.

Sam had the work well organized. As trees fell, he had them cut to 24-foot lengths for future hewing and stacked to best promote drying. The two packhorses came in handy for this backbreaking job. The branches were cut and stacked for use as firewood the next winter, though they didn't bother to take the time to split them now. They worked through the morning and into the afternoon until they took their dinner break. After that, they took up arms and fanned out around the worksite to allow Lewis, Henry, Miles, Charles, and Marie to come in and get their dinner.

"I thought I would head back home after we finished eating," Marie announced once everyone had their food before them.

"Alone? Haven't we been through that once already?" Henry asked in mock horror.

"Stop it, you," Marie said jokingly back at him. "Seriously, I'll be alright. I'm within sight of the blockhouse when I clear the rise and you can see me from here to there."

Looking to Lewis, Henry just couldn't let it go, "I thought she wanted to help us look for Indian sign and protect our laborers so they could work. Now she's ready to quit before the job is done?" Turning to Charles he continued, "Cover your eyes and ears, I don't want you picking up any bad habits from your Aunt Marie!"

They all laughed at Henry's antics but Lewis wasn't sure Marie's laugh went all the way to her eyes.

"Fine, you can go, but ride quickly. Just because you're within sight doesn't mean we can get to you in time should some hostiles have worked their way around our perimeter. That's the same rise we know they've used to observe the fort in the past, so they are very familiar with the territory here."

"There you go, 'perimeter,' you're sounding more and more like Edward every day. And we've seen no sign of any 'hostiles' all day so I hardly think it likely there's any about. But thank you for your permission. I'll remember your generous consideration at supper this evening," she concluded with mock formality that sent Charles into another bout of laughter and the men grinning broadly.

After they had eaten, Marie went to mount and Lewis joined her. "I'm serious, you don't need to gallop but move quickly back to the fort. All joking aside, there is no need to take unnecessary risks. We can't assume the snow that had father close his school impeded any Shawnee intent on raiding. I'm confident they're not within our circle, but they could be lurking just outside it waiting for their chance."

Marie appreciated his sincerity, coming after the teasing she had received during the meal. She really should be used to it by now, this Jewett sense of humor, but sometimes she still let it anger her a little even though they never meant anything by it.

Reaching up to give him a kiss, she had to settle for a quick peck. No, Lewis never would be comfortable kissing her in front of others, especially his brothers, no matter how long they were married.

They restarted their patrolling with Lewis taking Marie better than halfway up the rise, then letting her cover the remaining distance alone while he watched as she safely disappeared over it. Then he turned his horse to the right and began his circuit while the sounds of axes rang out in the woods.

They had decided to quit in time to be back at the blockhouse before sunset, leaving Sam to gauge the time they needed for repacking the tools and starting back. The riders would then form back on them just like they had come out this morning, only this time, Charles was to take the lead and Lewis would ride trail. Lewis always wanted to make sure the boys, Charles or Philip, were in the position that best afforded them a chance to get away from danger.

As they climbed to the top of the rise, Lewis wasn't exactly paying close attention, thinking more of how this had been a very long day in the saddle and how tired he realized he was. A shot off to his left rear brought him out of his musings with a start.

Everyone had stopped and they had all turned and were looking in the same direction, the direction of the shot. Lewis turned back and signaled to Charles and Sam to go on toward the fort. They started to move and quickly, despite their fatigue from the day's labors. Miles and Henry held their positions on each flank until the work party was well over the rise and then they converged to where Lewis sat looking anxiously in the direction the shot had come.

"Who had the afternoon patrol?" asked Henry when the three were together.

"Let's see, it was McCrary and the McNultys this morning so I think it was Gordon, Bennett, and Stuart this afternoon," answered Lewis.

Henry thought for a moment. "It could be the patrol in trouble, if they were heading this direction, possibly to warn us."

Then they heard a second shot.

❧ Chapter 10 ❧

Edward feigned ignorance of the situation at Fort Oswego while knowing full well it was a decrepit trading post Major General Shirley ordered fortified in the fall to serve a base of operations for his planned assault on Fort Niagara in the spring. At the end of a tenuous supply line, it was as likely to starve itself out of existence as to fall to the French.

"I was sure you had the Northern Campaign well in hand, General, and would have no need of my meager abilities."

"How I wish things had gone well. Niagara should have been ours before winter. But enough of this kind of talk. How are things with you? I hear you've taken up residence on the fringe of the frontier in Virginia. Now, had you returned to Rowley, I could have used you here before now."

As they moved to the table and dinner, Edward gave the General a brief review of his family's situation in the Valley and their efforts to defend themselves and their neighbors. George remained quiet through this, wishing Edward would get to the point but not wanting to insert himself for fear of ruining Edward's strategy for approaching General Shirley.

Through the first three courses, the General explained in some detail the success his New England troops had in Nova Scotia. He also outlined his orders to relocate the Acadian population after their refusal to swear allegiance to King George II. As disturbing as Edward found this, he kept it to himself for he needed the General open to their request and it wouldn't do to irritate him at this point.

Retiring so the servants could clear the table for the dessert course, General Shirley brought them around to the reason for their visit.

"So, Edward, I'm sure you didn't make such an arduous journey just to enjoy a chat with an old comrade in arms. What business brought you here if it wasn't to volunteer for a command?"

"Actually, General, it is a complication resulting from last year's Royal Proclamation placing all provincial officers of any rank falling under any Regular officer, no matter how junior."

"I'm familiar with the issue. That Proclamation has caused me no end of trouble. I try as best I can to organize Provincial troops in units far removed from the Regulars. It's inefficient, but no Provincial senior officer will consent to serve if any pimple faced ensign can order him and his troops around. I didn't realize it was a problem for you, though, as you hold an active Regular Commission in your own right. In fact, I believe you rank every other Colonel in His Majesty's Service at this point."

With the conversation going exactly as he wanted, Edward explained the issue between George and the self-proclaimed Regular Captain in Maryland and what effect it was having on the security along the Virginia, Maryland,

and Pennsylvania frontier. When convinced the General's head nods were in all the right places and his instincts told him he was making his case, Edward tossed out his strongest argument.

"My confusion comes from two aspects in this issue. The first is that this Captain has letters telling him Colonel Washington is acting on my behalf. This should have resolved the situation right there. Instead, he persists with his claims and issues orders with regularity and has now threatened Colonel Washington with charges for not obeying. This in spite of the fact this same Captain resigned his commission at the end of the late war, so how he can now claim it as the basis for his seniority is beyond my comprehension."

To George's delight, Edward's approach brought the General to the same conclusion.

"You are absolutely right, Edward. This young pup has no right to claim seniority over a corporal's guard. Good on you for calling him on it." He then signaled his aide, standing by the door. "John, you've heard all this. Prepare an order for my signature placing Edward here in command of the Virginia, Maryland frontier and all forces…"

"That should be Colonel Washington, General, as I am assigned as the advisor to Virginia's Governor. To place me in command on the frontier would make me unavailable to do my duties as assigned by Lord Halifax and the Duke of Cumberland."

"Quite right. Did you understand all that, John? Good. Make four copies, one for both Virginia and Maryland's Governors, one for us, and one for the young Colonel to carry away with him." Turning to Edward, "Of course that same argument would make you unavailable for command at Fort Oswego. More's the pity. But I won't let this stand for long. I will ask the Duke to release you so your talents can more effectively be employed at the discretion of the Commander here in the Americas. I can't have the senior Colonel, and one experienced fighting on the frontier, sitting out this war in Williamsburg!"

Edward bowed politely, "I am at your service, General, and, as soon as I am released from my current obligation, I will serve where you best think my meager talents can best benefit His Majesty."

This had the desired effect on the General and he returned to the table in a jovial mood. The conversation for the rest of the evening remained light and joking as the two recalled humorous episodes from their previous service together. While feeling a bit left out, George didn't mind at all for he would leave with the order he had sought.

Taking their leave two hours later with the order in hand, George turned to Edward as soon as they were seated in the carriage. "I don't mind telling you that I was becoming quite impatient and nearly ruined everything by speaking up. You were brilliant how you maneuvered him into basically bringing up the topic himself."

"Patience, George, is a virtue. Many a man has gotten an answer he didn't want by forcing the subject into the fore of the visit, placing the senior in a defensive posture. As you saw, by engaging the General on other subjects, he relaxed with us and we were able to handle it amicably. The General will also remember this issue the way we want him to, positively toward us, even if unlikely to recall the specifics of our arguments."

"I have learned a considerable amount from you already, and, just when I think I've learned all you have to offer, you surprise me with another lesson. I am indebted to you, Edward, for more than I can ever repay."

"I'm not so sure, George. Now that you have the authority, you will also incur the blame. Remember the old adage 'Be careful what you wish for, you just may get it.'"

The next morning, good to his word, General Shirley sent Edward a copy of his letter to the Duke of Cumberland requesting Edward's release from his present assignment and requesting the Commanding General in the Americas decide where best to use him.

"I'm afraid by helping me I have placed you in an awkward position, Edward. I'm sorry for that."

"It was bound to happen. Lord Halifax only made me an advisor to get me positioned where he thought he could use me later. I have actually been expecting it and, had General Braddock lived, it would have happened long before now. He prepared the same request, dying before he had a chance to sign it."

As Edward went to dress for his dinner with the Faircloths, Aaron pointed out they had not brought suitable clothing, aside from his Regimentals, for the occasion. Edward acquiesced as he had little choice.

Arriving on time and in his Regimentals, Edward was shown into a very comfortable drawing room by an overawed servant where he was greeted in short order by Captain Faircloth.

"Colonel Jewett, welcome to my home, sir. What has it been now, twenty years, since we met at your brother's wedding?"

"Captain Faircloth, I am honored to be remembered."

Mrs. Faircloth and Captain Faircloth's mother, the Widow Faircloth, joined them and they passed a pleasant hour reminiscing before dinner was announced. During the meal, Mrs. Faircloth asked about Marie and Lewis and it was two courses later before Edward had satisfied her curiosity.

"Your nephew sounds delightful," the Widow Faircloth said. "I wish he was my great grandson instead of the problem we have."

This gave Edward the opportunity to ask after Hannah and how he could deliver the letter Marie had written to her.

"Gone, she is. After failing at everything here, her husband decided to uproot them and now they are in Albany. He thinks the Dutch will put up with his laziness. Hah! Not any more than we did here in Boston."

The blunt statement surprised Edward. His experience had the better sort more circumspect airing any discord within their households. Then again, Captain Faircloth was well known for speaking his mind.

The Widow Faircloth continued in this vein. "Colonel, I'd value your opinion. My great grandson is becoming more like his father by the day. Do you think finding him a position in the army would help mold him into a man? Can you advise me on this?"

"Mother, you remember how poorly he did as a cabin boy. I can't imagine him succeeding as a soldier." Turning to Edward, Captain Faircloth explained, "I shipped him with my best Captain on one of my own ships for a short trip to Bermuda and back. When he brought the boy back, the Captain said he would quit the sea before he would accept my grandson on his crew again."

"Well, Captain, the boy is now what, thirteen?" They all nodded and Edward continued, "My experience tells me a boy that young would have a very difficult time in the army, even more so if he were headstrong. I can't recommend that course to you. Had he some education he might fare as an apprentice clerk, but even that would require some discipline."

"It's just as well," Mrs. Faircloth said with a sigh. "As his father is unlikely to agree to any plans of ours, especially now that he has the two of them clear out in Albany and feels he is out from under any obligation to us. I just feel so for Hannah."

The conversation paused awkwardly at this point and, when it resumed, it was back on Marie, Lewis, and Philip, a much more comfortable subject for Edward. As he left, he entrusted Marie's letter to Hannah with Captain Faircloth and returned to his lodgings.

The next morning, they got an early start back toward Virginia. The weather was better, the snow having stopped, and, as they moved south, it improved as they went. Their pace was more leisurely and they chose to stop in Philadelphia to rest the horses for a day. Besides, Aaron developed a boil from riding in wet clothing and riding was now uncomfortable.

After a physician lanced Aaron's boil and he was resting comfortably, Edward went to stretch his legs and chanced upon Benjamin Franklin on the street.

"Why, Mister Franklin, I don't suppose you remember me, but…"

"Not remember you, why Colonel Jewett, I am so glad to see you. We had first heard you were lost with General Braddock but I was gratified to learn those rumors were false."

"Well, it seemed a close thing for a while, but I have fairly recovered from my injuries."

"Listen, while you're here, I would like to give you some copies of my Almanac to take back with you, for your family. Perhaps it will provide you some amusement on a winter's evening. My shop is just across the street, do you have the time?"

Edward graciously accepted the Almanacs after offering payment for them, which Benjamin absolutely refused. They then retired to a nearby coffeehouse to continue their conversation, Benjamin quite interested in hearing firsthand of the events along the Monongahela. When he learned that George was also in town, Benjamin insisted they both dine with him.

Both Colonels found Benjamin in a jovial mood that evening and the conversation was lively and humorous, full of his witticisms and quips much like those he sprinkled throughout his Almanacs. They did take their leave early as they planned on starting before dawn the next morning, Aaron now much improved and ready to resume their journey.

The rest of the trip to Mount Vernon was uneventful, though hard on man and beast, both because of the distance and the still cold weather. On preparing to continue their journey back to the Valley, Aaron found their horses had recovered well while in the care of George's people at Mount Vernon. Over breakfast the next morning as they prepared for a more leisurely departure, George had one more surprise for them.

"Edward, it is a shame to have such a fine stallion and not have equally fine brood mares to go with him. I'm sending two back with you so Marie can see to the improvement of your horses, making them something more appropriate for such a prominent family as yours."

The offer stunned Edward and George rather enjoyed seeing his friend caught by surprise, speechless and sputtering. Placing his big paw of a hand on Edward's shoulder, he brought them eye to eye before continuing.

"It doesn't matter what you say, I'll not argue with you. The brood mares are yours and that's final."

Edward's protests to George fell on deaf ears. Nothing he could say would persuade the young Virginian either that his gift of two brood mares was too much or to accept payment for them. George just waved off every argument Edward made.

"I've lost more in bad bets to gentlemen I had no fondness for," he concluded. "So take them and I'll listen to no more protests." Then, with true affection, "I can't thank you enough for all you've given me, Edward. Let me give you this as a token of my esteem."

That was an argument Edward had no counter for so, reluctantly but very moved by the sentiment, he acquiesced. The two tall men then said their heartfelt goodbyes and Edward, Aaron, packhorse, and two brood mares, began their journey back to the Valley.

❧ Chapter 11 ❧

Lewis had a good fix on where the shots had come from, even seeing a little white smoke marking the second point of discharge. It was just inside the woods that covered the top of the next ridge to the west, the one that marked to boundary of their grant, and in the general place they would have expected the patrol to be if they were making their way to the Jewett's little fort.

"Let's spread out, Henry to the left, Miles you go to the right. Stay about a hundred yards out and let's move carefully. We don't know what this is," Lewis said with far more confidence than he was feeling. A quick look over his shoulder told him the others had disappeared toward safety. He checked his priming and refreshed it, as did Henry and Miles, following his example. With a deep breath, he looked left and right, then nodded and started his horse forward, Lewis heading directly toward where they had seen the now dissipated gun smoke.

It was with more than a little trepidation that Lewis entered the narrow band of woods at the low point between the two ridges before starting up the open ground toward the woods covering the upper slope of the ridge in front of them. He paused as he came back into the open, waiting until Henry and Miles were also through before all three continued forward. The ground was such that Lewis could see both Henry and Miles while each of them could only see Lewis. It all depended on him.

They had covered half the open space, with about a hundred and twenty-five yards left to go, all of it now within rifle shot of the woods, when Henry shouted to hold. Lewis stopped Miles and then looked back to see what was happening with Henry on his left. Movement caught his attention beyond Henry. It was a rider, coming fast along the narrow wood line they had just exited a few moments earlier. Lewis again checked his priming and pulled the hammer back to full cock.

Henry did not flee in front of the rider, making Lewis think he must know who it was. One rider, could it be that the other two members of the patrol were down? When the rider reached Henry, Lewis could see it was Ben Gordon and he was talking to Henry while making gestures toward the woods in front of Lewis. Lewis lowered the hammer of his rifle back to half cock. That's also when he realized he had been holding his breath. Then both Ben and Henry were riding fast toward Lewis and motioning for him to move back toward the woods behind him. Turning, he signaled to Miles and they all converged at the point Lewis had left the woods several minutes before.

"Lewis, I'm glad I caught you in time. Matt Bennett and I have been watching five Shawnee in those woods for the past hour or more. We sent Stuart back to spread the alarm. Listen, they've been watching you work clearing these woods and after you finished, just before you made it over the rise, they fired that shot. Although it stopped you, I guess your hesitation unnerved them and they fired a second shot hoping it would bring you back to check things out. They're luring you into an ambuscade sure as I'm here telling you about it."

Lewis looked back to the woods they were approaching and realized just how close they had come to becoming victims. The thought frightened him for a moment until he shook his head and regained control of his faculties.

"You say five, are you sure there are only five about and this isn't just a group scouting for a much larger war party?" asked Lewis earnestly.

"We'd completed our entire circuit and these are the only tracks we found. I think if there had been more, we'd have come across their sign. I guess you could say I'd stake my life on it, because if I'm wrong, I'm as dead as you'll be."

"Alright, they obviously saw you ride to warn us and know their plans have been discovered. Where did you leave Matt? Tell me, don't point!"

"He's at the top of the ridge, just in front of where Henry would have entered. He's on their back trail for when they turn to leave. He picked a spot among some rocks that gives him a good view down the hill."

"And behind him? Can he see what's coming up the ridge from the west?" Lewis did not even trying to conceal the concern in his voice.

Thinking and scratching the back of his neck, "Oh, I see what you're getting at. No, he can only see what's coming at him from this side of the ridge, not the west side."

"He's in a bad spot, Lewis," said Henry with a look of concern on his face. "If those Shawnee pull back now, Matt will have his hands full of trouble, and if there's more of them, they'll come right up behind him and catch him in the middle."

"That's right," Lewis said, thinking fast. "Henry, you go with Ben and get back to Matt. Swing wide to the left so you don't give away Bennett's position. Miles, you come with me, we're going to swing to the right about two hundred yards. At the least it should split them up a bit. Now, Henry, when we make the woods, we're going to dismount and move toward the top of the ridge. Once there, we'll move left toward you. Get to Matt and then hold your position until we come to you. If we're lucky, we might surprise them like they planned to do to us. If not, we'll at least be moving to the same spot."

Nods all around confirmed they thought it a sound plan. Henry reached out and grabbed Lewis's shoulder, "You be careful, brother. I'll be waiting for you at the top of the ridge."

With that, they scattered, two left and two right, riding fast. When Lewis calculated they had covered the two hundred yards, he turned sharply left and made straight for the woods covering the ridge, Miles staying close up with him. He headed for a small patch of cedars among the bare hardwoods and, as soon as he was among them, reigned in and dismounted quickly. In the few minutes it took Miles to tie the horses, Lewis positioned himself behind a rock outcropping at the base of a large cedar and was scanning the woods for movement. He saw none.

Miles was breathing heavily when he joined Lewis. "That was fun. What do you have in mind now?"

Scanning the woods slowly, a plan formed in his mind. "See how this outcropping we're behind continues nearly unbroken all the way to the top?" Miles looked and then nodded. "Staying low, you move along it a ways, but not too far, while I stand ready to deal with the Shawnee. I'll then move to and beyond you while you watch for our visitors. You then do the same while I watch, and we continue like that until we reach the top."

Miles nodded and began to move low and slow. After twenty-five or thirty yards, he found a spot he was comfortable with and whistled softly to get Lewis's attention, so intent was he on the woods to their front that he wasn't watching Miles at all.

Before he started, Lewis thought to himself, "I'm getting too old for this." He then moved slow, low and steady to Miles, paused, and continued on another twenty or so yards where he found a good spot to wait and watch. Just as he was about to settle in, a shot rang out and stone chips were knocked into his face. Lewis hadn't even had time to drop behind the rock when he heard Miles fire.

His face stung from where the rock chips had cut him and there was dirt in his eyes. Even so, with Miles's gun now empty, he knew he had to get into position fast. Blinking rapidly to clear the dirt from his tearing eyes as he brought his gun to rest on the top of the rock, he was quickly ready should the Shawnees move on Miles.

Miles reloaded, staying as low as possible as he did so, and then moved up to where Lewis waited.

"That leaves four, if Ben can count. Are you alright?"

"Some stone chips got me. That was too close."

"Yes, sorry. I saw him shoulder his gun and he had the round off before I could get a bead on him. He was fast."

With that, Miles patted Lewis on the shoulder and moved further up the ridge. After what had just happened, they started moving more cautiously, leaving less distance between them, more like ten yards rather than twenty or more. In time, they reached the top and paused together to plan their next move.

"My guess is we now have about two hundred yards to cover to join the others, assuming they're near where Ben said they'd be."

"Yes, but we'll be silhouetted against the sky if we move along this ridge top, and I'm not of a mind to make things that easy on the Shawnee."

Lewis looked around, taking stock of the landscape. Climbing up, it looked like the ridge was rather steep and he assumed it was the same on both sides. Now that they were on top, Lewis realized it had a rather broad, rounded summit, making their situation difficult. Of course, he thought, I've been over this ridge before, only circumstances were different and I wasn't thinking of silhouettes and stalking an enemy. He did note, however, that there were other rock formations spaced along in the direction they wished to travel.

"What do you think of this, we do essentially the same thing we did getting here, moving from rock formation to rock formation? This time, whichever one of us is moving, needs to first move down the slope," Lewis continued, indicating the west side of the ridge. "Otherwise, we risk being seen as a silhouette against the skyline. Once down the slope, move from tree to tree, coming straight up the slope to the next rock formation. We're probably going to have to pick up the pace or we'll run out of daylight and be at their mercy."

"Are you sure you haven't done this before? Alright, as you came up with the plan, I'll move first. I'll drop down a bit right here, signal when you're ready."

A slight nod of Lewis's head sent Miles moving quickly. The recent snow had left the woods damp, allowing them to move quieter, faster than if the leaves had been dry. Coming up to the rock formation from the west, Miles carefully looked around before signaling Lewis he was ready. Lewis fairly flew as he made his way beyond Miles. Thinner and taller than Miles, he was quite nimble on his feet.

Once in position, he not only carefully checked the woods to their front, he also paid attention to the next rock formation, the one Miles would be heading toward next. Just as he was convinced all was clear, movement among those rocks caught his attention and he put out a hand, palm toward Miles, to hold him in place.

Was it a bird or squirrel perhaps? Lewis just wasn't sure and he couldn't send Miles racing toward it until he was. He waited and watched, the tension building. There it was again, definitely not an animal, too large, but it was gone again. Lewis studied the rocks with an intensity he didn't realize he was capable of, trying to distinguish between rock and man. And then he could see him, a Shawnee amongst the rocks so as to be nearly invisible. Now that he saw him, though, he could hardly believe it had been so hard to distinguish him from the rocks. Looking carefully, the Shawnee appeared focused on Miles and seemed not to have seen Lewis make for the closer rock formation. He took careful aim, breathed, held, and squeezed. The quiet of the woods was once again shattered by the roar of a rifle.

Miles was beside him before the smoke cleared and they could see the Shawnee sprawled on his back, no longer able to bother them. Lewis quickly reloaded and they both scanned the woods and rocks around them. All seemed quiet.

"That would have hurt," Miles observed before moving off to occupy the rocks so recently vacated by their adversary.

Because of their recent experience, Lewis joined Miles instead of leapfrogging to the rocks beyond. Both then spent some time looking carefully all around, now in-cluding the slope to the west as well as the east.

"Have I mentioned I'm getting too old for this?" Lewis whispered to Miles.

"Oh, you have a good way of hiding it, if you ask me," Miles chuckled under his breath. "You move pretty good, old man, and a lot faster than I can."

"I'm off," Lewis whispered.

With that, Lewis started toward the next rock for-mation. He had moved down the gradual west slope and just turned to make his run south when several shots rang out in front of him and he dropped heavily to the ground, face down.

∞ Chapter 12 ∞

After his sons left with the laborers to cut timber, Robert joined Esther in his cabin for a leisurely breakfast with Sarah, Jenny, and Rebecca. He enjoyed the company and was in fine humor, making all the women laugh with his stories. Now he had some new material to work with, Ronald Samuel and his forgetfulness being a favorite topic these days. Even though he was making them laugh at Ronald's expense, all could sense the affection Robert felt for his new friend. It cheered Esther to see her father so happy. After they'd finished eating, he left to make his rounds.

Robert had taken to spending part of every morning visiting with the off duty soldiers who were stationed at their little fort. Over the months, he had learned them all by name, knew their parents' names, if they had brothers or sisters and their names, and the circumstances of their families. Occasionally, one or another would ask him to write a letter to their parents, not all of them being able to read and write. He had even taken to teaching those who wanted to learn how to read and write for themselves. One young man always sat nearby when Robert was doing the lessons, though he said he didn't need the lessons as he could already read and write. Robert doubted it but, as was his nature, never challenged the soldier on it.

He also spent time on the second floor of the block-house with the pair of soldiers always on duty there. Ever mindful not to cause a distraction so that they might miss something, he nonetheless helped them pass their monotonous watches with a bit of humor or good natured conversation. And he always carried the spyglass to check out any distant movement. While on watch, he didn't want the soldiers using the spyglass as that would focus their attention on too narrow a field and they might miss something important just to the left or right of where they had the spyglass trained.

Today, with so many to include all of his sons out of their little fort, Robert decided to hold his lessons with the off duty soldiers on the second floor, where he would be nearby if anything were to go wrong.

Esther had arranged with Sam's wife, Rachael, and Jubal's wife, Sally, both former slaves, to go through the laborers' cabin to note what needed mending or replacing. With everyone but the women gone, this was the best time to do it. If the men were around, they would sometimes hide their mending out of embarrassment. They preferred Esther not always see where their clothes were wearing out. Or else they would take to making bawdy jokes to distract the women from their task. Today, the only man in the house would be Rachael and Sam's son, Joseph, not yet two.

When she arrived at the cabin all the laborers shared, Rachael met her at the door. Esther had found the two women very reserved around her and the other family women and hoped to use this opportunity to draw them out more. Inside, Lewis had insisted on dividing the cabin to allow the two married couples some modicum of privacy from the six unmarried men. Still, the two couples and Joseph shared one long, narrow open room down one side from front to back with the one smaller fireplace, not overly private but better than all being in one big open cabin with the unmarried men. Sally had hung a couple of old blankets on a rope to divide her and Jubal's space from Rachael and Sam's and give the couples their own privacy.

They started in the large room, going through the clothes of the single men. Esther sat at the table and made a list of who needed what mended or replaced, the other two women not being able to write. It wasn't long into this process when all three found themselves laughing about the habits and ways of these men, the humor at times turning a bit bawdy for Esther's usual taste. She chose not to protest and go along as it was drawing these two women out more and more.

They finished in the large room and moved into Sally and Rachael's portion of the cabin. This was where the women at first got quiet, looking slightly embarrassed to have Esther see their meager belongings. To overcome the awkwardness, Esther noted the fine stitching done on the old blankets, where Sally had folded them over the rope and stitched them to form the room divider. She complimented Sally and asked if she could teach her to do such fine work, as she considered her sewing to be rather inferior. Sally warmed up immediately and brought out some more of her work to show Esther while Rachael did the same. They really were both quite good with their stitches. That gave Esther an idea.

"If we had some cloth sent in with our next load of supplies from Williamsburg, would you be interested in earning some money turning that material into clothes?"

"Oh, Miss Esther, you don't need to pay us for making clothes for these men here," Rachael said, somewhat surprised by the suggestion.

"No, you misunderstand me. The rest of us are also in need of clothing from time to time, and I daresay some of our neighbors are downright desperate for them. If you had the material and one of us wanted something sewn, we would then pay you for your work. It would be a way for you to make a little money on the side," adding with a wink, "money your husbands wouldn't need to know about unless you decided to tell them."

This really broke the ice and the three excitedly explored how Esther's plan could be put into effect. Her list finally made, Sally and Rachael set out to do the mending while Esther would order the new articles needed. She also would order various types of cloth to make shifts and shirts, trousers, breeches and weskits and blanketing to make coats. Leaving the laborers' cabin, Esther felt really good about the progress she'd made that day.

She hadn't gone far when someone called her name. It was Mister Agner.

"Miss Esther, with most everyone gone today, your father busy with the soldier boys, and me not having any work to do, I was wondering if you would see fit, if you had the time that is, to sit and chat with me a spell, to pass the time before dinner."

Feeling a bit nervous, still Esther responded with, "Well, I'm not overly busy right this minute, Mister Agner. I suppose we could sit and chat for a little while. But mind you, it can't be too long as I have father's dinner to prepare."

They sat on opposite sides of the bench outside the door to Robert's cabin and chatted. Mister Agner actually did most of the talking, seeming rather nervous and not wanting there to be any silent moments. Esther learned how he acquired his knowledge of milling and preparing millstones, though he did go into a bit too much explanation of the process of making millstones. She also learned of his first wife and how she had died trying to give birth to their first child, who also did not survive.

When she announced it was time for her to see to dinner, he stood and awkwardly doffed his hat and bowed, thanking her for sitting with him. Esther smiled as she went inside, knowing she had learned a lot about him but he had learned nothing new about her.

"I saw that, Aunt Esther! I believe Mister Agner is sweet on you!" teased Sarah as soon as Esther had closed the door behind her.

Blushing, Esther shot right back, "Yes, and you also saw how a lady talks to a gentleman, with plenty of space between them!" Now they were both laughing. "Not that Mister Agner could pass for a gentleman, mind you."

"Maybe not, but he is trying to improve himself. I could almost smell the castile soap from in here." This did nothing to diminish the laughter, which continued off and on as they worked to prepare dinner.

Dinner was almost a repeat of breakfast, with Jenny and Rebecca joining them again and Robert telling more of his humorous stories. After dinner, he sat with Sarah and Rebecca, repeating his reading and writing lessons for them. One thing he had always insisted on was that the Jewett women know how to read and write. Sarah had fallen behind when Henry and Mary had removed to Boston, but she was bright and picked it back up quickly. Rebecca was a new learner and not quite as fast as Sarah but she worked hard and she felt a little pressure because of Sarah's abilities.

When the girls finally finished and left, Robert turned to Esther, "So, what did you and Mister Agner find so interesting this afternoon? You surely talked a good long time."

"Oh, he was lonely with no one else around to pester, so he decided to pester me. I took it as his way of getting even with me for that time I knocked him into the mill pond and tossed him a bar of soap," Esther said, trying to make light of the situation and hoping her father would drop the subject.

"Is that what it was, because from my angle it looked like you were enjoying the company? Ah, well, I was all the way up in the blockhouse and could be mistaken…"

They were interrupted by the sounding of the alarm.

"Quick, Esther, find Sarah and Rebecca and get to the blockhouse," Robert said as he rushed out the door.

Running to the blockhouse, he asked the soldier who had just finished hammering on the piece of shovel they used as an alarm bell, "What's the matter?"

"We don't really know, sir. We heard a single shot from over there," pointing to the west. That's when they both heard a second shot.

"We've got the slaves coming over the rise now," the Sergeant shouted down at Robert, who immediately corrected him on his use of the term "slaves."

Robert hurried up the ladder to where he could get the spyglass on the ridgeline. He could see Charles leading and the laborers coming quickly behind him with their packhorses. What he couldn't see worried him. His sons and Miles weren't to be seen on either flank and, watching as the group made their way into the narrow strip of woods along the creek at the bottom of the rise, they still hadn't come into view at the top.

With everyone now in the blockhouse and the soldiers manning the loops, Robert went down to open the gate. He was worried, where were his sons?

As they came up out of the creek bed, Charles moved to one side, letting all the men on foot pass while he sat there with his rifle at the ready. Although still worried, Robert also felt a twinge of pride at how his youngest grandson was acting more like a man with each passing day.

The laborers were all heavily winded and Robert grabbed Sam and Jubal. "Sit everyone down here until they can catch their breath. No one followed you over the rise so we have time." He then called for water to be brought from the blockhouse and saw it passed around.

When Charles entered and dismounted, Robert didn't even need to ask the boy what had happened. Charles just began at the beginning.

"We were starting back when we heard a shot from the boundary ridge, well to our rear and left. We stopped, at first thinking it may be the patrol in trouble. I didn't move to talk to Uncle Lewis, staying in the lead where he had put me, so I don't know what he was thinking, but he motioned for us to move on, and from his signal I took it to mean to be quick about it. I saw Miles and father join Uncle Lewis before we made it over the rise and I couldn't see them anymore. That's about when I heard the second shot. It was off in the same direction as the first and sounded about as far off. What I do know is the second shot didn't come from father, Uncle Lewis, or Miles." Charles paused to take a sip of the water Esther offered him, thanking her.

"So, you have no idea what your uncle planned to do about those shots or even who was doing the shooting?"

"I'm sorry, grandfather, but Uncle Lewis's signal, I couldn't disobey."

"No, no, Charles, I wasn't being critical of you or your actions, not at all. Why, the way you handled yourself here, at the creek crossing, I'm proud of you." Robert's soothing voice calmed Charles instantly.

"So, what of your Aunt Marie? Did she also stay behind with your Uncle Lewis?" asked Esther, concerned.

"Aunt Marie?" said Charles, now looking confused. "She headed back here about two hours ago. We watched as she cleared the rise. You mean she isn't here?"

❧ Chapter 13 ❧

Henry followed Ben Gordon as they retraced his path back south. He hoped they could get to Matt Bennett before the Shawnee discovered his hiding place. After riding hard for about two hundred yards, Ben turned sharply right and started across the open meadow, heading for the woods covering the boundary ridge at a full gallop. Henry didn't see it at first, but soon noticed Ben was heading for a small cut in the ridgeline that would provide some cover for them as they, hopefully, passed by the Shawnee more or less unnoticed. At least, that was the plan.

Crossing that open meadow knowing there were Shawnee in the woods caused Henry to tense up. He expected a shot at any moment, to feel again the searing heat of a lead ball piercing his flesh. This sent a shiver up his spine. By focusing back on the woods in front, he was able to if not exactly shake the feeling, at least push it back in his mind.

Ben reined in when they reached the woods, setting a slower pace as they moved higher and higher up the little cut. In this way, the horses didn't make as much noise as they would have had they continued the fast pace through the trees and laurels of this little vale. Henry knew why he slackened their pace, and appreciated it, but not being able to see over the top of the banks, being so closed in, didn't give Henry any more comfort than riding across that open meadow. In some ways it was worse now. At least in the meadow you had a chance the Shawnee brave would have difficulty hitting a moving target at a distance. Here, if they suddenly appeared at the top of the bank, it would be like shooting fish in a barrel, and he and Ben would be the fish.

That's when they heard it, the report of two rifles, one closely following the other, some distance off in the direction where Lewis and Miles should have been. They stopped and listened for several minutes but heard nothing else beyond the normal forest sounds of squirrels and birds, so they moved on again, as quietly as they could. The little valley they'd been using gave out in a bowl containing a spring and Matt Bennett's horse. Here they dismounted and tied their horses beside Matt's before climbing cautiously out, Ben in the lead.

Their movements were those of both hurry and wait. They would dash from tree to tree, but wait and watch the forest around them before moving to the next tree, ever fearful they would be spotted and intercepted. Henry's only comfort at this point was the knowledge Lewis had been right. The Shawnee had either split up or, worse case for Lewis, all gone after Lewis and Miles.

A few more trees and Ben pulled his wing bone turkey call from his hatband and gave three soft clucks on it. This was answered by two clucks coming from a rock formation at what appeared to be the top of the ridge. Henry hadn't noticed it as such at first for it was fairly buried by leaves and masked by laurels from this side of the slope.

Henry only hoped the view from inside the formation was better than the view of the formation.

They had reached Matt and he knew they were there. Henry breathed a little easier now, when the thunder of another shot, closer, rolled through the woods. Ben and Henry wasted no time joining Matt among the rocks, taking up positions to watch both sides of the ridge. Matt had chosen well and they had a good view of the slope now to their front, even if the position had been hard to distinguish as they approached, the masking laurels didn't impede their view.

Here is where Henry noticed the ridge was more rounded than abrupt at its summit, the ground sloping off and rising again. Of course he knew it did that, but in his mind, as they were working their way to the top, he thought of it more as a sharp peak. Lewis had been right. Matt would have been in a terrible fix had the Shawnee come up behind him. The damp leaves would have made their movements all but undetectable until they were right on top of him.

Turning his attention now to the forest surrounding them and generally off toward the sound of the last shot, Henry saw a series of rock outcroppings spaced along this level of the ridge. They would make good cover for Lewis and Miles moving toward them, but would also make good hiding places for the Shawnee, possibly to let Lewis and Miles pass before coming in behind them. Could that be what caused that shot? And was that shot Lewis, Miles, or one of the Shawnee? And who was it that made the other two shots earlier? These questions and the waiting increased Henry's tension until he thought he'd burst.

That's when he saw movement. Not coming from the direction of the last shot, more to their right, down the slope more. Henry pulled his rifle in tight to his shoulder, pulled back the hammer, and got ready while still trying to make out what the movement was. After a few moments, as the movement paused and restarted only to pause again, he could see them, three Shawnee working their way from tree to tree up the slope toward them just as he and Ben had done earlier. The Shawnee were cautious, wary, as if they expected Henry and his companions only they didn't know where they would appear.

Matt, to Henry's left, had also seen movement and, out of the corner of his eye, Henry saw he was also ready. Ben was out of position, being situated more to watch the reverse slope, and any movement he made now would give them away.

Henry waited. The Shawnee weren't presenting any targets they could shoot at and to fire prematurely would only give away their position, so he waited. A trickle of sweat coursed its way down his back, under his shirt, almost tickling him. Still he waited and, with each passing moment, they drew closer. His cheek was now against the stock of his rifle as he moved his sights along with the Shawnee movements.

The Shawnee seemed concerned about the rock formations to Henry's left, where he at any moment expected to see Lewis and Miles. Were they coming and had the Shawnee spotted them? He certainly wasn't going to raise his head to find out. All he knew was they were running out of trees between themselves and Henry's rifle.

Just as all three cleared the last of the trees, Henry heard it, a metallic snap, just one but unmistakable to anyone who had ever pulled the hammer of a rifle back to full cock. Matt had just cocked his rifle and, for just an instant, the three Shawnee froze with their eyes fixed on Henry's little hiding place. Then five rifles spoke nearly as one and the Shawnee were lost in a cloud of white gun smoke.

Henry thought of reloading but pulled his belt axe and knife instead, one in each hand and not a moment too soon. Out of the guns' smoke came two Shawnee, leaping into the rocks with them, making their hideous shouts as they did so.

Caught in the act of reloading, Matt was driven to the ground by his assailant while Henry met his head on. A thin man, Henry caused the Shawnee to miss as he swiped at him with a knife by turning sideways and pushing his hips back. The Shawnee had miscalculated badly and now he was partially turned away from Henry. Taking quick action while he had the advantage, Henry had just brought his belt axe down on the Shawnee's neck when he was startled by another shot from very close by, so close he was hit in the face by chips of rock and sharp pieces of lead.

Thinking it was the third Shawnee, Henry dropped to one knee, placing the rocks between him and where he had last seen the Shawnee. That was when he saw that the shot had not been from outside the rocks at all. He understood now. When Ben heard Matt and Henry fire, he had moved around the rocks just in time to save Matt from a killing blow from a Shawnee tomahawk.

So, where was the third Shawnee? Henry searched with his eyes around the rocks and beyond as he quickly reloaded his rifle. Then he saw him, seated against a tree, head down on his chest. One of their initial shots had been true. He also saw more movement.

Bringing his now reloaded rifle back to his shoulder and sighting where he had seen it, Henry knew he would have to be sure because Lewis and…

It was Miles, moving cautiously toward where he had heard the Shawnee war cries. Henry lowered his rifle but not his guard. For all he knew, there were still at least two Shawnee out there, somewhere. His eyes continued to scan for movement as Miles moved closer. When Miles was clearly in view, Henry raised his hand as a signal to Miles, who acknowledged it by raising his hand. Both men continued to scan the woods around them for several minutes, minutes that seemed much longer than they really were.

Ben was busy now with Matt, who had taken a knife to his shoulder and was bleeding badly. Ben tried to stem the flow using Matt's sash. Henry knew both of those rifles were empty, so having Miles appear when he did provided Henry a measure of comfort and security. The only problem now was that they were both facing the eastern slope. Any Shawnee to the west who had heard the fight could be working their way up behind them.

Henry had no sooner thought to move to watch the west slope when a hand gripped his shoulder, causing him to about come out of his skin.

"Don't shoot me, baby brother. I've been shot at enough for one day, thank you."

"Lewis, am I glad to see you," Henry whispered back. "I'm concerned we can't see the west slope from here."

"I just worked my way up from that direction and there's nothing moving. How many did you get here? We shot two as we made our way up."

"We have three here. That accounts for the five Ben and Matt saw, assuming they got a good count."

"You stay put and keep a sharp eye out. I'll slip back around and watch the west face for a little while longer. We're about to lose the sun anyway. Then," looking to where Ben still worked on Matt, "we'll see to getting Matt back to the fort."

After dark, Henry struck a light to a small bit of candle he carried in his pouch, allowing Ben to continue to work on Matt. He moved off a little ways and was joined by Miles and Lewis.

"I haven't seen anything else moving," Miles whispered.

"Nor is anything moving on the reverse slope. That makes me think we're now alone in these woods," Lewis concluded. Turning to Henry, he then chuckled, "You about scared the life out of me when you all shot at the same time."

"Why, what happened?"

Miles picked up the story. "When those shots sounded your brother dropped like a sack of rocks. We were close and I thought they'd gotten him for sure. I don't know what scared me more, the thought of being in the woods alone with the Shawnee all around or facing Marie and telling her we'd gotten her husband killed off. Then I saw him move."

"Hey, I didn't know they weren't shooting at me, now did I? I dropped so they'd think I was down and would start looking for Miles. Once I thought they'd have their eyes off me, I rolled behind a big chestnut and signaled Miles I was alright. You should have seen his face. He looked so relieved!"

"That's about the time we heard the war cries and knew the shooting must have been at you all here," finished Miles. "We could see the cloud of gun smoke so we worked our way here and you know the rest."

Ben joined them. "I got the blood stopped, but he's lost a lot of it. I'm kind of afraid to move him as it might start the bleeding all over again. I have him wedged into the rocks to keep him from moving and removed the bodies so they won't bother him."

Thinking, Lewis said, "We probably should stay, only I'm concerned father will think us all lost if we don't get word back to the fort. Henry, is your horse nearby? Good, why don't you ride for the fort and tell them not to worry. We'll stay here with Matt and come in tomorrow."

As Henry worked his way through the dark woods toward where he had left his horse, he wondered whether he was given the better assignment or not. Maybe Lewis was sending him because he didn't want to make this night ride and risk approaching a fort full of tense people expecting a Shawnee attack.

Hey, he thought, have I just been set up by my brother, again?

◌ **Chapter 14** ◌

R obert wasn't prone to worry and took most things quite calmly, keeping them in perspective. Now, however, he was worried and there was no denying it as he paced the second floor of the blockhouse, moving from loop to loop hoping to see Marie or his sons, preferably both, coming home.

He had distributed his small force around the little fort, placing two of the laborers each in his and Edward's cabin, the center of the street and on opposite sides. The other four laborers were in their cabin at the opposite end of the street from the blockhouse. He had the Sergeant and six soldiers plus Charles with him in the blockhouse. Without their neighbors seeking shelter in the fort, and with so many of the family outside its walls, they were very thinly manned and Robert knew it wouldn't take a too large or determined Shawnee war party to overrun them.

They heard two more shots off in the distance to the west, distinct but very close together. This did nothing to alleviate Robert's worries. And he still couldn't understand what had happened to Marie.

"Charles, you're quite sure you saw your Aunt Marie come over that rise heading back here?" he asked Charles again.

One of the soldiers spoke up at this point, "Sir, you're asking about Mistress Marie? I saw her come over the rise, then angle more east. I thought she was going to the barn at first but then realized it was more like she was going to pass beyond the mill pond and the mill. I just thought she'd swing back around the mill to the barn, only I haven't seen her since and that was about two hours ago."

"Why am I..." Robert started with some anger in his voice before catching himself. This soldier was here in the blockhouse when he was outside questioning Charles and couldn't possibly have known they were concerned about Marie. "No, son, I'm sorry. You say she was riding across the face of the rise, there?" he asked, pointing out the loop.

"Yes, sir, she was moving kind of across and down like she was going just beyond the mill. I lost sight of her about there," he said, pointing to where the trees along the creek obscured their view of the slope.

"I could go look for her, grandfather, now that we know generally where to start," Charles volunteered.

"No, Charles, we don't know why she didn't return and I won't risk losing you by sending you out alone like that. You've done great today, but you've also done enough. Now, find a loop and keep a close eye out."

"Here she is," the Sergeant called. "Coming up toward the barn from the east."

Charles and Robert rushed to the loop and, sure enough, there she was, trotting toward the barn.

"What is she doing?" Robert asked to no one in particular.

Marie went straight to the barn and stripped the saddle off her horse before going inside. That's when those in the blockhouse heard another shot from off in the same direction as the others. From what they could tell, the shot wasn't any closer than the earlier ones and maybe it was a little further off. This Robert found as puzzling as to why Marie was acting the way she was, as if nothing was wrong. Coming out of the barn with two handfuls of hay, Marie began to rub down her horse.

Talking again more to himself than anyone nearby, Robert asked, "Didn't she hear that shot? What does she think she's doing out there?"

"We could fire the wall gun as a signal," the Sergeant volunteered.

"No, that was the signal to Lewis and Henry that we were under attack. I won't have them confused like that, especially not knowing what they're facing at this moment."

"I can go get her now, grandfather," volunteered Charles, again.

"Yes, you go and bring her here, quickly. We'll watch from here but I want you to keep a close eye on the trees along the creek. We don't know that there aren't Shawnee lurking there." Robert put a hand on each of the boy's shoulders, "Be careful."

That was when they heard a loud report of several guns firing at nearly the same time.

"What's this? It sounded like a regular volley," the Sergeant observed, quite surprised. "You don't think there's French Regulars out there sneaking up on us, do you Sir Robert?"

"Right now I don't know what to make of any of this...look! That got Marie's attention!"

Marie had heard the volley of shots and first looked confusedly toward the rise she had crossed earlier that afternoon. Looking then back toward the little fort, she realized the gates were closed and, turning her head further, realized all the stock was gone, perhaps inside the stockade like they did when there was trouble. That's when she felt the fear rising up within her. Grabbing the horse's lead rope, she turned the horse and started moving quickly toward the gate.

"Did you see how big her eyes got?" asked one of the soldiers.

"Keep your mind on your business, if you please. Watch the trees along the creek and make sure she's not being followed," ordered the Sergeant.

"Charles, run and open the gate for your aunt." Then, in a louder voice so all in the blockhouse could hear him, "Look sharp, we're opening the gate to let our straggler in. Guns at the ready."

With that, every loop that they could man had a gun protruding from it. This was not lost on Marie and she quickened her pace, the horse slowing her progress. As she approached within twenty yards of the gate, it opened and Charles came out past her, gun in hand, and backed slowly through the gate behind Marie and her horse, closing the gate behind them.

"That boy's got sense," remarked the Sergeant to Robert. "He knows how to cover an open gate as well as men afoot crossing a creek and open ground. He's a smart lad."

"Thank you, Sergeant. He is a smart lad," Robert responded. "And I am very proud of the man he's becoming. Now, could you see to things here while I go and have a talk with my daughter-in-law?"

The Sergeant smirked as he nodded, making a mental picture of what awaited Marie when Robert got her alone, where the presence of others wouldn't inhibit his language. Of course, the language the Sergeant was imagining was what he would use, not necessarily the words Robert was likely to choose.

Robert met Marie at the door to the blockhouse just as she was entering. "Marie, would you come with me, please?" he asked sternly, much to her surprise. He then led her to the nearest empty cabin, which happened to be Lewis and Marie's.

As soon as he closed the door behind them, Robert turned and fixed a stern eye on Marie, who wilted under the stare. "Just where have you been?"

"I'm sorry, father, I decided to take a ride. All we were doing up there was walking the horses in circles and I thought the exercise would be good for me and the horse. I didn't know anything was wrong. What's happened and where's Lewis?"

"You didn't know anything was wrong because you were off riding alone, again! We didn't know where you were and Charles was even ready to leave this fort to try and find you, only I wouldn't risk his life that way."

Marie was very taken aback by the upbraiding she was getting. Robert rarely scolded, making this all the more painful to her. At first she wanted to strike back, to tell Robert it wasn't any of his business, but she couldn't do that. Not just because Robert was the family patriarch, but because she respected him too much. That's when she felt the tears start to well up, her pride forcing them back.

"Charles tells us there were two shots fired from a distance as they were returning here. Lewis, Henry, and Miles went to investigate while Charles came back with our laborers. We've now heard a total of six shots plus the volley you also heard. We don't know what's going on, only that my sons are out there, in trouble, while you are off pleasure riding!" He nearly choked saying this, he was so mad at that moment.

Here he turned away from her, gripping the back of a chair, trying to regain his composure before proceeding. While he did this, Marie just stood there, her head down, eyes fixed on the floor. She had never seen Robert mad like this in all the years she had known him and now realized she was becoming a little afraid of him.

"Marie," Robert's voice was calm now. "I apologize for losing my temper. We can discuss this matter later, when Lewis has returned."

"And if he doesn't?" Marie asked without thinking.

Robert snapped his head around, anger flashing in his eyes again, "You had best hope he does!"

Marie jumped when the door slammed hard as Robert left the cabin. Too late she had realized just how bad her rejoinder would be received by her father-in-law, a man who loved his sons and daughter more than life itself. She slumped into a chair, asking out loud, "What have I done?"

It was dark now and the temperature was dropping quickly. Robert paced the width of the little street trying to regain his composure before entering the blockhouse. When he finally did, Esther met him just inside the door.

"Are you alright, father?" she asked in a soothing voice.

"I'm alright, daughter," giving her a hug that lingered a bit longer than normal. The discussion with Marie had gone badly and he felt terrible for having lost his temper not once but twice.

"Esther, do you think you could see that everyone gets supper at their posts this evening? We don't know the nature of the situation and I would rather we didn't let our defenses down until we do."

"Of course, father. Leave it to me. Do you think you could lie down for a few moments? All seems quiet enough now and the Sergeant has everything under control here."

Patting her arm, "Not just yet, daughter, not until I know what's happened to your brothers." Then, almost distractedly, he climbed the ladder to the second floor.

Esther watched with concern, concern for her father and concern for her brothers. Two were out there where there had been shooting and the third was making a hazardous and extended winter ride, all the way to Boston. She also knew if it was concerning her, it was far worse for Robert.

The women set to work putting supper together for the fort's defenders. Mattie and Betty went to Mattie's cabin and brought back the biscuits they had baked that morning, enough for a couple of days under normal circumstances. Esther and Jenny went to their cabins and returned with leftover venison roasts. With Sarah and Rebecca helping, biscuits and roasts were sliced and put together to form a nourishing, if dry, supper while Sally and Rachael drew mugs of sweet cider from the barrels they kept in the blockhouse. Once all was ready, they started distributing it around the blockhouse. Sally and Rachael then took the evening's fare to those in Robert and Edward's cabins while Esther, Rebecca, Sarah, and Jenny did the same for the laborers' cabin at the end of the street. Robert had forbidden them to take food to Marie, telling them she could join them in the blockhouse if she was hungry.

Returning, Jenny remembered some cheese she had in her cabin and bid the others to go on while she stopped in to get it. Entering her cabin, she lit a candle by blowing the coals in the fireplace to life. She stood with her hands on her hips for a moment, looking around the kitchen portion of her cabin until she saw what she was looking for, went and picked it up.

"Jenny," came a whisper from the darkness at the back of the cabin.

Jenny jumped, startled, and dropped the cheese back on the table. Almost as fast as she dropped the cheese, she grabbed the knife that had been next to it and spun into the shadows, stepping away from the candle and toward the door, her only escape route.

❧ Chapter 15 ❧

Lewis was standing alone in the darkness, looking off down the slope to the west where Henry had disappeared. He had heard Henry stumble, heard the horses when he reached them, and then heard him as he walked his horse further west toward the meadow and home before losing the sounds altogether. Now he was enveloped in the dark with hardly a sound to be heard. Miles and Ben were seeing to Matt among the rocks behind him, their movements exaggerated against the rocks and trees by the small light of Henry's candle, yet their sounds were muffled. It was very quiet in the Virginia woods at night in the middle of winter.

He started thinking of all that had happened today, of the plan to keep the laborers safe while they worked, of Marie's impatience at the task of guarding them, the near thing they had when they first went to investigate the shots, how Ben had saved them from a certain death, and then the woodland fight. A sudden sharp prick of pain from his stone chip scarred face reminded him of just how close death had come. This thought sent a shiver through him. Pulling his hunting frock closer about his neck, he tried to shake off the fear as he moved back toward the rocks and his companions.

He found them again trying to stop Matt's bleeding. Every time he moved, the wound would open and they would start the process of stemming the flow of blood all over again.

"It's going to be a cold night, Lewis," Ben said as Lewis moved into the small circle of light from the stump of a candle. "I thought I'd go down to the horses and bring up the blankets. Both Matt and I have one, so that makes two. It should keep us for the night."

"Ours are some distance off and I'd hate to try to get there and back in the dark," observed Miles dryly.

"We'll collect our horses in the morning," Lewis assured him. "In addition to the blankets, do you have any food with you? All I have is some venison jerky and parched corn."

"That's all we have, also, just trail food. We weren't expecting to be out long so we only brought what we normally would, just in case we had to overstay in the woods. Guess it's a dry supper this night." You could just make out Ben's grin by the candle, which was almost gone. "I'll go get those blankets. Promise not to shoot me when I come back?"

"We promise, you'll have our only blankets."

They listened to Ben as he moved clumsily through the woods toward the horses. On a dark night like this, there was no moving quietly.

"Lewis, I'm worried about Matt. That wound is as bad as I've seen, even if it is in the shoulder. Maybe if we had something to sew it up, but lacking that, it starts bleeding again, bad, every time he moves."

From his belt pouch, Lewis pulled his piece of candle and a small leather pouch containing a small ball of sinew and a couple of needles. "Will these do? It's not cotton thread and will leave large stitches, but it's all I have with me."

"That it will. We can worry about the fevers later. Right now we need to stop the bleeding."

With Lewis holding the candle, Miles set to work sewing up Matt's wound. It wasn't an easy task, still bleeding as much as he was, but the bleeding subsided as Miles drew the last stitch tight and tied it off.

"Well, that will hold him for now."

"It looked like you knew what to do, well enough."

"I'm no ship's doctor, but I've seen them do this many a time in my days at sea. His wound's cleaner than those you get on shipboard, where the big splinters can leave a nasty, dirty wound."

They wrapped the wound as best they could with what they had. Matt's blood-soaked sash now useless as a bandage, Lewis contributed his, holding his hunting frock closed with just his belt.

Ben returned with the blankets and went about cutting some cedar boughs to use as bedding. Then they fished out their meager rations and sat and ate in the dark, preserving what was left of the candle. Not much was said as they chewed, and chewed, and chewed at the dry, tough jerky. Each man followed the parched corn with a couple of swigs of water out of their water bottles before putting away what was left of their rations for the morning.

"I'll take the first watch," volunteered Lewis.

"Wake me and I'll take the second," Ben said as he stood and moved to lay the blankets out.

Miles and Ben positioned themselves on each side of Matt and arranged the two blankets over the three of them, in frontier fashion. They would have been warmer and more comfortable had they time to gather leaves to make a bed under them, but the few cedar boughs Ben had gathered for them to sleep on would just have to do.

Matt had roused a bit so Ben gave him some water and, as he warmed, he seemed to revive more. Chuckling softly, "Good thing this is just a two dog night as there isn't enough blanket to bring Lewis in if it were cold enough to be a three dog night."

Ben said to Miles, "So, now we're just dogs he's let under his blankets to keep him warm. Some gratitude. Maybe I should have just let him bleed."

"Nice talk," added Miles to Matt. "So maybe the next time I'll just sew you up with my vent pick and the strap off of my horn. That would suit someone as ungrateful as you."

"You mean you didn't this time? Sure felt like you did!"

Lewis, who sat off a ways but could still hear them, chuckled to himself. Even though severely wounded, Matt could still joke. These were hardy men, here on the frontier, hardly the sort he was used to around Rowley. No, the frontier was far different than anything he'd been used to before. He was starting to fit in, to become useful to these men. And yet he would never be like them, never totally accepted by them. They were from different worlds.

While they would never possess the frontier skills bred into these people, his family was now respected by them for what skills they did have. Robert and Edward were from the beginning respected for their leadership and that respect had grown as their neighbors realized they could count on them in a crisis. And now Lewis found these same men were showing him some of the same deference when he made suggestions to them. He had never imagined his life would turn out like this and he would have been perfectly comfortable remaining in Rowley, among all things familiar. That said, he would not have traded his current life, finding it richer in many ways than life in town.

Philip had picked up more of the frontier skills than he likely ever would. The boy could read sign and tell how many Shawnee there were, track deer and bear, and had sharp eyes to see game or trouble when it was waiting at some distance. He was growing up and not just taller, though that was also true. Lewis hoped the blend of schooling and frontier skills would make Philip into a better man, one respected by all like his grandfather and uncle. No, watching how Philip was actually thriving and how having property had opened doors for him, Lewis knew their decision had made a better life for his son.

But it had come with a price. He saddened as he thought of Joseph, his adopted son cut down in a Shawnee ambuscade, and his sister-in-law, Mary, who had been driven mad by her fears and had perished in the snow trying to escape the madness. He, his father, and Henry all bore the scars from the tough fights they had already had and Edward the mental scars from his. Marie missed the more civilized life of Rowley, preferring their snug house over the log cabin, even if the Jewett cabins were the only ones in the area with wood floors instead of dirt. She didn't see the dangers like he did, didn't understand why they couldn't build regular houses and stop living in the little stockade.

As he sat there musing, passing the lonely time listening for sounds he hoped not to hear, he realized that in spite of it all, he was pleased with himself and his life, or rather with what his life had become. He lived surrounded by his father, brothers, and sister, his son was learning how dear a thing family is and becoming very close with his Uncle Edward, and, to Lewis, there was nothing better in the world than that closeness of family.

The moon rose and cast its eerie glow, allowing Lewis to see about him and not rely only on sounds to alert him of trouble. He knew he should wake Ben to stand watch but found the peace after the day's excitement and exertion to be very relaxing. Finally, he had relaxed sufficiently. He knew if he didn't wake Ben, he would succumb to sleep, leaving them without a watch and seriously harming the reputation he had been working so hard to earn as one to be counted on. So he made his way back into the rocks and quietly woke Ben before taking Ben's still warm place under the blankets.

They woke with first light and found Matt had taken a fever during the night. They conversed in low tones about the next course of action and agreed there was little that could be done for him here, so Miles and Ben went off to gather Matt and Ben's horses, then go and reclaim Miles and Lewis's from where they had been left the day before.

Lewis tried to get Matt to drink some cool water, but was only partially successful. The first sip went down but he choked on the second and they gave up for fear of opening up his wound again. Lewis didn't want to risk further choking, so he didn't give him any jerky or parched corn. Hadn't Aunt Bess said you starved a fever? He never could remember just how that saying went.

When Miles and Ben returned, they sat and discussed how to get Matt back to the fort while they chewed more of the jerky and crunched the parched corn. Breakfast done, they set about gathering up the guns, powder, and lead from the Shawnee before heading home.

Ben mounted his horse, sitting behind the saddle, and Lewis and Miles lifted Matt up to sit on the saddle in front of him, wrapped and tied in his blanket. Ben would hold Matt in the saddle as they slowly worked their way toward the fort.

Miles led out first, walking his, Lewis, and Matt's horses while Lewis followed leading Ben's horse and picking the easiest way through the woods as Ben held Matt in the saddle. Once in the meadow below, all mounted and they began riding slowly, letting Ben set the pace. Lewis had Miles ride scout for them, still not sure if the five Shawnee they had dealt with the day before were all there were in the area.

Matt groaned a little from time to time, otherwise making no conversation. When they came through the woods the Jewetts had been working in the day before and started to climb the rise, Ben's horse shied and Matt shifted to where Ben was about to lose him. Lewis, riding to Ben's right, lent a hand to check Matt's fall until Ben could get him situated in the saddle again. As Lewis put pressure on Matt's right shoulder, Matt let out a scream, though that was all.

"I don't like this, not at all," Ben said to Lewis once they had Matt situated again. "His fever is worse and he doesn't seem to know what's going on around him."

"It's not good, Ben, not good at all. We've done our best for him, so now we just have to hope once at the fort we can break this fever and he'll start to recover." Even as he said it, Lewis wasn't at all confident Matt would recover.

Miles joined them. "Everything seems quiet between here and the fort, and Matt's scream didn't seem to get anyone's attention. I think we're in the clear."

"Ride ahead to the top of the rise, where you'll be plainly visible, and try to signal the fort that we're coming in. There's no point getting shot at by our own folks." Then, to Ben, "Even with Henry bringing the word last night, all it would take would be one nervous man with a gun to ruin our day."

⟡ Chapter 16 ⟡

Jenny backed toward the door, feeling for the latch with her left hand behind her back while holding the knife in her right hand in front of her, toward where she heard the whisper calling her name. With her eyes, she tried to penetrate the dark shadows at the back of the cabin, out of the small pool of light provided by the candle on the table. She didn't panic, didn't scream, instead reacting quickly and calmly like the woman of the frontier she was.

"Jenny, are you there?" the whisper came again. This time she recognized the voice, though that recognition raised more questions in her mind than it answered. Henry was out with Lewis, fighting who knew what, and there was no way he could have slipped back into their cabin, nor would he have come stealthily and not told his father he was back.

"Jenny, can you hear me? I'm here, outside, under the shooting loop."

The fear now gone, Jenny rushed to the back wall and stepped up on the bench that doubled as a shooting platform for the loop set high on the wall so someone out-side couldn't use it to shoot in.

"Henry, I'm here. What are you doing out there? Why haven't you come into the fort?" she asked, also keeping her voice down, not knowing why Henry was whispering.

Still whispering, "I don't want to get shot and thought if I just rode up to the fort, someone would shoot me off my horse."

"But how…?"

"I left my horse tied in the trees along the creek and crept up here. When I saw the light through the loop, I took a chance it was you. Can you get my father? Tell him I'll wait here, where no one can shoot me, until he opens the gate for me."

"Wait right there, I'll be right back," Jenny said as she quickly moved back to the cabin door and out into the street. At the next cabin, Robert's, she went in.

"Sam, listen, Henry is outside, along the wall, and whatever you do, don't shoot him! I'm going now to tell father."

Sam was surprised, first by the sudden visitor and then by the news she carried. He'd been looking as hard as he could but it was so dark he hadn't seen anything.

"Yes, Missus Jenny, we understand and won't shoot," his reply following her as she went back out the door on her way to the blockhouse.

"Father," she shouted from the door. "Henry is out-side the walls. We need to get him in without getting him shot by one of us."

Robert rushed down the ladder almost too fast, missing the last two rungs and landing with a hard thump at Jenny's feet. "What's that you're saying? Henry's here? How do you know?"

Quickly relaying what had just happened at her cabin, Jenny explained Henry's fear of being shot and how he had approached the fort. Robert then sprang into action.

"Sergeant, pull your men off the loops and make sure no one shoots. Henry is outside our walls and I'm going to bring him in. Charles, bring a lantern. We'll open the gate ourselves. Jenny, you're sure Sam knows not to shoot? Good. Sergeant, is everyone away from the loops? Good, I'll tell you when we're inside."

Jenny went with them as they exited the blockhouse and took the few steps to their gate, located under the protection of the blockhouse walls. Jenny took the lantern while Charles opened the gate and took a defensive position just outside the opening and against the wall. Robert did the same at the opposite wall.

"Henry, are you there? Stay close to the wall and come to me at the gate, son."

"I'm here, father," came the reply as Henry came into the lantern light, staying very close to the wall.

Jenny beat Robert to Henry and threw her arms around his neck, giving him a big kiss before hastening him inside the gates. Charles and Robert quickly closed the gates behind them and then it was Robert's turn to give Henry a welcoming hug. The gates had barely thudded shut when Esther, Sarah, and Marie appeared, eager to welcome Henry home and hear what had happened.

"And what of your brother?" asked Robert. "You're alone. This doesn't mean…?"

"Lewis is fine, father, Marie. He sent me back knowing you'd be worried." Catching sight of another exiting from the blockhouse, "Miles is fine, also, Mattie. But Matt Bennett has been wounded, badly it seems, and they with

Ben Gordon have stayed with him. They plan on bringing him in tomorrow, when they've controlled the bleeding."

"Charles told us of the two shots. Who was shooting and what were all the shots afterward?" Robert asked anxiously.

Henry told all gathered about the cunning ploy the Shawnee had tried to draw them into an ambuscade and how it had very nearly worked if it hadn't been for Ben Gordon and the afternoon patrol. He then told what he knew of the ensuing fight and how they had taken care of the five Shawnee the patrol had counted. They just didn't know if this was all of the Shawnee in the vicinity.

The lantern light reflected off the tears of relief and joy on Robert's cheeks as he learned the two sons he had been worrying about for the past several hours were safe and one was actually back here with him. His legs felt suddenly weak and, if it weren't for Esther's firm grip on his elbow at just that moment, he might have fallen. Recovering slightly, Robert gave Henry another hug.

"Jenny, why don't you take this son of mine home and patch up that face of his? Henry, you really are a sight, you know." He then passed the word around the little fort, establishing a strong watch but letting most get some much needed rest, especially the laborers who had been working hard all day.

Sally and Rachael took the watch from their shared cabin at the end of the little street, allowing all of the former slaves to sleep. The Sergeant was going to keep three men on watch in the blockhouse but Sarah and Rebecca volunteered to watch with just one soldier, letting the other two sleep. The Sergeant was hesitant at first, but saw Robert's nod and agreed to the unusual arrangement. With the two ends covered, Robert felt comfortable enough to let everyone else return to their homes and beds.

Robert slumped onto the edge of his bed, suddenly feeling drained, too tired to even undress.

"Father, can I get you some tea? It might make you feel better," Esther asked, concerned.

"No, daughter, I'm too tired to drink it. I'm just so tired." He paused, thinking, before continuing. "I'm afraid I lost my temper with Marie this evening, something I'm not proud of."

"I know, but I'm sure you didn't say anything that didn't need saying," Esther said, trying to calm her father's feeling of regret.

"Still, I shouldn't have lost my temper. I hate it when I do that."

"You don't lose it very often, I can't even remember the last time, so when you do it makes a lasting impression. I'm sure Marie heard you and will remember better what her transgressions were because you did lose your temper tonight. At least I hope so, she needs to remember! Now, let me help you into bed."

Esther helped him out of his coat and weskit and then lifted Robert's legs as he twisted back onto the bed. Before covering him with the blanket, she removed his shoes. Placing them on the floor, she looked back and saw that Robert was already asleep, snoring lightly.

She worried about Robert. He was really quite old, tonight one of those few times he looked his age, and took on way too much for a man of his years. In Rowley, most men his age would have retired to their parlors by time they reached Robert's age, but even there Robert had refused to do likewise. He liked to work, to be busy, to feel needed and depended on. She realized tonight for the first time that this is what kept him going, what he lived for, to be needed and depended on. Oh, and to be surrounded by his family.

Esther then returned to the blockhouse to stand her own kind of watch. With her two nieces and one soldier on duty, it wouldn't do for there not to be someone to chaperone the three young people. From the look of things, her arrival was timely as Rebecca moved quickly to one side, away from the now red faced young soldier.

"Oh, don't mind me, I'm just too worried about Lewis to sleep and thought I'd just sit up with you three for a little while until I feel sleepy." Of course, she never felt sleepy enough to leave the three of them alone.

Henry and the Sergeant saw to it the loops were manned before first light, allowing Esther and Rebecca to return to their cabins, Sarah choosing to remain with her father. Robert normally saw to this but Esther insisted they let him sleep. It was after sunrise when he finally did wake, looking refreshed and in good spirits.

"What, the sun's fully an hour up, why didn't you wake me?"

"Father, there was no reason. Henry saw to things and you needed your rest after yesterday and last night. It's fine, now come eat your breakfast."

Robert ate quickly and then set off to make his rounds, hoping no one had noticed his tardy start to the day. He found Henry in the blockhouse, his face puffy and red where the stones and lead had cut his cheek.

"I see your experiences of yesterday did nothing to improve your looks, son," Robert said good-naturedly.

"Funny, Jenny thought it quite an improvement," Henry laughed back, the Sergeant joining in the laughter.

"Any sign of Lewis yet?"

"No, and I wouldn't expect them just yet. They would need to collect his and Miles's horses, which were some distance off, then move slowly with Matt. I'm sure they'll be here by noon or so."

Robert then moved to the other cabins, making sure all were well and prepared for any emergency. This was something he always did when they were under arms and expecting hostile action.

They kept up a heavy watch but otherwise went about their business as usual. Henry and Charles guarded Marie as she took the horses and stock to the creek to water them before returning them to the pen they'd built next to the stockade. It had proved much better than having them in the streets all the time.

Marie continued to avoid Robert. She was still smarting from his harsh words the night before, words she wasn't used to hearing from anyone, especially from her father-in-law. Normally he was a very mild mannered man and had always treated her very affectionately. She really couldn't understand what had caused his outburst last night. All she had done was take a nice ride after that boring job of guarding the men cutting timber. How was she to know there were Shawnee about?

They were barely back inside with the stock when a tired looking Sarah rushed out of the blockhouse door and started banging on their alarm. Everyone rushed to their positions. Robert jogged to the blockhouse door.

"What have you seen, Sarah?" he asked, slightly out of breath but still in the calm, soothing voice he always used with his granddaughter.

"There's a rider at the top of the rise, waving his arms. We think it's Miles."

Henry appeared at the door and confirmed it was, in fact, Miles. He moved with Robert and Charles to the gate, opened it, and then all three stood in the opening, waving back at Miles so he knew they were expecting them. Robert turned to Sarah and asked her to tell everyone in the other cabins that Lewis and Miles were coming in and not to shoot.

Once the four men were inside and the gate closed, Robert turned his attention to Matt Bennett. Lewis and Henry had lowered him from his place on the horse in front of Ben and laid the limp body on the ground. Robert, Jenny, Betty, and Esther gathered around the form.

"Is he dead?" Betty asked after seeing the Matt's pale gray face and colorless lips.

☙ Chapter 17 ❧

Margaret Samuel sat reading her Bible. From time to time she'd look up from her reading and watch the young man across the table busy with his schoolwork. She liked having Philip in the house. He was very polite and courteous, quiet except when he and Ronald got to laughing about some nonsense or other. It was good to hear the two of them laugh like that. It would always bring a smile to her face as well, even if she did fuss at them once in a while for being loud. Having him here had worked out better than she had ever imagined and she had grown very fond of the young man.

The door to the cabin burst open, destroying the quiet moment, and in rushed Elam, all excited. "Philip, I found where some turkeys are roosting. Let's go do some spring turkey hunting before it gets too dark."

"Elam, shush, can't you see the boy is studying? Maybe if you didn't assign him so much work he'd have time for hunting and such."

"Oh, don't be such an old woman, he's fine. What do you say, Philip?"

"Well, if you say it's alright, Aunt Margaret, I only have a little reading left and I can do that after supper. I could use a break from reading."

How Margaret wished her own son was that courteous. "Then it's fine, Philip. Make sure you dress warm and don't be out late, you know when I serve supper."

Philip thanked her, marked his place in the book he'd been reading, and kissed Margaret on the cheek before climbing to the loft to change into his hunting clothes.

"What a nice young man. If only my own son had turned out so well."

"Humph," was Elam's response to his mother's jab. After a pause, "He's also a very smart boy, top of his class. I only give him as much reading as I do to better prepare him for William and Mary. He's already starting on this fall's assignments." Then, getting a playful look in his eye, "What's for supper? Maybe I'll join you."

"Join us if you like, but you'll eat whatever I fix if you do."

Philip returned, dressed for the woods, said goodbye to Margaret and the two left the warmth of the cabin for the cool spring air.

"How will you ever get a turkey close enough to shoot wearing that red frock?" Philip asked, curiously.

"Why," said Elam, his eyebrows raised and pointing skyward, "I will use the superior human intellect, outwitting a bird that relies only on instincts and not reasoned thought for its survival."

"Instincts are one thing, sharp eyesight is another," chuckled Philip, finding it hard to be as respectful of Elam in the woods as he was in the classroom. "I think I'd take a turkey's sharp eyesight over your red frock any day."

"Why, I would have thought you'd like my frock, it being the uniform color of your beloved Regulars and all."

"Just my point, they only wear those red coats when they're hunting men. When Uncle Edward is trying to outwit a turkey, he wears browns or greens. Nope, one can only sneak up on the 'superior human intellect' dressed in red like that," Philip retorted mockingly.

"Ah, we shall see, my young companion, we shall see."

"Alright, only don't sit next to me!"

Elam led them to where he'd seen the turkey sign and Philip saw droppings indicating several toms were among them. They then each picked their spots and sat down to wait. Philip had chosen to sit behind some laurels, downhill from where Elam had chosen to sit. He reasoned he might be able to get a bird shying away from that red frock Elam was wearing.

Pulling a wing bone turkey call from his hunting pouch, Philip let out three clucks. From Elam's reaction, he knew he'd fooled his teacher into thinking the turkeys were coming in. He waited a little while, then did it again, only this time it was answered by a clucking drake coming back from feeding to set her nest. Just as Philip thought, she spied that red frock and changed course, coming downhill right to him. A couple more drakes did the same maneuver before a tom came in. When he shied and moved to Philip, he waited until the tom was within twenty-five yards before taking his shot.

Elam joined Philip as the young man began field dressing the bird. "See how well my plan worked. I sent that tom right to you."

With his face to his work, Philip rolled his eyes before saying, "You did do that, I must admit. I think if you were to ask nicely, Aunt Margaret would invite you to dinner tomorrow to thank you for all your help in bringing home such a fine bird."

Elam was chatting away as they walked back toward the house, until Philip put a warning hand on his arm, listening intently to the woods around them. Then he signaled Elam to drop behind a large oak while he chose another tree nearby. They hadn't waited long before a lone Shawnee came into view, obviously trailing them. Philip watched as the Indian paused, pretending to look away after it appeared to Philip he'd seen something in Elam's direction, probably Elam's red frock. Philip saw the Shawnee moving his hand slowly as he very cautiously brought the hammer on his gun to full cock, the whole while feigning rapt attention off away from Elam. When Philip heard the sound of the heavy lock dropping into the full cock notch, that's when Elam's gun spoke and the Shawnee was toppled over backward by the heavy turkey load.

Running now, they returned to the village and passed the word to the watch that they had seen and dispensed with a Shawnee close to the village. Elam remained to join the militia as it was called out while Philip returned to the Samuel cabin with the turkey.

Margaret met Philip at the top of the steps just as Ronald came out of the cabin, an ancient musket in his hand.

"And where do you think you're going, old man?"

"Can't you hear the bell calling out the militia? They might need me!"

"If they need you, we're all in more trouble than we can get out of. Now, put that thing away before you hurt yourself with it."

Ronald did as he was told and returned to hear Philip's news of their encounter with the Shawnee.

"I suppose my shot at the turkey brought him up on our trail. We had no idea any Shawnee were in the area."

"Well, the militia will find out what's going on soon enough, I suspect," Margaret concluded.

"So, you say Elam shot the Shawnee and you shot the turkey? Hmmm, I'm partial to turkey, so I think you made the better shot," Ronald said, a glint in his eye told Philip he knew the response it'd get from Margaret, which came as soon as he said it.

"There wouldn't be a turkey if that Shawnee had got the two of them, now would there? Sometimes you say the silliest things." Throwing up her hands, she went back into the cabin, muttering to herself the whole way.

"So, you say you heard the Shawnee trailing you? I thought they moved pretty quiet in the woods," Ronald asked, anxious for the details.

"Not so much heard, really, as sensed. As we went into the woods, you'd hear the birds start chirping again behind us, after we passed. Coming out it was the same way at first, only then they stopped and didn't restart. That made me think someone or something was behind us. Uncle Edward taught us never to pass off these kinds of warnings."

"You know, you're a pretty smart kid," Ronald chuckled.

Not so very smart, Philip thought to himself. Not smart enough to have reloaded after shooting the turkey. Uncle Edward had taught him better than that, better than to be caught with an empty gun.

Elam returned after an hour, telling them the militia had found no additional signs so had doubled the night watch. With that, he plopped down across the table from Philip and asked, "What's for supper, mother?"

The next day, the boys all carried their guns to class, leaning them against the side walls when they took their seats. Mister Alexander came and addressed them, telling them that if there was trouble, the school would be where they would remain and defend as one of the places the townspeople would come to for safety. If trouble started after they dismissed for dinner, they were to return as quickly as they could. The militia, less Elam and definitely without Ronald, was back out scouring the woods on all sides of town looking for signs of more Shawnee about.

All of the excitement made it difficult for the boys to concentrate on their lessons, but Elam and the other teachers worked hard to keep them at it. Things were starting to return to normal with the teachers firmly back in control when it was time to dismiss for the day. Mister Alexander reminded all the boys as they headed back to their lodgings about returning if the alarm sounded.

Elam and Philip walked home together, as was their custom, and arrived to find the Samuel cabin smelling wonderfully of roasting turkey. Margaret looked tired as they entered, but also pleased.

"I am so glad you two are here finally. That old man is about to worry me to death, always wanting to lift the lid and check the bird. He's been constantly underfoot all day."

Ronald was just sitting at the table, grinning. "Well, I can't help it, I'm hungry and it smells so good."

"Yes, and if you hadn't lifted that lid when I told you not to, it would have been done earlier. It's just a good thing the boys are a little late is all. And if you're that hungry eat a biscuit." She then turned and grinned broadly at Philip and Elam, letting them know she and Ronald were just up to their normal banter. "Now, get ready for I'm about to put the bird on the table."

As they sat around eating, Margaret told Philip what a good turkey he'd brought them. "Fall birds are plumper, a bit more meat on them, but a spring bird tastes just as good."

"Hey, I helped get this bird, too, don't forget!" interjected Elam, grinning at Philip as he said it.

"Oh, the way I heard it was you got the Shawnee and Philip got the turkey. I think the turkey's better eating, but that's just my taste," Ronald tossed out, which got them all to laughing, all except Margaret who just sighed.

A knock at the door interrupted their good time. It was Mister Alexander.

"Elam, I thought I heard your voice in here. I'm just letting all the teachers know what the militia found. Seems there were only two or three, a scouting party and not a raiding party. The militia will keep an extra guard out for a few days at least. We'll have school tomorrow as normal." Then, looking at Philip, "That means the students shouldn't need to come to class armed tomorrow."

"Yes, Mister Alexander," Philip responded automatically, just like in the classroom.

"Oh, and Elam, can I talk to you for a moment, alone?" Elam joined Robert Alexander outside, closing the door behind him. "Just because the students need not bring their guns to class, I think it wise if you and the other teachers came armed, just in case. This whole business has our militia Captain rather nervous and he's sent a messenger to Fort Loudoun advising Colonel Washington of what's happened and asking for some help up here."

⊙ Chapter 18 ⊙

"**I** don't think he's dead, not just yet, anyway," said Ben as he dismounted and joined the little knot formed around Matt Bennett.

Betty and Jenny took to examining Matt's wound. "It's full of fever and we'll need to drain it before it'll heal," Betty said to Jenny.

"Yes, and we'll then need to apply a hot iron to stop the bleeding after it runs again. Do you think he'll survive it?" was Jenny's reply.

Robert stood listening, very concerned for their neighbor's survival. "Lewis, you and Henry should go and bring Missus Bennett and the children here. She'll want to be nearby and they shouldn't be at their cabin alone."

"Mister Robert, I can go," volunteered Ben. "And have the morning patrol bring them here. It was Jim Rice and Tom McCrary again, wasn't it?"

"Thank you, Ben, yes, Jim and Tom." Robert then turned back to the wounded man. "Can several of you lift him gently and take him to my cabin? Betty, Jenny, you can treat him there. Let Esther know if you need anything, anything at all."

Four of the laborers picked Matt up and carried him into Robert's cabin, placing him on the table. Before gathering towels and bandages, Esther put the poker into the fire, adding some more wood to revive the bed of coals, making it into a good, hot fire.

"Will you need needle and thread?" Esther asked Betty, softly so as not to disturb Matt.

"No, I think we'll need to leave the wound open after applying the iron. Can we use your father's shaving bowl to catch the poison?"

When Esther returned with the shaving bowl, Betty and Jenny began removing the stitches, opening the wound and allowing the poison to drain. When it ran with clear blood once again, Esther brought them the now red hot poker, which Jenny laid into the wound while Esther and Betty held Matt down.

The hot poker revived him, if only momentarily, and it was all the two women could do to hold him still so Jenny could keep the poker in place long enough to stop the flow of blood. When the bleeding stopped, they packed bandages around the wound, leaving it open to the air, and called for help moving him to the bed. The four laborers had been waiting outside Robert's door, ready to move him. Esther had him moved to Robert's bed where the women covered him and tucked him in to restrict his movements. And now all they could do was wait and pray.

Robert had been watching his cabin door closely from the bench outside Edward's cabin, where he was discussing events with Lewis and Henry. When he saw Esther come out and take a seat on the bench, he excused himself and went and sat with her.

"How is he?"

"Too soon to tell," Esther answered, feeling a bit sick herself, now that it was over.

"We have to talk," Marie hissed at Lewis as soon as Robert moved away and barely before Lewis heard the news about Matt. She then led him to their cabin and abruptly closed the door behind them.

"So, I suppose your father has told you all about what he considers my transgressions," Marie began, unable to conceal her anger.

"What are you talking about? Father said nothing about you. What did you do that he would consider a transgression?"

With that, Marie told how she had decided to take a ride after leaving him the day before and when she returned, she found the fort closed and heard gunshots in the distance, her first indication that something was wrong. She then told how Robert had become unreasonably angry and yelled at her, as if she'd done something wrong.

"Well," she asked when Lewis remained silent, "aren't you going to say something? Don't you see how your father is losing his mind?"

"Marie, my father had a right to be angry with you. You've been told not to go off riding alone, and what is worse, you lied to me when you said you were coming directly back here. Don't interrupt. I would have thought the lessons of three years ago would have lasted longer. That time you went riding alone and Joseph died, along with Jenny's husband and two sons. How many more will you kill so you can enjoy your rides?"

Marie was horrorstruck at Lewis's reaction. Her eyes wide and mouth open, at first she didn't know how to react. Lewis didn't normally speak so harshly to her and the look in his eyes, she'd never seen him this angry before. As the weight of his words sunk in, along with the memory of her capture and their adopted son's death, she turned her head and started to cry. She jumped when the door slammed, looked up and saw that Lewis had gone, and cried harder, slumping against the table.

Lewis found his father still sitting with Esther. "Father, Marie tells me you were angry with her last night. What did she do that made you so angry?"

"Well, Lewis, I did lose my temper with her, not something I'm proud of, and thought we could discuss the matter at some point so adjustments could be made for everyone's safety."

"I understand that, father. I just want to hear from you what happened."

Robert told his side of the incident, Esther prodding him to include how Charles volunteered to go find her. Esther finally became frustrated by how unemotionally Robert had presented the situation and interrupted.

"Lewis, we had no idea what was going on other than you were in a fight to the west and Marie was missing. We all thought she was taken once again and were worried sick."

"Now, Esther, Marie had no way of knowing what was going on, anymore than we knew what Lewis and Henry were facing. Let's be fair."

"Thank you both, I now know what happened here. Thank you," patting his father reassuringly on the shoulder before returning to his own cabin.

Lewis's sudden reappearance caused Marie to jump just as his departure had. She also noticed the firm set to his mouth and cold look in his swollen eye. Only then did she really see how cut and swollen his face was.

"So, did your father make up some terrible deeds I've somehow done to make him so angry as to yell like that?"

Lewis's fist pounding the table caused her to jump again and really frightened her. "No, in fact, aside from how worried he was about your safety and how Charles offered to go to your rescue, it matched pretty much what you told me."

This surprised Marie, both that Robert had been so even in his telling of the incident and that they were actually worried as much as they were. Now knowing this, Lewis's reaction, his barely controlled anger, was even more mystifying to her. "So you know I did nothing wrong."

"Wrong," Lewis spit back, louder than he intended. "You lied to me. You told me you were coming back here. Instead you went off doing whatever you wanted. Well, from now on you can go anywhere you like, but the horses belong to Edward and you'll not ride again until he says you may borrow one of his horses." He again turned to leave.

"But Edward isn't here to ask!"

"Exactly!" Lewis again slammed the door behind him.

Marie had never feared Lewis would strike her, as was so common, especially among the frontier families. She knew Robert would never tolerate one of his sons treating a woman that way. This was the only time she ever thought Lewis looked like he wanted to strike her and she thanked Providence his self control had prevented it.

"Miles," Lewis called once outside. When Miles joined him, nearly in front of Robert and Esther, Lewis continued. "You are employed by my brother, right? Good. In his absence, I want you to look after his property. I need you to see to it that his horses are kept safe here at the fort. Only Henry, you, and I are to have riding privileges, oh, and father," he added, turning and nodding toward

Robert. "Do you understand what I'm saying and will you do it?"

"Oh, I understand you alright and there'll be fireworks for it, but I'll do as you say and protect my employer's property, best as I can." Miles had a knowing smirk on his face, Mattie having told him of the events from the night before.

Robert looked to Esther and whistled lightly under his breath. This was as mad as he'd ever seen Lewis, angrier than Robert had been the night before. But he had to admit, he was also relieved Lewis was taking firm action to keep Marie safe.

"It's for her own good," Esther whispered to him, as if reading his thoughts.

The Bennetts arrived before dinner and Robert set about entertaining the children while Missus Bennett went to see her husband. Mattie brought over some clear broth she'd made from the bones of a turkey in case Matt woke and could try to eat something. She also brought a plate of food for Missus Bennett.

Matt healed slowly over the next couple of weeks. He had lost a lot of blood and remained very weak from his ordeal. He progressed from the broth to solid foods and finally was strong enough to walk, though he needed someone to steady him. His biggest concern was his arm as he found he only had limited use of it.

"Good," observed Betty. "That way you won't be waving it around before you're healed." But to Robert and Robert only, she worried, "That wound was bad and, though the men did what they could in the woods, they didn't apply an iron right away when it wouldn't stop bleeding. I'm afraid he'll never have full use of it again. Only time will tell if he'll have enough use of it to continue to work his homestead."

It was springtime now in Virginia and they set to work planting fields near the fort and planning on how to make more of the meadows productive. They also continued to keep a sharp eye out for further Shawnee intrusions.

While on patrol with Tom McCrary one afternoon, Lewis came across sign of what appeared to be a few, maybe three, Indians enter their vicinity from the northwest and make their way to the boundary ridge, avoiding the homesteads along the way. Going only as far as where Lewis had arranged the bodies of their five victims, this group then retraced their steps, exiting the Valley by way of Kerr's Creek and the Cow Pasture River by the time Lewis called off the scout. He was convinced they were looking for their friends who had not returned.

Robert was worried, however, as these Indians, if they were in fact Shawnee, seemed to know where to go looking for their friends, as if watching the little Jewett fort was their stated purpose before leaving their tribe to come to this area. That could mean there were plans to attack them, though he also thought the loss of their scouts would send a strong message and delay any attack. He hoped Edward returned before any more trouble came their way.

Marie did not like being unhorsed, but could do nothing about it. Miles was good to his word and guarded the horses jealously. She thought he seemed almost to enjoy keeping her on foot. He'd even moved her saddle into his cabin for safe keeping. Of course, it really wasn't hers. Again, it was Edward's that she'd been using for several years so she thought of it as hers.

She had also been working hard to mend things with Lewis. It was harder than she expected. He really didn't like being lied to and was responding slowly. She thought if Philip had been here, she might have had more luck as Philip always found a way to put Lewis into a good mood with his antics. But, no, she had to do this herself.

And things were better, even if Lewis did remain a bit aloof and wouldn't even consider it when she asked to be allowed to ride again. In fact, the couple of times she had brought this up it had set her efforts on mending things back, so she learned not to mention how much she detested walking, not to ask how long her punishment of being unhorsed would last.

"Lewis," Robert asked one day, "how long are you going to keep Marie guessing?"

"Oh, I don't know, father, I'm getting rather fond of the extra attention and you must admit, she is behaving herself better than ever before."

"Yes, but you don't want to break her spirit in the process. Just be careful, son."

Charles was sounding the alarm that drew Robert, Lewis, and Henry at a run.

❧ Chapter 19 ❧

Edward and Aaron traveled south out of Mount Vernon heading toward Williamsburg. The Burgesses would have convened their spring session by time they arrived and Edward had not reported to Governor Dinwiddie in person for many months, not since the Governor left him with General Braddock in Alexandria late last spring. Anxious as he was to return home, Edward always had a strong sense of duty and usually placed duty ahead of his own desires.

The weather was only cool now, but wet as early spring in Virginia usually is. Ferries had begun their operation again, only occasionally suspended while uprooted trees floating by formed a hazardous obstacle. Aaron was enjoying this leg of their journey as there were ample taverns for rest and refreshment along the way so that they didn't suffer from sleeping out of doors or eating trail fare.

They arrived to find the city bustling, the Burgess and the Court bringing in people from throughout the Colony. Unable to find lodging at the taverns, Edward took a chance and called on John Dandridge, who had housed him and his father on a previous visit. John and his wife,

Fanny, were thrilled to see Edward again and offered him his old accommodations in Fanny's father's office, situated adjacent to their Williamsburg home. They passed a pleasant afternoon in conversation while Fanny had the office cleaned and prepared. They spoke of old acquaintances and of their daughter, Patsy, who now had two children but still rode her London carriage too fast through the Williamsburg streets when in town, or at least Fanny thought so.

Once his quarters were ready, Edward excused himself and went to freshen up and pen a note announcing his arrival to the Governor. Calling on Aaron to take the note to the Palace, he was surprised to find Aaron not alone.

"Colonel, the tailor is here and Mister Prentiss has sent over a couple of shirts for your approval."

"Tailor? What, or rather why?"

"Well, Colonel, we left without proper clothing for a visit to Williamsburg and Mister Nicholson here assures me he can have a suitable set of clothes ready by mid-morning tomorrow."

So while Aaron took the note over to the Governor's Palace, Edward suffered through a tailor's fitting and fussing. Mister Nicholson made the task as easy on Edward as he could, obviously knowing his business well enough to overcome the impatience of gentlemen clients. Aaron had previously selected the fabrics so Edward was not bothered with that detail and, by the time Aaron had fairly returned, Edward's ordeal was over.

That afternoon, Edward chose to take his dinner at Mister Weatherburn's tavern. Still dressed in his traveling clothes, he nonetheless fit right in with those already gathered at that establishment. Mister Weatherburn recognized Edward right off and ushered him into his private dining room so Edward could partake of the better fare with the better sort, or at least that is what Mister Weatherburn said as he left him. Gathered in the room were various planters, some enjoying a bowl of punch before dinner and others enjoying their pipes while they conversed, sometimes rather heatedly.

Considering his time among the Royals at Court, Edward inwardly smiled and wondered if either those or this really represented the "better sort." Somehow he seriously doubted it.

Scanning the room for an empty seat, he saw James Bordon signaling him from across the room, motioning to an empty chair at the table he was occupying. Making his way there, Edward saw several other Burgesses he recognized from his previous dealings with the House.

"Colonel Jewett, I didn't expect to see you here. I had heard you were on your way to Boston or some such nonsense, though I gave it no credibility. No one would go to Boston in the dead of winter unless they had to, I say."

"And you would be quite right, Mister Bordon, only I had a duty to go so I did. I have just returned and will call upon the Governor before heading home to the Valley. How are things there? Have you any news?"

"Oh, we're faring alright, I suppose. Some Indian scares from time to time. It is Thomas Lewis who is feeling it the worst and Nelson Beverly to a lesser degree. Thomas has had his tenants all but driven out of some of the western and northern valleys, such as along the Cow Pasture and Bull Pasture Rivers, and many others have left simply out of fear alone. Nelson has had fewer attacks, but like me, has lost many a tenant to fear. Why, of my entire holdings, the area near your Grant is the only one where I can honestly say everyone is remaining on their homesteads."

"So there have been no attacks in that region?"

"Not so. There was a small party of Shawnee, probably more a scouting party than a real raiding party, just before I left to come here. Your brothers handled them well enough. Why I heard not a single savage survived and there must have been ten of them, maybe more!"

Now somewhat concerned, Edward asked, "And my family, were they injured?"

"One of my tenants, your neighbor as you refer to them, was badly injured, not sure what became of him, but your brothers were fine, the way I heard it, and they took care of things some distance from your stockade, so none of the rest of your family were in any danger at all."

Edward was relieved to hear his brothers and family were fine, though concerned that Shawnee had been in the area. He and James continued an amicable conversation through dinner. Edward concluded he would finish his business with the Governor and return home as soon as he could. If the meeting with the Governor went well, he would leave the following day.

Two notes waited for him when he returned to his lodgings. One was expected, Governor Dinwiddie asked for him to come to the Palace at eleven. He would wear his Regimentals for that meeting, he thought to himself. The other was from John Dandridge requesting he join them for a light supper this evening. Aaron had made notes to both invitations letting Edward know he had already accepted for him.

Supper was a pleasant diversion, though Edward thought John Dandridge tired too easily to be well. Even so, he appreciated the early evening as he was fatigued from his trip and retired early. The next morning, good to his word, the tailor appeared shortly after breakfast with a suit of clothes for Edward to try. They fit and Aaron saw to payment while Edward dressed in his Regimentals for his meeting with the Governor.

"Edward, it is so good to see you. You don't know how dismayed I was when first you were reported lost with Braddock. That old peacock nearly cost us everything," was Governor Dinwiddie's warm welcome before they sat down to business.

"We've had a good year in the House. They've seen fit to give us $55,000 for defense. Of course, you heard the fall session authorized the Regiment be raised to fifteen hundred men, well now they've enacted a draft law to go along with it."

The Governor was excited and animated at the good news from the House of Burgesses, but Edward was thinking, here's another friend who's not looking at all well.

"The law isn't the best, I'd hoped for better. I daresay we could have had a better law if I only had you here to talk to these infernal eastern planters, to convince them it's in their interest to defend the frontier, not just ours. But still it is a start and a lot more than Maryland is doing. Did you hear they're abandoning Fort Cumberland, moving the frontier all the way back to Fort Frederick?"

"I had not heard that, but find it disturbing, living on the frontier as I do. We had a bit of luck with General Shirley and he agreed with our arguments, so Captain Dagworthy won't be bothering Colonel Washington by issuing orders again. In fact, our Colonel Washington is now responsible for the frontier in both Colonies. You should have a copy of the General's order to that effect with the next dispatch boat."

They then started reviewing the provisions of the new legislation in some detail, discussing various points of interest or gaps in the legislation. Edward raised his concern over the split in military funding, the bulk going to supply the militia with the Virginia Regiment, actively engaged on the frontier, taking the smaller portion. Yet both men agreed, they couldn't complain as they did finally have funding and a draft law, no matter how imperfect they might be.

Their discussions continued through dinner, as Edward had suspected from the timing of their meeting. Their business concluded, he excused himself shortly after dinner and returned to his lodgings where another invitation awaited him. Several of the Burgesses requested he join them for a private supper at Mister Weatherburn's that evening where they wished to honor his service with General Braddock on behalf of the Colony. Edward let a small groan escape his lips as he read Aaron's penned comment that he had accepted, yet he knew there was little other choice in the matter.

"Aaron," Edward called and when he appeared, "I don't plan to make this a late night, so let's leave for home tomorrow morning, as early as you think we can be ready. Sunrise is good for me, but we have more stock to get ready for this trip, so I leave the timing up to you."

Although lean from his travels, Edward cut a fine figure dressed as he was in his new shirt and clothes. The private dining room at Mister Weatherburn's was crowded with Burgesses, mostly from the western counties but more than a few from the east as well. It was with the western counties that Edward held the most sway, the large planters accepting him mainly for his connections to Court and his understated wealth.

For every toast offered to his honor, of which there were far too many for Edward's liking, he countered with one for Colonel Washington, the Virginia Regiment, Major General Shirley, the Regular Regiments who were with him at the Monongahela, or others in that vein. As was his custom, he drank sparingly while most of his companions drained their glasses with each toast. It wasn't long after supper that Edward was able to take his leave with his assorted hosts too in their cups to really notice.

Breakfast was brought to his room before first light and Aaron had everything in readiness for their departure shortly after sunrise. As the Dandridge's were not about at that hour, Edward left them a note thanking them for their kindness. Although he had drawn his back pay from the Colony's Treasurer, he knew not to leave any funds for lodging or boarding his five horses as it would have insulted John Dandridge. Instead, he stopped by to see Mister Prentiss and gave him money to put against the Dandridge account. Mister Prentiss noted it in his ledger as if John Dandridge had made several smaller payments himself, assuring Edward that the aging man would never know the difference, and certainly wouldn't hear from him how his account had managed to shrink. Mister Prentiss watched Edward leave, as impressed with him as he had been his father on meeting him four years before.

Edward left feeling better. John Dandridge was a middling planter thrust into the upper level of planter society with his daughter's marriage. He was thus expected to entertain and conduct himself well beyond his limited means, as really all of the upper class of planters did, only it was harder for John. The Governor and Edward had frequently discussed how most of the eastern planters were land and slave rich but cash poor, many overwhelmingly in debt to London merchants, due to their lavish lifestyles. The Governor thought that would be the ruination of the Colony.

Although the roads were deep with mud from the rains and leading two brood mares and a packhorse was occasionally difficult, Edward and Aaron still managed to make reasonably good time. Both men were anxious to be home again and the animals were well rested and ready for the journey.

The redbuds were just blooming and the dogwoods not quite when they crossed the North River ford and made their way over the hill and into sight of the little stockade they called home. The watch in the blockhouse had evidently announced their arrival as the whole population turned out to greet them, some coming from the fields, some the barn, and still others the stockade itself.

Robert was the first to greet his eldest son and welcome him home with a big hug. This was followed by hugs from his brothers and sister while Aaron slipped to one side for his own welcoming hug from Betty.

As Charles, Jenny, Sarah, and Rebecca finished greeting Edward, Marie, who was much too preoccupied examining the brood mares, asked, "Edward, wherever did you get such magnificent mares?"

❦ Chapter 20 ❦

"These fine brood mares go with my stallion. It won't be long before I have the finest stable west of the Blue Ridge," Edward told Marie in particular, but all gathered in general and not without a little pride. "I think if we expand the stock pen, add some sheds to serve as stalls, it will serve us until this crisis is over and we can start building proper farms and barns," he said with a sideways look at his father. They were all anxious to begin normal lives outside the stockade but also understood Robert's caution.

Miles took over from Aaron, seeing to the needs of the stock, so as to allow Aaron time to be with Betty after his long absence. He made sure to double tie all the horses now, so there could be no contamination of blood lines until proper arrangements could be made.

Marie followed right on Edward's heels all the way to his cabin before saying what was on her mind. "If you want me to see to the breeding of your horses, you'll need to allow me to ride," she said with a touch of defiance in her voice that Edward did not especially understand nor appreciate.

"Oh, not to worry, Marie, I won't burden you with such a task. Aaron is a fine man with horses and can see to their care and breeding. There's so little for him to do when we're here, with Betty taking care of me, that it'll be good for him."

Marie was struck dumb by Edward's response, not being at all what she had hoped for. Turning to leave, he stopped her.

"Aren't you curious about your friend Hannah?"

The mention of Hannah brought Marie back and with the change of subjects was also a change in her demeanor.

"Oh, yes. Did you see her? How is she? Did she tell you why she hasn't written? Maybe she sent a letter with you?" she asked excitedly, all thoughts of horses now gone.

"Whoa, slow down. No, I didn't see her. I don't know how she is only how she was. I have no idea why she hasn't written and she sent no letter back with me. Did I answer all your questions?"

Marie looked confused. Robert, Lewis, and Henry had arrived just in time to hear Marie's questions and Edward's answers. They looked amused at Marie's confusion.

"I did have dinner with the Faircloths, though, and entrusted your letter with Captain Faircloth," Edward now continued in a more soothing voice. "It seems her husband chafed under the Captain's watchful eye and has up and moved the family to Albany. I hadn't realized Hannah had chosen so poorly in marriage until the Captain and his mother explained things to me. It seems Hannah's son, Luke, has also begun to be a burden to his mother."

"Albany?" Marie asked. "What in the world are they to do in Albany? Isn't that the frontier?"

"Well, not as remote as all this, but, yes, it is the Old Dutch trading center and very close to the Iroquois. The frontier is a bit further west and north, although these days with the French stirring things up…" he looked back at his father and brothers before continuing, "but I'd guess she has it a bit better than you do here."

Not catching Edward's last comment, Marie stated, "Hannah isn't used to that. She's used to the finer things," finishing with more emphasis, "Oh, that Daniel Davies will have a lot to answer for, taking her out of Boston."

The horse situation totally forgotten now, she left to let the men get caught up.

"There is obviously something about Marie and riding that bothers her so much she was trying to get me to agree to do something without reviewing the bidding. Care to fill me in, Lewis?"

Lewis gave a sketch of what had happened with the Shawnee scouting party and Marie's ride and its aftermath. "She's been walking, or I should say stomping, around here for a month now, not liking any of it."

"Alright, brother, I won't interfere with your domestic issues, but tread lightly."

They spent the next two hours reviewing all that had been happening, both in Virginia and in Boston. When Esther finally interrupted to announce supper would be in Robert's cabin for all of them, Edward caught her before she could leave.

"I've something for you, dear sister, well, really for everyone but I'm giving you first read. Doctor Franklin sent along four of his Almanacs and, knowing how much you like something new to read and hearing they really are quite witty, I thought you'd like to read them first." With a flourish, he produced the four and handed them to her. "I'd be careful, though, as Doctor Franklin can be a bit bawdy in his humor at times, or so he is over dinner, so not everything in these may be suitable for an unmarried maid like you."

Despite Edward's humor and the laughter coming from her other two brothers, Esther heard none of it and only saw the Almanacs. She thanked Edward and carried them back to Robert's cabin as if she was carrying solid silver. It was going to be so good to have something new to read, she could hardly wait. She put them aside to savor later and then saw to the final preparations for supper.

As they ate, they continued to discuss the business of their little village.

"I passed the carts bringing our spring shipment. At the rate they're traveling, father, I suspect they won't be here until day after tomorrow, at the earliest. Mister Prentiss sends his regards and asked me to deliver your latest account books. You seem to have ordered a lot this year, by the looks of those carts."

"Yes I did. I got to thinking that the families around here have so little and no way to acquire items they need. So this year I ordered extras so I could set up a little store for them. While Greenville has a small store, you really need to go all the way to, what are they calling it now, Staunton, to replace a pot or skillet. I guess I forgot to mention it after your return, what with everything else we had to catch up on."

"Not to worry. As long as you know what you're getting yourself into, I'm fine with it."

In two days time, when the carts arrived, Robert found there was much more than just what he ordered. There was also a list of "diplomatic gifts" to be distributed to the northern bands of Cherokee, Governor Dinwiddie's attempt to sway the Cherokee into joining the English against the French and their Indian allies. The bureaucratic letter of instruction from one of the Governor's underlings convinced Edward the Governor had no hand in how these gifts were to be distributed, explaining why he hadn't mentioned the Jewett's role when Edward was with him in Williamsburg. In his usual way, Robert inventoried every item, separating those for the family, the store, and the Cherokee, before releasing the carts for their return to Mister MacDonald at the landing.

It was only two days after the carts departed when the morning patrol came riding hard and fast for the little fort, raising the alarm.

"Colonel, Indians coming in," shouted Jim Rice, breathlessly after his hard ride, pointing back to the south where, sure enough, a band of Indians were making their way over the rise and into view.

Robert took a close look with the spyglass and then handed the glass to Edward as the others made their preparations for a fight.

"Cherokee," Edward said.

"Agreed. I assume they received word to come and pick up their gifts. They're not painted for war and we've had no trouble with the Cherokee over the years."

"Jim, you and Tom spread the word that the Cherokee are here at the fort. Keep everyone on their guard but away from here unless the Shawnee strike."

"And then what do we do, Colonel?"

"And then we improvise," Edward responded with a sly grin.

As the two riders headed west, Robert passed the word for everyone to be on their guard, but not to act in any way hostile toward the Cherokee. From the looks of it, it was a large party and, should hostilities commence, it was unlikely they'd prevail.

The last one into the little fort was Mister Agner and Edward couldn't help but chuckle as he watched Mark awkwardly hurrying up from the mill toward where Edward was waiting for the Cherokee.

"That's a lot of Indians, Colonel. Sure hope you know what you're doing."

"That makes two of us, Mister Agner, that makes two of us."

As the Cherokee crossed the creek and started up the rise toward Edward, Lewis joined his brother. "We did this together last time, thought you could use the company again." Edward just smiled at his brother and nodded.

"Great Bear, Wise Owl, greetings old friends," came the call as the Cherokee headmen approached.

Edward and Lewis greeted the Cherokee amicably and after the usual ceremonial beginning, the Cherokee showed Edward a letter from Governor Dinwiddie's agent telling them he had sent gifts to the Jewett Grant and they should come and claim them. Of course the letter went on to ask that they reconsider their position and join in the fight against the French and Shawnee, but the Cherokee didn't mention that part and Edward chose not to bring it up until later.

They had brought nearly their whole village, including women and children. Lewis showed them where they could set up their camp so as not interfere either with the security of the Jewett fort or trample the crops they had already planted.

While they did this, Edward had the awning moved out beyond the stockade and set up for the meeting with the Cherokee. Robert began moving the diplomatic gifts from the first floor of the blockhouse to the awning and joined Edward and Lewis for the next meeting with the Cherokee. Good to his word, the Governor had obviously made the trip to the Jewett fort profitable for the Cherokee, including blankets, shirts, pots, and even powder, flint, and lead, though no guns.

When the Cherokee returned from setting up their camp, the process of inspecting and accepting the gifts proceeded quickly. With the exception of the powder, flint, and lead, which the headman kept control of, the men came in and made claim to items in what to Edward appeared to be in order of importance. The trinkets, mirrors and the like, were tossed to their women waiting outside the awning, but the blankets and shirts, pots, axes, and the like were inspected and taken away by the men.

The gifts finally disbursed, as if on cue, Mattie and Esther came out of the fort carrying a large pot of venison stew between them, followed by Rachael and Sally with biscuits and jugs of sweet cider. This met with obvious approval from the Cherokee and the three Jewetts sat and broke bread with half a dozen of the senior Cherokees.

The meal finished, the Cherokee had a question for Great Bear. "We have furs and hides to trade. Would the Great Bear have goods to trade, in addition to the gifts? We are poor and need many things."

Robert spoke up, saying that they did have some limited items that could be traded. He had more pots, axes, blankets, shirts, and cloth.

As a Cherokee ran back to have the furs and hides brought forward, the headman asked about guns. Here Robert deferred to Edward.

"I am sorry to say we received no guns from the east and only have those that we need to defend ourselves against the Shawnee."

The headman didn't seem surprised at the answer, brushed it off, in fact, and the trading began. Robert whispered to Lewis that he wasn't a very good judge of furs and hides, though he had done some trading for them in Rowley. He therefore elicited Lewis's help in the bartering process to see that both sides came away with a fair bargain.

By time they had finished, the atmosphere around the Jewett fort had taken on a festive feel. The Cherokee women and children had joined the men as they bartered for what items Robert had to trade. Games began spontaneously around the meadow with the Jewett women and laborers taking part. At the same time, Charles, Miles and Aaron remained locked in the blockhouse with the Sergeant and all six of the soldiers, keeping a sharp eye out for any treachery.

Just like in their previous dealings, the Cherokee remained friendly, even when Robert ran out of trade goods and they ran out of furs and hides. The games and interaction continued very friendly until sunset when, on a signal from the headman, the Cherokee stopped what they were doing and everything fell deathly silent.

❦ Chapter 21 ❦

Hannah Davies sat on a mended chair next to the little cabin's fireplace. In her lap she had two sealed letters, one from her mother in Boston and the other from her best friend, Marie, somewhere on the Virginia frontier. Although she had received them two days earlier, she hadn't found herself able to open them. Instead, whenever she had a quiet moment like this, she just sat cradling them, feeling sad and lonely.

"Where's breakfast?" asked Daniel Davies, her husband, as he returned from the necessary. "Is Luke up yet? We really had a time of it last night…"

"There's some cheese and bread on the table and there's about a pint of small beer. That's all the food in the house," Hannah responded curtly. "And I really do wish you'd not take Luke when you go to the taverns. That's no place for a boy."

"Ah, stop acting like he's a baby. He's thirteen now and it's time he started learning about being a man."

"Drinking, smoking, and gaming won't make him any account of a man, Daniel Davies, any more than they've contributed to your success," the sarcasm heavy in her voice.

Daniel took a step toward Hannah but halted when another voice came from the loft. "Are you two fighting again?"

"No, Luke, now come down here and eat something," Hannah said reassuringly and not a little relieved at the interruption.

The three of them ate what little cheese and bread there was in silence. Daniel drank the last of the small beer while Hannah and Luke settled for the foul smelling water from the well.

When they finished, Daniel rose, "Luke, what say we go over to meadow and see that race they were talking about last night. With what we heard we can't lose."

"I was hoping to continue Luke's reading lesson this morning, the one you put off yesterday to take him to the cock fight, I believe it was. Besides, I've no money for food and we've eaten the last of it. You don't think you could find a way to earn some money instead of going to a race?"

"I thought getting you away from Boston and that family of yours would end your constant complaining. Here, there's three shillings and one, two, four, no five pence, I can spare that much for food. The rest of my winnings from yesterday are my stakes for the race. After today, with what I learned about the horses at the tavern last night, I should finally have my due. You'll see, I'll come home with a full purse."

"Yeah, mother, you'll see, once father wins it big on today's race," added Luke, much to his mother's horror.

Both of them fairly strutted out the door, leaving Hannah alone with her fears of how Daniel was turning Luke into a small version of himself. She lifted the shawl she had thrown over the letters when Daniel came in, sat back down, and cradled the letters.

They had moved from Boston to Albany at Daniel's insistence when her father had denied him further loans. Having little, they had rented this small cabin from the local Patroon and Daniel was to find work. So far they'd been here eight months and the only work had been gambling, winning just enough to keep them from starving and to stake his next wager.

She hadn't opened the letters for fear of what they said. Her mother's would be full of disapproving comments about Daniel and Marie's would tell of her new, hard but satisfying life on the frontier. Hannah didn't think she could deal with either of the letters just now, and yet she longed to see both of them, and her father and grandmother as well. Looking around the room she saw the scant things left to her, a bed in need of new roping and bedding, a linen press holding what clothing she had left, a rough sawn board table with three stools around it, a pantry with broken door, and the mended chair she was sitting on. No, life was not turning out as she had planned.

Going to the linen press, she opened it and took out her last treasure, her Bible in its painted box. She set it on the table, opened it, and removed the Bible, placing the letters in its place. Sitting again, she opened the Bible and began to read. These days it was her only joy.

She read for nearly an hour when a hard knock on the door startled her. Answering it, she found the Patroon, accompanied by two of his men.

"Mistress Davies, we're here seeking your husband," the Patroon said with his heavy Dutch accent.

"I'm sorry, he isn't here. He said something about there being a race in your meadow this morning."

"And I don't suppose he's left you funds to settle your rent, now has he? No, I thought not. Well, he hasn't paid rent in six months and I'm here to take him before the Magistrate for payment or imprisonment. Stand aside while we search for him. If you're hiding him it'll go bad for you, as well."

"Search all you want, he's in your meadow, I tell you," Hannah said firmly and with what little dignity she could muster under the circumstances.

While his men looked in the loft, under the bed, and in the yard, the Patroon stood looking at the meager sight around him. He saw the money on the table and moved to seize it, but hesitated. Seeing there was no food in the pantry nor on the table, he stopped and turned to Hannah, who had been watching him closely.

"Is this all the money you have?"

"That's all I have, and that was to buy food. But if my husband owes it to you, take it." Hannah had lost some of her defiance and most of her dignity by this point.

Hannah had always impressed the Patroon as perhaps coming from a family of means. That was really the only reason he had consented to rent this cabin to them in the first place, assuming it would be temporary until her husband could establish himself in some way.

"No, Mistress Davies, if you say it is yours, then it is not mine to take. My issue is with your husband, not with you." Signaling his men, "We will go and find your husband at the race and not bother you further."

After they left, Hannah replaced her Bible in its box and put the box back in the linen press. Picking the coins off the table, she put them in her embroidered pocket, which she usually wore on the outside of her skirt. Now, however, with all the money she had in the world inside, she untied her pocket and retied it under her skirt where it would be safer. Wrapping her shawl loosely about her shoulders, she left the cabin and started walking slowly toward the Magistrate's house.

Good to his word, the Patroon had found Daniel at the meadow and was just about to enter the Magistrate's when she saw them. Daniel was firmly held between the two men who had searched for him at her cabin earlier. Luke was following, yelling at them to let his father go, while tears streamed down his face. Seeing his mother, he ran to her.

"Mother, do something! They're dragging father before the Magistrate. You must stop them," he pleaded.

"Luke, think son, how am I to do that? Unless you're holding sizable winnings from today's race, I haven't nearly enough to pay his debts, let alone the fines that will likely go with them," she said firmly, taking hold of Luke's arm to keep him by her side.

"No, I haven't got anything. Father lost today, stupid horse, it should have won. Last night they said it would win, and with good odds, too."

"Then there's no sense in blaming me. You were there and saw him lose all the money we had. Now, we just have to wait and see what the Magistrate says."

After they'd waited anxiously for nearly half an hour, a boy ran out of the Magistrate's office and down the street toward the army camp on the outskirts of town. He returned leading a Sergeant and two soldiers carrying iron manacles. They entered and when they came back out, Daniel was manacled and being led away.

"Sergeant, wait, at least let me say goodbye to my son and wife."

The Sergeant paused, looked toward Hannah and Luke, and then nodded to the two soldiers who led Daniel to where Hannah and Luke stood.

"Hannah, it was debtor's prison or the army for me and I chose the army. The Sergeant said they'll take me out of the manacles when we're well on our way to Fort Oswego with the next supply. I lost today so I've nothing to leave you, you'll just have to make out the best you can…" the soldiers grabbed Daniel up short and started leading him away. "Goodbye, son, remember what I taught you."

"This is all your fault, mother," Luke screamed through the tears.

"How is it my fault your father can't pay his debts?"

"If you'd made grandfather give father the money back in Boston like you should have, none of this would have happened," he shouted before running off down the street after his father and the soldiers.

The Patroon was standing on the stoop and heard this exchange. "Mistress Davies, as I said earlier, I have no issue with you and the boy. If you would like, I could use some help in my household. In that way you can stay in the house and I would pay you the balance so you'd have some little money for food and things."

Hannah thought for a moment. Becoming a servant in the Patroon's household was not something she relished, but the alternative at this moment was being thrown out on the street and starving to death. "Thank you, sir, thank you very much. I'll be by tomorrow to start working. Is sunrise a good time?"

Hannah stopped by the grocer on her way home and was able to buy some food for her and Luke. It wasn't much but it would have to do for now. Before leaving, she asked if the grocer needed any help her son could do in return for food. Assured there was, she told him Luke would be by in the morning.

When she returned home, Luke was sitting on one of the stools with his head down on the table, crying. She went to him, placing a hand on his shoulder while she stroked his hair to comfort him.

"Leave me alone!" he sobbed. "It's because of you they've taken father away to the army. And you stood there and did nothing to stop them."

"Now, Luke, be fair. I asked you then what was I to do. There were only three choices, pay the Patroon, go to prison, or go to the army. Your father chose to gamble away what little money we had left, not I, and your father chose the army, not I. Now, you just sit there and think about that while I make us some dinner."

Luke remained sullen through dinner. After cleaning up, Hannah told Luke about the job she'd arranged for him and that he started the next day.

"Job, what do I need a job for? Father always says a job is for those who weren't smart enough to make a living on the labors of others. I don't want a job!"

"Yes I know, but your father is now in the army for failing to pay his debtors what he owes them. It's a simple matter of we need a place to live and food to eat. I'm going to work in the Patroon's house, also starting tomorrow, which will allow us to keep this cabin. You're going to work for the grocer and he's to pay you in food. Now, no more of your arguing."

The rest of the afternoon Hannah had Luke working around the cabin, sweeping, cutting kindling, hauling water for her, anything she could think of to keep him busy and his mind occupied. Still, it only had a marginal effect on his mood as he remained sullen through their cold supper, after which he went to bed.

Hannah sat in the growing darkness, thinking and listening to Luke toss and turn on his pallet in the loft.

He eventually settled down and she could hear his heavy breathing, indicating he had fallen asleep.

Going back to the linen press, she again took out her Bible box and set it on the table. From their hiding place under the Bible, she took the two letters and set them aside as she lit her last remaining candle by blowing life into a coal left banked in her fireplace. Moving her chair into the candlelight, she lifted the two letters from the table and held them for a few moments before, with resolve, she broke the wax seal on her mother's letter and began to read.

☙ Chapter 22 ☙

"**H**old steady! No shooting unless I order it! Wait for the signal from the Colonel!" shouted Miles to the soldiers manning the loops in the blockhouse.

There had been a festive atmosphere in the meadow outside the little fort just moments before, and now all was silence. The Cherokee women and children had joined the men in standing silently, stoically, upon a signal from their headman under the awning with Robert, Edward, and Lewis. Miles didn't like it, but Edward had made it perfectly clear before going out that Miles was not to start any hostilities, only react should the Cherokee start something. While Edward may have doubted any hostile intent, Miles didn't trust any Indian. Cherokee or Shawnee, they were all the same to him.

Out under the awning, Robert and Lewis were startled by the sudden change in atmosphere. Only Edward seemed unaffected as he stood facing the Cherokee headman, every bit as stoic as the Cherokee and looking the headman square in the eye.

Solemnly, the Cherokee headman began by ceremoniously thanking the Jewett men for the gifts, the meal, and the fair trading. He then invited them and their women to the Cherokee camp that evening where he had two deer roasting for a festive supper. They would sup together, he announced, and the Cherokee would depart for their lands in the morning. When the Jewett's accepted his invitation, he extended his arm first to Edward, then Robert and Lewis in turn, and they gripped forearms in Cherokee fashion before the headman and his entourage turned and departed, the rest of the tribe following.

"Well, son, they had me worried there for a moment," Robert said as they watched the last of the Cherokee disappear over the rise to the east.

"I shouldn't say this, but for a moment I shared your worry. It would appear they take their ceremonies very seriously and don't want them intruded upon by screaming, laughing women, children, and young men," responded Edward as they turned back toward the gate.

Sam and Jubal came out after the Cherokee had moved out of sight to oversee the gathering of the furs and moving the awning back inside the fort before being invited to join the Jewett men, Aaron, Miles, and the Sergeant discussing how they would handle the evening's invitation.

"I think Henry and Jenny should remain here," Robert offered. "Henry was not with them today and now that Jenny is with child – don't look so surprised, I've known for a couple of weeks – they should remain here with Charles."

Henry turned a bit red faced and seemed to be checking the condition of the toe of his boot, choosing not to look anyone else, particularly his brothers, in the face.

"I agree," Edward said, after a pause and seeing Lewis's nod. "Sergeant, you and your men will remain at your posts, of course. Miles, what say you of you and Aaron?"

Looking at each other, Aaron spoke up for both of them, "If it's alright with you, Colonel, we'll stay here."

In the end, they decided Robert, Edward, and Lewis would be joined by Esther, Marie, Sam, Rachael, Jubal, Sally, and Mark Agner. Everyone else would remain within the fort and the gates would remain closed. Sam, Jubal, and their wives were elated about being included, as the big grins on their faces confirmed. They were curious about the Cherokee, that was part of it, but mostly it was about being included.

"So, little brother," Edward began with a wide grin on his face, quickly picked up by Lewis, "you've gotten Jenny in the family way, have you? Haven't I told you that you're too old to have screaming babies around the cabin? Why, at your advanced years you need all the rest you can get!"

"Well, I know you're too old! That's why you passed up the chance to have Jenny for yourself. Your loss is my gain, big brother!"

Through the laughter that followed, Lewis was able to get out, "That was pretty quick thinking, little brother, though you might want to tread lightly there. You never know how these old men will react." This only increased the laughter as the two brothers congratulated Henry in their good humored way.

The Cherokee greeted them kindly as they approached their camp and a festive evening ensued. Edward didn't really enjoy parties much, but he did enjoy this one. For all their stoic reputations, the Cherokee did know how to enjoy themselves. They were especially intrigued with Sam, Rachael, Jubal, and Sally, being more used to seeing English settlers than those of African descent. As a result, these two couples found themselves more the center of attention than they had expected. They conceded they'd probably enjoyed the best evening of revelry of their lives, as they all walked back home after the festivities were over.

At sunrise the next morning, Robert joined Edward at the top of the rise. From there, they watched the Cherokee as they broke camp and started moving southwest, crossing the creek just below the mill. The headman waved just before disappearing into the strip of woods along the creek and they waved back.

"Father," Edward started as they walked back toward the fort, "just because Jenny is now with child we don't want Henry to think he can use that to get out of work around here. What do you think of sending him and Charles with your newfound wealth of furs and hides down to Mister MacDonald's landing to sell them?"

"I think that would be a fine idea, son."

So Henry and Charles took four packhorses loaded with furs and hides to the landing while the rest of the little fort worked to get in the first cutting of hay. The Cherokee camp had destroyed that field of productive hay, so instead they moved further out and cut the meadows to the southwest where they had been cutting timber earlier in the year and the meadows to the east toward the ford they used to cross the North River. When Henry returned, Robert was surprised at how much Mister MacDonald had been willing to give for the furs and hides, resulting in a tidy profit from the undertaking.

While there were rumors of Shawnee and Delaware attacks along the Greenbrier, Jackson, and Cow Pasture Rivers, these were many miles north and west of their little settlement. The summer was progressing quietly with little or no Indian sign turned up by any of their patrols. This encouraged Matt Bennett to move his family back to their homestead in spite of the limited use of his right arm. He had come to grips with the fact that he would likely never regain full use of it and would just have to learn to live with it.

Lewis, Henry, and Charles accompanied the Bennetts back to their homestead and saw that they were fairly settled in. Matt's arm was weak and he had little feeling in his hand, making the simplest of chores difficult and slow. Of major concern was his inability to use his rifle. Just pulling it to his shoulder caused him pain and he didn't have enough feeling in his fingers to pull the trigger without jerking it so badly he could never be sure of his aim. Reloading was also difficult as he tended to drop the ball due to the numb fingers and hadn't the strength in his right arm to force the patched ball into the muzzle of the barrel, let alone drive it down against the powder.

All of their children being under the age of eight, this left the family pretty much defenseless. Lewis and Henry didn't like leaving them in this state, but Matt insisted. They did make sure all of the patrols knew to get word first to the Bennett's in case of trouble, giving them the most time to seek shelter of the little fort. Beyond that, there was little else they could do, so they returned home, feeling a bit dejected.

Colonel Washington continued to visit on occasion, using the excuse of checking up on the troops stationed with the Jewetts to see Sarah and continue their courtship. From what Edward could tell, and Robert confirmed, the courtship was going very slowly, with Sarah being the one unwilling to commit herself to the tall, handsome Virginian.

Sitting together in Edward's cabin one evening, as was their custom, Robert brought up the subject of George and Sarah.

"Your niece sees qualities in George she likes very much, but she also sees qualities she doesn't like. She shared with me that he is maybe a bit too sure of himself now, no longer the shy young man she fell for. She questions her strength to stand up to such a man and fears she'd lose herself to his personality."

"It sounds like your granddaughter continues to come to you for advice, father. It shows she is a good judge of men," Edward chuckled.

"What do you think, son? Should I steer her toward George or encourage her to use caution as I have been? If she were to send him away, would it affect you and your relationship with the young man?"

"George is a fine man who would make a fine husband, for the right woman. Sarah is correct in that he has become a bit headstrong, as he needs to be if he is to succeed in the army. It seems he is also smitten by pretty women a bit too regularly these days, so I would suggest she proceed cautiously, as you've recommended. And please assure her that nothing that occurs between her and George will have any effect on me at all. The more I think on it, the more I'm convinced what George needs is to find a young widow, one who knows how to stand up to him. I should suggest it to him."

Robert nodded, thoughtfully, and after a long pause, "Perhaps we've not been fair to Sarah, bringing her out here. It might be wise for me to take a trip to Williamsburg, take her with me, and introduce her around to some of the quality men of the Colony."

"Are you sure you'd be up to such a trip, father? You tire easily these days. Perhaps I could make some inquiries when next I'm there on military business. It would be far more discreet than arriving in town with Sarah on your arm. Your suggestion might just take on the air of an auction!" Robert had to agree as both men laughed at the thought. "Or we could ask of Misters Bordon and Beverly when next we sit on the court, see if they know of any young widowers of property we could look into. Naturally, before we do any of this, Sarah will need to decide about George, and tell him her intentions toward him. No man in his right mind will come near her now that the Colonel of the Virginia Regiment is courting her."

"No, no, you're quite right. Now, as for Rebecca, she seems to like one of the soldiers and then there are the McNulty boys she flirts with. I've suggested to Jenny she'd do better to find Rebecca a young widower with a little property, though there doesn't seem to be much in the way of prospects for that right now. I suppose I should have listened to my own advice when considering Sarah. I want Rebecca to marry well but, given her status, I suspect her prospects will be more limited. I was hoping for more for Sarah, though. I would like to see both marry well, only…" Robert paused awkwardly, not knowing how to continue.

"I think I understand, father. It's wonderful how you've welcomed Jenny and Rebecca into the family, but your first concern remains Sarah. That's only natural and nothing to feel bad about. But what of this soldier Rebecca seems drawn to? I can't say I approve of that!"

"Oh, there's nothing to worry about there. Esther keeps a close watch on both Sarah and Rebecca, as does Jenny, so between the two of them our young women are well chaperoned. Why, Esther has even gotten Mattie and Rachael into watching. No, it's as well regulated as our watch and patrols are. As for Rebecca and the soldier, I think it no more than a young woman's fancy, same as with the McNulty boys, nothing serious and nothing likely to develop out of it."

A shout of alarm and the sound of hooves inter-rupted their conversation, both men grabbing their guns and stepping into the street in time to greet a mounted courier in a Virginia Regiment uniform.

"Dispatches and letters for Colonel Jewett," he an-nounced, dismounting and handing his dispatch case to Edward, who had stepped forward and identified himself.

"You look tired, soldier, and your horse has had enough. See the Sergeant in the blockhouse. He'll see you fed and bedded for the night. We'll take care of your mount." With that, Edward turned to go back inside, mo-tioning to Aaron to see to the courier's horse. Marie, who had remained afoot all spring and now well into the sum-mer, looked sullen when she was not asked to see to the courier's horse, but she shrugged it off.

Lewis and Henry joined Robert and Edward in Ed-ward's cabin, sitting quietly while Edward read through the dispatches. As he read, his face showed concern.

"England has declared war against France, and France has reciprocated," he began. "Then there's this bit of terrible news. It seems Admiral Boscawen failed to inter-cept six French men-of-war that have now been seen mak-ing their way up the Saint Lawrence toward Quebec. That can only mean heavy reinforcements for the French. This dispatch informs us of the arrival of Major General James Abercromby who has relieved Major General Shirley of command. He is the newly appointed deputy and awaits the arrival of the commander, John Campbell, fourth earl of Loudoun. Then here are orders placing me under the command of Lord Loudoun to use as he sees fit while ad-vising me to remain of assistance to Governor Dinwiddie until such time as Lord Loudoun reassigns me. And final-ly George has asked me to call on him at Fort Loudoun." Pausing and tossing the stack of papers onto the table,

Edward then continued, "It would seem this little frontier war of ours has taken on a whole new dimension."

"With all this going on, Edward, do you suppose it would still be alright for me to go to Timber Ridge tomorrow, as planned? They are dedicating their new church and I so wanted to be there."

"I see no reason you shouldn't, just on account of this news. Our patrols still aren't showing any sign of Shawnee or Delaware incursion so we're not anticipating any danger here. I'll even ride there with you on my way to Fort Loudoun. Why don't you take Lewis with you and you can then go on to fetch your grandson. It is nearly time for school to dismiss, isn't it?"

☙ Chapter 23 ❧

"**L**uke, are you up there?" Hannah called toward the loft as she came inside the little cabin. "You'd better answer me!"

"I'm here. So what do you want?" came the surly reply.

"You get down here right this instant!"

Luke Davies took his time to climb down the ladder from the loft, not at all disturbed by the effect it was having on his mother. Quite the opposite, in fact, he rather enjoyed annoying her.

"Mister Kuipers tells me you didn't show up for work this morning, and that you've been disappearing early. Is that true?"

"Well, it's sort of true and it sort of isn't true."

"What?"

"Well, I sort of didn't show up for work today"

"How do you 'sort of' not show up for work? I walked you there myself."

"That's what I mean, I showed up, only I didn't stay, so actually he's wrong that I didn't show up. I see where he might think that because he didn't actually see me, only you know that I did show up for work because, as you said, you walked me there yourself."

His logic made Hannah's head hurt. "Enough. What about the part of not staying the full day, of leaving early? I suppose you have an answer for that as well?"

"I suppose if one had a watch, which I don't, they could say I left work early. But without a watch how am I to know if I leave early or if other days I don't leave work late? It all depends on who's looking at the watch and because I don't have a watch to look at, I can't say I've left early and I can't say I've left late. All I can say is that each day I do leave work."

"Enough of this! Listen, you are to go to work and stay at work until Mister Kuipers tells you that you can leave. Do you understand me, young man? It's all we can do to keep food on the table and here you go skipping work. And don't roll your eyes at me! If you won't work willingly I've half a mind to apprentice you out. That would fix you."

The threat of being apprenticed out had the desired effect on Luke. The last thing he wanted was to be signed on with a master who could work, use, and abuse him as he saw fit, some man who wouldn't be as easy to manipulate as his mother and who would be physically capable of beating him. Oh, she might think of beating him, but he was nearly her size, even at thirteen, he didn't see it as much of a threat anymore.

Having his attention, she felt a bit bolder. "Now, you go right down to Mister Kuipers's store and apologize to him for missing work. Then you stay and do anything he asks you to do until he tells you to come home. Do you understand? Then go, and I'll be standing right there watching to make sure you make it into the store this time. Go, he's expecting you!"

She watched as Luke went slowly down the street. He looked back before entering the store to see if she was, in fact, watching. Finding she was, he went inside. Hannah knew if she hadn't been standing there, he would not have gone in.

With Luke out of the house, she took her Bible box out of the linen press, sat it on the table, and pulled the two letters out from under the Bible. Sitting wearily on the mended chair, she started to slowly read again the letter from Marie. Hannah didn't know how many times she'd read the letter over these past few months, only that in reading of the life her friend had somehow comforted her. She could sit and dream of that life as if it was her own.

Not that Marie hadn't included the hardships faced by frontier families, she had. She also had a husband who cared for her, an extended family who saw to her safety and needs. Why, she even had a wood floor in her cabin, Hannah thought as she looked at the packed dirt floor of her little cabin. Marie also had a son who listened to her and was now off in school, learning to be a gentleman. Aside from not yet having the large house, she was living the life they had talked of so often as children, the life Hannah herself longed for. It was all there in Marie's long, newsy letter.

Hannah sighed, then rose, put the letters back in the Bible box and the box back in the linen press. It was getting dark and time to fix some supper. Luke would be home just after dark, Mister Kuipers had told her he'd keep him until then doing the sweeping and straightening up he hadn't done that day.

Supper ready and it was full dark and still no Luke. Hannah went out and looked up the street toward Mister Kuipers's store and saw the store was dark. She felt her temper rising again as she reached back inside for her shawl and started walking up the street. The store was dark and locked so Hannah knocked on the door to Mister Kuipers's home, which shared the same building.

"Mister Kuipers, I'm sorry to bother you, but Luke hasn't come home for his supper. Did you see which way he went after you let him go?"

"I'm sorry to have to tell you this, Mistress Davies, but instead of heading home he went uptown, toward the taverns."

Hannah had expected as much, so she thanked Mister Kuipers and returned home to eat her own supper, alone. She then put everything away, determined that Luke would just have to go to bed hungry.

Before she went to bed, Luke did come home, smelling of the strong tobacco smoked in the taverns and asking about his supper. When told he would get none tonight, he gave her an awful look, one that frightened her, before he climbed the ladder to his loft, making as much noise and raising as much dust as possible.

At breakfast the next morning, he remained sullen and wouldn't speak to her at all, though he did eat everything put in front of him and would have eaten more if more had been available. He continued in silence as she walked him to Mister Kuipers's store, only today she didn't walk on until she saw him actually enter the store. She knew once he was inside, Mister Kuipers would keep him working. She then walked on to the Patroon's house and her job.

The Patroon had not treated her badly, not at all. In fact, he had given her only light chambermaid duties instead of scullery maid as she had expected. Still, being a chambermaid was something she had never seen herself doing. Even though she had written back to her mother, told her of Daniel's troubles and that he was away now in the army, she hadn't told her of how she was now forced to live. And Marie, well, she hadn't responded to her letter yet. She really didn't know what to tell her, didn't want Marie to know just how bad things had turned out for her in Albany.

She busied herself with her work, airing out the bedding and carrying the chamber pots down to the scullery for the scullery maid to empty and clean. Although she noticed a lot more commotion around the house today, she didn't pay it any real attention. She had learned not to bother herself with the Patroon's business, that it didn't concern her. That is until the Patroon and his wife called for her to join them in the parlor. This was highly irregular and at first Hannah thought she was being accused of something.

"Hannah," the Patroon began in a calm voice. "It seems I have some bad news for you." He looked to his wife for encouragement. She nodded for him to continue. "I just received this," showing her a letter. "Our forces at Fort Oswego have been overpowered by the French and their Indian allies and forced to surrender." He paused, waiting for the meaning of his words to register on Hannah's face, before clearing his throat and continuing. "I'm afraid your husband has been listed as one of those killed in the fighting. Before you ask, I sent a boy to Fort Edward as soon as I heard and he's just returned confirming this news. Your husband was killed and not captured."

Hannah tried to stop her hands from trembling, tried to say something, but couldn't do either. She just sat there, staring at the Patroon until his wife came over and put her arm around her, comforting her. After a few minutes, she seemed somewhat recovered, though still confused. So many thoughts were racing through her head, thoughts about where they would go, what they would do, how she would tell Luke, too many thoughts for her to deal with, so she continued to just sit there.

"Mistress Davies, you may of course go and tell your son. Your work here today is done," the Patroon announced.

"Go and see your son, girl. And tomorrow you can decide what's to become of you both. No need to do that today." The Patroon's wife had an even thicker accent than the Patroon, so much so that Hannah could just make sense of what she was saying.

Hannah just nodded, then rose and left the Patroon's house, heading toward Mister Kuipers's store and Luke. When she arrived, Mister Kuipers had already heard the news, so he expected her. He had said nothing to Luke, leaving that for her to do. When Mister Kuipers called him to the front of the store and he saw his mother, Luke was confused, he didn't know why Mister Kuipers was letting him go when he had so much work to do, didn't know why his mother was here or why she looked so strange, but he went with her because he knew something was wrong. Besides, it was better than working, or so he thought.

Once at home, Hannah had Luke sit at the table. She sat opposite and reached to hold his hands, only he withdrew them. This caused her to hesitate before beginning, "Son, we received terrible news today," she started, paused, then continued. "Your father, he's been killed, in a battle with the French."

Luke jumped to his feet and recoiled, his face contorted in a look of shock, horror, and disbelief. "No, it isn't true! It can't be true!" His look then changed to anger, "You, you did this to him! You're the reason he went into the army! This is all your fault!" And, with that, he ran from the cabin.

Hannah wanted to cry, felt she should cry, only she couldn't. Instead, she went to the linen press and retrieved her Bible box from its shelf, carried it to the table, and sat in her mended chair, reading her Bible for hours until she lost the light and could read no more. She started to nod off when there was a knock at the door and she went to answer it. There was Mister Kuipers and Luke, the boy reeking of strong tobacco smoke.

"Mistress Davies, I brought him home to you from the tavern, thinking he needed to be here tonight."

"Thank you, Mister Kuipers. That was very kind of you."

Mister Kuipers guided a subdued but reluctant Luke into the cabin and gave him a little push toward the ladder. The boy climbed to his bed without a word or an argument, which Hannah appreciated tonight. She didn't think she could deal with either one. She didn't know what Mister Kuipers had done to make Luke so docile, and she wouldn't ask, so she just thanked him for his kindness and he left, joining his wife waiting quietly for him in the street.

That's when she realized she hadn't eaten since breakfast, so she lit a candle and went about fixing both of them a cold supper. When she called him to eat, Luke did come down, ate, and went back up to his bed without a word, never even looking at his mother. For her part, she chose not to speak to him, either, and, after cleaning up from the meal, she went to bed.

She was up at first light the next morning, not knowing what she would do only that there was one thing she must do first. Taking paper, pen, and ink from on top the pantry where she kept them, she sat down and began to write, starting with "Dear Marie…"

In her letter, she poured out all that had befallen her since she last wrote from Boston. Her father's refusal to extend any more loans to Daniel because he never re-paid them, their hasty move to Albany, the squalor they lived in, Daniel's gaming and debts that resulted in his ar-rest, her being forced to serve as a chambermaid, Luke's disobedience, all of it, and then news of Daniel's loss. As she wrote, she felt better, as if a curtain was being lifted and she now knew what she must do.

With a bold hand she closed the letter "…today we'll leave for Boston as soon as I post this. You may write me, if you still wish to, at my father's…"

⤳ Chapter 24 ⤳

They made a leisurely start the next morning, Robert not needing to be in Timber Ridge until noon. It was just twelve miles to Timber Ridge and they could comfortably cover that in three hours time. Aaron came along to accompany Edward to Fort Loudoun and Charles, at the last minute, wanted to go with his grandfather, so Henry consented.

They made for the Virginia Road and from there turned north. Traffic on the road had slowed to a trickle since the war began, as had work on the road, now that so many had fled east seeking safety in the more settled portions of the country. They rode along the rutted road, seeing no one, until about halfway to Timber Ridge when they saw a rider coming toward them. At a distance something seemed odd about him, so Edward and Lewis moved to the front, rifles at the ready.

Coming closer, they saw the comical figure of Ronald, riding awkwardly on his old sway backed horse. No one could ever mistake him for a horseman, which explained why something appeared so odd from a distance.

"Ronald, what are you doing here?" Robert asked as they came together.

"Hello, Robert, I could ask you the same question," came the response, with nods to Edward, Lewis, and Aaron. "I just received in yesterday's post a new diversion," he continued, excitedly. "It's called 'The Game of Goose' and I have it right here in my sack. I thought, that is, if you weren't busy, we could play a game or two."

"And you were riding all this way, alone, just for a diversion? What of the dedication of the Timber Ridge Meeting House?"

"That's today? Oh, it is today! I'd completely forgotten. You see, I received this new diversion in the post yesterday and thought I'd bring it along to show you," Ronald continued, now a bit confused. "No, wait, let me see, no, I did leave this morning bound for Timber Ridge. That's right, but I rode right past it, didn't I?" he said, turning his head and looking back up the road. It was hard for the Jewett party to stifle their chuckles, so his turning away came at a good time.

"Charles, why don't you ride Uncle Ronald's horse and let him ride on the chair with me? That's a good lad."

Ronald looked somewhat relieved to be off the horse and seated next to Robert and, as they continued on, he talked at length of the rules for "The Game of Goose."

"Now, I haven't played it yet, so that's just the way I remember them. We can figure it out as we go along," he chatted contentedly.

"You know, Ronald, we're coming to gather up Philip after the dedication today, so if you'll put us up for the night, we'll have plenty of time for your new diversion this evening, after the dedication," Robert assured him.

Lewis just looked at Edward and shook his head, causing them both to laugh. Now riding behind the riding chair, they were able to do this without Ronald seeing them. They had no desire to embarrass the old gentleman, actually finding him quite charming, if a bit eccentric. Charles, however, riding next to the riding chair, was unable to contain his laughter, which rather than embarrass Ronald, only encouraged him and his chatter became even more animated and humorous.

They arrived at the Timber Ridge Meeting House early, which was good for Robert hated to be late to anything. While Edward and Aaron stretched their legs and eased their horses before continuing on, Robert and Ronald introduced Edward around to the other Presbyterian Elders gathered for the dedication. In addition to the Timber Ridge Elders, there were Elders from Greenville, in addition to Ronald, and the New Monmouth Meeting House. Robert was an Elder while he lived in Rowley but the Timber Ridge and New Monmouth churches were each twelve miles from the Jewett's home. This was too far to make for regular services or for them to ask Robert to be an Elder in either of them. Instead, the Jewett's neighbors prevailed upon Robert to conduct monthly services for them at the Jewett's fort. As a consequence, and because of his role as a Justice in the County Court, the local congregations afforded Robert the status of Elder all the same.

Here in the Valley, the little Presbyterian Churches were thriving. They had been recognized by the Virginia Colony as an authorized dissenting church, known as "Dissenters" in the eastern counties, since the time of King James, who was the King of Scotland and a Presbyterian before becoming King of England, Scotland, and Wales. What made the Presbyterians thrive here was not only the numbers of Scots-Irish inhabiting the Valley, but also because there was no Church of England for them to support. Even though they did not belong, in the eastern counties Dissenters were still required to tithe to the Church of England, the Colony's official Church.

After meeting what seemed to Edward like every Elder in the Colony, plus the itinerant preacher who made a circuit of the churches, he bid his father, brother, and nephew goodbye and he and Aaron mounted, moving on down the Virginia Road.

Reining up at the Samuel cabin, they were greeted by a much taller Philip in the yard.

"Uncle Edward, it's so good to see you! Hello, Aaron. Have you come to take me home? You didn't bring a horse for me? Am I to ride the packhorse?"

"Calm down a moment. You may now be near as tall as a man but you've still to learn patience!" Turning toward the steps to the passage, he continued, "Good day to you, Aunt Margaret, see I did recall what you said to call you. You may rest assured that we found your husband wandering down the Virginia Road, apparently heading toward our place, though I doubt he could have found us. He has been delivered safely to the Timber Ridge Meeting House and my father will bring him home to you tonight. I hope you don't mind house guests this evening?"

"Oh, thank goodness. I told him to wait until Elam could ride with him, but you know Elam. He's off now terrorizing the creatures of the forest, trying to teach them his Locke, Bacon, and Newton. Ronald became impatient and all I did was turn for a second and he was off. I've been sitting here worrying about him ever since."

"Well, dear woman, he is safe. And as for you, young man, your father and grandfather will be here this evening to escort you home and they have your horse tied to the back of your grandfather's riding chair. Even Charles came along."

"So you didn't come for me?" Philip asked, looking disappointed. "Then why have you come at all?"

"I didn't say I hadn't come to see you, only that I won't be escorting you home. I'm off to see Colonel Washington on military business up at Fort Loudoun. Besides, it gave me a good excuse to slip in here before your grandfather and father arrive so I'd have you all to myself for an hour or so while we water and rest the horses."

The horses had gotten a good rest at Timber Ridge and were in fine shape, but it was a good excuse that brightened Philip up immediately. They sat on the top step talking over school, the happenings at home, and the war while Margaret brought out light refreshments and sat in her porch chair nearby, listening. It wasn't long before Edward announced he must be moving along. Philip walked with him to his horse and Edward gave his nephew a big hug before mounting and riding on.

"You love your uncle very much, don't you Philip?" Margaret said as she put her arm around the young man.

Trying to hide his tears, he replied, "Yes, Aunt Margaret, very much." He found that was all he could get out at that moment, but Margaret understood and just held him tighter as they both turned to watched Elam walk toward them.

"Was that the Colonel I saw riding off just now?" he asked, looking down the road at the lingering dust left in their wake.

"Yes and it's about time you got back. You were supposed to take your father to the dedication today. He was worried he'd be late and finally slipped out when my back was turned."

Elam now looked concerned. "You mean he left, alone? I'd best ride after him."

"No need to bother yourself. The Colonel and his family found your father wandering well beyond Timber Ridge and gathered him up with them. They'll bring him home this evening, no thanks to you." With that, Margaret turned and stormed back into her cabin, leaving Elam looking rather shocked.

"I did manage to get us four fat squirrels. Should have been six but I think this fowler of mine is shooting a bit high," he mused with Philip.

"Well, at least it wasn't a total loss. I'll help you skin them while we wait on my father and grandfather to show up." He then got a playful look on his face. "Maybe I'd better bury those skins when we're done or your mother may try to feed them to you instead of the meat." This sent them both laughing as they moved around to the shed to start preparing the squirrels for the pot.

In the classroom, Philip showed Elam all the respect due a teacher, but, around the house, the two had become friends. In many ways, Elam was like his father and could be a bit forgetful, a bit childlike at times, but good natured and always ready to laugh. The two sat on upturned pieces of firewood and saw to the chore of dressing out the squirrels while Elam related every moment of his hunt, all of which he managed to find references for from Locke, Bacon, or Newton, something Philip had learned to accept and was starting to find humorous since school let out.

Robert, Lewis, and Charles brought Ronald home just before sunset, having spent the afternoon at the dedication. They had taken a break between the sermons, which lasted for over three hours, for a dinner provided by the women of the Timber Ridge congregation.

"Ronald, what were you thinking going off on your own like that? If you hadn't come upon Robert on the road, what would have become of you, old man? That's right. Edward stopped by and told me how they found you, nearly six miles past Timber Ridge!"

Ronald just sighed and said, "Yes, yes they did. But," his face now became animated, "Robert is interested in playing my new diversion this evening and there's also Philip and Charles to play," he said, cheered by the thought.

"You and your diversions," Margaret said with a wave of her hand. She then busied herself getting better acquainted with Charles until Ronald called him to the table for "The Game of Goose."

Elam joined them for supper, bringing a pail with the squirrels already soaking in mild brine. He gave them to Margaret to become their dinner the following day and she thanked him. Already their company was putting the house into a festive mood and Margaret couldn't resist joining in.

The next morning was much more subdued as Philip said his goodbyes to the Samuels. He had grown close to the couple. Yet while saddened at leaving, at least until classes started up again, he was also very excited about going home. He was now close to a foot taller than Charles, rail thin, and his mother hadn't seen him since he was about Charles's height. He was enjoying his new size advantage over his cousin, making as if that was the reason Charles was riding in the riding chair while he rode a horse.

"I don't see where you're better off than Charles is," Ronald offered. "I found this riding chair to be far more comfortable than sitting astraddle a horse. No, I think Charles may have been the smarter of the two in claiming the chair over the horse."

"No way," was Philip's only response, which had Robert and Lewis still chuckling as they departed for their trip home.

They made good time on the way home, meeting the afternoon patrol just as they were about to leave the Virginia Road to head easterly toward home. Jim Rice and Tom McCrary reported all as being quiet with no sign of Shawnee about. And yet Lewis was left feeling there was something else that they weren't saying, almost as if they had a private joke between them that the Jewetts weren't included in. So, Lewis asked what else they weren't saying.

"Oh, you'll see soon enough, I suspect," Jim said. Then the two rode off, still chuckling to themselves.

"Now, what do you suppose that was all about?" Robert asked before shrugging his shoulders and clicking his horse ahead, across the meadow and up toward the wooded summit of the boundary ridge.

Lewis was still regaling Philip with the story of his fight with the Shawnee months earlier along this very spot when, upon coming out of the wood line on the far slope and near where Lewis and Miles had left their horses during the fight, they saw a rider coming toward them from the southeast. The rider pulled up quickly on seeing them, paused, then turned and galloped for the tree line across the open meadow before them and in the general direction of the Jewett's fort.

"I don't believe this!" Lewis exclaimed.

❦ Chapter 25 ❦

"Colonel, Colonel Jewett is here," George's orderly announced. George rose and came around the sawhorse and boards he used as a desk.

"Colonel, I am so glad to see you, sir. That will be all, Hastings."

After waiting for the orderly to close the door behind him, Edward greeted the younger man warmly, "George, it is good to see you again. But I must confess, your command is looking, while well disciplined, a bit threadbare."

"Oh, don't I know it! All of the running around trying to defend the Valley is wearing out shoe leather faster than I can procure replacements. The same applies to their clothing. Desertions are a constant, though the numbers are not great."

"Don't look so dejected, George!" said Edward, encouragingly. "You are doing a great job. Why, aside from the problems with the quartermaster, I've seen few Regular Regiments as disciplined and well led as yours. Plus you are successfully parrying the Shawnee and, here further north, the Delaware. Short of carrying the fight to them, which we tried with Braddock and you'll remember how that turned out, you've done remarkably well."

"Yes, but it galls me to be at their mercy like this! And now there is even more disturbing news, the reason I asked for you to come here rather than me to you. Have you heard of Fort Granville?"

"Why, I know of it, of course. It and Fort Frederick are the two best forts on the frontier. While you've laid out a strong and workable fort here, those are regular works, with bastions and outworks well formed for the defense. You can't compare your works here against those designed by Royal Engineers."

"I'm afraid I've taken advantage of you, Edward, and will apologize for it." George pulled a leaf of paper from the stacks on his desk. "This is a dispatch announcing that Fort Granville has fallen to a combined French and Delaware force, burned, and destroyed."

Edward was stunned by the news. He sat there a few minutes as the entire state of the frontier defenses raced through his mind. "George, this means that Fort Shirley is Pennsylvania's westernmost defense. That fort is nothing more than George Croghan's old trading post that's been fortified. It can never stand without Fort Granville."

"And that's this dispatch, notifying me Governor Morris of Pennsylvania has evacuated Fort Shirley as indefensible. The fort at Carlisle now becomes the Pennsylvania frontier. They did launch a punitive raid on the Delaware at Upper Kittanning town on the Allegheny River and managed to kill the Delaware war chief most responsible for the attack on Fort Granville. They accomplished little else than to lose more to casualties than they inflicted."

Waving his hand, Edward said, "A raid, no matter how successful, is of little value when compared to the loss of two fortified positions and an entire frontier. You've basically lost your entire right flank past Fort Frederick."

"And that's why I called you, Edward. How am I to deal with this? I feel bad calling on you for advice like this, but I'm in a bit over my head."

"Think nothing of it, George. I'm assigned as an advisor, so I advise. And besides, you're young yet. Most Royal Colonels are twice your age and have spent nearly as many as your twenty-four years learning their trade. You've learned fast, but you can't know everything. Why, most men your age are Lieutenants or, at best, Captains."

The two men then sat in silence for a long while, Edward in thought and George watching his friend closely. Finally, Edward looked like he might have an idea. He rose and moved to study the map on the wall, tracing lines with his finger until he summoned George to him.

"George, we need to think of this as one would on the battlefield. Look at what I mean. You've been flanked and your right has retired. One could look at it as a 're-fused flank' situation. If Pennsylvania would take the measure of building a string of stockade forts, quick to build though not as strong as a Fort Granville, along this line, here, between Frederick and Carlisle, as you have done from Fort Loudoun south to defend the Valley, you still have your right protected."

George studied the map, tracing the line Edward had just done with his own finger. "And, in fact, that line could be seen as an extension of my own, falling mostly within the Cumberland Valley. It would also improve communications between posts and give them the same defensible situation we have here and to the south. That's good, but does this help us?"

"Don't you see it, George? Fort Granville was attacked by the Delaware, a tribe that lives in the northwestern portions of Pennsylvania Colony and into the northern portions of the Ohio Country. They're attacking in this direction," Edward indicated a northwest to southeast direction with his hand. "Pennsylvania's old line of forts, protecting the frontier basically ran north to south, cutting across all these mountain ridges and allowing the Delaware to get on their northern flank. With the line we just discussed, the forces are facing directly toward the direction of attack."

George nodded, "I see. And being essentially in the same valley, as I have tried to do here, the Pennsylvania forces will be in support of each other in case of attack."

"Now, for us, our threat is primarily from the Shawnee, in our own western provinces and the southern Ohio Country. Their direction of attack is also from northwest to southeast, against your line that you've arranged northeast to southwest. The key position for us is our center, Fort Frederick, which is very strong and in supporting distance from you here, just as their center at Fort Duquesne is very strong. Now, with this plan, our lines now conform to each other's. What forces are now at Fort Frederick?"

"Still the Maryland forces, but Lord Loudoun has just dispatched a battalion of the 60th Royal American Regiment there, commanded by Colonel Stanwix. I will fall under him. They should be arriving from Philadelphia soon."

"Well, John Stanwix is a good man, good officer, and you can learn from him. He'll understand this plan very well. And having a battalion of Regulars protecting this one northern approach to you here will be comforting."

George turned back to the map, "So if I can just convince Pennsylvania to reform their line of defensive positions to ours, thus, they'll still form my right and I don't have to worry about being struck in flank and rear."

"Now you've got it, George," Edward said, slapping the younger man on the shoulder. "We can compose a suggestive letter to Governor Morris that couches it as being to his best interest, which it is, and he can't help but act."

"You mean Governor Denny. Morris has been replaced."

"Denny, you say? That wouldn't be Major William Denny, would it?" Edward inquired.

Rummaging through the papers on his desk until he found the one he wanted, George read, "Lieutenant Colonel William Denny, do you know him?"

"So, Billy Denny is now Governor of Pennsylvania. Oh, yes, I know Billy. He's the youngest son of a prominent family, one closely tied with Lord Loudoun, so it's hardly surprising." Smiling now, "Tell you what, George, I'll write the letter to Billy, if that's alright with you."

They spent the rest of the afternoon drafting the letter, Edward choosing his wording carefully to have the right impact on his old acquaintance. Once both men were satisfied with the result, they handed it off to George's clerk to be put into final form before Edward signed it.

Over supper in George's quarters that evening, talk of the war situation continued.

"Just be glad the Delaware participated in both the Fort Oswego and Fort Granville attacks, George," Edward observed between bites.

"I don't follow, Edward. Of what significance is that to us?"

Taking a sip of wine before continuing, Edward explained. "The Delaware captured a large store of arms, extremely large when you combine what they got from the two forts. Knowing the Indian nature, they will have hauled these back to their own tribe, to strengthen themselves against their enemies. It is unlikely any will fall into the hands of the Shawnee. But had the Shawnee participated in one or more of these attacks, you'd be facing our own muskets and a well armed adversary."

George let his silverware clatter onto his plate as the realization of just how bad these defeats had been to the English cause, and how much worse they could have been for his situation.

Over breakfast the next morning, the conversation was somewhat lighter, George's mood having improved considerably since Edward's arrival. Like most young men, when their mood is good, their thoughts turn toward women and George was no exception.

"So, Edward, has Sarah spoken of me? I would have preferred to come to see you, rather than drag you up here, for the opportunity to see your niece again."

Edward remained thoughtful as he chewed his food, stalling before answering as he wondered just how honest he should be with his young friend.

"George, let's be honest with each other. My niece is a very attractive young woman, it is true, but she is also very young and inexperienced in the way of the world. You have become very successful, Commander of the Virginia Regiment, young officers jump when you growl. Frankly, as your personality has become more confident, she has become less confident of her own ability to be of any real use to you as a wife."

Now it was George's turn to pause for thought. Edward pretended not to notice as he continued to eat, giving his friend time to contemplate the information he'd just received.

"Edward, as a friend, would it grieve you if I were to call off my courtship of Sarah? I have for some time felt there was something amiss between us and, as you so well expressed it, I have developed a rather brusque officiousness since I first met her on that trail up the Blue Ridge."

Edward smiled, "It would not grieve me. The issue is between the two of you. Were I to advise you, George, it would be to seek a lively young widow, one that knows how to handle your, what did you call it, officiousness?" This sent both men to laughing.

"Ah, yes, Edward, but I would have made a rich woman out of her, you must admit that."

"Yes, George, you would have done that, but she'll not want for anything as it is so that isn't the only consideration here. I would suggest even Sally Fairfax would have difficulty handling you these days."

It was nice to see that there were still some things that would make George turn red in the face, and Edward had hit on one of them. Edward knew George continued to court Sally on his frequent visits to see her father, the man singly responsible for making George known and successful among the first families of Virginia. He hadn't revealed all he knew to Sarah, biding his time until either George made his choice or he needed to step in to keep Sarah from being hurt.

"Oh, come now, George, it's hardly a secret that you've caught the eye of several eligible, and I might add beautiful, women since you've risen to such prominence in the affairs of the Colony. Relax, my friend, Sarah knows nothing of it unless you yourself revealed it to her." For some reason he liked seeing the young man squirm this morning, but he wouldn't keep him squirming long. He then changed the subject back to the business of the war.

Returning to George's office, they found the letter to Governor Denny ready for their final review before Edward signed it with a flourish.

"There, that should do nicely. If Billy listens to the advice, he can both firm up what is left of his frontier and cover your flank and rear. I should also let John know of this. No point having your new commander upset with you, George, when he can be upset with me, should he choose to be upset at all, which I doubt."

"Shall I have my clerk prepare another copy for Colonel Stanwix?"

With Edward's nod, George called his clerk in and gave him instructions to make two copies of the letter, one for them and one for Colonel Stanwix.

While George had been giving these instructions, Edward had been thinking.

"Now I have a favor to ask of you. Knowing Lord Loudoun is at his headquarters in New York, I must go and report to him, to allow him to assign me as he sees fit. And you now have a reason to visit my home, that matter with Sarah requires it. Don't look so pained, it's not something you can do by letter, you must go to her. And as you must, you can tell my father that I have gone to New York to report for duty."

∽ Chapter 26 ∾

Marie met them at the gate as they arrived back home, giving Philip a big hug and kiss as he dismounted. To Lewis, her greeting was more restrained and she looked a bit embarrassed.

"Philip, your mother will take care of the horses for us. Let's go see what's being put out for dinner," Lewis said as he draped his reins over Marie's shoulder.

Robert noticed that Marie seemed about to protest but checked herself. Lewis didn't see any of this because he had immediately turned his back and started walking toward the awning with his arm around Philip's shoulder, the other members of their little community greeting Philip as they went. Although out of character for Lewis, Robert knew his son was angry, and now Marie knew it also. No, these two would deal with it later, in private.

"I'll take care of your horse, grandfather," Charles offered after being warmly greeted by Henry and Jenny, completely unaware of any problems between his aunt and uncle.

As Charles moved off with the riding chair, Henry had a moment alone with Robert. "So, I take it from the chill in the air that Lewis knows Marie slipped out riding again?"

"Yes. She miscalculated and we saw her up near where you encountered the Shawnee this winter. I don't know how Lewis will handle this, but for now it's best we stay out of the line of fire," he chuckled as he tapped his youngest son's chest with his finger.

Turning his attention now to Jenny, "And how are you doing?"

"As well as can be expected given I'm as big as a cow."

"Well, you look lovely to me all the same. And from the looks of things, it won't be long now."

"That's what Betty and Rachael both tell me, any time now," she smiled back at Robert. He gave his daughter-in-law a hug and they all started walking slowly toward the awning for dinner, arm in arm.

Seeing to the horses made Marie late for dinner and they had not waited for her. She joined them, sitting next to Philip and listening to his stories of school, marveling at how he was growing into a man, now nearly as tall as his father, and apparently enjoying herself. That was what she wanted everyone to see. Inside she was stalling, hoping to put off the inevitable private conversation with Lewis she knew was coming. His reaction at the gate had confirmed to her that he had recognized her in the meadow, as hard as she had tried to get away without that happening.

It was not until after supper that they found themselves alone. Lewis had suggested Philip spend some time with his grandfather, who had missed his company. This was true, but Philip also knew his parents and had recognized his mother galloping across the meadow as well as his father had. He knew she was not to be riding so this was one evening he really didn't want to be around the cabin.

Once they were alone, Marie started chatting, about the weather, wondering about Hannah and why she hadn't written back, any subject at all that did not pertain to horses. Lewis just sat there, watching her, saying not a word for what to Marie seemed like hours, though it couldn't have been more than ten or fifteen minutes.

"Well, aren't you going to say anything? I asked you how long you thought a letter from Albany would take to reach us."

Lewis cleared his throat. "I neither know nor care. What I do know is that you were out riding, alone, far from these walls, and when you'd been told you were not to ride because of your irresponsible behavior when you do ride, putting yourself and others at risk for your pleasure. I'm not finished! As you've decided to do what you want with no regard for anyone but yourself, so be it. You may do as you wish, ride when you wish and where you wish. Don't interrupt! But as you ride remember this, I will not allow anyone to risk their life to rescue you. If you run afoul of the Shawnee, it will be up to you to deal with it, for we won't be coming to rescue you. If you are out when there is an alarm, no one will come to find and warn you."

"May I speak now?" Lewis nodded. "Those are very harsh things to say to me, Lewis Jewett. Don't you care what happens to me? Why, what would you do if I were to be taken, what would you say to our son?"

"I would tell him it is one thing for someone to inadvertently fall into the hands of the Shawnee and that it is quite another when his mother actually goes looking for it to happen." He then smiled, "And as for me, perhaps I'd find a pretty young widow, like Henry's done."

That had more of an effect on Marie than Lewis could know. While he was expecting a reaction to his finding another woman, Marie's mind immediately raced, making the link from Henry and Jenny to Henry's first wife, Mary, and how she had died running away, heading "home" to the east. She hadn't thought of her own actions quite in that light before, how she really was tempting fate every bit as much as Mary's wild ride over the mountain in a winter's storm. Really, as she thought about it, a winter's storm or a Shawnee raiding party, they were both forces of nature that could show no mercy for someone who failed to respect their power.

Although he found her silence and wide stare puzzling, Lewis waited, again saying nothing. No, he told himself, it is her turn to respond, wait for it. When it did come, her reaction surprised him. Instead of more defiance, she admitted he was right, promised not to defy him again, and started to cry. At first he hesitated, but not for long before he was moved by her remorse and went to her side. The rest of the evening was spent quietly, sitting close to each other while each remained lost to their own thoughts.

Charles pounded on Lewis and Marie's door very early the next morning, before it could really be called morning at all.

"Aunt Marie, come quick! Father says the baby is coming and mother needs you."

As quick as that, Charles was off in search of Betty at her cabin across the little street. Marie dressed quickly and met Betty, carrying her little girl barely six months old.

"I've sent Charles to have Mattie start boiling water. Let me leave little Eunice with Rachael and I'll be right there," Betty said as they hurried down the little street.

Arriving at Henry's cabin, Marie found Henry beside himself with worry, pacing and wringing his hands.

"Look at you, Henry. It's as if you'd never had a child before. You've been through it now twice before. Why don't you and Charles go keep Lewis and Philip company? Betty will be along and we'll tend to things here," moving past Henry when she heard Jenny's scream. "And take Sarah and Rebecca with you," she called from Jenny's side.

Henry paced while Lewis stoked a fire to make tea for those now assembled in his cabin. It really wasn't a long time waiting, at least not for anyone other than Henry who continued his nervous pacing and hand wringing. Marie returned to announce Henry and Jenny were parents of a fine baby boy.

After Henry rushed out of the cabin, Lewis asked, "Is Jenny alright?"

"Oh, she's tired, but she's fine. This isn't her first and things went quite well."

They had not disturbed Robert until after the baby had been born, but now Lewis woke his father and Robert and Esther joined Henry, Jenny, and their children, congratulating the new parents. It was hard for Jenny to tell who was the proudest, father or grandfather, as both men cooed over her new boy.

As for Jenny, she felt the hole left in her life by the death of her husband and two sons grow smaller. It had started to mend when she had married Henry and now she felt like her life really was moving on. Henry had made her happy, but the baby now made her content.

Around the Jewett fort, life returned to its early fall routine. The final cutting of hay was brought in for the winter feed, corn was either milled or laid aside as animal feed, gardens were harvested and the beds prepared for winter, and firewood was stacked so as to be handy when the first blasts of cold air arrived.

George Washington arrived before the first freeze and was greeted warmly by the Jewetts. He brought news that Edward, finding Lord Loudoun had arrived in New York, had gone to report to his new commander, taking Aaron with him. No one was really surprised by this news. Anticipating his summons to Fort Loudoun meant more active duty for him, he had prepared them all for another of his long absences.

Robert, Lewis, and Henry got George alone and asked of the war situation. The news was grim and yet the Virginia frontier, their Valley in particular, remained fairly quiet. Most of the raids had been further west, in the small mountain valleys where a few hardy souls still remained, though most had fled. It appeared the presence of the Virginia Regiment and their few successes over the past year had encouraged the Shawnee to focus on these more isolated, more defenseless homesteads rather than risk raiding the Valley.

George keep his comments focused on the Valley and the Shawnee, finding no reason to worry these good people with the amount of arms and munitions that had fallen into the hands of the Delaware. He did, naturally, tell of the fate of Forts Oswego and Granville, but didn't dwell on their consequences. It was at dinner that Marie picked up on the mention of Fort Oswego.

"Colonel, isn't that in New York Colony? Is it far from Albany? You see I have a friend in Albany who hasn't written and I'm much concerned about her safety."

"Oh, I shouldn't think there is much to fear in Albany. It is protected to the north by Fort Edward, a strong post and our main fort in that region, and a smaller but no less stout fort named William Henry. Fort Oswego was far to the west, on the lake, and fairly isolated at that."

This made Marie feel somewhat better but she remained concerned with why Hannah had not written her. She had even written to Hannah's mother, who had responded assuring Marie that she had forwarded her letter to Hannah. Marie found the silence from her best friend confusing and concerning.

As they finished dinner, Robert, with a smile, turned to George. "George, I really must apologize, but our supplies have just arrived from Mister Prentiss and I really must see to them. I will need Lewis and Henry's help, I'm afraid. I don't suppose you'd be content with Esther and Sarah as your company this evening? We will, of course, rejoin you for supper and you'll stay the night in Edward's cabin."

"I'm afraid I can't stay and will need to be off soon. I'll make sure to say my goodbyes before I leave."

George had actually been putting off his conversation with Sarah, glad for the distraction of talking war and military matters with the men. He still wasn't sure exactly what he would say, only that he had to find a way to say what was on his mind without hurting the young woman's feelings. In the few seconds before he rose from the table, he looked at Sarah and was again struck by her beauty.

Moving to a seat opposite Esther and Sarah, George began innocently enough. "It would seem your father and his sons have abandoned me this afternoon, ladies, and I was wondering if you might keep me company until I need to depart back to the fort."

"Why, Colonel Washington, I'd love to keep you company," replied Esther. "Only I have chores that will keep me busy. Perhaps my niece could sit with you a while." She then took her leave, acknowledged George's bow, and moved off, busying herself but continuing to keep a close eye on the young couple.

"It is good to see you again, Sarah. I'm afraid my military duties have kept me quite occupied of late."

"I know how busy my Uncle Edward is with military matters so I do understand, George." She paused, looking down at her hands in her lap before she continued. "I have been hoping you'd come to see me, for you see there is something I need to tell you." She paused again, only this time she looked up directly into George's eyes before continuing. "You see, George, I really don't think it will work out between us and I don't want you wasting more of your time courting me when I really can't reciprocate your affections."

George arose as Sarah stood and moved away, too dumbfounded to utter a word. Here he was, all ready to tell Sarah he could not continue their courtship, and she up and told him! Not at all sure what to do, he clamped his hat back firmly on his head and fairly plopped back down on his stool. Now it was his turn to study his hands in his lap as he thought about what just happened. As the shock subsided, a feeling of loss replaced it. Perhaps he was more fond of Sarah than he realized. And perhaps he needed to be less carefree with his attentions toward women.

It was a more somber George who bid his goodbyes to the Jewett family as he made preparations to leave. Sarah was noticeably absent from the gathered family. Mounting, George noticed Philip and Charles were once again huddled together in serious discussion off to one side, out of earshot of their parents. And this was not the first time he'd noticed this during his short visit. No, they were up to something, those two.

☙ Chapter 27 ❧

E dward and Aaron started from Fort Loudoun heading northeast on the Virginia Road. Their plan was to make for where the Virginia Road met the road to Philadelphia before turning east. Although longer, they thought they might come across the battalion of the 60th Regiment bound for Fort Frederick. George had insisted Edward travel with an escort befitting his rank and status, so instead of just the two men, there were fifteen. Accompanying them were a Lieutenant and twelve mounted soldiers from George's command.

"Well," Aaron observed to Edward. "We make a fine spectacle traveling like this. No self respecting tavern keeper will put us up now."

"Are you already longing for a hot meal and soft bed? We've hardly started," was Edward's sarcastic yet good natured reply.

In spite of the disadvantage of traveling with such a large escort, they were able to make good time. Their mounts had recovered during their stay at Fort Loudoun and, while the escorts' horses weren't the best quality, they were also fresh. Late on their second day out, they came upon the advance guard of the 60th and were passed through to main body where they found the Battalion Commander conversing with Colonel Stanwix.

"Well, here's someone I didn't expect to find in the wilds of America! How are you, Edward, and what brings you to these detestable forests? Last I saw you was at Whitehall, right after you had been presented to the King." John Stanwix greeted them.

"How are you, John? And congratulations on your promotion and new command."

As the Battalion Commander busied himself establishing camp for the night, the two Colonels spent the time getting caught up since they last served together. Edward also showed him the letter he was carrying for Governor Denny and the two discussed the plan.

"What you say makes good sense, and I'll defer to your understanding of the situation here, and to the geography. I've found the maps in this country to be all but worthless, drawn apparently by men who have never laid eyes on the terrain and who have relied solely on what they're told by others, who it seems have also never seen it. Once I get to Fort Frederick, I'll send a party out to start the first of the stockade forts about the same distance to the northeast as Fort Loudoun is to the south-southwest."

"If you would, could you add that as an endorsement to my letter to the Governor?"

John Stanwix complied and, in a few minutes time, the letter was safely back in Edward's dispatch case. The two Colonels then continued their friendly discussion as they waited on their meal. For a spot in the middle of the American wilderness, Colonel Stanwix set a fine table, worthy of any in Philadelphia, with fine china and silver, a real linen tablecloth, all under a tent fly and served by his servants. As the two men ate and chatted, Aaron discovered even his meal, taken with the servants, was far better than he'd get at a common tavern.

Taking their leave the next morning, Edward proceeded toward Philadelphia while John Stanwix continued on to Fort Frederick.

"So tell me, Colonel, do all Royal Colonels live as well as our host of last night?"

"Oh, not at all. What you witnessed last night were primitive field conditions. Most Colonels manage to live much better than that," Edward responded with a smile as he watched the reaction on Aaron's face.

"Is that the way you used to live?"

"I served mainly in Europe where we lived much better than what you just saw. As I said, last night was a primitive camp situation and in Europe we rarely had to endure a primitive camp. Normally we had our choice of a grand manor or small castle to rest and refresh ourselves."

They made Philadelphia in good time, dismissed their escort to return to Fort Loudoun, and took lodgings near the Governor's residence. Edward sent a note to both the Governor, requesting an audience, and to his acquaintance, Benjamin Franklin, announcing his arrival in his friend's city. By the time they'd cleaned the trail dust off their clothing, they had answers from both notes. Benjamin asked for Edward to join him for supper that evening and the Governor asked him to call at ten of the clock the next day. That out of the way, Edward prepared for his evening with Doctor Franklin and gave Aaron his leave to enjoy his evening as he saw fit.

Any evening with Benjamin Franklin was bound to be interesting and this evening was no exception. Edward enjoyed a lively discussion about everything from the weather, as befitting the publisher of the most read

Almanac in the Colonies, science experiments Benjamin was conducting on a wide variety of issues, and, of course, the war.

It always came back to the war these days. Benjamin was able to give Edward a good feel for the state of politics in Pennsylvania. Now that the Quakers had removed themselves from the political scene, they were trying to open a dialogue with the Delaware, proposing peace with the Delaware and other Ohio Indians to let the two European nations conduct their own fight without the Indians being a party to it. Benjamin was actually optimistic about their chance for success, though he doubted there would be quick results. He reasoned that as the Indians absorbed more casualties, they would lose their ardor for helping either the French or English.

As always, Edward left Benjamin's house in good humor. He found the chubby, balding man so disarmingly charming that he could lure the unwary into forgetting his superior intelligence. No, Edward actually pitied anyone who felt they could survive, let alone prevail, in a battle of wits with Benjamin. Anyone who tried would soon find he had brought a knife to a gunfight.

The next morning found Edward at the Governor's Mansion at the appointed hour, dressed in his best set of Regimentals, not the ones he'd been traveling in.

"Colonel Jewett, I was both pleased and very surprised when I received your note last evening. This is a pleasure. How long has it been, five or six years, since I served in your Regiment as one of your Battalion Commanders?"

"Six, I think, but you've done quite well for yourself since then while I have remained just a Colonel and you've been promoted from Lieutenant Colonel to Governor."

"Oh, Colonel, your modesty is too much," Governor Denny said with a laugh. "You've become a wealthy man here in the Colonies, and well respected if all I've heard is to be believed. Why, Benjamin Franklin speaks quite highly of how you assisted this Colony in avoiding the wrath of General Braddock. Is it true you survived the slaughter along the Monongahela with Braddock?"

The two men sat and discussed that fateful battle for a while before Edward brought up the subject of defending the frontier. He showed Governor Denny his letter and let him study it, moving with the Governor to the map that was mounted on the wall.

"As John Stanwix noted to me when I met him on the road, the maps are inadequate. What is missing from your map is the line of mountains, basically an extension of the Blue Ridge in Virginia that runs just here," running his finger along the map to indicate where he meant.

"Ah, then with that vital piece of information, the proposal makes all the more sense. So what you're saying is to use this valley, backed up by this ridge of mountains, as a line of defense. Well, I'm so used to taking orders from you I feel unqualified not to accept your plan. And with Colonel Stanwix adding his endorsement, who am I to argue?"

The two men continued their discussions, moving from their experiences together to the current situation and back again in an almost random fashion, until early afternoon. As the Governor had dinner plans, meeting with the key political leaders in the Pennsylvania government, Benjamin Franklin included, Edward took his leave.

The next morning, he and Aaron continued on to New York where Lord Loudoun was making his headquarters.

Although a busy port city, New York was nothing compared to Philadelphia, the latter second only to London itself in size. New York was mainly a city of wooden houses and warehouses serving the port. There were a few fine residences, of course, and that was where they found Lord Loudoun's headquarters.

As was Edward's custom, he and Aaron found lodging not far from Headquarters and Aaron delivered Edward's note announcing his arrival and placing himself at the General's disposal. Something Aaron found a little unusual this time, he was beckoned to wait and returned with a note requesting Edward immediately wait on the General at Headquarters.

Although he barely had time to wash the trail off and change, Edward made his way to Headquarters. He was ushered into Lord Loudoun's office where the General was busy with his staff, issuing orders and studying dispatches. Edward waited patiently as the aide whispered his presence to the General. As Edward expected, Lord Loudoun kept him waiting as he continued with his business. Finally, the General motioned Edward to approach, which he did, stepping quickly.

"Colonel, it's good of you to report for duty. I congratulate you on your willingness to help us in this war. I've found so many of these colonials are reluctant to do their duty unless there's a lucrative profit to be made. And I understand you are also a colonial, though I hadn't realized it before when your name was appearing in so many dispatches during the late war."

Edward knew the General's disdain for the colonials was genuine and not aimed personally at him, so he did not react defensively. The General was gauging Edward's reaction and, when satisfied Edward would not bristle at his slights against Edward's countrymen, he continued.

"For the time being, I find your assignment advising Governor Dinwiddie to be the best use of your talents. If you can keep Virginia stable in this matter, I can draw troops from there to the north, where the real fighting will take place."

"I will naturally do my best in that regard, General, and I thank you for showing such confidence in my poor abilities." General Loudoun waved off the polite response. "I assume, then, that your Lordship plans on cutting off the Saint Lawrence and strangling the French into submission."

Lord Loudoun, for as much as he didn't want to, was finding this tall Colonel quite charming and knowledgeable. Maybe he would have to find some other use for his talents. If only his name hadn't been associated in London with the now discredited William Shirley.

"I intend to first take Fort Louisbourg while at the same time my deputy, Major General Abercromby, moves up the New York lakes toward Montreal. We'll meet at Quebec."

"That was the strategy urged upon General Braddock, who felt compelled to strike at the tail of the snake and leave it free use of its head. I'm afraid General Braddock found the head to be the part of the snake with fangs."

Lord Loudoun found himself chuckling. No, he could grow to like this Colonel. Too bad they hadn't served together in the last war. They talked strategy for several more minutes before work forced them to end their interview. Lord Loudoun dismissed Edward to return to Virginia and even gave him an order allowing use of one of the ships pressed into army service to ease his trip home.

The next morning, Edward and Aaron made their way along the docks to find a ship to take them to Williamsburg. The Harbormaster told them where they would find the ships pressed into army service and they began their search there. They had barely started when Edward heard a familiar voice. Looking around, he found the source of the voice was on one of the nearby ships.

"Master Cole, is that you?"

"That's Captain Cole," came the quick rejoinder. "Oh, sorry Colonel, I thought you were one of the...Well bless me if it isn't Colonel Jewett. How are you, sir? Come aboard, come aboard, and welcome."

Shaking hands, Captain Cole explained how his old Boston packet had finally succumbed to worms and sank at her moorings. He went in search of another and was offered this new ship by Captain Faircloth, so now he was working for him instead of being his own master.

"It's actually been better for me, and I was able to bring all of my old crew with me, or at least those who wanted to work. And I have a fine new ship of increased tonnage under my feet and regular pay to boot. Life is good."

"So, do you still haul tobacco for Colonel Byrd?"

Laughing, "Well, yes I do, though I swear it was the Virginia waters that gave the old packet the worms."

"Listen, I'm in need of transportation back to Williamsburg and, if you feel up to the trip, it would be good to travel with someone I know and trust."

"My pleasure, Colonel, only the army has me on a short leash right now. I'm to wait on their pleasure."

"So, am I to take it you have no assignment at this moment, because I have a release from the Commanding General for a ship to see me to Virginia, if you're interested."

"Interested? How soon do you want to leave?"

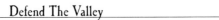

❧ **Chapter 28** ❧

In the early morning darkness before first light, a turkey clucked three times, sounding very loud in the small street of the Jewett fort. Charles felt very self conscious, looking around to see if anyone noticed the clucks he'd made on his wing bone turkey call. The sound of the wooden latch as the door opened in front of him startled him.

"Oh, Philip, it's you," he whispered as his cousin appeared out of the darkness.

"Shhh, someone will hear you," came the hushed response.

The two boys made their way out the gate, closing it behind them, and led a packhorse toward the south and the wooded creek bottom. Once across, they felt they could now whisper without being overheard.

"Well, we made it. Won't everyone be surprised when we bring a deer or two back?" Philip asked his younger cousin.

"I just hope they're not too mad that we slipped off like this, deer or no deer."

"Well, we leave for school tomorrow and this is our last chance. If Uncle Edward were here, he'd take us hunting. Neither of our fathers really enjoys hunting all that much, so you know they wouldn't take us."

"Oh, that's not it. It's the slipping off without telling them they're likely to focus on," Charles said, yawning.

The two boys made their way over the rise before stopping to wait on first light. As soon as they were able to see shapes, they moved on south. They'd been hunting the area now for several years so they boys intended to move further south to an area where they hunted less, hoping for better success. They continued to whisper as they went.

"So, how is it living with the Samuels? Are they nice?"

"It's actually fun. Uncle Ronald is a character. He's always forgetting things, which drives Aunt Margaret simply to distraction. He likes to have fun, though, and we laugh a lot. He loves his diversions and, if you ever want to get out of doing your assignments, just mention you'd rather play one of the diversions and he'll forget all about you having schoolwork to do."

"And how's Aunt Margaret?"

"She's great, but she remembers things! She's more likely to remember you have studies to complete and chase you back to them. Then there's Elam, Professor Samuel when you're in class. If he stops by and you're playing a diversion with his father, he'll ask to see your assignment or ask you to recite your lesson. Then you're in for a lecture!"

"Is it hard living with your professor?"

"You've been living with yours, only he's also your grandfather. It isn't that much different except that Elam is younger. He likes to roam the woods and will take us along with him for company. It is a bit hard to hunt with him because he's always talking, and not in a whisper, either. And it's always about one of his favorite philosophers, Locke, Bacon, or Newton. Or else he's arguing against the King and Parliament holding the Colonies in submission to their wills." Philip rolled his eyes, though Charles couldn't yet see his facial expressions.

"I'm not really looking forward to living away from father and grandfather."

"I can't say I like that part very much, either. When I'm there, I miss father and grandfather so much I can hardly stand it. Then Uncle Ronald will do something that reminds me of grandfather or something silly that makes me laugh and it seems alright again."

They walked on in silence in the growing light, now able to see their way clearly. They started to move more cautiously, so as not to frighten the deer before they could see them and maybe get a shot off. They started to see deer, but these remained too far off for the boys' light guns. While Philip was now tall, he still couldn't quite handle his father's short rifle as he was slight of build. Charles still hadn't grown very tall and was now a little stout, built as he was more like his mother than his very thin father.

As the sun rose over the Blue Ridge to their left, it lit up the high clouds with pinks and purples. The boys paused to watch until the sun cleared the top of the ridge and put them in full sunlight. Now they could see clearly and were ready to get into the spirit of the hunt.

They saw quite a few deer across a clearing and decided to tie the packhorse to a tree so they could better move up to where they were within range of the deer. Watching the wind direction to make sure their scent wouldn't carry to the deer, they worked their way around the clearing, staying just within the wood line and where they could still see the deer.

About halfway around, Charles, who was following Philip, stopped and tapped his cousin on the shoulder. Philip was too focused on the does in the clearing and just waved Charles off. Rather than pay any attention to this slight, Charles made ready to fire off to their right, deeper into the woods. His shot so startled Philip, he fell against a tree, which saved him from falling completely to the ground.

"Charles, what are you doing? Now, look, the deer have all taken flight and we'll have another hour or more before we find more."

"Well, not all have taken flight. The buck I just shot staggered before I lost sight of him," Charles replied, all the while reloading his gun.

The look of surprise on Philip's face told all Charles needed to know. Philip had been so focused on the does, he hadn't even seen the buck hugging the cover and also approaching the does, much as the boys were doing.

"How big was the buck?" Philip asked, whispering again.

"Big," was all Charles could say, as he replaced his wiping stick back in its place under the barrel.

Now Charles led the way as the boys moved slowly toward where he had last seen the buck. "He was standing right about here," Charles said as both boys started looking around for either the downed deer or signs of blood on the ground.

"Here's blood, you got him!" Philip said, no longer whispering.

The boys followed the trail only about twenty-five yards when they came to the downed buck.

"You were right, he's big," Philip said, impressed.

"He's bigger than I thought!" Charles replied. "Good thing we brought the packhorse. I don't think I could get him back home on my own."

"Well, you start to field dress him and I'll go get the horse. Don't roll your eyes, you know Uncle Edward's rules. You shoot it, you clean it!"

By the time Philip returned with the packhorse, Charles had done all he could do without Philip's help. Together they finished the job and then struggled to put the buck on the horse's back, a horse that wasn't all that thrilled with the idea of having a dead animal that smelled of blood draped over its back. They finally did manage to get the buck situated to where they could tie it securely to the pack saddle, then sat down, tired from their exertions.

"I sure wish we'd have thought to bring some food along. I'm hungry now," said Philip.

"Well, you may have forgotten, but I brought some cheese and bread with me. If you're nice, I'll let you have some," was Charles reply, enjoying having the upper hand on his older cousin. Not only did he bring along some food, he had also made the first kill of the hunt, and an impressive buck it was.

The two boys sat and enjoyed the food and a few swigs of water from their water bottles before deciding they needed to move on. They were now determined to find another buck for Philip before they returned home.

Having found the one buck in the woods, they decided to stick to hunting the woods. Both boys were enjoying their hunt, time in the woods together, feeling less like boys and more like the young men they were becoming. But after two more hours, they were starting to lose heart that they would find another buck for Philip.

"Let's move a little west and deeper into the woods. We just have to find something, and soon, if we hope to make it home in time for dinner," Philip said as they were resting against a large tree.

"You know we're not likely to see more deer before late afternoon, and we need to be closer to home by then."

"I know. I'm just not ready to give up yet. After all, how do you think it would look for me if you brought home the only deer, little cousin!?"

"Stop with the 'little' comments! You may be taller, but you're skin and bone while I have more muscle."

The boys knew better than to talk loud or laugh while hunting in the woods, but this last comment by Charles almost had them laughing out loud. Recovering and resting a little longer, they decided to start back by sweeping around to the west and then north rather than just retrace their steps. They had just about given up when Philip stopped short and threw up his hand, signaling Charles to stop.

Something up ahead had caught Philip's attention. Only, from where he was, Charles couldn't see what it was. Philip moved as quietly as he could back and whispered directly into Charles's ear.

"Tie off the horse here and follow me, quietly."

Doing as he was told, Charles moved in behind Philip, both boys moving as stealthily as they could. Then Charles saw it. Up ahead and digging honey out of a hollow tree was a bear, the biggest bear Charles had ever seen. He reached forward and grabbed Philip's arm.

"No, he's too big and our guns are too light to bring him down," he whispered as low as he could and still be heard.

"We can do this. All we have to do is make sure we hit him in the right spot. I'll shoot first and, if my shot doesn't bring him down, you shoot while I reload. Remember where Uncle Edward said to hit a bear? Good. Aim there and squeeze the trigger. Today is no time to miss."

As the two boys moved into position, the bear's head snapped up and he began sniffing the air. In their excitement, the boys had forgotten to keep the wind in their faces and now the bruin had their scent. The boys treed, as they'd been taught, and watched as the bear stood, sniffing in their direction. They had known he was big before, only now he was a lot bigger standing than they originally thought.

Philip looked at Charles to make sure he was ready. He then took careful aim and a deep breath, let some out, held it, and squeezed the trigger. The report shattered the silence of the woods, followed almost immediately by the howl of the now wounded bear. Philip dropped the butt of his gun to the ground and grabbed his powder horn to start reloading.

Looking up from the now full powder measure, he saw the bear was charging them. The report of Charles's gun was comforting and Philip saw the bear react. He didn't stop his charge, though, just jerked his head to one side, missed a step, and came on right toward the boys, who now had only empty guns.

Loading fast as he had been taught, Philip got the powder down and then spit the ball down the barrel, not bothering to patch it. At about that time, he realized the bear would reach him before he could get primed and he knew Charles was behind him in the loading process. Now he was frightened and knew Charles had been right about leaving the bear alone.

As the bear reached him and raised his huge paw, Philip dropped to his knees and pulled his large belt knife, determined to go down fighting.

⌒ Chapter 29 ⌒

Edward and Aaron arrived early dockside so they could be loaded and Captain Cole could ride the receding tide out of the harbor at noon. As Edward had requested, a boarding plank had been rigged between the ship and dock to allow the horses to be brought on board more comfortably, without the use of the normal method of slinging them on board. Edward always found the sight of a horse in a sling, high above the deck and in near panic, a disconcerting sight and he didn't want his animals treated in such a manner.

Once aboard and secured in corrals designed to keep horses or cattle secure on a sea voyage, Edward was satisfied. He then joined Captain Cole in the Captain's cabin.

"Well, all secured and ready to depart? Good. I picked up the dispatches and post bound for Virginia and the Carolinas to deliver as well. You should be interested to find a letter for your sister-in-law amongst the post," Captain Cole chatted away at Edward, handing him a rather thick letter addressed to Marie.

"I know she's been waiting for this for some time now. It is from your employer's daughter and her best friend, Hannah Davies."

"Ah, yes, I know of her. The 'Admiral' wanted me to take that son of hers with me on this voyage, but I'd heard about that lad and had the good sense to decline. Oh, from what I've heard, he's very poorly disciplined and always up to no good. Not something you'd want to take willingly on board a small ship with a small crew. A crew is a funny thing and can be heavily influenced by the son of the ship's owner into forgetting their duties. No, I'd have none of that."

Edward changed the subject to one he felt more comfortable with than discussing the qualities of a boy he'd never met, the son of Marie's best friend. "Timing should be very good for you, Captain, what with the tobacco harvest complete and the drying almost done. You should be able to carry a full hold of hogsheads back with you to satisfy the army's craving for tobacco. But aren't you afraid to get worms in your new ship?"

Captain Cole chuckled, "Not at all. She's got copper plating on her, so no worms can get at her from the outside. It makes her a lot faster, too. You'll see."

Compared to the men-of-war they passed in New York Harbor, Captain Cole's ship may have been small, but compared to his little packet, she was grand. She was built to be a collier and thus had a good hold capable of carrying a lot of cargo. As they left the harbor, Edward could tell Captain Cole was quite proud of her.

Captain Cole asked after Edward's family, showing some sorrow on hearing of the loss of Mary and Joseph. He enjoyed hearing how well Robert was doing, though, and was thankful the elderly gentleman continued to enjoy good health. All in all, they had a fine time conversing as they made their way south.

They made good time and arrived within a week at the Queen's Creek wharf. Edward said goodbye to Captain Cole, promising to send Colonel Byrd down if he could find him in town, now already crowded for the fall Court and Burgess Sessions.

He went immediately to see John and Fanny Dandridge, not just because they had become friends but also in the hope they'd allow him to stay in their adjoining office again. The Raleigh Tavern was on their way so it only took a moment to find Colonel Byrd where they knew he'd be, enjoying an early bowl of punch, and tell him of Captain Cole's arrival. When they arrived at the Dandridge house on Duke of Gloucester Street, Edward noted Patsy Custis's London coach tied up in front and it was Patsy who answered the door.

"Oh, Colonel Jewett, have you come to pay your respects to my mother?"

"Why, Missus Custis, has some tragedy befallen your family? I've just arrived from New York and was calling out of courtesy."

"Then you haven't heard. My father passed away quite suddenly late this summer. Mother is absolutely distraught."

"I am so sorry to hear that, Missus Custis. Your father was a fine man and a good friend. Perhaps I should come back at a more convenient time."

"Who's there, Patsy? I thought I recognized Colonel Jewett's voice, only I know he's still off on the frontier," Fanny Dandridge called from the parlor.

"Oh, do come in now. If I told her I'd sent you away, she'd be ever so upset with me." Patsy ushered Edward into the parlor.

"Missus Dandridge, you have my deepest sympathies on the loss of John."

"Thank you, Edward. You were always so kind to him. Oh, don't think I don't know about your paying some on our account with Mister Prentiss. John never knew, but since his passing, Bat, my son Bartholomew who's handling his father's affairs, found it out from Mister Prentiss when the books didn't exactly match. It was very kind of you to think of his pride like that."

"Well, you've found me out, Fanny. I hope you're not offended, but I couldn't just stay with you and not find a way to compensate you for your kindness."

"Nonsense, John would have thrown a fit, but I appreciate it especially as John owed so much. So, tell me, have you lodgings yet? No? Well, you shall have your usual accommodations and I'll not take no for an answer."

After chatting for nearly and hour, Patsy saw Edward to the little office. "Thank you, Edward. Your visit seemed to brighten her more than any of us have been able to for simply weeks. Will you join us for dinner? My husband will be joining us."

It was a pleasant dinner where Edward got to know Daniel Parke Custis better and Fanny Dandridge seemed more her old self. As they chatted afterward, Aaron interrupted to inform Edward Governor Dinwiddie was expecting him for supper that evening.

Dressed again in his Regimentals, Edward made his way to the Governor's Palace in the twilight of the fall evening. He found Governor Dinwiddie looking old and tired from all of his worries and efforts to keep the Virginia Regiment supplied and Virginia's interests protected during this war.

"I tell you Edward, if Pennsylvania hadn't lost most of its frontier after the fall of Fort Granville, the Lords

Proprietors would have been badgering the King to place Virginia's western lands under them. I see it as a blessing they saw fit to settle the Quakers in their Colony. Their pacifism overcame good common sense and now the Penn family has lost their frontier. Now we must make sure to preserve our own frontier and prestige or we could lose those Ohio lands yet."

"Governor, you work yourself too hard and worry too much. George is doing a fine job on the frontier defending the Valley, if a bit discouraged from time to time with how little he gets from the Burgesses. You need to take comfort in having such a man in command and get some rest. It'll do no good for you to ruin your health. Virginia needs your firm guiding hand."

The next day and those that followed saw Edward making the rounds of the taverns and committees of the Burgesses, trying as he might to gain interest in supporting the frontier and the Virginia Regiment and taking some of the pressure off Governor Dinwiddie. With his firsthand knowledge of the military situation, having just come from Lord Loudoun's headquarters, he had instant credibility, although not instant relief for young George Washington. By Edward's being in Williamsburg during the meeting of the House of Burgesses, Robert Dinwiddie put most of the burden on his military advisor and did take the advice of getting some rest. They supped each night together so Edward could keep the Governor informed on the goings on, but, beyond that, the Governor left it to Edward.

Captain Cole stopped in to see Edward before he set sail back to New York. Colonel Byrd had provided him with a full hold of tobacco hogsheads at a price Captain Cole couldn't believe, but accepted quickly before Colonel Byrd had an opportunity to reconsider. No, he told Edward, he would make enough to secure a good profit for his employer and a tidy sum for himself and the crew. The soldiers were willing to pay well for good Virginia sweet tobacco, even if the market for tobacco in general was depressed, and Captain Cole knew just the right merchants to get the best price for his cargo. He left Virginia a very happy man indeed.

Just as soon as the fall session concluded, Edward and Aaron made their way west toward the Valley, but not before Edward sat down with Bat Dandridge and satisfied himself that, while deeply in debt, Fanny Dandridge had the means to support herself. He also made fair recompense for his lodging in the Dandridge office. Bat refused to accept what Edward first offered, finally agreeing on an amount that satisfied both men.

They were fairly down the road toward Richmond when the sound of thundering hooves and creaking carriage gear coming up quickly behind them got their attention. It was Patsy Custis in her London-made carriage racing to catch them.

"Colonel Jewett, Edward, Bat told me of your repeated kindness and I couldn't let you leave without thanking you personally. You see, father left some large debts and while mother will be taken care of, that is only because Bat and I will see to it. Were it not for my ability to satisfy her creditors, I'm afraid she'd have lost all by now."

"I've done nothing I need to be thanked for, Patsy. Your mother has always shown me and my family every kindness and I simply paid for my lodgings, as I would have done had I stayed elsewhere in Williamsburg."

"Well I thank you all the same, for no matter how light you make of it, it is uncommon enough these days that it can't go unnoticed. And mother says that whenever you're in Williamsburg, if you don't stay with her she'll be very upset with you."

Edward grinned, "Thank your mother for me and tell her that upsetting her is something I shall always endeavor to avoid."

After the coach turned around and headed back toward Williamsburg, traveling just as fast as when it was trying to catch them, Edward noted, Aaron spoke up.

"I'm glad to hear you paid for all the fodder these animals ate. They were telling me in the stables that Missus Dandridge has had to sell several of her slaves to satisfy debts. Most have luckily gone to Mister Custis, so they've kind of stayed in the family. It's such a pity."

"Well let that be a lesson to you on how quickly even a landed man can get himself into financial difficulties trying to live a lavish lifestyle."

"Seems to me, from what I saw with Colonel Stanwix, that you led a pretty lavish lifestyle before taking up residence on the frontier, Colonel. So how is it you managed to avoid having such large debts, or do I just not know of them?"

"You've seen me take wine and punch, have you not? Well, then, I've managed my funds the same way. I make the appropriate appearances of living a lavish life like I do drinking with these planters. They drink heavily while I drink modestly. In the end, they're convinced I've drunk as much as they only I'm the one still on my feet."

"I think I understand you."

"Well, you should ask Esther to loan you the copies of Poor Richard's Almanac. Doctor Franklin includes many tips for preserving and increasing wealth. Did you know he started as a runaway apprentice? No? Well he did, running away from his brother's Boston printing shop to Philadelphia where I think you'll admit he's done quite well for himself. Remind me next time we see him and I'll suggest he gather his suggestions on gaining wealth into a single pamphlet. I think it would sell very well, not that Doctor Franklin really needs any more money."

The two men chuckled as they rode along, thinking of the jovial Benjamin Franklin and trying to picture him as a runaway apprentice.

∽ Chapter 30 ∾

Henry lightly knocked on Lewis's cabin door in the predawn darkness. When Lewis answered, he was already dressed.

"Did you know our sons have slipped off, out of the fort and into the night?" Henry asked in a hushed voice.

"Well, I didn't know all that, but I knew Philip had slipped off after I heard a turkey call. I heard Charles practicing with it last evening so I figured they were together."

"What with the baby and then my legs aching again, I was awake when Charles dressed and slipped out, thinking he was being very stealthy. That boy will never learn that I know all the tricks, tried most of them out on father when I was his age, and was no more successful than Charles is." Both men chuckled at the memory of Henry's attempts to rebel against their father's firm but loving control of his household.

"Philip was the same way. I thought I heard him but it was the turkey clucking that gave it away. Haven't seen a turkey in our little fort since we built it and don't think one would live long enough inside to cluck, what with how hungry those soldiers always seem to be." Lewis could hardly contain a laugh at the thought.

"They took a packhorse and headed out. What do you think they're doing, running away? Tomorrow's when they're supposed to go back to school."

"No, Philip enjoys school too much, so I doubt they're running away to avoid that. Besides, he likes the Samuels. It must be something else."

"What do you propose we do?"

"We go after them, of course. No sense leaving before first light, though. In this darkness we could walk right past them and never know it. Let's saddle the horses. Just because they're walking doesn't mean we need to." With the ache returning to Henry's legs with the cold weather, he appreciated Lewis's suggestion.

The two men saddled their horses and made ready to go out as if going on patrol. Lewis made sure the Sergeant knew they were going out and told him briefly why so he could tell Robert. No sense in waking their father now or having him worried needlessly when he found his sons gone. As soon as it was light enough to see, they left the fort.

"Well," Henry said in a hushed voice. "It won't be any trouble following them until the sun burns off this frost. I can see right where they went, knocking the frost off the grass."

The two men followed at a leisurely pace, knowing the boys were on foot. Even after the sun melted the frost, it wasn't hard to see where they had gone. They even found where they had evidently waited for first light.

"Sitting down on the frosty grass, those two now have wet seats. That should make them uncomfortable for a while," chuckled Lewis to Henry's nods of agreement.

"Say, you don't suppose they've decided to go off hunting, do you? They were talking some about hunting yesterday only I didn't put it together," Henry asked.

"That just might be. Philip did mention his disappointment a few days ago about Edward being gone right during the prime deer hunting season. And that would explain the packhorse. They must be counting on a successful hunt."

It didn't take them too long before they had the boys in sight. They stayed far back so they didn't alert the boys to their presence, content to watch from a distance to see what they were up to. Several times, they saw the boys stop and look and point, they were even able to see the boys were pointing to deer far off, out of their range. That's when Lewis and Henry knew for sure the boys were out on a hunt.

"What do you think? Now that we know what they're up to, we could just leave them to it and go back for some hot tea. It's chilly out here," Henry suggested.

"We could, only I'd feel better if we stayed with them. It wouldn't take much for them to get into something they'd have a hard time getting themselves out of."

"You're right, like always. That hot tea would have tasted good, though."

They closed the distance between them and the boys once they made it into the woods. The cover the woods provided still kept the boys from detecting them but the fathers would not have been able to keep watch on them from any great distance for the same reasons. Eventually, they came to where the boys had tied the packhorse and, looking out across a small meadow, they saw several does feeding on the far side. A little movement to their right showed where the boys were working their way closer to the deer through the woods.

"Well, they'll be coming back for the packhorse, so it wouldn't do us any good to leave our horses here. Let's take them back to that stand of cedars we passed and leave them there," Lewis suggested.

Their horses safely hidden from view, Lewis and Henry moved quickly through the woods to get the boys back in sight. Henry's hand on his shoulder halted Lewis and his point showed where he'd spotted the boys. That was just about the time they saw Charles get waved off by Philip, then take aim. Despite craning their necks, they couldn't see what Charles was aiming at. Then he fired.

Henry dropped behind a tree, hand on his mouth trying desperately to stifle his laughter. Lewis moved close by, also trying not to give their position away.

"Did you see Philip jump?" Henry clucked when he had recovered a little of his composure. "Had the branches of that chestnut been lower, he'd have hit his head on them!"

"Shush, you'll get me to laughing with you," chuckled Lewis as he watched what the boys were doing. Oh, how he wished he was close enough to hear what they were saying. Philip was obviously not pleased with his cousin, but after some explanation, he looked a bit excited and the two moved off in the direction Charles had shot.

"If you've composed yourself enough where you think you can walk, the boys are heading toward whatever it was Charles shot," Lewis asked, barely able to contain his own laughter, not a little due to the effect of Henry's desperate attempts to control his.

Partially controlling themselves, the two men moved off after the boys. Evidently the boys found what they were looking for because they could see them stop and examine something on the ground, move on a little bit, then stop again, this time paying close attention to something the men couldn't see because of the distance and undergrowth between them and the boys. Then they saw Philip turn in their direction.

Quickly ducking into a stand of pine saplings growing in a small patch where a downed chestnut allowed more light to penetrate to the forest floor, they were barely concealed when Philip walked pass, muttering.

"It just figures he'd go and get the first deer, and it would have to be a huge buck. Well, this hunting trip isn't over, not until I get mine," or at least that's what the two men thought they heard him muttering.

After waiting quite a few minutes, they saw Philip coming back leading the packhorse. They were quite safe where they were hidden as he was focused on making his way through the woods and not on looking around him.

Charles had been mostly out of sight while Philip had been gone, his head coming into view occasionally, as he went about what the men assumed was field dressing his kill. When Philip joined him, they first discussed something and then the two of them bent out of sight. When next they stood erect, Philip moved to bring a reluctant packhorse closer, tying it to a tree close to where they'd been working.

Finally they got their first look at what it was Charles had shot. The boys were both working together to lift the head portion of the deer and boost it over the packsaddle.

"Your son shot an impressive buck, Henry," complimented Lewis. Henry just clucked in response, very proud of his son.

It was then that the scene got interesting. The two boys were struggling to boost up the deer, the packhorse was trying to avoid them, and it became a dance, with the boys struggling and the horse shying and whinnying.

Henry patted Lewis on the shoulder but, by time Lewis turned, Henry had turned his back and was moving down into a little hollow behind them, his head down into the crook of his arm.

Lewis wasn't sure what was wrong, but when Henry sat down on a large rock and buried his head in his folded arms, he became concerned and moved to his brother's side.

"Henry, are you alright?" he asked in a low whisper.

Henry looked up and Lewis knew immediately what the problem was. Watching the boys "dance" with the horse was more than Henry could bear. He was laughing so hard tears were running down his face and he was trying so hard not to make noise that would give them away. That was all it took to send Lewis over the edge as well. The two men sat there in the middle of the forest, laughing as hard and as silently as they could possibly laugh.

By the time they had recovered sufficiently to look again, the boys were putting the finishing touches on tying off the deer. Philip took off his hat and wiped his hand across his brow and said something to Charles.

"He just told Charles that he was sweating," Lewis told Henry, who looked surprised. "He always does that after he's worked up a sweat. Haven't you noticed? It's like he wants you to know he's been working hard enough to sweat."

"That's your boy!" was the whispered response.

They waited until they saw the boys were sitting down, evidently eating something, before hurrying back to retrieve their horses. By time they returned, the boys had moved on, sticking to the woods now and definitely not heading back toward home.

"Now what do you suppose they're up to?" Henry asked.

"It's Philip's turn. You don't think he'd be content to head home with Charles making the only kill of their big hunt, do you? No, he'll want to try to get a deer of his own before heading home."

"He is that way, isn't he? Must get that from his mother," Henry chuckled.

"You won't mind if I told her you said so, would you?" Lewis chuckled right back. All he knew was this was turning out to be the most fun he and Henry had had together in longer than he could remember.

Not surprisingly, considering the time of day, there wasn't a lot of deer now out to be seen and the boys eventually started working their way more westerly than southerly. This encouraged their fathers into thinking they were now going to work their way back toward home. Then the boys stopped.

Both men watched as the boys held a very short conference before Charles tied off the packhorse and both boys moved cautiously forward.

"Well, Lewis, it doesn't look like your boy will be coming home empty handed after all, at least not if he can shoot straight."

"Can you see what they're stalking? I can't from this position." Henry shook his head. "Let's leave the horses and move closer."

Moving in, they saw the boys stop, looking at something just out of their sight. They continued closer. About the time they saw Charles shake his head, they saw the bear.

"Oh, he's not thinking of…"

With that, they saw Philip raise his gun and Charles do likewise. Both men moved forward quickly, no longer trying to mask their movements. They saw Philip fire and the bear begin its charge, then saw Charles fire and his shot be shrugged off. The men now instinctively stopped and brought their guns up, firing nearly simultaneously just as the bear reached Philip.

The two heavy balls hit the bear just as he was about to take a swipe aimed at Philip's head. The reaction caused the swipe to do no more than knock Philip head over heels into Charles, leaving both boys piled in a heap, the bear lying now dead on the spot Philip had just involuntarily vacated.

Lewis and Henry reloaded before moving forward, not trusting the bear to truly be dead and not wanting any more surprises. When they did make it to the boys, they found them starting to untangle themselves from their collective heap, Philip shaking his head trying to clear his vision.

"How bad are you hurt, Philip?" a concerned Lewis asked while Henry made sure the bear was truly dead.

"Father? Where, how…?"

"Never mind that, are you hurt bad?"

"I'll be alright. He hit me hard, though."

"I'll say he did," chuckled Henry, now that he knew the boys, while rattled, were basically fine. "At least he got you where it'd do the least harm."

The tension now relieved, the two men were laughing at the boys, who were still trying to recover some of their dignity. Once they were both up and functioning, Lewis sent Henry to bring up all of the horses while he stayed with the boys.

"Well, Philip, you'd best get started."

"Get started, what do you mean, father?"

"I mean you don't think I'm dressing out your bear, do you? Now, get to work. Charles can help you when you need it. I'll sit right here and keep watch."

The two boys reluctantly started in on the task and were nearly done when Henry returned.

"How do you propose we get that thing back? Neither of these horses can carry it, even field dressed. It must be a three hundred pound bear."

"I know, but once the boys finish the field dressing, they'll skin and bone it. We can wrap just the meat up in the hide and it should then be manageable for one of the horses then."

Philip and Charles looked at each other, eyes wide, realizing their work was just beginning.

"You could help, you know," Philip said to his father.

"Oh, you're doing just fine with Charles's help. Henry, do you have any of that jerky left? I'm a little hungry."

They two men sat and munched while the boys worked. Finally, when the bear was reduced to just its hide and meat, they loaded it up on Lewis's horse and started walking.

"Boy, just wait until they see the bear hide when we get home," Philip said excitedly to Charles. Now that the work was done, he was in a much better mood.

"Boys, the people at home aren't going to see that hide," Lewis told them. Turning to Henry, "I think Matt and his family will really appreciate having this meat to help see them through the winter, don't you?"

Henry now understood what his brother was up to, smiled and nodded, "Yes, they sure will appreciate you boys hunting up meat for them, now that Mister Bennett can't do his own hunting."

∽ Chapter 31 ∾

Edward and Aaron arrived home on a windy, raw, yet sunny late November day. In spite of their sojourn in Williamsburg, both men were trail weary and Robert was concerned by how worn out and gaunt Edward looked. Aaron had fared some better, but his face too was showing how fatigued he was. Edward's big black stallion was also fatigued, making Aaron's horse and the packhorse nearly spent. None of the three would be up for anything strenuous until they'd recovered.

As was their custom, Robert, Lewis, and Henry escorted Edward to his cabin so the four of them could catch up on all the news, both from New York and from their own little settlement. Before entering, however, Edward called for Marie to join them. Surprised, she entered and remained in the background as the men talked while Edward peeled off his powder horn, shooting pouch, haversack, dispatch case, waist belt with pouch, and sash before he could even begin removing his greatcoat. The whole time he was listening as Lewis and Henry laughingly told of Philip and Charles's final hunting trip before going off to school.

Once comfortably dressed for the warm cabin, Edward pulled his dispatch case from the pile of gear on the table and summoned Marie forward.

"Marie, I believe I have something here that you've been waiting a very long time for," he said while sorting through papers in the case. "Ah, here it is. A letter from Boston in a lady's hand and from the heft of it there is only one person I can think of who this could be from."

Marie's eyes shone bright when she reached for the parcel and recognized Hannah's neat hand on the address. "This is so exciting!" she exclaimed to no one in particular. "Oh, thank you very much, Edward. I've been waiting for this for so long now I just can't wait to read it." She turned to leave, not taking her eyes off the parcel and only absentmindedly saying goodbye to her husband in response to his goodbye to her.

"Well, you've made her a very happy woman. You realize, of course, that all I will hear about for days now is 'Hannah this' or 'Hannah that.' But thank you anyway, Edward. You've really made her day," Lewis said, grinning broadly.

"I also have another letter here, but, before I deliver it, I thought we should discuss it. Father, first you need to hear some sad news. John Dandridge passed from this life in August, very suddenly, though I think I told you I didn't think he looked well when I was there in the spring." Edward paused while Robert absorbed the news. John was a much younger man, Edward's age, and his passing gave Robert pause as he considered how much older he was.

"The other letter is from Bartholomew Dandridge, John and Fanny's son, Patsy's brother. Well, he's twenty-one now and has completed his studies in law with Mister Wythe. He is doing quite well for himself. And, in spite of John's heavy debts, he has been able to save his father's plantation from the creditors, though it will require some rebuilding as he had to sell most of the stock and slaves to preserve the property."

"Oh, poor Fanny, she must be devastated," observed Robert, still absorbing the news of John's death.

"It would seem Bat, as Fanny and Patsy call him, remembers Sarah from when she passed through four years ago and asked me if it would be alright for him to write her. He is as yet unmarried and has shown the good sense to shun the local beauties for someone he feels would be more frugal and understanding, in other words more like he is. If, after exchanging a few letters, should things go well, he thought he could visit us and the two could determine if there might be a future for them. I, of course, won't deliver it unless you, Henry, and father agree it would be alright. And then there is the issue with George, has he been by?"

"Several times," Robert answered quickly.

"Yes, but he's been all business. Sarah has told him there is no future for them and he has accepted this. If you ask me, the two of them enjoy each other's company more now that the courtship has been called off than they did while courting," observed Henry. "I think giving her the letter would be fine, provided you vouch for Mister Dandridge's character. I can't say I remember him."

"Well, even if you did, you'd be remembering a seventeen-year-old boy. I was much impressed with him. He has a sound head for figures, has moderate habits, and comes from a good family we know. He is not wealthy, but with what he's been able to do on his own and through preservation of his father's estate, he is comfortable."

"Henry, would you be alright with it? I'm in favor of it, knowing his parents and sister as I do. I, of course, remember him from my last trip to Williamsburg, but he was nineteen then, studying law," offered Robert. Henry nodded his agreement.

"Then, Henry, I'll give you his letter and let you give it to Sarah."

The four men then spent the next two hours discussing the war, how badly it continued to go for England, and what had happened at home during Edward's absence. He learned he was an uncle again, congratulating Henry on his new son, and that they had a good fall harvest unmolested by the Shawnee.

As they finished, Marie reappeared holding Hannah's now opened letter.

"Oh, you should hear all the terrible things that have befallen Hannah. No wonder she hadn't written, poor girl. Daniel treated her terribly and their move to Albany was simply terrible for her. But, here's the interesting part, Daniel was killed in the fall of Fort Oswego," looking to Edward who nodded, confirming he knew of the fall of the fort. "She's moved back to Boston and is temporarily staying at her parents. It's a pity she's lost Daniel, but it's also a blessing. Now that she's back in Boston, we can write each other regularly again. Isn't it exciting?"

Marie then left as abruptly as she had appeared, not waiting for any response as she wasn't looking for any. The four men looked to each other and could only chuckle. Edward's brothers left but Robert hesitated.

"You know, Edward, it really isn't good for you to be alone. I remember Hannah and she's a fine woman from a good family. You should consider…"

"Father!"

"You know, Edward, I'm only saying this because you really do need to hear it. Maybe not Hannah, but you should find someone. You've been alone too long and it isn't natural."

"And you? Just how long have you remained a widower?"

"It's not the same thing, Edward, and you know it. I had you boys and Esther to look after, and I also had Aunt Bess helping me, and now Esther."

"Now that you bring it up, though, you are not young anymore. If you thought it better for your health, you could remove to Williamsburg where life is kinder. Perhaps take up with a recently widowed old friend?"

Robert chuckled, "I hadn't considered that. Perhaps I should." Continuing seriously, "No, I think I'd prefer a shorter life here, surrounded by my children. A longer life removed from them, even with a woman as charming as Fanny, holds no allure for me." Then his eyes sparkled again and he concluded, "You, however, have no such excuse for remaining unattached."

The cold November led to a colder December, the little fort falling into its winter routine. Sarah responded favorably, if a little cautiously, to Bat Dandridge, sending him a response that started a fairly regular correspondence.

On a cold late December day, while the boys were home during the Twelve Night period, Thomas Lewis and his son, Jeremiah, arrived at the little Jewett fort. Thomas was Colonel of the Augusta County militia and a prominent landholder who sat as a Justice on the County Court with Edward and Robert. He had not been to see the Jewetts since the detachment of soldiers transferred from his militia command to George Washington's Virginia Regiment. The Jewetts greeted him warmly and, while his son, a militia Lieutenant, went about inspecting the soldiers, Thomas retired to Edward's cabin.

"Edward, I wonder if you'd let Jeremiah stay with you for a month or so. Let him learn military drill and discipline here with you. Besides, things are bad around Fort

Lewis, what with the Shawnee prowling about all the time and all, and I'd just as soon have him out of harm's way for a while."

"Certainly, Thomas, he's welcome to stay. But, I sense you've not told me everything. What else is wrong?"

Thomas began by clearing his throat and acting a bit uncomfortable. "Alright, you've found me out. Truth be told, I've taken him east with me trying to find him a suitable marriage, only to be snubbed by those eastern planters who act like they're royalty or something. I recalled you have a couple of young women of marrying age here and thought, perhaps, if he were to spend some time here, something might develop that would be beneficial to all parties. You know he has a fine estate. This would allow you to gauge his character without needing to commit to a courtship. You'll find him much more prudent than I, he takes more after his mother that way. And you have one of the finest families in the Valley. I just thought…"

"Relax, Thomas. We've had our differences but what you say is true. Your son has fine prospects and would be a good match. You know my niece Sarah has been courted by Colonel Washington. Oh, you hadn't heard? Well, no matter, as there is also my niece Rebecca. Both are the same age and Rebecca is also quite handsome. We'll put your son up and see if anything develops. If not, he'll at least have learned a thing or two about military matters."

Thomas Lewis remained a few days with the family before taking his leave. Edward, naturally, informed Robert, Henry, and Jenny of the low pressure approach Thomas had proposed for his son and Rebecca to get acquainted. From the looks of things, Rebecca was quite taken with the youth and it wasn't long before Esther and Jenny had their hands full keeping an eye on the young couple.

Edward used the Twelve Night school break to re-acquaint himself with his nephews, taking both out, separately of course, for some late season deer hunting and then delivering their success to the Bennett homestead. Neither boy brought up their hunt together before school started, assuming Edward knew nothing of their adventure. In fact, Henry had taken great pleasure in telling and retelling it for Edward while Lewis would sit trying to control his laughter. Each time the three brothers couldn't get to end of the story without breaking into uncontrolled laughter at the boys' expense. All agreed, though, not to let the boys know Edward knew anything about it.

All three brothers rode the boys back to Greenville at the end of their school break, leaving Robert in charge at home. He would have normally gone along with his sons and grandsons but the weather was especially cold and Esther didn't want him out traveling in it. She was getting more watchful over her father's health these days and Edward made a mental note to ask her why.

"He told me he feels he's running out of time, that he won't be with us too much longer. I ask but he says he feels fine and I can find no indication of poor health. And yet he says it remains a feeling."

Edward also became watchful of his father after that. The two kept their father's feelings of impending death to themselves, though, and didn't share them with their two brothers.

By the time Thomas Lewis returned for Jeremiah, he and Rebecca were getting along very well, well enough that Thomas and Jeremiah approached Jenny and Henry for permission for Jeremiah to court Rebecca. Before answering, Jenny and Henry wanted to discuss the matter with Robert and Edward.

"Jeremiah seems a fine young man and Rebecca is quite smitten with him. But do you think it's a good match for Rebecca? I'd like to hear your opinions before I speak mine," Jenny opened their discussion.

Robert and Edward looked at each other before Robert took the lead in answering her.

"Jenny, you know I want to do right by Rebecca. Jeremiah will bring to the marriage a fine estate, so from that perspective, it is a very good match, better than she could likely have enjoyed had not..."

"I understand what you mean, father. And you, Edward, your thoughts?"

"Well, I've watched Jeremiah closely these past weeks and he seems a fine man. Oh, there could still be hidden traits that would cause me concern, but I've detected none. He is much better mannered than his father and I've seen no sign of a temper as he's worked with the soldiers. I must agree with father, this looks to be a very good match for Rebecca."

Jenny nodded before stating her opinion. She was actually quite thrilled at the prospect of her daughter marrying one of the wealthiest young men in the Valley, having come from such poor beginnings. This settled the issue and Jeremiah was given leave to formally court Rebecca.

By time the Virginia weather turned to spring, Edward and Aaron had to return to Williamsburg for the spring session of the House of Burgesses. They rode with James Bordon, who represented Augusta County and, in spite of the miserable condition of the roads caused by the thaw, they made reasonable time.

Arriving at the Dandridge house, Fanny surprised Edward by telling him his sea captain friend, Captain Cole, had just days before brought a woman to Williamsburg who had been asking how she might travel to the Jewett Grant.

❧ Chapter 32 ❧

Jacob McNulty was angry as he rode away from the Jewett's fort with his father and younger brother. They had just finished the evening patrol and letting the Jewetts know they'd found nothing. That wasn't what made Jacob angry. It was Rebecca Thompson. She had always flirted with him when he'd been to the fort and today she was nothing more than polite. It was true she had also stopped flirting with his younger brother, but he had always seen her flirtations with him as just her way of getting at Jacob. And then there was the soldier she flirted with, again, Jacob thought, just to make him jealous.

No, now there was Jeremiah Lewis and he was coming courting. Just because her widowed mother had married Henry Jewett, that didn't make Rebecca any more than she was, just a poor man's daughter. Why, they'd practically grown up together and he'd always considered her to be his girl. Now this rich man's son makes advances and she doesn't want anything more to do with him, starts putting on airs like she's better than him. She's got some nerve. Only this wasn't over, not yet, and he intended to have the final say.

"Did you notice how angry Jacob was when he left?" Sarah asked, hardly able to contain her giggles.

"I can't say that I noticed Jacob McNulty at all, let alone whether he was angry or not," Rebecca replied with a feigned air of indifference.

"Now don't tell me you hadn't noticed, everyone did and I mean that to include you. You were just rubbing his nose in it, weren't you? How he's always treated you as if you were his property," Sarah said with some disdain. "Now, though, you have that nice Jeremiah Lewis and you just couldn't help flaunting it in front of Jacob, now could you?"

Rebecca gave up the indifferent act and giggled herself, "No, and it serves him right. Whoever told him I was his anyway? It wasn't me! But you're right, he was very angry, wasn't he?"

Watching the two young women as they walked toward the awning to start putting dinner out, Esther was concerned by what she saw.

"Father, I'm afraid there may be trouble with Jacob McNulty."

"Why, daughter, the McNultys are good people and we've never had trouble from them before. Why now?"

"Well, you know how Rebecca has always flirted with Jacob. Today he found out about Jeremiah and he left here not at all happy. He's not going to let Rebecca choose anyone other than him without first fighting for her. I don't know why I think it, but I just do."

Robert stopped and thought for a moment. "You're probably right. I'd best talk to Henry and Jenny on this, so they're aware of the situation." And then, smiling, "You'll just have to keep a sharp eye on Rebecca to make sure no trouble hurts her. You can do that now, can't you?" Both chuckled at Robert's humor.

Although he had made his little joke, Robert knew this was no joking matter. Frontier families were a harder lot than those he'd lived with most of his life in Rowley. They saw things differently and tended to take matters into their own hands more readily. And an angry young man was also an impetuous man, prone to do almost anything. If only Jacob was more like his father and grandfather. Both men were hard men, but neither had a violent temper or impetuous nature. No, Jacob got his temper from his mother and would need to be watched.

Springtime was planting time around the fort and everyone was busy putting their old gardens and newly cleared fields into production. They had decided, after the events of the previous winter, to focus their clearing efforts more to the east and southeast, toward the river and ford, placing the little fort between their work parties and any Shawnee scouting parties. This had allowed them to get far more timber cut than the previous winter, and more cut timber also meant more cleared ground.

This was good ground. As the sun had been blocked by the trees, it had not gone to sod, so, once they removed the stumps, they only had to contend with roots and rocks as they plowed the rich dirt. Unlike most who planted a lot of tobacco, the Jewetts planted none, putting their fields into wheat, oats, and corn. Plus, in a small area, tightly picketed against deer, this year Robert had set out apple seeds. Next spring he hoped the resulting saplings could be replanted into a regular orchard.

This little garden plot became Robert's personal project. He tended to it daily, pulling any weeds or grass that appeared, keeping the soil moist but not too wet, and keeping the pickets in good repair so neither deer nor rabbits could reach the tender young plants. And whenever Rachael lost track of Joseph, she knew she'd find him "helping" Mister Robert in his garden. For his part, with his two older grandsons off at school and his new grandson still an infant, Robert appreciated the company of their foreman's toddler.

The patrols continued to find no sign of hostiles in their area, aside from an occasional problem with white ruffians looking to take advantage of the unsettled state on the frontier. As for these, most learned quickly enough that they weren't welcome in this district and moved right along. Usually the patrols discovered their presence before any mischief could be done and they were given "encouragement" to keep moving. Others still had heard of the regular patrols and generally secure situation of the district and avoided it altogether. They were not looking for a fight, they were looking for easy spoils and none was to be had in this region.

Mister Agner's presence around Esther was becoming so commonplace that it stopped flustering Esther when he'd approach and seat himself near her. He was always careful to be proper around her and, in fact, had taken to showing improved manners as a matter of course. Jim Rice and Tom McCray both complained of the loss of their best customer for the product of their still, the one Mister Agner had sold them. While Esther did nothing to encourage his attention or improve his habits, she also did nothing to discourage it, either. At best, one could say she remained politely indifferent.

Jeremiah Lewis was a regular visitor now, frequently bringing along the post from Staunton and letters for Sarah from Bat Dandridge. They had yet to meet and already Sarah and Bat seemed to have developed an understanding. If handling his mother's affairs permitted, Bat planned to travel back with Edward when he returned from Williamsburg. It seemed to Robert that both his granddaughters, for he always considered Rebecca as such, had found suitable suitors.

There came the day when the inevitable happened. Jeremiah was visiting when the McNultys came to report the results of the afternoon patrol. When introduced, the other McNultys greeted the young Lieutenant cordially, but Jacob just stared at him and declined Jeremiah's extended hand. To see Rebecca paying Jeremiah attention and totally ignoring him was more than Jacob could stand and he vowed to himself that he'd do something about it.

On his way home, Jacob made the excuse to his father that he had forgotten his water bottle at the Jewett's spring when he had gone to fill them. Not to worry, he'd ride back and get it, then probably remain there the night as it was nearly dusk and would be twilight when he made it back to the fort. Mister McNulty found the reasoning plausible and consented, telling his son to ride home with the morning patrol and not, under any circumstances, to ride home alone.

Jacob actually had left his water bottle by the spring inside the Jewett's blockhouse, only he left it there on purpose after having offered to fill his father and brother's bottles when he went to fill his own. He'd also used the time alone in the blockhouse with the jilted soldier to elicit his help in the project. So the closer he got to the Jewetts, the better he was feeling about his plan.

Lewis met him at the gate and accepted his story of the lost water bottle, especially when Jacob returned from the blockhouse with it. Curiosity satisfied, Lewis had gone to join Robert and Henry in Robert's cabin to discuss the day's events and the plans for tomorrow. Jacob McNulty had been around the fort often enough that there was no reason for Lewis to be suspicious of him. Why, they'd even rode the patrol together a few times when Jacob's father had brought him along. Tonight, he offered to put the lad up in his house, but Jacob declined, saying he'd just stay in the blockhouse with his soldier friend.

Everything was coming together just as Jacob had seen it in his mind. Jacob stood in the shadows watching Rebecca and Jeremiah as they sat on the bench outside Henry's house. Jacob didn't see anyone else around until the soldier came out of the blockhouse, stopped to nod at Jacob, then move to the Lieutenant, say something, and return with the Lieutenant to the blockhouse. Jacob moved deeper into the shadows and was thus unnoticed by the young Lieutenant.

Jacob caught up to Rebecca as she was crossing the street toward where the awning occupied the corner of the little fort. Dropping the reins to his horse, he grabbed her from behind, clasping a firm hand over her mouth.

"Rebecca Thompson, you're my girl and you're coming away with me, now, so there's no use fighting," he whispered in her ear as he spun around with her and started toward his horse. Instead of quieting her struggles, it seemed to have the opposite effect and she fought harder. "Stop that, I tell you, or I'll have to tie you up." He froze as he felt a hard, painful jab with a sharp object in the middle of his back.

"Jacob McNulty, you let her go or I swear I'll run you through with this poker. I swear I will," Esther said in a loud voice.

Jacob went to spin back around, thinking he'd get Rebecca between him and his assailant. But as he went to move, Esther jabbed the poker even harder against his spine and he stopped.

"I warned you I'd run you through! Don't make me do it!"

The commotion in the street now brought Esther the help she hoped it would. Robert, Lewis, and Henry came out of Robert's cabin, the laborers came from their cabin behind her, Miles from her left, and the Lieutenant, Sergeant, and several soldiers came out of the blockhouse. His escape route past the blockhouse now sealed, Jacob loosened his grip on Rebecca. As soon as she spun free, Sam, Jubal, and Miles quickly seized the young man, immobilizing him in their strong arms. Mattie came up to Esther, whose knees now felt weak, and supported her as Mister Agner came up and patted her shoulder comfortingly. Rebecca, as she spun, found herself in Robert's comforting arms and started crying.

"What was the meaning of this, Jacob?" Robert demanded. "By what right do you enter our home and manhandle one of our women in such a manner?"

Lewis and Henry had never seen their father this angry, only Marie had and she trembled at the memory.

Jacob's confidence was starting to wane as he realized there was no escape. "I came for Rebecca, to take her as my woman. She's always been mine only lately seems to have forgotten her place," he said, still with some defiance in his voice.

"She is not nor ever was yours and what you've done here this night is proof why I would never consent to her being yours," Robert spit back, not even trying to conceal his anger.

Jeremiah had now come up beside Robert and Robert passed the crying Rebecca into his arms. Understanding Robert's intent, Jeremiah moved back with her, joined by Jenny, taking Rebecca out of the center of the scene playing out in the middle of the little fort.

Jacob, watching Robert's face, was now scared. He had known Robert as his teacher, as the patriarch of the most prominent family in their district, even as the commander of the blockhouse during a Shawnee attack, but nothing had prepared him for the Robert who now stood before him.

"Miles," Robert commanded in an icy tone. "Get a rope."

∞ Chapter 33 ∞

While Aaron saw to getting them settled in the Dandridge office building, Edward rode to the Queen's Creek wharf to find Captain Cole. He was confused by a woman looking for how to reach his grant, had no idea who this woman might be or what her business with his family was.

"Colonel, now before you get angry with me, I told them it was a bad idea coming unannounced but no one listened," a flustered Captain Cole began while Edward was still walking up the plank to his ship.

"Captain Cole, good to see you again," Edward replied. "Now, what's this I hear all over town, something about a woman looking for a way to reach my grant?"

"That would be me, Colonel."

The sound of a woman's voice coming from the direction of the ship's main cabin was somehow out of place and startling. Edward turned and saw a young woman, thin, attractive, dressed well in traveling clothes, who somehow looked vaguely familiar to him.

"I'm afraid you have me at a disadvantage, madame."

"Has it been that long since your brother's wedding that you've forgotten me, Colonel?"

"Hannah?" Now knowing where he should know her from, he was able to place the face. Yet it was no wonder he didn't recognize her, she was much thinner now than he remembered her being twenty years before. "Hannah Davies, is it?"

"Why, Colonel, you do remember. I'm flattered you remembered. I must say I'm surprised you came to escort me. I was expecting it to be Lewis. Did Marie come with you?"

"No, Marie's not here and I didn't come to escort you. Escort you where?" Knowing who the woman was had not exactly answered all of Edward's questions, rather, created new ones.

"Why, to your Grant, of course. It was so kind of you all to offer me a place to live. It has been very hard since Daniel's death, what with my son disrupting my father's household and all. And then to hear how much you welcomed the idea of us coming to live with all of you, why, it couldn't have come at a better time."

"Welcomed the idea? Why, this is the first I've heard of it! What made you think...Ah, Marie wrote and invited you, didn't she? Now I'm beginning to understand," the realization of what must have happened brought with it clarity.

Now Hannah was embarrassed and it showed. "Oh, then you mean she wrote without discussing it with you first? Then I've placed you in a very awkward situation and must apologize. If I had known, I never would have come all this way..."

A wave of Edward's hand halted Hannah's apology. "We'll work something out. You'd best gather your belongings. I'll speak with Captain Cole then will ride back and arrange lodging for you. Is your son with you? Alright then, for him as well. I'll return later with a conveyance to bring you and your things into the city."

Understanding that her interview was over, Hannah curtsied and returned to the main cabin, allowing Edward and Captain Cole to talk in private.

"She's the daughter of my employer so what would you have had me do, Colonel? I hope you're not too upset with me for bringing her here."

"Oh, I don't blame you, and you shouldn't blame yourself either. What's done is done and now we must make the most of it."

"There is something else you should know. Captain Faircloth was most firm that I was to bring her and the boy here and under no circumstances was I to return with them. When she said her boy disrupted Captain Faircloth's household, she didn't tell you the half of it. I learned on the trip down, that boy is no good, I tell you."

Edward smiled at his friend and patted him on the back to assure him of their continued friendship. "Now, I best be about the business of finding them lodging. Have her belongings hoisted to the wharf. Will I need a cart or a freight wagon when I return?"

Assured Hannah and Luke's belongings were reasonable, Edward rode back to the Dandridge house, where he found Bat waiting for him.

"Ah, Bat, I'm glad you're here. I've something to discuss with you and your mother."

Explaining the situation, Fanny Dandridge immediately offered to allow Hannah and Luke to stay in her house, with Bat agreeing. Edward wanted three things well understood before they accepted the Dandridge hospitality. Hannah would be a paying lodger or he'd seek lodging elsewhere. He was not about to have them take advantage of Fanny's friendship with the Jewetts. Next, this could be a long term arrangement. And, finally, he explained what he knew of Luke and how he had somehow disrupted his grandfather's household.

"I intend to tell the boy that should he misbehave under your roof, I will immediately apprentice him out to Mister Anderson at the forge. And if he doubts me, he'll be sleeping in the forge loft by the time he realizes his mistake."

Lodging arranged, Edward returned to the wharf with a carriage and cart. Meeting Luke now for the first time, he explained in front of Hannah exactly what was expected of the boy and what would happen should he fail to live up to those expectations. His firmness left no doubt in Hannah's mind that Edward not only meant what he said but would follow through without hesitation. For the first time in a very long time, she felt like someone finally knew how to handle Luke. Marie was right. This was going to be good, for both of them.

As they rode back, Luke studied the tall man on the black horse riding erect alongside the coach. His warning and resolve had frightened him. This man was different, somehow, than his father or grandfather. There seemed to be no bluff, no bluster, just cold facts delivered icily with no room for doubt. He would be good to his word and, if Luke wanted to avoid a miserable apprenticeship, he'd best watch himself around the Colonel.

Fanny invited them to all join her for supper that evening. Hannah began the evening very nervous over Luke's behavior. She so wanted to make a good impression on the Dandridges and Edward. And, for some reason, since first seeing him on Captain Cole's ship, she so wanted him to have a favorable impression of her. Yet it was just that fussing that seemed to have the opposite effect before the meal was even served.

"Hannah, stop, the boy is fine," Edward told her, finally having enough of her fussing about. This caused Hannah to sit down at her place rather embarrassed.

"Finally," Luke said almost under his breath, and then to Edward, "I thank you, sir."

The conversation allowed all to get to know one another. Luke was very quiet, answering questions asked of him with short answers, always remaining watchful of Edward's reaction, trying to gauge the kind of man he really was, and always coming back to the same conclusion he had come to in the coach. This was not a man to trifle with.

"So, Missus Davies, Marie is an avid equestrian. Are you as well?" Edward asked.

"Oh, heavens no! And it's Hannah, please do call me Hannah. Marie got me on a horse once, it threw me and I broke my shoulder! No, I'll ride a cart or walk rather than mount a horse."

"Spoken like a sensible woman, my dear," Fanny intoned. "I don't know what it is these days with women riding horses. One sees it all the time. Why I remember when a woman was only rarely seen mounted, and then only the lower sort of women."

Bat also used the time to determine if he was reading too much into Sarah's letters or if there really was some understanding developing between them.

"I'll never pretend to understand what a woman is thinking, but from what my niece is saying to her grandfather, it would appear she is quite taken with you, for a man she's not seen in five years and even then only in passing. No, but we'll fix that soon enough, that is if your mother can spare you for a couple of months." Fanny agreed immediately, welcoming the chance her son might find a wife with a family who had treated her and her husband so kindly over the years.

That settled he then turned his attention to Luke. "Tomorrow, after I've finished with the Governor, I'll enquire about a classical school for you, young man. There are several in town so I believe we can find one with an opening."

"School!? Why do I need to go to school?" He looked first to Edward and then to his mother, hoping for her assistance in avoiding school. Much to his surprise, his mother was looking approvingly at Edward, not taking up for him at all. "What if I don't want to go to school?"

"Well, it's a simple matter. A boy your age and in your circumstances has but two choices, school or an apprenticeship. If you'd prefer, I could take you over to Mister Anderson's yet this evening."

Seeing his error, Luke changed his tone and demeanor instantly, continuing very respectfully. "Oh, no sir, a classical education would be a wonderful thing to have. I just didn't expect to have the opportunity is all."

The next day, after he had spent the morning and taken his dinner with Governor Dinwiddie, Edward returned to the Dandridge house and delivered another shock to Luke.

"I've located a classical school with an opening and you can start tomorrow. Now, if you'll clean yourself up, I'll take you over to introduce you to the headmaster this afternoon."

As Luke climbed the stairs to change, Fanny saw that Hannah had something on her mind, so she excused herself to see to her servants and allow Hannah a chance to talk freely with Edward.

"This is very good of you, Colonel, but I'm afraid I don't have money for tuition. I'm not without funds, mind you, only they are limited," she said, her embarrassment showing. "Father didn't think I'd require more than traveling money."

"I anticipated as much and took the liberty of settling the question of his tuition. I'll also see to the cost of your lodgings. The Dandridges were friends and Fanny has found things difficult since her husband died last year, so I help her out where I can. That's why you're staying here and not elsewhere, I'd rather see my funds go where they're needed and to people I care about."

Edward's generosity shocked Hannah and at first she just stood there, not knowing what to say. "I don't know how to thank you, Colonel. Really, though, I can't have you incurring debts on our account. I'll send a letter to my father and I'm sure he'll reimburse you."

Edward passed it off with another wave of his hand. "Nonsense, I am incurring no debt on your account, simply parting with something found very dear in these parts, coin. You see, I am amply supplied with coin of the realm, unlike most who deal in pounds of tobacco. I've found most are so in need of coin, starved for it you might say, that they are quite willing to grant me significant discounts over their normal fee paid in tobacco." Then Edward got a twinkle in his eye, "And besides, I can always charge it against Marie's account. It was she who invited you, after all."

Luke started school and, for all outward appearances, was a changed boy. He did once begin to argue with his mother in Edward's presence, over supper one evening with Fanny and Bat, and Edward put an instant stop to it. Still, there were times when Hannah would see Luke's thinly veiled anger, would see Daniel in the boy's face, and it made her tremble. She was just glad Edward's influence kept Luke's anger from bursting out of control.

Edward did not allow the distraction of Hannah and Luke to impact on his duties. During the Burgess session he talked, discussed, cajoled, argued, and did all those things necessary to try and persuade the eastern planters to vote for much needed funding for the Virginia Regiment. He also kept the Governor and his counsel advised of what was happening and, being in Williamsburg, was able to keep up on all of the latest news of the war and how it was progressing. He even offered his services as Lord Loudoun built up his forces to attack Fort Louisbourg, a place Edward was very familiar with from the last war.

His services declined, it came time for them to depart for home and summer in the Valley.

❧ Chapter 34 ❧

As soon as it was light enough to see in the pre-dawn darkness, Robert had Lewis and Henry riding toward the McNulty cabin to bring Mister McNulty back to the Jewett's. When they returned, they had both Jim McNulty and his father, Matthew, with them.

"Sir Robert, Lewis and Henry told us what Jacob did last night and I can't apologize enough. If I'd have known what he intended, I never would have let him come back after his water bottle." Jim McNulty was anxious to appease the head of the Jewett family, a family who had helped the McNulty family when their cabin had been burned out and just about every other family in the district at one time or another.

"Jim, Matthew, I can't tell you how sorry I am for what I had to do last night. Why, I taught Jacob to read and write, how to do basic mathematics. I've always thought highly of the boy."

The McNultys could see the honest regret in Robert's face, knew he was sincere in his regret for their pain. That was what set this family apart from the other major landholders they'd come into contact with. They didn't lord over their poor neighbors like some did. That's what made this all the more embarrassing for the McNultys.

"Now, Sir Robert," Matthew McNulty inserted. "You don't trouble yourself one bit. You did what had to be done, and that's all you did. There's no sense all of us feeling bad, it was the boy who did this terrible thing. So if you'd just take us to him, we'll take him home to his mother."

Robert sadly nodded and then signaled to Henry who led the McNultys into the blockhouse. There they found Jacob and the young soldier who was his accomplice, firmly bound hand and foot with a guard, one of the laborers, standing over them. When Jacob saw his father and grandfather, he began to give his excuses but they cut him off.

"Not a word out of you, boy! You've shamed us enough as it is, don't shame us more by making excuses." Turning to Henry, "If you'll untie his feet, we'll be on our way. No need to untie his hands, though."

Henry nodded and the laborer set his gun against the log wall and untied Jacob's feet. While Jacob had found being bound humiliating, having been guarded by the laborers, former slaves all, was even worse on his pride.

"So, what's to become of the other one, the soldier?" Matthew asked.

"The Sergeant is sending him up to Fort Loudoun to stand before a military court. He says it'll go badly for the lad. I suppose he's right, but it's Edward who knows of military things and he's not here for me to ask."

"Well, you have my deepest regrets for what my grandson did. Please, tell your daughter she has nothing more to fear from him. And if you would, convince her we're still the good people she's known for most of her life. Just because I have a fool for a grandson doesn't mean we're all bad people."

Henry put a hand on Matthew's shoulder in a re-assuring way, "She already knows that, Matthew. And we thank you."

Jim and Matthew put Jacob on his horse and led him out, with his hands still tied and his horse on a lead rope.

Robert stopped them, putting a hand on Jim's leg and telling him, "I'm sorry it came to this, Jim, truly sorry I had to treat your boy this way."

Jim McNulty took Robert's hand and shook it firmly. "You'd have been within your rights to have hanged the boy, or sent for the Sheriff and let the court hang him. I thank you for not doing either and letting us handle him ourselves. I've the morning patrol tomorrow, so I'll see you after when we make our report. Goodbye, friend."

The ordeal she'd gone through did have an impact on Rebecca. It made her more committed than ever to make things work out between her and Jeremiah. She had remembered how her father had treated her mother and thought that was the way things were. Then she saw how Henry treated her mother and found it didn't have to be that way. When Jacob tried to force her with physical violence to have his way, she knew she didn't want to go back to a life with people who looked on violence toward their wives so casually. She wanted something better and her mother's remarriage to Henry was giving her that chance. She may be a poor man's daughter but she didn't have to be a poor man's abused wife, not now.

Edward returned with the flowering of the dog-woods and they all turned out to greet the tired entourage that rode through the gate. As always, Robert was the first to greet his son, followed by Lewis and Henry and then the others, all greeted warmly, including the laborers.

"Mister Dandridge," Edward then said with a flourish. "May I present my niece, Miss Sarah Jewett, and her father, Mister Henry Jewett. Sarah, Henry, Mister Bartholomew Dandridge."

As Bat moved off with Henry and Sarah, Edward turned to Betty and Aaron. "Aaron, I may need to find a new traveling companion if you keep having children."

The obviously pregnant Betty blushed and dropped her eyes while Aaron just grinned with pride.

"Now, Lewis, Marie, we need to talk. Father, you'll want to hear this as well."

Once the four of them were seated in Edward's cabin, Edward handed Marie a letter.

"Oh, good, another letter from Hannah," cooed Marie. Then she spotted the word Williamsburg on the outside and she immediately turned red.

"That's right, Marie, your friend Hannah is in Williamsburg. Now, would you like to tell your obviously surprised husband why your friend from Boston might just happen to be in Williamsburg, or shall I?"

"I'm sorry, Edward, I was going to tell you, honest I was, only it never seemed to be the right time…"

"Tell us what?" Lewis said, a little louder than he had intended but nonetheless conveying his mood.

"I, well, you see…"

"It seems your wife wrote Hannah telling her we'd all love to have her come live with us, here on the frontier. Taking Marie up on her offer, after her son all but destroyed his grandfather's home life, she came to Williamsburg, asking how to get from there to here. It seems your wife also failed to mention that the frontier is not anywhere near Williamsburg."

"You did what!?" Lewis was not at all amused.

Ignoring Lewis for the moment, Marie focused back on Edward. "So, she's in Williamsburg. Why didn't you bring her with you? You didn't send her back, did you?"

"No, I didn't send her back and I could hardly have brought her with me. Surely you're joking, a widow traveling for two weeks through the countryside with a man not her husband? I had no choice but to leave her in Williamsburg." Turning to Robert, "She's taken lodging with Fanny Dandridge and I've enrolled Luke in school there."

"Now wait a minute! You did what!?" Lewis interjected toward Marie again, having been ignored the first time.

"Well, I was going to tell you about it, I just never got the chance is all."

"The time to tell me about it was before you wrote the letter, not after she's arrived in Williamsburg and become a burden on my brother."

"Well, you know what, it just didn't happen…"

"You two can discuss this more fully later, in private," Robert reminded them.

"So, how does she look? Did you recognize her?" Marie turned her attention back to Edward, glad to have been saved from further explanations to Lewis, at least for the moment. And just when she thought things were getting back to normal between them, this had to come up. Oh well, she thought.

"I did, though she had to remind me where I knew her from before I could put name to face. She's much thinner than I remember from your wedding."

"Is she still pretty? Did you think she was pretty?"

"Marie, enough!" Lewis had finally had all he could stand. "Leave us, now!"

Marie hesitated and then rose to leave, half whispering to Edward from the door, "We'll talk more later."

As soon as the door closed behind her, Lewis started, "Edward, I'm really sorry for the awkward situation Marie put you in."

"And it really was awkward. I'm sure it started all the tongues wagging when it got around Williamsburg that I had a pretty young widow show up on a Boston trader, her son in tow, looking for me. She actually was looking for the Jewett Grant, but I'm sure that's not how it is being told around dinner tables all over the Colony right about now. And of course it would be while both the Burgess and the Court were in session, so there isn't a part of Virginia that won't have heard of it by week's end," Edward said in mock horror.

That had the desired effect of cutting the stress Lewis was feeling over his wife's actions and allowed them to discuss the other news, both from Williamsburg, the war, and what had been happening here, in more normal fashion.

"Have you had any trouble with Jacob since?" Edward asked when Robert finished the sad tale of Jacob McNulty's assault on Rebecca.

"We never see him. Jim McNulty always sends him home before coming to make patrol reports and he's stopped coming for lessons. I did hear his mother was the most upset, fairly wearing him out with a knotted plow line. She has a temper, that one. Still, it's sad something like that had to happen."

"And how is Rebecca?"

"Oh, Henry and Jenny will tell you, so act surprised when they do, she and Jeremiah Lewis have agreed to wed," Robert concluded with a big smile on his face.

Bat Dandridge spent six weeks visiting the Jewett fort. Edward had warned him of their primitive conditions, but he found them not nearly as primitive as he expected. And Sarah was every bit as charming in person as he'd found her to be in her letters and far more beautiful than he'd dared imagine. The young couple was quite smitten with each other, so much so that Bat asked Henry for permission to marry Sarah and Sarah agreed. Henry took the matter up with Robert before granting his permission, but insisted on a long engagement where Bat would repeat his visit twice before any wedding would take place. When Bat left for home, he was a very happy man indeed.

One evening in mid-summer, when Edward and Robert were alone in Edward's cabin doing nothing more than quietly enjoying each other's company, Robert brought up a delicate subject once again.

"So, Edward, now that you've had some time to get to know Hannah, have you thought any more about what I said before?"

"Are you going to bring that up again, father?" Edward asked with a little irritation in his voice. "You know I am far too busy with this war going on to even consider taking a wife. Why, I don't know from one day to the next that I won't be ordered to join troops in the field. I just can't do that to another woman."

Robert was quiet for a few moments, remembering how Edward's first wife had taken her own life those many years ago.

"Well, you also know that madness ran in her family, so you can't keep blaming yourself for that," he said firmly. "Why, even Mary, her younger sister, went mad. Besides, that was a long time ago and you did tell Marie you found Hannah to be pretty. We already know she's from a good family and well situated, even if her father is currently being a little tight with the funds because of Luke."

"And how difficult do you think it would be on poor Lewis, to have me marrying his wife's best friend? Wait a minute, here's a thought, he might just like having company in his misery!" Edward chuckled even though Robert saw no humor in it. So Edward continued, "And then there's the other side of this discussion, Hannah. I'm sure she found me overbearing and opinionated, not to mention too old for her." Reading his father's thoughts in his face, Edward gave in, "All right, I'll consider it. But that's all I'll say for now, that I'll consider it. And don't be telling Marie any of this."

Late in July, as the family was anxiously awaiting the return of their two boys from school, a dispatch arrived for Edward. Robert, Lewis, and Henry gathered in Edward's cabin to hear the news, and it was bleak. The fleet of a hundred ships carrying six thousand troops Lord Loudoun had sent to retake Fort Louisbourg had been thwarted by a stronger French fleet and then scattered by a hurricane. The failure left open the Saint Lawrence for French resupply and reinforcement.

❧ Chapter 35 ❧

I n late July, Ronald and Elam brought Philip and Charles home for the summer break from Augusta Academy. Charles would be returning in the fall but Philip had completed his course of study and would be taken by his father and uncle to the College of William and Mary for the fall term. He was both excited by the prospect of living in the city and saddened at leaving not only his family, but also the couple who'd become his second family, Ronald and Margaret Samuel.

It was a grand homecoming when the boys made it to the little fort. Everyone turned out to greet them and there was a big feast prepared, giving it a very festive atmosphere. Rebecca's fiancé, Jeremiah, also attended, meeting the boys for the first time. And Charles's younger half brother, Isaiah Jewett, seemed to enjoy himself although no one really thought he understood what was going on. Most of the neighbors came by over the next couple of days to welcome the boys home as well. Overall it was a grand few days.

Robert was just as proud as could be of his grandsons, and it showed. He spent most of a week with a grandson on each arm as he went about his normal chores, like he didn't want either out of his sight. Charles had grown and, while still not quite as tall as Philip, was catching up with him and had thinned out as well, although he remained heavier built than Philip. One might not recognize them as related, they didn't look that much alike, but both bore enough resemblance to Robert that, with him in the middle, it was obvious they were related.

Philip was a little frustrated in that he didn't really have his grandfather or uncle alone that first week. Ronald was always with Robert and Elam spent much of his time with Edward. Instead, he contented himself spending time with his father, yet always looking for the opportunity to catch one of the others alone.

"You heard about the aborted attempt to take Fort Louisbourg. There is yet another example of how inept Parliament and the King are at ruling from such a distance, don't you agree?" Elam badgered Edward, looking for validation.

"I'm not sure I see where Parliament and the King had much to do with it. It looks to me more like poor planning and bad luck with the weather more than an inept government," Edward countered.

This type of conversation between the two men went on for hours each day. When the Rice family came to pay their respects, Jim mentioned the rock bridge to the south of the Jewett Grant. This drew Elam's interest and he questioned Jim closely to the point of making Jim a bit uncomfortable, not really understanding Elam and his odd ways. Elam began pressing to be taken to see what sounded like a marvelous natural formation and, before the visit was over, Edward had agreed to take Ronald, Elam, Jim, and Caitlyn to see it. Before long, it was half the fort going and Edward just rolled his eyes. In truth, he welcomed the break from talking the war situation with Elam and just hoped the rock bridge would prove enough of a distraction to see him through to the end of the Samuels's visit.

They set the day and Jim and Caitlyn arrived an hour after sunrise. Jim, the three Jewett brothers, and the two boys would ride as guards, Sarah and Rebecca would accompany Caitlyn, Esther would ride with Robert in his riding chair, and Ronald and Elam rounded out the company. There hadn't been any sign of Shawnee for months, so they weren't overly concerned about their security, yet they always remained cautious. Jenny and Mattie prepared a dinner for them and tied it onto the back of the riding chair just before they all set out.

Edward and Jim rode point with Elam tagging along, talking the whole time. Lewis and Philip rode the right flank and Henry and Charles rode the left. When they arrived at the rock bridge, Edward, Lewis, and Henry first compared notes on what they saw on the way there. None having seen any sign of hostiles, they allowed everyone to dismount and, aside from the three brothers who remained vigilant, they began sightseeing. Philip and Charles regaled Elam with the story of George Washington carving his initials, which they showed everyone, and throwing the stone over the rock bridge. So incredible did Elam find the rock throwing tale that only when Edward nodded that it was, in fact, true did he consent to its validity, with reservations.

Elam was like a child in his wonderment over the natural formation. He admired it from every angle and asked if he could view it from above. Edward consented so Henry, Charles, and Philip accompanied him as he rode out from the little gorge, up the left bank, across the top, stopping to admire the view, and then back down the right bank. Elam actually crossed the rock bridge somewhat hesitantly, not at first convinced such a formation would hold their weight.

Returning, he observed, "This is an incredible sight. Who would have believed nature could form such a magnificent monument?"

"I wish mother was up to traveling. She would love to see this," mused Ronald to no one in particular.

While Caitlyn took in the sights like the others, she was more interested in talking with Sarah and Rebecca. The subject was, naturally, their intended husbands and it wasn't long before the soft giggle of the young women echoed off the walls of the little gorge. Esther sat with them, quietly, until Sarah observed that she, too, had a man interested in her, Mister Agner. Now the soft giggles became outright laughter as Esther protested and Sarah and Rebecca countered each of her arguments, showing how Esther had misinterpreted what had happened and that they actually proved the younger women were right.

Edward, Lewis, and Henry just looked at each other, smiled, and rolled their eyes. None of the brothers, however, had any intention of coming to their sister's rescue, not this time.

Dinner was unpacked and all ate well, leisurely enjoying the coolness of the gorge compared to the warmth of the late-July day. All too soon it was time to pack everything back up and start back for the fort if they were to arrive before sunset.

"I'll take Jim with me and we'll ride a wide flank, looking for sign further out from what we did coming down. Alright, Elam, you can come along, but you'll have to be quieter than on the trip down here. Lewis, Henry, why don't you do the same on the river side?" Edward suggested. All three brothers were fairly confident no Shawnee were in the area.

"I want to ride with grandfather," Philip inserted, seconded by Charles.

"I'd much rather you rode with your fathers, to keep an eye on them so they don't fall into trouble," Robert said firmly but with a little grin at the end.

Edward was cautious and didn't care for this idea. Robert remained firm so Edward relented and allowed the main party to continue with just Robert's gun for protection.

"Don't look so worried, son, things will work out just fine and in accordance with Providence's plan," Robert told Edward just before they split into three groups to make their way home separately.

Ronald rode next to the riding chair, talking with Robert, the three girls riding further ahead still talking and Esther sat in the riding chair only half listening to her father's conversation with Ronald. The two older men continued to enjoy each other's company and the conversation was wide ranging, if a little random, as it bounced from subject to subject.

Robert's horse perked its ears and started looking left, slackening its pace just a bit. Ronald continued to talk, not noticing, but Robert noticed and started paying more attention to the animal. In a few moments, he was satisfied he knew what was bothering the animal.

"Ronald," he said in a soft voice Ronald could just barely hear. "I think we have unfriendly visitors nearby. Listen closely. I want you to ride forward and warn the women. Do it naturally, not too fast. When I fire my gun, you are all to ride as hard as you can directly to the fort. Don't stop for anything. Do you understand?"

Ronald's eyes were about to bug out of his head. At first he couldn't understand what Robert was saying. Then it hit him, they were potentially in trouble. He didn't know how Robert knew, it was enough that he spoke so confidently. He went over his instructions in his mind, made sure he understood what he was to do and say, then he nodded his head to Robert indicating he understood and was ready.

"Go ahead then, not too fast, but ride like the wind as soon as you hear my gun. We'll follow. Esther, here, you take the reins."

Ronald rode forward as he had been told, coming up to the right of the three women. Their giggling stopped almost as soon as Ronald began to talk. Sarah looked over her shoulder at her grandfather with a worried look on her face. He gave her a reassuring smile and a nod before she turned forward again.

Robert continued to watch his horse's reaction closely. He was becoming more nervous and, when Robert felt the time was at hand, he quickly raised his gun and fired a shot into the air.

With the shot, everyone spurred their horses forward and Esther slapped the reins, sending all of them into a reckless flight toward the fort and safety. The sound of the gunshot had barely stopped reverberating when they heard a loud Shawnee war cry very close by. Robert and Esther caught a fleeting glance of a painted warrior in the laurels to their left as they dashed past him, leaving him behind.

Robert looked back forward, now starting to feel confident they'd make the fort ahead of the hostiles. Besides, he knew the shot would bring his sons to their aid, alerting them to the proximity of the danger and giving them a general idea of where he was with the women.

Sarah was out front with Caitlyn close behind. Rebecca, not as good on a horse, was following a bit behind, and then there was Ronald. If it weren't for the danger, it would have been comical watching him ride. At least Edward had insisted he ride one of the Jewett's horses instead of his old sway backed horse. Robert doubted that animal could even remember how to gallop, regardless of the motivation.

Then his eyes widened in horror as he saw Sarah's horse go down with a shrill cry, throwing Sarah hard to the ground. Caitlyn, following too close behind, also went down as her horse first shied to avoid the downed animal in front and then, now riderless, continued on. This caused Rebecca and Ronald to slow, looking back at Robert to see what they should do.

Robert waved them forward and they turned to continue their flight. Dropping his rifle to the floor of the riding chair, he then said to Esther, "Keep going, daughter, and don't look back all the way to the fort. Remember that I love you." With that, he leaped from the riding chair.

Esther was horrified at what she was seeing. Sarah and Caitlyn in a heap on the ground by Sarah's screaming horse and now Robert moving toward them. She hesitated, not wanting to leave them there. Still, she would be of no help to them so she did as she was told and slapped the reins down on the horse's back again, increasing its speed as she continued on after Ronald and Rebecca.

Robert strode to where the girls were with quick, purposeful strides, smiled at them and took in the scene. Sarah's horse's left front leg was still in the groundhog hole and was obviously seriously broken. He then turned his back to them, facing the Shawnee warriors, now visible, running toward them, and crossed his arms in front of his chest.

Sarah, now hugging Caitlyn, heard her grandfather's familiar, calm, and reassuring voice. Thinking he may be giving them instructions, she listened closely to hear what he was saying. It wasn't instructions, it was something else. She recognized it, but from where, then her eyes grew wide as she realized it was the Twenty-third Psalm.

"…Yea though I walk through the valley of the shadow of death, I will fear no evil; for thou art with me…"

Then Caitlyn screamed.

⚮ Chapter 36 ⚮

Edward Jewett led Jim Rice and Elam Samuel out from the narrow valley containing the rock bridge and to the north, heading toward the ridge that formed the northwest boundary of the Jewett Grant. Turning northeast on gaining the ridge would put them on a course parallel to Robert, Esther, and Sarah Jewett, Ronald Samuel, Rebecca Thompson, and Caitlyn Rice. In this way, they would likely find signs should there be any hostiles in the area to threaten them. This they all considered unlikely as there hadn't been any Shawnee trouble for months and the Delaware didn't venture this far south. Still, Robert's use of the term "Providence" bothered Edward and he kept looking to his right as if trying to see through the trees to where his father was with the others. As they moved up the ridge, Jim saw the Virginia Road just off to their left.

"I didn't know the Virginia Road passed this close to the rock bridge. Why, I could bring Melinda down to see it and it'd be an easy trip," Jim observed.

"Mother would like to see this, but she doesn't travel much these days," added Elam. "Perhaps one day I could borrow your father's riding chair and bring her

down. Or better still, I could get your brothers to build another riding chair for my parents. They'd love that! Maybe
you'd put in a good word with them for me, you know,
make them more amenable to the suggestion."

"Just a minute there, Elam," Edward said with a
wide smile on his face. "The building of riding chairs is my
brother Lewis's business and I stay out of it. He doesn't
tell me how to ford a river under fire and I don't tell him
how or for whom to build a riding chair."

"I understand, completely, it's just that both my
parents have so admired your father's chair, especially
since the Timber Ridge dedication when my father actually got to ride in it."

"Yes, and just as soon as I help you convince my
brothers to build the chair, you'll be working on them to
help convince me your parents need a better horse than
that old, sway backed mare and how I should sell you one
of mine. I can see it now, 'preferably that great black stallion of his!'" Edward said as he patted his horse's neck.

Elam laughed, "Oh, you have things figured out
pretty well, Edward, only one thing you got wrong. My father needs a much gentler horse than that lively stallion
of yours. Why, by time he figured out where it was he was
supposed to be going, he'd be miles past it!"

This set them all laughing. While Jim didn't know
Ronald as well as Edward did, the few times he'd seen him
and today's experience had taught him just how forgetful
the pleasant old man could be.

"Now, Elam, let's set our minds to our task at
hand," Edward said seriously as he moved ahead, checking woods and ground in a studied, systematic way. Jim
did the same, only less intensely.

They continued on up the ridge with Jim explaining to a questioning Elam what the patrols looked for in

order to spot whether Indians, particularly the Shawnee, were in the area. Listening to Elam's questions, Edward realized just how much he'd learned about living and surviving on the frontier over the past five years. What's more, having spent a lot of his time away, how much more his nephews had learned. Those two were far better at reading sign than Edward or either of his brothers, often able to tell with near certainty how many Shawnee, or deer for that matter, had passed a particular place, just from the prints on the ground.

Remembering back, he also recalled Lewis and Marie's adopted son, Joseph, and how his life had been cut terribly short when he blundered into a Shawnee ambuscade after Edward had thought he'd sent the boy away from danger. Edward frequently looked back in quiet moments wondering what he could have done, should have done, differently to have prevented that tragedy. It was the only thing that had caused him to doubt his decision to share his frontier grant with his city raised family, moving them from the lives they'd known onto the frontier that had almost immediately erupted into violence. Only Robert knew the events of that day still haunted his eldest son, having found him more than once in the pre-dawn darkness standing by Joseph's grave on the little rise that had become their cemetery. They would never speak on those occasions. Robert would just put a comforting hand on Edward's shoulder and they'd stand there together, remembering.

To shake his melancholy, Edward turned to Elam, "So, are you by way of being a drinking man, Mister Samuel?"

"Oh, I'll confess that in my youth I was occasionally an intemperate man, but not to the extent I'd call myself a 'drinking man,' sir, though sufficiently to embarrass my parents who hold no store with strong drink. But I've given it up and found I don't miss it. Besides, drinking and teaching are two things that do not mix well when one works for that old Scot Mister Robert Anderson and his Augusta Academy. Why do you ask?"

"Why, it's because you're talking to one of the proprietors of the finest stills in these parts. Jim Rice there, with his partner, Tom McCrary, distills every kernel of corn he can lay his hands on and sells what few drops he can't drink himself."

Seeing Elam's eyebrows raise until they nearly touched his cap, Jim felt obliged to clarify. "It's difficult and costly to transport our surplus grain to the eastern markets. It seems that once it's distilled, it is not only by way of being much reduced in bulk, it is also a commodity more in demand. I do enjoy a sip once in a while, though the person who had to make a living off my drinking would starve in short order. That's all. Although the way Edward just said it, you'd think I was the district's local drunkard."

"So you ship your devil's brew east then?"

"Oh, no, we'd normally ship our surplus corn east, but the still's output we were hoping to sell locally, to travelers on the Virginia Road. Now with the war and all, we're distilling more than we have customers for."

Elam was silent for several minutes, thinking, before his face lit up and he became animated. "Have you ever thought of selling it to the tavern keepers in Greenville and Staunton? I know for a fact Mister Steele complains of the high cost he must pay to obtain suitable refreshments for his guests and that what he does manage to acquire is of inferior quality."

Edward rolled his eyes. This conversation was not going at all where he had expected. Jim had completely stopped looking for signs and became fully engaged with Elam on how such a plan could be carried out and what, exactly, needed to be done. If there was one thing Jim was not, it was a businessman. He knew how to make his concoction and how to drink it, but had no idea how to go about distributing it beyond the stall he and Tom had set up along the Virginia Road. Of course, Philip could have told him that Elam was one to capitalize on an idea, but Edward did not know Elam that well and only thought to have some amusement at Jim's expense.

"Oh, I don't drink anymore, but I've nothing against those who do. My father would rather not associate with those who do take drink. That, I'm afraid, he's found impossible. Now, if I were to help you find tavern owners willing to purchase your product, what would be in it for me?"

"Elam, I am surprised at you!" Edward finally had to interject as all three came to a halt. "You'd be interested in becoming a whiskey merchant? I'm sure your father would have plenty to say about that!"

"That's true, and then he'd forget what it was I was doing. It's mother I'd have to worry about," Elam said, now laughing.

That's when Jim became distracted and Edward noticed his friend was not enjoying the merriment. "Edward, look over there, two riders just coming out of the wood line."

Looking to where Jim pointed, Edward and Elam could both see the riders. They were moving cautiously, looking around and at the ground. Because Edward always insisted on riding along a wood line or below the actual crest to where he would not be highlighted against the sky, the two riders hadn't spotted them yet. Edward used his knees to encourage his big black stallion behind some laurel bushes that provided further cover. His companions did likewise.

The two riders came on slowly, rifles held in readiness as if they expected trouble at any moment. Watching them, Edward was convinced they had not been spotted so he wondered what had these two so skittish. Jim knew silence now was critical, so when Elam went to ask him a question, he silenced him with a look and shake of his head.

When the riders moved close enough to be recognized, Edward urged his horse forward, raised his hand, and said in a voice just loud enough to carry to them, but not loud enough to be heard at any distance beyond them. "Well, Daniel, what brings you to Virginia?"

The two men had been startled when Edward showed himself. As soon as Daniel Boone recognized Edward, he raised his right hand in a wave, holding his tongue until they had closed the distance between them. Jim and Elam also joined Edward.

"Colonel, you about scared me into shooting you!"

"I'll take that as a compliment to my increasing woodland skills, as you don't scare easily if memory serves. Let me introduce Elam Samuel, a teacher at the Augusta Academy, and I think you know Jim Rice. Aren't you a customer of his?" Daniel just grinned. "Gentlemen, this is Daniel Boone, from North Carolina. And I can tell just by looking that your companion must be a brother."

"That's right, Colonel, this is my brother Squire Boone."

"So, what brings you to Virginia?"

"Actually, we were on our way home. I took my furs up to Philadelphia to sell and to see those of my family still there. You remember my uncle and cousins, don't you?"

"And Rebecca sent me along to see that he brought some of the money home this time," Squire added, laughingly.

"Rebecca? Then, Daniel, am I to assume you've taken a wife?"

"Oh, Daniel's gone and married the prettiest gal in the Yadkin Valley. What she sees in him is anyone's guess!" Squire grinned broadly and slapped Daniel on the back.

The brotherly jesting reminded Edward of how he and his brothers jested with each other. He had missed that all those years he'd spent away in the army. He also noticed that the whole time the two brothers had been talking and, in spite of the humor, they had remained ever watchful, as if anticipating something.

"So, I assume she's blind and has no sense of smell to put up with the likes of Daniel," Edward added. "But before we get too carried away, you've moved off the Virginia Road and were moving very cautiously when we saw you. Something's wrong. Care for some help?"

"Actually, Colonel, I'm glad we ran into your patrol. We saw signs of twenty Shawnee crossing the Virginia Road from the north, heading south, and decided we'd follow a ways to see where they were headed before coming to warn you. Colonel...?"

Edward had already spun his horse around and was spurring him over the ridge when they heard the shot.

⌒ Chapter 37 ⌒

Philip wasn't at all pleased as he rode along with his father, Uncle Henry, and cousin Charles. For that matter, neither was Charles. Both boys had wanted to ride back with their grandfather and neither could understand why he had been so firm in refusing, in telling them to ride back on the flank with their fathers. It just didn't make any sense as they'd spent the last week, the three of them, nearly inseparable.

"What's bothering you, Philip?" Lewis asked as he reined up beside his son. "You're lost in thought and not paying much attention to the ground around us. Some help you are in looking for any signs of hostiles."

"Oh, father," came the annoyed reply. "You know as well as I do that there aren't any Shawnee around. That's why I can't understand grandfather insisting Charles and I ride flank with you instead of riding with him."

"So, you'd rather ride with your grandfather than with me," Lewis said in mock horror. "Some son you've turned out to be!"

"I'm having the same problem with my ungrateful first born son," Henry said, getting into the act of cheering up the boys. "Only I have an advantage on you, Lewis, in that I now have a new son. If this one keeps giving me such trouble, I'll just disown him."

"Father, stop it!" Charles said, not at all amused.

"Seriously, boys, I'm sure your grandfather has his reasons. Perhaps he feels like he's dominated your time since your return and is simply trying to make it up to your fathers," suggested Lewis.

The boys looked at each other, both thinking Lewis's explanation made some sense. It would be just like their grandfather to think of something like that. Now that they had a reasonable explanation, they started to feel better and act better, paying more attention to their task and talking in low tones with their fathers.

"I don't think I'd have gotten along with Elam if Philip hadn't explained his ways. He can be both demanding and funny at the same time," Charles observed as he told the two men of his first year experience at school. "I've liked having Philip there with me and am not looking forward to going back by myself."

"But it'll be fine," Henry told him. "When you first went there last fall, Philip was the only boy there you knew. Now you have friends in class with you, so it won't be so bad."

"Well, maybe, but I'm still not looking forward to it," Charles said with some finality in his voice that made the two men smile.

"Think about poor Philip. He's off to William and Mary where he'll be expected to wear a student's gown to class and conduct himself like the gentleman I wish he was," chuckled Lewis, although Philip didn't see any humor in it.

"It was bad enough being in Greenville, but at least there I was close enough for you and grandfather to come up for a visit every once in a while. And I could come home each time we had a week or more off from classes. Now I'll be stuck in Williamsburg, truly on my own except when Uncle Edward comes in the spring and fall to see the Governor," Philip pouted.

That's when they heard a shot off to their left and a little behind them. They paused just for a moment before spurring their horses and heading toward where they thought the shot came from, taking as direct a course as the ground would allow. As Edward had taught them, the two men rode in front and the boys followed behind, close and yet far enough back they could turn and make their escape should it be an ambuscade.

Coming up out of the North River valley and into the field they'd cut hay off of just six weeks earlier, they saw two riders and the riding chair heading fast toward the fort. As soon as these three saw Lewis and Henry, they slowed their pace and angled their course to meet them.

"Esther, where's father?" demanded Henry as soon as they were within earshot.

Reining in, Esther answered as best she could, given her excitement, "Sarah's horse went down, taking Caitlyn's down with it. Father jumped out to be with them and told us to leave them, to flee for the fort."

"But why the shot, why the dash for the fort?" asked Lewis, a little frustration showing in his voice.

"Shawnee! Father knew they were there before anyone else and fired the shot to bring you. I saw one and heard his cry as we at first made our escape. Then the horse went down, father jumped out, and … oh, Lewis, Henry, you must hurry!"

"Boys, take your aunt to the fort and stay there!" Lewis ordered.

"No!" both boys responded in unison. "We're going with you," Philip finished their thought.

"Lewis, we've no time to argue, let's go and take them with us if we must, but let's go!" Henry said as he spun his horse to head back the way Esther and the others had just come.

"Oh, alright!" Lewis growled as he spurred his horse to catch up to his brother, the boys following as before.

Under other circumstances, the boys might have felt pleased with having won the argument, but not this time. There was no time for that. This was deadly serious business and they both knew it, felt it, and they were too preoccupied praying they'd reach their grandfather in time all the while knowing from their frontier experience it was unlikely.

They rode along the top of a rise that dropped off gently on both sides but steeper to their left, toward the river, than on the right, which gradually sloped toward a creek about four hundred yards off. Lewis slowed them as they approached where the woods rose to nearly meet those on their left, knowing there was a steeper drop to a spring just on their right. This was a good place for an ambuscade for the unwary.

Passing through the small band of woods that touched both sides of their trail, Lewis reined up sharply as he saw men and horses in the little meadow beyond and to their right. All four now came to where they could take in the scene. Four men stood to one side, guns at the ready, holding five horses. A fifth man stood a short distance away, back toward them, erect yet head down and hands in front. That's when they saw, on the ground in front of him, two bodies, one of a man and another of a horse.

There was a collective gasp as the realization of what they were looking at hit each at nearly the same time. They dismounted, reluctantly, not wanting confirmation of what they dreaded. They were drawn forward, each feeling he had to know what he already felt to be the case.

"Boys," Lewis said in a choked, quiet voice. "Stay here." He and Henry then walked forward, toward where Edward stood, the boys following behind in spite of Lewis's order.

Stopping short of where Edward stood, evidently in prayer, they all looked at the form of Robert on the ground at Edward's feet. He was laid out straight, a bow and two arrows laid across his chest. The left side of his head showed where he had been struck but there were no other wounds. He had not been mutilated or scalped. His assailants had evidentially respected the grey-headed man's courage to leave him thus, with weapons he would need, in their belief, as he made his way to their spirit world.

As tears welled up in their eyes, Edward said a quiet "Amen" before kneeling and patting his father's right shoulder. "We will all miss you very much, father, very much." He then stood, still with his back to Lewis, Henry, and the boys, for a few moments before turning.

"We met Esther and the others. She told how..." Lewis's voice choked and he had to pause before Henry continued.

"It was the Shawnee. Did you find Sarah and Caitlyn?"

To the confused look on Edward's face, Lewis continued, "Esther said father stayed behind when Sarah's horse broke its leg and Caitlyn's threw her."

"No, they weren't here," Edward said tiredly before turning back toward Robert's body. After a moment taking in the scene, Robert, the horse with its leg still in the groundhog hole and its throat cut, he drove his right fist into his left palm.

"Lewis, Henry, wrap father in my blanket and put him on my horse. It isn't his riding chair but it's the best animal here. Father deserves to go home riding the best." After another pause, he turned back toward them and continued, "Philip, is your powder horn full?"

At first Philip, in his grief, didn't understand what was being asked of him. When the realization did hit, he was able to refocus from the terrible loss they'd just suffered. "Yes, sir, just as you taught us, 'always leave the fort with a full horn.'"

"Good, let me have it, please."

Philip instantly understood what was happening, his father and Uncle Henry still standing, staring at Robert's body, not realizing Edward's intentions. As he slowly removed the horn, he looked at Charles who seemed, like him, to understand what Uncle Edward was about to do.

"You'll need to ride back doubled up with Charles as I'll need your horse, your stirrups being set longer than Charles's." Taking hold of the reins and turning back toward Lewis and Henry, he continued, "Lewis, you'll find father's will in my cabin, in the center compartment of my field desk, with my own. Bury him next to Joseph, he'd like that."

It hit Lewis like a heavy blow as Edward turned to lead the horse away. "No, wait, where are you going?"

"Sarah is out there, somewhere, and I'm going to try and bring her back."

"We're going with you," responded Lewis.

"No," Edward said, loudly and firmly. "This I do alone. Take the boys and," in a softer voice, "father," he paused before continuing firmly again, "back to the fort and see to your families." He then mounted. The Boones and Jim also mounted.

"Edward, she's my daughter," insisted Henry. "I can't turn back while she's still out there. I must either go with you or in your place! Think clearly, you can't do this alone!"

"We'll go with you, too," Philip said while Charles nodded emphatically.

Edward dismounted and walked toward Henry, placing a hand on his shoulder. "Henry, I know Sarah is your daughter and you love her very much. I understand you want to go and bring her back. Listen to me careful-ly," he said in a quiet, comforting yet firm voice. "You also have to think about Charles, little Isaiah, and, now that Jenny's with child again, another son. I can't raise them for you, only you can do that. But what I can do for you, for father, is to try to bring Sarah back."

Henry dropped his head and nodded. "All you say is true. And yet…and yet that's my little girl out there, somewhere, afraid and alone. I have to try! For Sarah I've got to try!"

"Then listen to a more practical reason. I have a chance, slim though it is, of bringing her home if I do this alone. If you are along, I'll be distracted trying to keep you from sharing father's fate and that could get all of us, including Sarah, killed. Do you understand what I'm saying?"

Henry again nodded, hesitantly, and then looked to Lewis, who nodded at him reassuringly. Looking back at Edward he said, "Alright, Edward, we'll do it your way. Just bring my Sarah home to me safe."

Edward patted Henry on the shoulder and then gave him a hug before he remounted. Turning again to face his family, he leaned forward in the saddle.

"Listen to me, all of you! You have things you need to do as do I. Yours takes you all," pointing to each of his brothers and nephews in turn, "all, back to the fort. Mine takes me after Sarah and Caitlyn. None of our tasks are easy, but all must be endured." With that, he spun the horse and quickly started off in a southerly direction, where a clear trail showed the Shawnee had headed.

Daniel Boone moved his horse toward Lewis and Henry. "Don't worry about the Colonel, he's a tough old bird. Besides, my brother, Squire," indicating his brother, who nodded at Lewis and Henry, "and I are headed home and that takes us in the same general direction he's headed. I think we'll just ride along a piece. Who knows? He might just find us a good Indian fight."

As they moved off, Jim rode forward, "Tell Melinda I'm off after Caitlyn. And Henry, don't worry, we'll bring Sarah home to you," spurring to catch up with the Boones, who were riding a respectable distance behind a grieving Edward.

"No you don't, Elam," Lewis said in a loud voice. "You're wanted back at the Academy. You come with us." As Elam removed his foot from the stirrup where he'd just placed it, Lewis turned to Henry, "Finally, someone listened to me!"

They all turned and watched Edward, Jim, and the Boones disappear into the woods. With the clouds billowing up from the southwest indicating a storm, none of them were sure if what they were hearing off in the distance was gunfire or thunder, but they could definitely hear one or the other.

✐ Chapter 38 ✐

Esther watched as her brothers and nephews disappeared over the rise and into the woods. She realized she was trembling and felt sick. The riding chair was not designed for racing over rough ground like she had just done and she felt like every bone in her body had been shaken loose. Looking up at Ronald Samuel and Rebecca Thompson, she realized they were looking to her for instructions. She nodded and slapped the reins against the horse's back again. From here to the fort, she set a brisk but no longer breakneck pace, Ronald and Rebecca riding with her and instead of out in front. With her brothers between them and the Shawnee they'd seen, they felt comfortable preserving as much of the horses' strength as they could. As they came into view of the blockhouse, they heard the alarm being sounded inside the little fort. Not knowing for sure why the alarm, she urged the tired horse to quicken its pace once more, although it had very little strength left.

Entering the fort, one of the laborers closed the gate tight behind them. Esther and her companions were nearly as spent as their horses. Jenny helped Rebecca to the bench outside the blockhouse door while Marie did the same for Ronald. As Esther turned to climb out of the riding chair, it was Mister Agner there to catch her as she nearly collapsed into his arms. Betty brought them water while Miles and the Sergeant waited for them to recover somewhat before launching into their questions.

Esther shared what she knew, leaving all in earshot in a state of shock. It was more than just the Shawnee, who had left them alone all summer. It was that Robert, Sarah, and Caitlyn Rice had fallen into their hands. Miles looked to the Sergeant, who let out a low whistle under his breath. Both knew it unlikely Robert would return to them alive and the fate of the young women may never be known. The Shawnee were well known for carrying off young women and children for adoption into the tribe while killing men and older boys who they generally considered too dangerous to risk marching back to the Ohio country.

Miles, Aaron, and the Sergeant discussed sending someone to warn their neighbors. The Sergeant was set against sending anyone out, not knowing for sure if there were more Shawnee lurking about or not. Not only would it weaken their defense, it could likely be a suicide mission for whoever undertook it. After giving it some thought, Aaron said he'd go. Their neighbors deserved a chance to get into the fort, and the more that did make it in, the more guns there'd be to defend the fort.

"Aaron," Esther, who had been quietly listening to the discussion, inserted herself. "Go to the Rice place first and take Melinda over to the McCrary's. Tom can see her safely to the fort while you go on to warn the rest."

"Yes, ma'am."

"And tell Melinda not to worry, that I'm sure Jim and my brothers will bring Caitlyn back safely."

"Yes, ma'am."

As Aaron turned, gave Betty a hug and kiss, and mounted the horse brought to him by a laborer, Esther sat thinking of what just happened. She'd given instructions and the response was "Yes, ma'am" just like they always replied "Yes, sir" when Edward or Robert gave instructions. She leaned her head back against the logs of the blockhouse and closed her eyes.

"Are you alright, Miss Esther? Do you feel faint?" asked Mister Agner, concern very apparent in his voice, enough to attract the attention of Marie, Jenny, and Betty standing nearby. "Would you like to lie down here on the bench?"

"No, no, Mister Agner, but thank you. I'm just very tired and very, very worried about father, I mean Mister Robert."

"We'll see she's alright, Mister Agner," Marie said, putting her hands on his shoulders to steer him up and away from Esther. "Would you be a dear and see to these played out horses while I sit with my sister? Thank you, you're a big help."

As Mister Agner led the horses and riding chair away, Marie turned to Esther, "He's really taken by you. All it would take is a little encouragement and he'd ask for your hand, you know."

"Marie," Esther said forcefully, her head coming forward and eyes opening to focus on her sister-in-law. "Now is not the time!"

And so they anxiously waited, and waited, and waited. Every minute seemed ten as the little fort waited to find out the fate of their patriarch and friend. Two hours later, from the northwest, Tom McCrary was seen coming in with his family and Melinda Rice. For the next hour, the neighbors arrived in their family units, having departed as soon as Aaron passed the alarm. Aaron accompanied the last family in, the Stuarts, and Betty finally felt like she could breathe again.

Close on the heels of the Stuart's arrival, one of the soldiers shouted from the blockhouse that riders were coming in. While everyone's first reaction was to race to the southeast face of the blockhouse to see for themselves, they made way for Esther, followed by Marie and Jenny. Using Edward's spyglass, she first saw Lewis and then Henry. The next sight caused her to slump against the log wall.

"What is it, Esther?" Marie asked, taking the spyglass from Esther's now limp hand. Looking, she said, "I see Lewis and Henry, there's Philip and Charles riding double, and Elam in that funny cap, and…Oh my God!"

"What is it? Tell me before I bust," shouted a frustrated Jenny.

"It's Edward's black stallion," Marie said, slowly. "And there's a wrapped body over the saddle."

There was a collective gasp from those gathered in the blockhouse before Aaron asked, "And the Colonel, where is he?"

"I didn't see him, did you, Esther?"

All Esther could do was to shake her head.

By the time Lewis led his little band to the gates, they were open and all but one or two soldiers who remained on watch were gathered to find out what had happened and who was in the blanket. As in the blockhouse, Esther found the group had made way for her to be out front. The looks of pain on all of the faces riding in told the news was not going to be good.

"Is that father or Edward?" Esther asked, almost reluctantly, not really wanting to know the answer.

Lewis dropped his chin to his chest before saying, "It's father."

The effect of this news hit all of them hard. Rachael and Sally screamed and dropped to their knees, crying, and most of the laborers also openly wept. They had thought quite highly of "Mister Robert." He had taught most of them to read a little and even write their own names, looked after their well being and elicited their opinions. They had never met a white man like him.

Miles and Aaron took the news a little more stoically, although even they had red-rimmed eyes when they finally looked up at Lewis and Henry.

"Mister Lewis, Aaron and I will see to your father. And Mattie and Betty will prepare his body," now looking to Esther. "You don't need to worry about a thing. We'll take care of it."

"Mister Lewis," added Aaron. "What's become of the Colonel and Mister Rice?"

Taking a deep breath, praying he could get through the explanation, Lewis spoke in as loud a voice as he was capable at this moment, hoping that all gathered could hear. "My brother has gone after the band of Shawnee who did this and who have taken Sarah and Caitlyn with them. Mister Rice and the Boones, Daniel and his brother Squire, who we happened upon, have gone with him." Turning now to face Melinda, "There was nothing to show that the girls had been harmed and we've every reason to hope Edward will be successful in gaining their release."

The crowd started to slowly disburse, gathering in little knots to quietly discuss what they'd just heard. Miles, Aaron and the laborers gently lifted Robert from the horse and carried him into his cabin, placing him on the table. Rachael and Sally joined Mattie and Betty in preparing the body for burial while Sam and Jubal built the coffin. They would not allow anyone to help, insisting on doing it all themselves.

Marie put one arm around Lewis and the other around Philip and guided them toward their cabin door while Jenny did the same with Henry and Charles. Although grieving themselves, the two women did their best to console their men. After a barely eaten supper, Lewis had rallied enough to ask the family, or, as he said, "what was left of it," to gather in Edward's cabin.

Once all were gathered around Edward's table, Lewis cleared his throat before beginning. He started first by opening Edward's field desk where he quickly found two packets in the center compartment. Looking at them, he saw one was labeled as Robert's will and the other as Edward's and both had been wax sealed.

"Before he departed, Edward told me where to find both father's will, and his own. As I cannot handle the thought of needing both of these, we will only open father's now. Before I do, please join me as I pray for Edward's safe return."

After the short prayer, Lewis opened Robert's will. Robert had named Lewis as the executor of his estate. It went on to make several specific bequeaths, setting aside the money for both Philip and Charles to attend William and Mary, the sum of £8 to each of the laborers with £10 going to both Sam and Jubal. There was some funds set aside for Esther, Lewis, and Henry, but as was expected and required, the bulk of his estate went to his eldest son, Edward, with a stipulation that he would take care of Esther's needs. It had been witnessed by Miles and Aaron, freemen.

As they sat quietly after Lewis finished, Jenny began humming a sad country hymn. Before long, they were all singing it as the tears flowed freely down their cheeks.

Everything being ready, at ten of the clock the next day, everyone gathered on the little rise that, since Joseph's death, had become their little cemetery. Sam and Jubal had crafted a fine coffin out of black walnut and Rachael and Sally had lined it with white linen. Lewis read from the family Bible and led the gathering in prayer before they lowered the coffin and everyone passed by, tossing a handful of dirt into the grave as they passed.

Lewis sat alone in Edward's cabin later that morning, feeling the loss deeply. Edward had been the first born, but he had spent most of his life in Europe. Henry had moved off to Boston for many years. Lewis, however, had spent his whole life near his father. They had been very close, talking and sharing on a near daily basis. He had sought out his father when he needed advice and his father had always gently guided him in the right direction, never simply telling him what he should do. That was not his way. He had been a gentle man, a gentleman in the truest sense of the word, although never really having risen to that class until Edward's grant had thrust him into it. He was humble, quietly hating it when those around him had applied "Sir" before his name, out of respect for who he was and how he treated everyone.

No, Lewis thought, there needed to be a way to ensure that Philip could still learn from his grandfather, learn how to be the man Robert had been. He must find a way to keep Robert's memory alive, for Philip, for Charles, and for little Isaiah.

He was startled from his thoughts by the sound of the alarm and the cry of "Riders coming."

☙ Chapter 39 ☙

Storm clouds were billowing up from the southwest and over Purgatory Mountain as Edward Jewett, Daniel and Squire Boone, and Jim Rice followed the trail left by the Shawnee and their two captives. Riding hard, they slowed their pace only when the wind blowing in their faces carried with it the sounds of gunfire.

"That's not too far ahead, Edward, probably along Purgatory Creek," Daniel observed. "We'd best move a little more cautious until we find out what we're riding into."

Edward simply nodded his assent, not having uttered a word since leaving the body of his father behind to try and free his niece. At least, thought Daniel, he has finally acknowledged our presence without ordering us off.

Daniel and Squire moved off to Edward's left while Jim moved to his right so now the four were riding abreast, spread out with about twenty-five yards between them. In this manner, it would be harder to ride into an ambuscade without one of the flanking riders spotting it. As they rode, the gunfire, which had been sporadic at first, picked up with shot following shot in rapid succession. Whatever they were riding into, it was obviously a fair-sized fight.

They all saw it at nearly the same time. The trail they had been following split at a point where the Shawnee had obviously halted and milled around. One trail headed south, the other continued southwest and toward the sound of gunfire.

"I make out seven heading south and the two girls are definitely with them. Another eight went on ahead," Daniel said to Edward, Squire nodding his agreement.

"Which do you want to follow? The odds are now much better for retaking Sarah and Caitlyn," added Jim.

Edward was torn. Ahead there was a fight going on and these eight Shawnee could tip the scales in their favor. To the south were his niece and her captors, the object of his mission. No, it was clear from the gunfire there was a desperate fight up ahead, one he couldn't ignore.

"You three can go after the group with Sarah. I can't ignore the group that continued toward the fight. If they were to come up behind a militia unit, it would go very badly for the militia."

"No, Colonel, we go with you. We can pick up your niece's trail again after the fighting's over," Daniel said firmly.

Edward looked from face to face, seeing assent from both Daniel and Squire. When he looked to Jim, he found his friend as torn as he was. Slowly, almost reluctantly, Jim nodded his assent.

Dismounting and securely tying their horses, the four quickly moved forward in the same open order they had used when riding. They had not gone far when they saw the Shawnee had begun to spread out, at about the point where they were clearly close to the fighting. Another four or five paces and they could see the Shawnee crouching before them and the clouds of white gun smoke just beyond.

Edward raised his rifled gun, taking careful aim at the Shawnee in the middle, the one who was giving hand signals to the others. Seeing his intentions, Edward's companions did likewise, picking their targets and drawing a careful bead. With all the gunfire, the Shawnee failed to hear the four locks coming to full cock behind them. The headman let out a loud whoop, his companions loosed a ragged volley, and four of them instantly fell from shots immediately behind them. The remaining Shawnee, so startled by the turn of events, disappeared in the undergrowth and gun smoke without continuing the attack. Then the rains came.

As soon as they had reloaded, Edward, the Boones, and Jim moved forward, cautiously, only to find the Shawnee to their front had vanished. Reaching where the headman had fallen, Edward could see a startled group of militia arranged along some deadfalls. Where the militia crouched, the Shawnee attack would have come on their exposed rear, although now they were all turned facing where the sudden attack had come from.

"Hello in the camp," shouted Edward.

"Come on in," came the reply.

Edward signaled for the Boones and Jim to wait for him, watching for any repeat attack from the rear. The rain was now heavy and darkness was descending quickly. He moved cautiously forward, right hand raised and his rifle gun held in the crook of his left arm.

"Is that you, Colonel Jewett? I'm Thomas Carter, we met briefly at the Timber Ridge dedication. I don't know what brings you out, but I'm mighty glad you came on us when you did. Why, if you hadn't broken up that attack on our rear, we'd have been in a bad way!"

"Mister Carter, gentlemen," Edward said, nodding to the others, now starting to mill around as the shock began to wear off and no other hostile sounds came from the woods to their front. "What happened here?"

Mister Carter explained the nature of a very large raid along Kerr's Creek and the area around New Monmouth, how they'd managed to follow this group of twenty, even though it was not the main Shawnee party, catching up with them at this point.

"I'm afraid Benjamin Smith, Thomas Maury, and Mister Jew are dead, several others wounded," Thomas Carter concluded. One of the militiamen came up and added that they'd found nine Shawnee bodies to their front.

As the darkness and heavy rain made further fighting unlikely, Daniel and Jim joined Edward and Thomas. Each man carried his own rifle gun, two trade guns, and extra powder horns.

"Took these off the ones we left back there, Colonel. Squire's gone for the horses."

"Good. Well, Mister Carter, the group we were following killed my father and took off my niece and Jim Rice's daughter. We made a detour to help you out here, but now must be off before we lose them altogether. Could you send word to my family that you saw us here and we were safe to now?" Thomas nodded and moved off to see to his own wounded.

"Now, Colonel, I'm no military man, as I proved on the Monongahela," Daniel said. "But I've hunted these parts some. Instead of following after them, I suggest we head north, up Purgatory Creek, then cut west around the south slope of North Mountain. I believe we could come out ahead of them. If we can keep them from going up the Jackson River, maybe block them and steer them up the Cow Pasture River instead, we'd stand a better chance. You know if they make the confluence of the Jackson and Cow Pasture ahead of us, we'll never get the girls back."

"Well, do you know this country?" asked Edward as Squire came up with the horses.

"Colonel, once Daniel's been over ground, he has an uncanny way of remembering it," Squire chimed in. "He's hunted around here and I'd bet my life on his ability to remember the lay of the land."

"Jim, are you up to a hard night ride?" asked Edward, seeing from the stiff movements and pained look that told him Jim's back was bothering him.

"Up to it or not, it sounds like a good plan to me."

All in agreement, Daniel led the four as they turned north up Purgatory Creek. To keep them together in the darkness, each man held onto the tail of the horse in front of him and followed, slipping and sliding on the wet, muddy ground. Continuing past the headwaters of Purgatory Creek, Daniel then led them southwest down what he called Hickory Hollow before turning north again. When the rain finally let up, they halted for two hours to let the horses rest and so they could get some sleep themselves. When they started again, the moon had broken through the clouds, giving them enough light to mount and move more quickly around the base of North Mountain, ever working their way north toward where the Cow Pasture and Jackson Rivers met.

They made their goal before noon the next day, where the sign clearly told of a large group of Shawnee having passed sometime after the rain had stopped.

"Don't look so concerned, Edward, these came in from the northeast and not up the river from the southeast. These aren't the ones we're after," Daniel observed. "That said, this was a very large group, over fifty, I'd say. If it's alright with you, I'd rather not tangle with them!"

"Is there any sign of captives with them?" Jim asked.

"It's hard to tell with so many tracks walking all over each other. I think I can see some of heel prints mixed in, indicating captives, only they're too walked over to tell for sure how many."

"So, what's the plan?" Jim asked nervously.

"Well, I'd say we take up positions just up the Jackson, blocking the trail, and force them back. Then we fall on their rear, harassing them at every crossing and pass until they give up Sarah and Caitlyn," Edward answered to the Boones' nods of approval.

As Squire moved ahead to pick their position, Daniel slid up to Edward and whispered so Jim couldn't hear.

"You know, if we press them too hard, they might just kill the girls."

"I know. We just have to find a way to keep that from happening."

"It's a long shot, but we're still with you, Colonel."

Clamping a hand on Daniel's shoulder, "I know that and I appreciate it, even if I neither wanted nor expected you to come along."

"Well, I'm kind of making a habit of looking after your scalp, Colonel. It would have been a shame, having saved it along the Monongahela only to watch you lose it in your own cabin yard," Daniel chuckled.

Squire found a good position where the spring's high water had tossed deadfall up against the rocks, forming a sort of breastwork. The horses were secured up the bank behind them, out of the line of fire and where there was good grass for them to graze. Each man now had two guns, his rifle gun and a trade gun taken the evening before from the fallen Shawnee. After taking their positions in their improvised fort, they took turns standing watch while the others got some much needed rest.

Nothing stirred that afternoon, so the four men kept up their watches through the night. Jim was discouraged, thinking perhaps the Shawnee had taken a different route back. Daniel assured him this was the most likely way and not to worry, they had just taken the most direct route while the Shawnee had to travel south before being able to turn back north for the Jackson River and safety.

Midmorning the following day brought the first sign of the Shawnee. Jim was on watch when he saw their advance scouts, three of them, move into view down the river. He let out a low call on his turkey call to signal the others. As they all watched, the main party moved into view.

"That's a larger group than I was expecting, Colonel," Daniel observed. "There are twenty of them and we can't even see their rear guard yet."

"Yes, but look there," responded Edward. "See the girls, in the middle? This is the bunch we've been waiting for. Don't shoot into the main party, concentrate on the advance." Having now seen Sarah and Caitlyn, alive and apparently well, Edward for the first time thought they just might succeed.

The Shawnee were moving confidently, evidently assuming they were well ahead of any pursuit, when one of the advance scouts spotted hoof prints and raised the alarm in the form of a whoop. It was his last utterance as all three scouts were felled by the ragged volley from behind the deadfall.

The effect was immediate as the main body of Shawnee recoiled and slipped into the woods on the northeast side of the river.

"Do you suppose the group we were following joined up with the group Thomas Carter chased?" asked Jim.

"It seems likely. Now, Colonel, it looks like they've taken the Cow Pasture, just like we wanted them to. See there, that's their rearguard just skirting the woods. We've got to move around to the north of this hill on our left or they could still get behind us and up the Jackson," said Daniel with some urgency in his voice.

"Alright, Jim, you and Squire stay here for another half-an-hour in case they double back, then follow us," Edward ordered as he picked up the trade gun and slung it over his left shoulder. "Daniel and I will cut them off and send them further up the Cow Pasture."

As Daniel and Edward moved quickly for the horses, Daniel chuckled, "Over twenty Shawnee and you intend for you and me, the two of us, to turn them. I've got to admire your confidence, Colonel, I really do!"

⤫ Chapter 40 ⤬

The occupants of the now crowded little fort gathered around Thomas Carter, all except the Sergeant and soldiers who were keeping a sharp lookout from the second floor of the blockhouse. Lewis, Henry, and Esther in front, Thomas looked at the gathered faces and started his story where he knew it mattered most.

"I met up with the Colonel last night and, when he left us shortly after dark, he, Jim Rice, and the Boone brothers were all in good health."

When the collective sigh of relief had subsided, he continued, "Yesterday morning, a large band of Shawnee, about sixty we figure, hit the Dennis homestead, killing Joseph, a child, and Thomas Perry. We couldn't find Hannah Dennis, so we must assume she was carried off. From there, they went to the Renick homestead, carrying off Missus Renick and her four young sons and daughter. Thomas Smith's was hit next, where Thomas and Robert Renick were killed and Missus Smith and Sally Jew were carried off. That's when the band split up, most heading back toward the Jackson River and about twenty heading south."

The settlers in the Kerr's Creek area were not well known to those gathered in the Jewett fort yet the impact of a raid this large sent chills up their collective spines. They all knew that it could just as easily have been their homesteads that were attacked, their men killed, their women and small children carried off. Only the Jewett and Rice families had suffered in this raid, but everyone gathered knew it could have just as well have been them.

"Twenty-two of us took off after the smaller group, knowing we'd have no chance against the larger, and caught up with them along Purgatory Creek, well south of here. We were doing well, dropping nine of them, when the group who killed Sir Robert came up behind us. If the Colonel hadn't interrupted when he did, I doubt I'd be here to tell the tale. As it was, their first volley took down Benjamin Smith, Thomas Maury, and Mister Jew, Sally's father, before the Colonel hit them hard, bringing down four of their number and sending the rest running."

"And of my daughter, what news have you of her?" asked an anxious Henry.

"None, really, other than the Boones having found her tracks among those of the Shawnee. She and the other girl are at least well enough to walk on their own. Beyond that, I have nothing else to offer."

Thomas accepted the offer of food and water, both for him and his horse, before continuing on to pass the word to the other settlements along the Virginia Road. Lewis thanked him before he left and accepted his condolences for the loss of Robert. As he left, the occupants of the little fort went about their chores, relieved in part but still worried about those still outside the protection of their stout walls.

For his part, Henry returned to the blockhouse where he had remained watchful, hopeful. He was worried about Sarah and Edward and grieving for his father. He could not tear himself away from the watch except for Robert's funeral and now the visit by Thomas Carter. The food Jenny brought him went untouched, taking only water and even then drinking with an eye to a loop, looking for some sign Edward was bringing his daughter home to him.

Ronald found Philip and Charles seated on the ground in a corner near the animal pen, dejected and stabbing the ground with their belt knives. Finding a stool used for milking nearby, he pulled it up next to the boys and sat down with them, at first sharing their silence.

"You two look like you've something on your mind. Anything I might be able to help with?" he finally asked.

While they liked Uncle Ronald, they really thought of him more as a peer than an adult, what with his sometimes childish ways and all. In response to his question, they just looked at him, shrugged, and went back to stabbing the ground. Ronald waited a few more minutes before trying again.

"Your grandfather was a great man. Oh, not in the sense they'll write books about him, but in how he had such a good effect on all those who came around him. I knew him as a good friend, my best friend, and feel his loss terribly. I'm sure you boys feel the same way, probably more so."

"We should have been with him!" Philip fairly shouted. "We could have protected him from the Shawnee. Instead, he insisted we go with our fathers and he ended up facing them all alone."

"Why didn't he let us ride with him?" added Charles.

"Why? The only answer to that is that it was the hand of Providence that sent you to be safe with your fathers and it was the hand of Providence that called your grandfather home." The boys had now stopped stabbing the ground and were paying closer attention to Ronald. "You see, if you had been there, if you had put up a fight, we would have buried you along with him, likely Sarah and Caitlyn as well. You could not have stopped it, only added to the tragedy."

Now the boys were thinking hard on what Ronald was telling them.

"So, what you're saying is, had we been there and put up a fight, it wouldn't have saved grandfather?" asked Philip.

"That's right. Two boys against, what did Mister Carter say, fifteen Shawnee warriors? Your grandfather faced them unarmed, we know that, and by the way they respected his person it tells us they thought him a brave and noble warrior to do so. And it likely assured Sarah and Caitlyn were only captured and not killed for none of their warriors were killed so they had no reason to exact revenge. No, it was the hand of Providence I tell you. It was as it was supposed to be."

"So, had Providence wanted us there, we would have been there?" asked Charles.

"Absolutely! No, Providence has other plans for the two of you, just as he had plans for your grandfather." Then, looking at each of the boys before proceeding, "Besides, your grandfather lives on, in your hearts and memories and those of everyone else he loved and touched. Always remember there is a little of your grandfather in each of you. He was proud of you and now it is up to you to carry on in his footsteps."

The boys both rose and gave Ronald a hug and then the three of them continued to talk about Robert. While there were tears at times, Ronald had broken the boys' melancholy and they no longer blamed themselves for not saving their beloved grandfather from his fate. Ronald also had a way of talking about Robert that soon brought smiles to the boys' faces as they remembered how much Robert liked to laugh.

Early the following morning, Lewis made what was becoming his daily walk to the little family cemetery. Only on that particular morning, as he approached, something was very different. There, in place of the simple wooden cross they had planted at the head of Robert's grave, was a stone marker, neatly carved with Robert's name, birth year, death year and a cross at the top of the carvings. The sight of a proper gravestone confused Lewis. Where had it come from?

"Ahem," Mister Agner cleared his throat as he came up behind Lewis. "Mister Lewis, I'm sorry to intrude on your thoughts. I hope you don't mind. I took the liberty of carving up a proper gravestone for Mister Robert. I'm not a regular stone carver, so it's a little crude, but it was the best I could do."

Tears filling his eyes, Lewis remained facing the gravestone as he responded, "Nonsense, it's a beautiful gravestone. Thank you, thank you very much, for all of us."

The two men stood in silence for several minutes before Mister Agner spoke again, "Mister Lewis, what will happen to your sister, I mean Miss Esther, now that your father's gone?"

Looking at Mister Agner quizzically, Lewis answered, "I'm not sure what you mean, Mister Agner. My brothers and I will look after her, of course, provide for her needs. That's what father wanted, so she shan't want."

"What I mean is, well, she's a fine woman. I lost my wife and child in childbirth and have roamed the world alone ever since, never finding anyone to measure up to my Lucy and watching my life spin downward. That is until I came here. Your sister is spirited and kind hearted and I've grown quite fond of her."

"Mister Anger, are you asking for permission to court my sister?"

"Well, sir," he said, a sheepish grin crossing his face. "I guess I am at that. Normally I know I should ask the Colonel, but with him being gone and all, that puts you in charge of things, so I thought I'd ask you."

Lewis was quite taken by surprise at the request and at first didn't know how to respond. Finally, as Mister Agner began to fidget, he found the words. "There is nothing my brothers and I wouldn't do for our sister, Mister Agner, you must understand that. So, if she's willing, I have no objection to your courting her. If, however, you ever hurt her in any way, you'll have the three of us to answer to. Do you understand my meaning?"

Now with a big smile on his face, "Yes, sir, I understand completely. And I thank you, sir."

"Well, don't thank me just yet. As you say, while my sister is kind hearted, she is also spirited and not one to suffer fools. Good luck to you, Mark, I think you may need it!" With that, Lewis extended his hand and the two men shook.

Walking back to the fort, the two men met Elam.

"Lewis, just the man I was looking for. Good morning, Mister Agner. Do you suppose I might have a word?"

Lewis could now see how his world had changed. All of the things that normally would have gone to his father were now being brought to him. It was a new role for him and he felt he could never do as well as his father had always done in handling the affairs of their little community. He prayed he would have the strength and wisdom to handle the responsibility adequately.

"Yes, Elam, what's on your mind?"

"Father is concerned about returning home. We were supposed to leave today, but with the Shawnee on the prowl and all, I told him it wasn't wise. He's worried, now that Mister Carter has spread the word, that mother will be worried about us and wants to get home as soon as he can."

"I don't advise travel until we know more about what is going on around us, Elam. With just you and your father on the trail, you'd be a tempting target for even a small raiding party. Right now I can't ask anyone to go along to protect you. Besides, with a raid of this size, I'm not sure there are enough men in the fort to see to your safety beyond our walls."

"I know, I told him that, but he's worried and when he's worried he works himself into one of his headaches. Maybe if you talked with him it would help."

Lewis did as he was asked and talked to Ronald, explaining how dangerous such a trip would be at this moment, assuring him that as soon as they thought it safe, he could be on his way. The clincher was when he added that Margaret would worry even more if she thought Ronald and Elam were out on the road at a time like this. Ronald finally accepted the ruling and went to lie down to sooth his headache. Lewis wisely sent Philip and Charles to ask Ronald if he would play some of the diversions he had brought along. This pulled Ronald out of his spell and soon all three were laughing.

Lewis didn't know what Ronald had said to the boys the day before, but whatever it was it had done wonders for their mood. Still grieving over the loss of their grandfather, they no longer blamed themselves and it looked to Lewis like they were now handling the loss. He only wished he felt like he was handling it as well as they were. No, the pain was still sharp and he was feeling very lonely, even with all those around him.

"Lewis, just what have you done? Did you give Mister Agner permission to marry me?" Esther asked, breaking into his thoughts.

"Oh, Esther, there you are. Well, not exactly. What I told him was that if you agreed, he could court you. The decision is yours and we will abide by whatever you choose to do."

"Did you ever stop to ask me before you gave your permission? No, of course you didn't!"

With a look of mock horror, Lewis was starting to have fun at his sister's expense. "Do you mean you don't have any feelings at all toward Mister Agner? And after all the harassment you've heaped on the poor, lonely man? Why, Esther, I thought it only fair to give him the opportunity to exact a little revenge for all you've done to him. And what better way to harass you than to come courting!" Lewis started chuckling when he saw how this frustrated his sister.

"Now, I made no promises for you and even told him he could court only if you were willing. So, you haven't answered my question. Don't you have any feeling toward him?"

Finally finding her voice again, Esther huffed, "That's not what I'm saying! I mean, oh, I don't really know what I mean!" She then turned and stormed back to Robert's cabin, slamming the door behind her.

❦ Chapter 41 ❦

Edward Jewett and Daniel Boone took positions to best block a Shawnee move around behind where Jim and Squire blocked the entrance to the Jackson River Valley. Their plan was simple, to turn the Shawnee back into the Cow Pasture River Valley, which would take them to the northeast, parallel to most of the Valley settlements and not away from them. If the Shawnee made it to the Jackson, they would be able to make it all the way to the Ohio and beyond. Since they had just dropped three more Shawnee warriors, as near as the two men could figure, they were facing nineteen warriors.

"Ten to one, is that your idea of good odds?" Daniel asked quietly as they waited.

"If we can simply turn their advance back on the main body, we should have much more even odds. This group has to be pretty demoralized with the losses they've suffered. I don't see them putting up a strong fight, not for just two captives."

"Sure hope you're right," Daniel whispered. "And here they come."

Through the forest moved five warriors, the advance Edward was hoping for. Armed with two guns each, Edward and Daniel waited until they were close before firing. When the smoke cleared, three warriors were down and another was being helped off by what appeared to be an unhurt warrior.

"That should confuse them. Now they have no idea how many of us they're facing or where we really are," Edward whispered as he began reloading quickly.

"I have to admit, if this works, you're one shrewd Indian fighter."

"Indians or Austrians, the element of surprise remains the same."

They both reloaded and waited, wondering if the Shawnee had, in fact, moved northeast or if they were once again trying the Jackson River where Squire and Jim waited. Two quick shots from the east only served to further confuse the two, knowing Jim and Squire were to their south. Still they waited. Their companions should have joined them by now. Both men looked about nervously, wondering what had happened and if their companions had survived.

Their wonderings were interrupted by the distinct sound of horses coming through the forest from the same direction as the Shawnee scouts had come. Into view rode Squire Boone with Jim close behind. Stepping from the laurels, Edward and Daniel hailed their companions.

"What…?" began Edward but he stopped when Squire raised his hand.

"I know, you said to wait thirty minutes and follow. We did, only decided to follow the Shawnee and I'm glad we did," Squire announced.

"Once they hit you two, they turned and tried to make their way back," added Jim. "We had moved in on their rear and sent the rear guard running. We only dropped one of them but they're fully committed now to the Cow Pasture River Valley."

"Great thinking," said Edward.

"Now," Daniel began. "We have to hurry. The next place they can break to the west is along Thompson's Creek. We've got to beat them to it."

Recovering their horses, Daniel and Edward joined Squire and Jim in a wild ride through the mountainous region, moving west of Little Mare Mountain to come out along Thompson's Creek. Daniel and Squire took a quick look around while Edward and Jim chose a good site to block the Shawnee from moving west.

"No sign they've passed. I think we've continued to stay ahead of them. If, as you say, they were shaken before, this should really make them nervous," concluded Daniel.

"Yes, but what do you think, will it make them nervous enough to kill their captives to affect their escape?" asked Jim.

Daniel and Squire both thought about the question before Daniel answered. "I don't think so. Thus far, it doesn't look as if their captives are impeding their progress. And from what we've seen, they're the only profit this group has for the loss of, what do you think, Colonel, twenty or so braves?"

"If we turn them here, Daniel, where do they head next?" asked Edward.

"They'll have to continue up the Cow Pasture until the confluence with the Bull Pasture. That's their next chance to slip west. If we turn them here, we'll have to turn them there as well. Thing is, they'll have to pass Fort Lewis about halfway to the Bull Pasture. Your guess is as good as mine as to what they will do there."

Taking up a strong position between the north-east face of Little Mare Mountain and the ridge opposite it on the north bank of Thompson's Creek, they waited and rested nervously. Each man was now equipped with four guns, which they loaded and placed all within reach, ready for a concerted effort by the Shawnee to pass. It took two hours for the Shawnee to make it to Thompson's Creek and, when their advance discovered the trap, they immediately turned back into the Cow Pasture River Valley without testing the defenses.

"Well, I'll be, you must have been right about them being shaken, Colonel," observed Squire. "They took one look and didn't even try to force their way through."

"Yes, but I still don't like it. At least we got another look at the girls and they seem to still be alright. I'm afraid of what will happen if they start to slow them down."

"We can talk later, now we need to move. I say we stay west of Tower Hill Mountain, keeping it between us and them. Bad part is we won't know what happens when they try to pass by Fort Lewis."

"It's a chance we have to take," concluded Edward.

Mounting, they took off again at a quick pace, following a dry run before coming out in a small valley that Daniel announced was close to the Bull Pasture River. It was now fully dark and they were moving by moonlight, and little of that what with the waning moon they were under. Edward called a brief halt to rest the horses and, after two hours, they moved to the Bull Pasture River. Daniel then led the little party to the southeast through a very narrow pass where they determined to set up their next ambuscade. With Daniel and Squire on the north bank and Edward and Jim on the south, they settled in to wait again, relishing the opportunity to rest.

After sunup, Daniel looked around for sign and then hurried over to where Edward and Jim waited.

"This isn't good, Colonel. A band of about twenty warriors passed through here sometime yesterday," Daniel told them.

"What? How did they get ahead of us?" Jim asked, incredulous.

"No, you misunderstand me. These were heading in the other direction. Instead of somewhere around twenty warriors, we're now facing forty! You still think ten to one good odds, Colonel?"

Letting his breath out slowly, Edward thought hard before responding. "I think we can still turn them here. Now, once we do that, is there a place we can get in front of them, to block their progress altogether?"

"Sure there is. About three miles further up the Cow Pasture, the river curves through a tight spot. If we can get there first, we'd have them blocked. But it would still be just the four of us against forty warriors."

"You don't need to do this, Daniel. You and your brother are free to go and no stigma will attach."

"You know, Colonel, you sure know some fancy words. I don't know what a 'stigma' is though my guess is it's the same as a coward. I guess you've done well by us so far, we'll just stick it out and see how you manage to finish it." Daniel shook his head as he made his way carefully back to where he and Squire were to wait.

It was several more hours before the Shawnee came into view. It was just a few scouts, not the main party and they spotted Jim as he moved, having become uncomfortable where he was situated and moving to relieve his back. With a whoop, they headed back toward the Cow Pasture River. After waiting half an hour, Daniel and Squire moved forward, then came running back.

"They headed up the Cow Pasture without testing us here. If we're to cut them off, we've got to move and move fast."

"If this is as narrow a valley as you say, we'll need to remain behind this mountain or they'll hear us for sure," observed Edward as the four made for their horses.

Riding hard on the northwest slope of Bull Pasture Mountain, Daniel led them through a saddle in the ridge-like mountain and down onto the Cow Pasture River. It was now late afternoon and, not finding any sign the Shawnee had passed, they tied their horses, took all their acquired guns, and moved cautiously south to where the river made a turn from northeast to northwest before continuing back to the northeast.

Again Daniel and Squire moved ahead to scout both for the Shawnee and for a position they could defend. Returning, Daniel looked pleased.

"The Shawnee have made camp on the south side of the Cow Pasture, near where it passes through this gap. There's a deadfall snag on the rocks on this side of the river. It is a good position, well protected on the front and two sides by large tree trunks. With the river forming our front, we just might be able to pull this off, Colonel."

"Okay, assuming we get the girls, then what?" asked Jim.

"Well," said Daniel, scratching his neck as he thought. "Behind us about eight or ten miles is the trail over Shenandoah Mountain. If we were to get the girls out, one of us could take them on the horses and head for the trail. Once over the mountain, you're in Staunton and relatively safe."

"And the other three?" asked Edward.

"Well, I didn't say it was a good plan, only that it was a plan."

"Actually it is a very good plan. Jim will be responsible for getting the girls over the mountain and to safety if you two will stay with me to keep the Shawnee off their tails."

"Colonel, you never do anything the easy way, do you?" observed Squire. "That said, count me in. Today's as good a day to die as any other." Daniel grinned as he nodded his assent.

"Good. Now, Jim, leave your extra guns with us. We'll be in the snag and I want you, where Daniel? Would the girls be better able to make the bank to the left or right of our position?"

"I'm with you now, to the left is better, easier for them to make cover."

"Jim, take one shot, then gather up the girls and ride as hard as you can for Staunton. Don't stop for anything, no matter what you hear behind you."

They moved quietly and cautiously into position. Well protected and with five guns each, Edward felt confident about holding off the Shawnee. Now all he needed was an opportunity to free the girls. It was the waiting that was the worst.

As the shadows lengthened in the narrow valley signaling an early sunset, two warriors brought the girls down to the river right in front of the snag where their rescuers waited. Edward looked at Squire and Daniel, unable to believe their luck. Believing their pursuers to be to the southwest, they felt safe allowing the girls to gather water behind their camp.

As the girls waded into the shallow river, having to come halfway across to find a pool deep enough to draw water from, the two warriors remained on the bank, chatting and watching their charges.

"Sarah," whispered Edward. "Caitlyn, don't look up but continue what you're doing, look natural. I want you both to move to the right of the snag. When I fire, run as fast as you can for the woods on that side. Caitlyn's father will meet you there. Nod your heads once if you heard and understood." Both girls nodded their heads once, then started talking and moving toward the opposite bank as they continued to fill the gourd containers that served as canteens.

Taking careful aim when he saw the girls' movements had alerted one of the warriors, Edward dropped him and Daniel dropped the second. A whooping from the camp signaled the Shawnee response would be swift.

The girls made the woods and relative safety just as the warriors made the opposite bank. The three rescuers began firing swiftly and effectively, dropping six more warriors while their fire harmlessly struck the large tree trunks forming the snag. Then it was over. The Shawnee pulled back from the bank and Daniel, Squire, and Edward began to furiously reload their empty guns.

"Great Bear, is that you, brother?" came a call from across the river.

Whispering, "Watch the river above and below as they'll try to distract us to get on our rear." Then, in a voice to carry across the river, "I'm here, Black Fish."

"Why do you kill so many of my warriors, Great Bear? I thought we were brothers."

"Does a brother send his braves to kill the father and steal the daughter of his blood brother?"

Black Fish was quiet for a moment. "My warriors were wrong and I have now come back to gather them up and take them home where they will suffer for their failures."

Squire fired twice, dropping two of three warriors trying to make their way across downstream from the snag and driving the third back to their side of the bank. A few minutes later, Daniel dropped another upstream, halting the crossing in that direction.

"Black Fish, how many more of your warriors must die today? What will the great chief of the Shawnee, Cornstalk, think when you return without captives and so few warriors? Will he ever allow Black Fish to lead the Shawnee on the war path again?"

Again Black Fish was quiet, but no more warriors attempted to cross the river that the well chosen snag commanded.

"They'll wait until dark and then move when we can't see them," observed Daniel.

"As soon as it's dark, we're pulling back as quick as our legs can carry us. Use your belt axes to break the cock of all but your rifle gun and one other. Those we take and leave the rest," Edward whispered.

"Great Bear," came Black Fish's voice once again, "Give us back the captives and we'll let you go in peace back to your people."

It now being dark, there was no answer from the snag. After a minute or so, the Shawnee raised a chorus of whoops as they surged across the river and over the snag.

∽ Chapter 42 ∾

"That is just so cute," Marie said to Jenny as they watched Mister Agner walk down the street in the little fort toward Robert's cabin.

He was wearing the new set of clothes Rachael and Sally had just finished for him and carried a bunch of wild flowers. His hair was neatly combed and tied in a queue and, except for his old broad brimmed hat, he looked the model of respectability. So intent were the two women on watching Mister Agner, they didn't even see Lewis walk by, heading toward the blockhouse and carrying two plates of food. With the crowd now in the little fort, they had started eating in shifts under the awning, although Esther and Henry had remained absent.

Knocking politely on the door, Mister Agner pulled himself up to his full height and placed his right hand at the middle of his back. As he assumed what he thought to be the stance of a gentleman, Marie and Jenny nearly laughed out loud.

"Oh, Mister Agner, it's you. This really isn't a good time for me. I'm not sure when would be a good time these days," Esther told him as he stood perfectly still in front of her.

"Nonsense, Miss Esther, there is never a better time than the present. Won't you sit here on the bench with me? With everyone able to watch, I'm sure it won't impugn your reputation any."

Hesitantly at first but then with a firm nod of her head, Esther stepped from the cabin and sat on the shady bench, picking her place at the very end and closest to the door. Mister Agner, taking a cue from her, sat at the opposite end, just as far away as the bench would allow. After a few moments of awkward silence that seemed longer to both, Mister Agner handed Esther his bundle of flowers and cleared his throat.

"Miss Esther, I think I've told you how I lost my dear wife, Lucy, in childbirth." Esther nodded. "Well, what I didn't tell you was that within a week, I lost Lucy, my child, and my parents. They died of the pox, you see. That's when I lost all hope. I started drinking and lost my position. I was a master miller but let myself go. I had to move from community to community until I ended up at Beverly's Mill Place, Staunton now. There I met your brother, the Colonel, and he gave me a chance when no one else would. That's when I cut back my drinking to just when there wasn't milling to do."

Esther sat, listening politely, not quite sure where Mister Agner was going with all this and not altogether sure she should be hearing it. Receiving no objection, Mister Agner continued.

"I was still slovenly in my appearance, but my work was again first rate. Then, as things happen, you dumped me into the mill pond and tossed that bar of soap at me. That's when I saw you as the spirited, sensitive woman you are, and I fell for you right then."

Esther's opened her eyes wide at this point, a little fear creeping into her mind as she contemplated just what Mister Agner was going to do next.

"Now, Miss Esther, you've lost your father and you're hurting. No one understands that better than Mark Agner, no sir, I mean ma'am." Turning a little red in the face, he continued. "What I'm saying is you need someone to care for you now. Not your brothers, I know they do, but they have their own families and lives. You can't sit alone in your father's cabin grieving or you'll end up bad off, like I did."

"Why, Mister Agner, I could never marry a man who pitied me."

"Oh, no, you misunderstand. It's not out of pity I'm here. Well, I've been trying to catch your eye for some time now and haven't been able to make any progress. Now, with you isolating yourself from everyone, I knew I'd have to take bolder measures to let you know just how I feel about you."

Esther remained a little afraid and yet was very moved by Mister Agner's sentiments. Looking him over closely now, she began to see that he really did have many good qualities. She also realized that by including him in her jesting, as if he were one of her brothers, she had encouraged him. Maybe deep down that's what she had wanted all along. Oh, if he'd only go away and let me think, she thought.

"Well, I can see I've burdened you enough for one day, Miss Esther, so I'll be on my way. I hope you'll let me call on you again," he ended, hopefully.

Esther heard herself say "I think that would be lovely" without consciously forming the words. It surprised her. And when they stood, she actually felt a twinge of sadness that he was going to leave her.

With an impressive bow, he did take his leave, not wanting to press things too hard while Esther was still grieving so over the loss of her father. As he walked away, his step was lighter and he had a smile on his face that, while his back was toward Esther, Marie and Jenny clearly saw. As soon as he passed, they rushed over to Esther and hustled her inside so she could tell them all he said, having been too far away to hear more than a word here and there.

While his sister met with her gentleman friend, Lewis made his way to the blockhouse door. As crowded as the little fort was, there was no problem getting someone to open the door for him as he juggled the plates of food. Climbing the steep stairs to the second floor, he found Henry, moving from shooting loop to shooting loop, searching the horizon for signs of his daughter. He was drawn and pale, his eyes red and the sockets dark from lack of sleep.

"Henry, come have some breakfast with me," Lewis called out in as cheerful a voice as he could muster. The soldiers moved away from where he set the plates on a barrelhead, giving the brothers some degree of privacy.

"No, no, you go ahead. I need to keep watch for Sarah. I don't want to miss her return."

"Henry, it'll do Sarah no good if you make yourself sick worrying."

"I know, but I should be out there. It should be me, not Edward, going after my little girl. And here I am, like a coward, penned up in a safe place while Sarah is out there in the hands of the Shawnee. Why did I listen to you and Edward, why didn't I go anyway?"

Lewis took Henry by the shoulders and guided him to the barrel that would serve as their table, pushing him down on the crate that was to be his seat. Taking a crate opposite, he looked Henry long and hard in the eyes until he was sure he had Henry's attention before proceeding.

"Henry, Edward is doing what he does best. He spent thirty years fighting in Europe, that's what he does. You, on the other hand, have spent just five years here in the wilderness. You've developed some skills, it's true, but Edward is still the best man among us in a fight with the Shawnee or the French."

"That doesn't change the fact that it was my daughter out there!"

"Yes, and you have two sons in here and a wife about to deliver you another child. Edward was right, your place is here and his place is out there. You must raise your sons and he'll do everything possible to bring your daughter home."

Henry slumped, "Then why does my being here feel so wrong?"

Lewis thought for a few moments before answering his younger brother. "If father were here, he'd tell you the same thing I am. You are where you are supposed to be and Edward is where he's supposed to be. You must accept that. And you must eat and maintain your strength for when Sarah does return. We have no idea how she's being treated and she'll need a strong father to lean on. Now, eat."

"I always felt she leaned on father more than me," Henry said dejectedly, as he put a piece of biscuit into his mouth, the first food he'd taken in several days.

"We all did, Sarah, you, me, Esther, and even Edward in his own way. Now she has lost her grandfather and will need you more than ever."

Henry nodded half heartedly and took a bite of ham. "I do believe this is Melinda Rice's ham. She knows how to put them up in the fall better than anyone I know, except maybe Aunt Bess."

Lewis felt relieved as he realized he had made it through to his brother. Watching, Henry began eating with more and more relish until soon his plate was empty. "Should I bring you more?"

"Oh, no, I can wait until dinner now." After a long pause, Henry looked into Lewis's eyes and said, "Thank you, brother, for being there for me, like father always was. I think I'll take a little nap now."

As the days passed, waiting for word about Sarah and Edward was taking its toll on those in the little fort. Esther was spending portions of every day in conversation with Mister Agner, but always with an ear cocked to hear the call of "riders are coming" or the sound of distant hoof beats on the baked August ground.

To help break up the monotony and to bring in much needed information, Lewis restarted morning and evening patrols. They always traveled in fours in case they ran into trouble, and Elam insisted on being part of the rotation as well. Not knowing how well Elam would be in a fight, Lewis always made him the fifth member of the patrol, making some little excuse about how this particular patrol was more dangerous than the others had been to sooth Elam's feelings.

Outside of the fort and the patrols, they knew nothing about what was going on beyond their little piece of Augusta County. Lewis found this especially frustrating. And Ronald worried more with each passing day what Margaret was thinking with him not there and no way to get word to her that he was safe.

To ward off Ronald's headaches, Philip and Charles tried their best to keep him occupied with his diversions or by getting him to tell them stories of his childhood, of

Elam's childhood, or anything else that presented itself. It was working and Ronald's headaches were few and far between. Having him here with the boys also helped them cope with the loss of their grandfather. He wasn't Robert, but they had grown to love him all the same.

One afternoon, Lewis, Henry, and Esther asked Ronald and Elam to join them in Edward's cabin. Once assembled, Lewis cleared his throat before beginning.

"Ronald, when we are able to send you home, we've been talking amongst ourselves and have decided we don't want you riding that old, sway backed mare to Greenville. That horse is plainly too old for you to be out riding her, and too dangerous should you need to flee from the Shawnee."

"But that's the only horse I have. If I don't ride her, how will I get home? I can hardly walk that far."

Lewis looked from the concerned, confused face of Ronald back at his brother and sister before proceeding. "Well, we've decided that father would want you to have his riding chair and horse. They'll be far more comfortable…"

"Oh, no, you can't part with Robert's riding chair! It was so much a part of him!"

"Nevertheless, we feel father would want you to have it. We're all in agreement, save Edward who we're sure would say the same thing. Now, it's settled and we want no more arguments about it."

Ronald was overwhelmed by the generosity and could only mutter a thank you as he shook their hands and shuffled out the door. Elam, however, waited until his father had gone before addressing the Jewetts.

"It's a wonderful thing you've done. I don't know how we shall ever thank you."

"No thanks are necessary," assured Lewis. "We are only doing what father would have wanted."

As the four stepped out of Edward's cabin, a shout of "rider coming" from the blockhouse energized them all. Henry ran to the blockhouse hoping to get the first look at his daughter while Lewis and Esther ran for the gate.

A breathless military post rider on a lathered horse reined up at the gate and shouted for all to hear, "There's been a running fight along the upper Cow Pasture River between Colonel Jewett and the Shawnee."

꩜ Chapter 43 ꩜

Edward's heart pounded in his ears and his breath came in hard gasps. His vision was blurred and his legs felt like lead. It was all he could do to put one foot in front of the other as he worked his way up the steep trace.

They had run all night, managing to stay just ahead of the Shawnee who trailed them. They had been able to keep track of the Shawnee by the whoops every time they found the trail Edward and the Boone brothers had left. True, Daniel could have used some of his tricks to throw them off the trail, but there really wasn't time for that. Plus the moonless night made it very dark and too difficult to keep their own way, let alone set false trails for the Shawnee to follow.

Covering the eight or ten miles to the trace that lead up over the pass in Shenandoah Mountain had taxed Edward's endurance. While he was in reasonably good shape, he was still fifty-seven years old, more than the combined age of his two companions. Until now, he had been able to keep up with them, but this steep grade was more than he could manage.

Since daylight, they had occasionally spotted a following Shawnee warrior and had been shot at several times. All of this served to propel them on. Now Edward felt it was over. He had no more strength left. The Shawnee would dispatch him here on this mountainside and leave his bones to be scattered by the wolves.

Then he felt hands, many hands, grabbing his arms and propelling him upward. At first he thought Shawnee, but they would have pulled him down. In his dazed, unseeing state, it seemed as if the angels had come and were carrying him off. So be it, he thought. At least we freed Sarah. Father would be surprised to find Edward joining him so soon, but at least they would be together again.

He began to realize he hadn't passed on when the same hands that had lifted him up set him gently against a tree and pressed something to his lips. Cold, refreshing water trickled down his parched throat and down his chin and neck. Opening his eyes, through still blurred vision, he thought he could see a man in uniform knelt in front of him.

"Colonel Jewett, I'm Captain Weber of Company F, First Virginia Regiment."

Edward feebly raised his arm as far as he could and managed to squeak out the word "Shawnee" as he pointed in a general downhill direction.

"Oh, don't you worry about a thing, Colonel," the Captain said as the sound of sporadic gunfire reached them. "I force marched my whole company up from Staunton as soon as Mister Rice brought the word. There are a hundred men between the Shawnee and you. You're safe now."

Edward's chin dropped back down to his chest and he sat there, for how long he didn't know. When next he woke, it was completely dark and he was laying flat. He sensed movement but, when he tried to move his arms or legs, he couldn't. He tried to talk, and couldn't. As he passed out again, his last thought, the only thing that made any sense to him, was that he was being carried into Hades for all he had done in the wars he had fought. No, he wouldn't be joining his father after all, he thought with regret.

His next sensation was of a hand raising his head, a firm yet gentle hand, the hand of a woman. Then something pressed to his lips and a burning liquid sent him coughing and sputtering as he got his elbows under him. Opening his eyes, he found he was looking into the calm, gentle face of Margaret Samuel.

"Normally I don't hold store by strong spirits, but they have their uses."

Edward shook his head, trying to clear the cobwebs from his brain, trying to make sense of it all. Then he managed to squeak out one word, "Sarah."

"Oh, she's right here, Colonel darling."

And then he was looking into Sarah's beautiful face as she moved to replace Margaret at his side. He studied her hard, at first unable to grasp that she was real. Her eyes then teared up and she laid her face against his chest and cried. He tried to comfort her but couldn't get the words out, settling to simply pat her hair.

"You need to eat something, Colonel, if we're ever going to get you back on your feet. I've made some nice broth for you. First, let's take care of that throat," she said as she shoved a spoon of something into his mouth. It had a strange flavor, honey maybe, and something more bitter, like vinegar. He wrinkled up his face as he swallowed.

"Sarah, would you be a dear and bring the broth from the table? Thank you," she said in a very kind voice. As Sarah moved off across the room, Margaret whispered to Edward, "She's suffering something fierce, Colonel, blaming herself for your father's death." As Sarah returned to Edward's bedside, Margaret continued in a louder, more cheerful voice, "As soon as I heard, I sent word to have you brought here so I could nurse you. No sense being nursed by strangers, or worse, army surgeons."

Struggling to speak, Edward asked, "Jim Rice, the Boones, and Caitlyn?"

"Oh, they all came here with you. I put the girls in the loft and Mister Rice and those Boones in Elam's cabin. Those Boones, they're a hard lot, though I try not to judge too harshly after what they did for you."

Margaret continued to chatter away as she fed Edward the broth and Sarah sat next to him and held his hand in both of hers. Once he had taken all of the broth he could, Margaret laid him gently back down, covered him up, and told him to get some sleep, she'd wake him when it was time for another dose of her throat remedy.

When next he woke, it was from being patted on his shoulder. Opening his eyes, he looked up into the grinning faces of Daniel and Squire Boone. Both looked the worse for their recent experience though not as bad off as he was.

"Colonel, you really do know how to put on a good Indian fight. That was mighty neighborly of you to invite us along," grinned Daniel. "Anytime you want to do it again, just let us know and we'll come running."

Mustering his strength, Edward managed to speak, the pain in his throat having subsided. "Daniel, Squire, I never could have done that without you. And Daniel, without your knowledge of the terrain, well, my bones would be out there bleaching in the sun right now. I can't thank you enough."

"Ah, forget it. You taught me a thing or two about fighting Shawnee on this trip, lessons I won't soon forget. You're a sly old fox, Colonel, and it was our privilege to have seen it. Now," looking around to see that Margaret Samuel was across the room, he lowered his voice, "we're off to the tavern for a wee bit of refreshment before dinner. We'll check in on you later."

As the Boones moved away, there was Margaret, shoving another spoonful of her remedy into his mouth. "Now, Colonel, how did the broth sit with you? Would you like some more or do you think you could try a little bread and cheese?"

Over the course of the next several days, Edward slowly regained some strength. He learned that there was a mounted squad in the yard and that, when he was ready, Colonel Washington had instructed them to escort Edward home. He also learned that, while Sarah and Caitlyn had not been treated harshly, they had suffered more than was common for young settler women. Jim came and sat with Edward for a portion of each day and he took great pride in retelling Margaret of their running fight with the Shawnee and his final mad dash over Shenandoah Mountain to bring the girls to safety. Edward never corrected Jim, even when some of the events seemed a little enhanced.

Sarah was always close to Edward as he recovered, though hardly saying a word. Finally, when he could stand her pain no longer, Edward pulled her close. For the next hour, he answered her questions, always assuring her that it had not been through any fault of hers that Robert had met his fate. Slowly and through many tears, she began to come to grips with her grief, began to blame herself less, and then she smiled for the first time as they recalled Robert together. It would still take a lot more time and a lot of comforting, but Edward now knew Sarah would recover from her melancholy.

As soon as Edward was strong enough to sit a horse, they started for home, Edward, Sarah, Jim and Caitlyn Rice, the Boones, and Edward's military escort. They made quite a spectacle as they rode down the Virginia Road. Before leaving, as he thanked Margaret for her kindness, he promised he'd send Ronald and Elam back with the military escort as they returned to Staunton.

Arriving at home, it was quite the homecoming. Everyone turned up outside the gate to welcome them home. Henry gave Sarah a huge hug and wouldn't let her go. Melinda was all in tears when she saw Caitlyn and Jim, smothering both with kisses and hugs.

After welcoming Edward home, Lewis stood aside as others greeted him, watching. He didn't like what he saw. Edward was gaunt and pale, not looking at all healthy. Worse, his eyes lacked the spark Lewis remembered them to have. Edward looked to have aged years in the few weeks he'd been gone and his smile never extended beyond his mouth. No, this was not the same man who had left there. He just hoped over time that they'd be able to bring the old Edward back.

The little fort took on a festive atmosphere as platters of food were brought out. Jim Rice told his version of their adventure over and over again, not telling it quite the same way with each retelling. After all had eaten their fill, the elder Mister Stuart brought out his fiddle and there was dancing in the little street. The Boone brothers danced with every woman in the fort, except Sarah. Henry wasn't letting go of her, not for a moment. Things didn't wind down until full dark when everyone slowly found their way back to their lodgings.

Early the following morning, Daniel and Squire Boone left to continue their interrupted return trip to the Yadkin Valley and home. As the military escort readied to return to Staunton, Ronald approached Edward, seated on the bench outside his cabin door.

"Now, you're sure it's alright for me to have the riding chair and horse? It really is a very generous gift, too generous."

"No, Uncle Ronald, the riding chair is now yours. We hope you enjoy it as much as our father did."

"Alright, as long as you're sure. I really can't thank you enough. Why, I can now even take Margaret for rides."

"Be careful, old man, or she'll be taking you instead!" chuckled Edward as the two men shook hands.

Between Betty and Esther, they made such a fuss over nursing Edward back to health that it was all he could do to stand it. Be that as it may, he knew they meant well and didn't protest too much. And slowly, his health did improve. He put some of his lost weight back on and gained some of his color back. He still didn't have his usual stamina, but he was getting stronger.

"So, Esther, what's this I hear? You're keeping company with Mister Agner?" he asked his sister one day, with the old sparkle in his eye.

"Yes I am, and don't you go scaring him off like you did all the boys when I was growing up. Why I'd be nicely situated today instead of an old maid if you hadn't considered every boy who came around not to be good enough for me!"

"Me? Surely that was one of your other brothers!"

"Now don't go making light of it. Mister Agner and I are coming to an understanding and, while he isn't exactly a gentleman, he's a good man."

Edward pulled his sister to him and patted her shoulder. "I'm sure he is, Esther. And I promised father I would take care of you, so you'll not want for anything. Just as long as you're happy, that's all I care about. Now, I suppose I should talk to him and set a few ground rules."

"No you don't, Edward Jewett! I know all about your 'ground rules' as you call them. Why, the Hardy boy you told if he ever raised a hand to me, they'd find his body floating in the marshes. I never did see him again. I don't think he stopped running until he reached Salem! And then there was Boston Carter, you remember him. Why, you scared him so bad he developed a stutter and would cross the street just to avoid me!"

Laughing, Edward raised his hand, "All right, guilty as charged. I won't scare off Mister Agner. Just make sure he knows if any harm comes to you by his hand, he will answer to your brothers."

"Oh, there might not be much left of him for my brothers to deal with. I'm pretty good with a hot poker, in case you hadn't heard." This sent them both to laughing. It was good to hear Edward laugh again, thought Esther. He still wasn't the same, but maybe now he could start to heal.

Several days later, Lewis and Henry sat in Edward's cabin as they went over dispatches delivered by military courier.

"It says here that the Marquis de Montcalm forced Fort William Henry to surrender, then he lost control of his native allies. If it weren't for those who made it to the protection of the French Regulars, the whole command would likely have been wiped out," Edward told his brothers. "Poor Lieutenant Colonel Monro, he's a good man and this will weigh heavily on him."

"And what of the Indian situation, do the dispatches give any hope of peace between us and the Shawnee?" asked Henry.

"Quite the contrary, it seems that the migration back across the Blue Ridge has stepped up since the July raids and the frontiers of Maryland, Virginia, and Pennsylvania are losing their population and settlements at an alarming rate."

The three sat quietly, absorbing all the bad news, until Henry broke the silence.

"Edward, I assume you'll be going to Williamsburg for the fall session of the House of Burgesses. I'd like to send Sarah with you, get her back east and near Bat, where they can really determine if their relationship is going to work out."

Edward thought for a few moments before responding. "Well, I'd need you and Jenny to go along then."

"I need to take Charles up to Greenville, remember."

"What if Marie and I went?" asked Lewis. "You know Marie has been dying to see Hannah and we do need to enroll Philip for the fall session of William and Mary. We might even leave Marie there to keep an eye on Sarah. I think she'd love that, more time to visit with Hannah. And then I could ride back with you."

Edward looked Lewis over closely. Ever since he'd returned, he sensed Lewis was trying to make things easy for him. Like his younger brother felt he needed taken care of. It mattered little that he might just have been right.

❧ Chapter 44 ❧

Governor Robert Dinwiddie was not a well man. He was quickly exhausting all his energy in an effort to save his Colony from being ravaged by the Ohio Indians allied with the French, to get Whitehall to understand the importance of reducing Fort Duquesne, and to convince the Burgesses to support the Virginia Regiments with more than mere words. There were some days he didn't know how much longer he'd be able to continue, his fatigue was so great. And yet he knew he must continue, for to let up for even a moment would be a grave blow to the fragile government of the Colony. That was why, when all reason told him he should resign or risk ruining his health forever, he stayed on.

Looking up from his desk in the dining room of the Governor's Palace, he had expected to be buoyed by the sight of his friend and military advisor, Colonel Edward Jewett. Instead, before him in dusty traveling clothes, was a tired old man, a man whose health seemed as shattered as his own.

"Edward, it is good to see you," the Governor tried to hide his dismay at the condition of the man before him.

"Governor, I came here as soon as I arrived so I hope you'll forgive my condition."

There was some of the old spark in Edward's eye, but it was very clear to the Governor that the man before him had in no way recovered from his harrowing experience of just two months back. The Governor decided to cut right to it without any niceties.

"Edward, you don't look a bit well. If I knew you remained ill, I never would have asked you to make the long journey. You could have sent me word, you know."

"Nonsense, Governor, I am here to serve."

Skeptically, Governor Dinwiddie turned to the task of bringing Edward up to date on the military state of affairs. "You've heard Lord Loudoun has returned to New York after aborting his attack on Fort Louisbourg?"

"No, I'm afraid I hadn't. That won't sit well with Whitehall nor does it give us any relief by cutting off French supplies and reinforcements from reaching the interior."

With the prospect for continued attacks all along their frontier, the two men talked for several hours, planning their strategy for how to approach the Burgesses. There were the requests for funding the military efforts needed to defend the Valley of Virginia followed by how they should respond to Lord Loudoun's repeated and most insistent requests for recruits and supplies. Seeing Edward was greatly exhausted by his travels and their business, the Governor concluded their meeting, feigning an "indisposition" and setting a meeting for the following afternoon.

As Edward shuffled back toward his lodgings at the Dandridge house, he made a little detour. Much to his surprise, as he entered the little Presbyterian cemetery, he found Lewis standing by Aunt Bess's grave.

"It seems we are of like minds, you and I," Edward said as he placed a hand on his brother's shoulder. Lewis only nodded.

The two stood silently, remembering, for quite some time before Lewis broke the silence. "Edward, you look awful. You should have rested before going to see the Governor. I'm sure he'd have understood."

"Perhaps you're right. I just don't seem to be able to do as much as I could just a short time ago."

"That's because you haven't allowed yourself to recover fully. Now, it's time for supper and Missus Dandridge is expecting us. She was most distressed when you went straight to the Governor without stopping to see her first."

When they arrived at the Dandridge house, Missus Fanny Dandridge greeted Edward warmly and not without a great deal of concern over his appearance. He assured her he would be fine once he got a good night's sleep. Fanny doubted his sincerity. Hannah's greeting was a little too familiar, Edward thought, but passed it off as a product of his exhausted imagination.

Over supper, Fanny informed her guests of the death of her son-in-law, Daniel Parke Custis. "It was quite a shock to us all. He just grabbed his chest, groaned, and sunk to the floor where he breathed his last. I can't tell you how hard Patsy is taking it."

After accepting their condolences, Fanny looked hard at Edward. "And if you don't start taking better care of yourself, Colonel Mister Edward Jewett, the same could happen to you. Perhaps what you need is a wife."

Sarah smiled as she lowered her eyes and blushed, seated next to Bartholomew Dandridge, while the other two women present, Marie and Hannah Davies, each seconded the suggestion, maybe a little to enthusiastically.

"You know, Edward, Patsy needs a good husband and you could do much worse than her. Besides, she comes with an estate of over seventeen thousand acres, White House Plantation convenient to Williamsburg, and a large house right here in town so you wouldn't need to keep making that long trek from beyond the Blue Ridge," Fanny said with all earnestness.

If others at the table had been looking at anyone other than Edward, they would have seen anger flash in Marie's eyes and disappointment in Hannah's.

For his part, Edward just brushed the subject off, "Oh, I'm afraid Patsy would find me much too old for her tastes."

"Nonsense, Charles Carter is already signaling his intentions and you're both practically the same age," retorted Fanny. "Truth be told, I'd much prefer you as a son-in-law over Charles Carter, not that there's anything wrong with Charles..." Fanny chatted on for some time trying to make her case for a match between Edward and Patsy while Edward sat politely and Marie fumed.

Edward retired immediately after the meal concluded, exhausted. The others sat in the parlor and listened to Lewis and Sarah tell of their recent trials on the frontier. Fanny was very distressed when she learned of Robert's death, calling him the finest gentleman she had ever met. Although their telling of Sarah's rescue lacked the finer, if somewhat dubious, details of Jim Rice's version, it nonetheless conveyed to the listeners the true desperateness of the situation.

Bat was both horrified at the danger Sarah had been in and gratified at the outcome of Edward's rescue. While Sarah seemed quieter than when they last visited at the Jewett fort, she had lost none of her beauty or appeal through her trials. Quite the contrary, he admired her strength, doubting any of the Williamsburg women who were trying to turn his head could have endured so much. No, she was stronger and more confident of herself than before the incident and he found himself even more drawn to her.

Edward recovered from the trip over the next few days in spite of the long hours he spent with the Governor. Once the Burgesses started arriving, he spent his evenings at the taverns, planting the seeds that he and Governor Dinwiddie hoped would result in better funding for the military effort. One of the topics these men, mostly eastern planters, seemed to never get enough of was Edward's own recent experience. Many of them knew Robert from when he accompanied Edward to Williamsburg and expressed their condolences before pressing him for the story of Sarah's rescue, which he told with great brevity and not the flair of Jim or even Lewis.

In addition to handling the legal affairs for his sister Patsy, Bat helped Lewis with settling Robert's estate while Lewis was waiting on Edward to conclude his business in Williamsburg. Mister Prentiss was very disturbed when he learned of Robert's death and called at the Dandridge house later to express his condolences to Edward and Lewis while offering his assistance to Bat in settling accounts with Robert's London factor.

Fanny took every opportunity to have Patsy around the house when Edward would be there, her attempt to push the two together not lost on anyone. For his part, Edward remained polite toward Patsy, not showing his disinterest in Fanny's plan while at the same time not giving Patsy too much encouragement. Truth be told, he liked Patsy, and, even in this time of sadness, she had a young, almost playful, air about her.

It began to appear to Edward that Hannah was always about. When he'd arrive back in his lodging in the adjacent office, there would be Hannah setting out light refreshments for him before excusing herself to the main house. When he'd go to the pleasant, if small, garden behind the house to take the air, she'd be there, sitting on the bench reading. After supper, when they would retire to the parlor, he would find her sitting at his elbow. And when he'd rise to go to meet with the Burgesses at the taverns, it was Hannah always helping him on with his cloak and handing him his hat. Edward wasn't sure he liked his sudden popularity with the ladies. Between Patsy, egged on by Fanny, and Hannah, he suspected egged on by Marie, there was a definite conspiracy against his bachelorhood.

One evening after supper, as they all sat in the parlor, the Governor's secretary arrived and requested Edward call on the Governor immediately. Following the secretary back to the Palace, all Edward was able to learn was that a packet of dispatches had just arrived by fast sloop, the contents of which had sent the Governor into a fit.

"Edward, you're not going to believe the news I've just received," Robert Dinwiddie said as the secretary ushered Edward into the Governor's dining room. "The Duke of Cumberland has surrendered his entire army to the duc de Richelieu."

The news hit Edward hard. For all his faults, and Edward knew many of them, the Duke had always treated Edward well. As the King's favorite son, he held sway in the Cabinet far above his position as the head of the Royal Army. Of late, he had been the only counterbalance to the Prime Minister, William Pitt.

"I know you corresponded with the Duke on my behalf and to good effect. Have you any influence now in the

Pitt camp that could serve to fill the void left by Cumberland's disgrace?" the Governor asked.

"I'm afraid not, Governor, though this may not be entirely a bad thing for us in the Colonies. The Prime Minister will now have unfettered power, it is true, but he will also be under extreme pressure to reverse the misfortunes England has suffered. Perhaps without the competition between the two, the Duke and the Prime Minister, the war will be prosecuted with more vigor."

They discussed events and composed letters to London well into the night, both retiring exhausted by their labors. For Edward's part, he prepared a proposal to be included in a letter from Governor Dinwiddie to the Prime Minister suggesting a three pronged offensive, one against Fort Louisbourg and then up the Saint Lawrence; a second up the New York lakes toward Montreal; and the third against Fort Duquesne to end the atrocities along their frontier.

The next morning, Philip sat in Edward's lodgings by the fire, pretending to be reading as he listened to Lewis and Edward discuss events of the night before. They were to depart for home the next day and Philip was intent on being with them as much as he could. Marie tapped lightly at the door before entering.

Seeing Philip sitting quietly reading, she put her hands on her hips, indignation on her face, and said, "Philip, what are you doing? Why aren't you out with Luke?"

Looking a bit sheepish, Philip responded, "Mother, I had some reading I needed to do so Luke went on without me."

"Is that any way to treat your best friend? Sometimes I just don't understand what's gotten into you!" she said before turning to leave, closing the door none too softly behind her.

"Father, can I ask you something?"

"Of course, Philip."

"Luke is off at a horse race and wanted me to go along. He goes there to place bets with the money he sneaks from his mother or winnings from previous bets. I don't want to go to horse races and I don't like betting. I haven't told mother any of this because I don't want to get Luke into trouble, but I just don't want to participate in it. What should I do? Go to the races just to please mother?"

"No, Philip, you do just as you are doing. Focus your efforts on your schoolwork and don't let yourself be distracted, by Luke or your mother, from what you know to be right. I'll talk to you mother before we leave."

Satisfied, Philip took his book and reluctantly went to his room in the main house when his father shooed him out.

"Look, Lewis, if you need to stay here, I can find my way home without you. I am anxious to get back and relieve little brother of the burden of managing our interests, but you needn't feel it necessary to go."

"Henry really did look overwhelmed when we explained what he needed to do while we were gone," said Lewis, chuckling at their youngest brother's penchant for avoiding things that put him in charge. "No, I'm going back with you. This is a small matter easily handled." Adding, after a thoughtful pause, "You don't think Henry has done too much damage in our absence, do you?"

❧ Chapter 45 ❧

"**S**o, what are you going to do? You have to do something!" Esther said.

"I don't know what to do! I wish Edward or Lewis were here. They'd know what to do!" replied Henry.

"Well, they're not here, you are, and they left you to look after things here. You can't just do nothing!"

"Esther is right, Henry," said Jenny in a more consoling voice. "Just ask yourself what your father would do."

"But it's not my land, not my money!"

"Not all of it, but some of it is yours. And if you don't do something, it'll be worth nothing," stated Esther emphatically.

Henry sat in his cabin wringing his hands, not knowing what to do. Afraid of doing something wrong, he had done nothing. Now he had to do something, but he didn't know what he should do. Make the right choice and things would be fine, make the wrong choice and…

They had been cooped up in the little Jewett fort for months now with no sign their neighbors would be able to return to their homesteads anytime soon. Yesterday, Matt Bennett had announced his intention to return east. Since his wound made it difficult for him to do the simplest of farm tasks and impossible for him to fire a gun, the frontier was no place for him and his family of small children. Now the others were talking, even Miles and Mattie, about leaving.

"Alright, I'll do something. I just hope it's the right thing." Henry then stormed out of the cabin and strode over to the awning where their neighbors had gathered, waiting on him. Esther and Jenny followed closely.

"Listen to me, all of you," Henry began, hoping he sounded confident even though he didn't feel confident. "It's understandable why Matt and his family are leaving. Matt can no longer work his place even if there were no Shawnee to threaten him, and his children are still too young to carry the load. But for the rest of you, I won't help you run away. No, I won't buy out your homesteads. That's right, if you run you will lose your land and, as there aren't any buyers for any land this far west anymore, you lose everything but what you carry with you. As it stands, your lands are worthless and I won't buy a single acre."

The crowd gathered was silent, several looking about to see the reaction of the others. They had asked, actually pressured, Henry to buy out their homesteads so they would have money to set themselves up east of the Blue Ridge. They knew Mister Bordon would show them no mercy. They both paid and occupied their lands or they forfeited them and their paid amounts back to him.

After they had absorbed what Henry was saying, he continued in a less forceful, more compassionate tone. "I know you can't work your homesteads while forced to live here. And without working your homesteads you can't make your payments. Anyone who wants to remain, I will guarantee your payments to Mister Bordon. Anyone who leaves, however, abandons his homestead and I can't, I won't, help you."

Jim Rice spoke first, looking at the plank table in front of him and not at either his neighbors or Henry. "That's fair, very fair, and I for one will take you up on your offer. We'll stay. The Jewetts have always been very good to my family and Henry's word of support is good enough for me."

"I'd feel better if the Colonel was here telling us this, that's true enough," said Tom McCrary, thoughtfully. "But I'm with Jim. My family will stay as well."

"Thank you Tom, Jim, for your confidence. I won't let you down. Now, the rest of you must make up your own minds. You leave, that's fine, but don't look to us to support you financially if you do." Henry then turned and returned to his cabin with Jenny.

As soon as Jenny closed the door, Henry sank into a chair by the fire and dropped his head into his hands. "I hope I did the right thing," he said sorrowfully.

Jenny came over and put her hands on his shoulders and she knelt in front of him. "You were magnificent, just magnificent." When there came a knock at their door, she added, "Time to put your confident face back on, darling. Are you ready?" When Henry nodded, she answered the door and let Miles and Mattie into the cabin.

"Mister Henry, we're in a little different circumstance than the others. We were given eighty acres for our service to your brother. What becomes of that land if we leave?"

"Well," Henry said, thinking hard. "It is not considered abandoned now because you live here, in reasonable proximity to the land. If you were to head back east, I would think the County Court would consider it forfeit and restore it to its previous owner or to the Crown. Of course, I'm not a lawyer or magistrate so I can't say for sure."

Miles scratched his head and looked at Mattie before responding. "Even though the Colonel isn't here, I assume we're still collecting our wages, same as before, if we stay?" Henry nodded. "Alright, then, I suppose we'll stay."

When they left, Henry let out a long breath and slumped back into his chair. "I hate this! I wish Edward were here, he'd know in an instant what to do and whether what I was doing was right or not."

Jenny was right back with him, her arm around his shoulders. "You've done fine, all of it, really. Not Edward or even your father could have done any better under these circumstances."

They sat together in their embrace for quite a while before another, softer, knock came at their door. Jenny let Esther in and the three sat at the table.

"You did really good today, Henry," Esther began. "Most of them are staying. Only the Bennetts and the Fishers have chosen to leave. The rest are staying based on your assurances. Good work, Henry."

Henry was starting to feel better about his decision and how he'd handled the little crisis. He looked again at Jenny, raised his eyebrows and nodded. Then Esther hit him with the bad news.

"I think you now need to talk to the laborers. They're as concerned as everyone else only they still think as though they are property. If you were to go to them in their cabin, I think it would go a long way in comforting them."

It never failed. Just when he thought he was finished, something else came up and he had to resume the role of leader of the little fort. Oh, how he missed his father and brothers who always kept these kinds of things off his back. Standing reluctantly, he then straightened his back and strode to the door.

Arriving at the laborers' cabin, just his presence gained him their immediate and undivided attention. "Each of you has a contract with my brother to provide seven years labor in return for his having bought your freedom." Looking around the room, he saw nods from all. "Then you must know, if you choose to leave now, and you can make that choice, you will break that contract and I'd have no choice but to return you to Mister Gladstone. I'm against it, but I don't see where I'd have any other choice open to me. Can you all understand that?"

Sam looked around before speaking up on behalf of all. "Mister Henry, your family has been very kind to us, and we all appreciate all you've done for us. It might be dangerous clear out here, what with the Shawnee and all, but at least here we're free. So if it's all the same to you, sir, we'd like to stay."

"Good, I'm very glad to hear that. And rest assured, you will continue to receive your wages, as agreed to, even if my brother isn't here."

Henry was exhausted when he returned to his cabin. He didn't know how his father had managed these kinds of decisions day after day. Esther was still sitting with Jenny when he entered and both women had a look on their faces that indicated they wanted him to tell them what happened, though were reluctant to ask. Once he reviewed what he told them, Esther rose and gave him a kiss on his cheek as she went to leave.

"You know, Henry, you're pretty amazing."

The Bennetts and Fishers left early the next morning, with the whole compound turning out to say goodbye. It was a sad departure, the little company having endured much together over the past five years. Still, none tried to talk them out of their decision. Under the circumstances, they all understood why they were leaving, even if they didn't necessarily agree. Henry asked Jim and Tom to ride along as extra protection until they made it across the ford and up to the road to Indian Trail Gap.

They remained pretty close to the fort that fall, only going out to bring in their crops and to the mill to grind their corn into meal, and then only under heavy guard. With no signs of Shawnee, Henry decided they could try to bring in some of the crops from the other homesteads, if they proceeded cautiously. This had a good effect on their neighbors. Jim and Tom even managed to bring back a few bottles of their special "medicine." Henry noticed that when they offered Mister Agner some of their product, he declined politely but firmly.

Things returned to their normal rhythms for those next several weeks, a fact Henry was quite pleased with. He was even more pleased when Edward, Lewis, and Aaron rode over the rise from the ford, taking the burden of running the place off his shoulders. As they sat in Edward's cabin catching each other up on what had happened, Henry came to the topic of their neighbors' departure and how he had handled it. He told what had happened tentatively, not knowing if Edward would approve of what he'd done or what he'd said. When he finished, he looked first to Edward, then to Lewis, then back to Edward and his brothers sat silently.

Edward broke the silence. "Well, Lewis, we could have wintered over in Williamsburg if we knew Henry had things so well in hand out here." Lewis grinned and nodded his assent. "You know, Henry, I have never doubted you and here's a great example of why. I can't say I'd have thought of as good a response as you did. I sometimes let my anger get the best of me when confronted like that. You did very well indeed. From now on, we'll leave you in charge here."

"Oh, no you don't! Next time you can take me with you and leave this all to Lewis!"

As the congratulations for Henry died down, a light knock came at the door. When Betty opened the door, Esther and Mister Agner entered, neither looking directly at the brothers gathered around Edward's table.

"So, sister, do what do we owe this interruption? Have you come to ask permission to marry?" asked Edward, a very large grin on his face.

Esther turned a bright red before sputtering, "How...who?"

"Why my dear sister, everyone in the fort has known for months! Everyone except you, that is."

❧ Chapter 46 ❧

Hannah sat in her room, too embarrassed to go down to breakfast. She had heard Lewis leave earlier, so she knew he and Edward had already started back to the frontier. Still, it didn't matter, she just couldn't face Missus Dandridge and the others after what had happened last night. She had tried so hard to make a good impression on Edward and all that effort she feared had now been for naught. Oh, what he must think of her now.

Luke failed to come home for supper the evening before so they had eaten without him. When he did come home, he reeked of tobacco and she suspected he may have been drinking. Edward had asked Luke and her to join him in the dining room and she had brought Marie with her because of the anger showing in Edward's eyes when he made the request, or, rather, the demand. When they had all arranged themselves at the table, Edward confronted Luke.

"I understand from your tutor that you regularly skip class and only do your work haphazardly, that you are basically failing."

Luke had said nothing, keeping his eyes trained down at his hands in his lap to avoid looking at either Edward or his mother. Edward then leaned forward and grinned, slapping Luke on the back and asking whether he'd bet on Colonel Byrd's horse in that afternoon's race.

Raising his head with a very pleased look on his face, "Why, sir, yes I did."

"Good for you, you picked the winner! I thought as much. So, tell me, how much did you win?"

Hannah and Marie sat dumbfounded by both the admission that Luke was betting on horse races and that Edward was taking it so well, basically praising the boy.

"I got fifteen shillings for the five I bet, sir," Luke said proudly.

"My, my, that's quite a lot of money for a young lad," Edward said as he pulled a piece of paper out of his weskit pocket and looked at it. "So you have twenty shillings in your purse, have you?"

"Well, no sir, I spent some of it already. I do have seventeen left," pulling his purse out to show Edward. "See?"

"Ah, yes, I see. It's no great fortune but it will at least start to repay your debts," he said, brandishing the paper as he snatched up the purse and its contents.

Luke had started to protest but instead of looking into eyes that a moment before had been playful, he was looking into hard, angry eyes again so he choked back his protest, his joy at winning now becoming fear.

"I paid your tuition for schooling, not horse racing, and will take this seventeen shillings as partial repayment for my money you have wasted. I have already spoken with Colonel Byrd, who happens to be an old acquaintance of mine, and you'll find any future winnings at the horse races will be held and passed to me to satisfy the remainder of your debt. Do you understand me, boy?"

Luke had been taken totally off guard. He was crushed and embarrassed in front of his mother and all he could think about was how he wanted to be somewhere, anywhere, but where he was with this hard man glaring at him as if at any moment he would reach out and snuff the life out of him.

"Luke, let me explain my purpose." Edward continued, his voice still hard but no longer loud with anger. "Your only future is through education or apprenticeship. I've continued your tuition for another year and, if you pass, you'll only owe me for the year you've thus far wasted. If it's gambling you want, Mister Anderson assures me he has need for apprentices and your mother can bond you over to him for seven years." Looking now to Hannah, "It is all arranged. All you need do is tell Mister Anderson and he'll come pick Luke up." Turning back to Luke, "That's all, boy. You can go to your room now."

After Luke had left the room, Edward gave the seventeen shillings to Hannah and advised her to put it somewhere Luke could not find it. Hannah tried to apologize but Edward cut her off with a wave of his hand. It wasn't about the money, it was about the behavior. He was not to enjoy the profits of his gambling and Edward had passed the word around to ensure the boy never collected on another winning bet.

"The boy doesn't listen to you, not at all, so there is little you can do to correct him. The best thing would be to let Mister Anderson teach him some manners and good work habits, but that would be a very hard lesson for him indeed for Mister Anderson is not a man to be trifled with. We can try one more time, but, if he doesn't come

around, I'm afraid he's heading down a steep and dangerous path."

Edward had been very brusque that night, not at
all what she had hoped for on his last night in Williamsburg. Not only was Luke ruining his life, now he was also
ruining hers. Right now, Edward was her best chance for
turning her life around and Marie had been very much encouraging the match. Now how could she ever face him
again? And it wasn't like there were other options here.
The Virginia planters had basically shunned her. Oh, they
had been polite, but she wasn't landed, didn't bring any
wealth to them, had a difficult son they'd have to deal
with, and basically had nothing going for her except her
fine appearance, so none had shown the slightest interest in her. If it wasn't for Missus Dandridge, she'd have no
social life at all.

There was a light tapping at her door and, when she
didn't respond, the door slowly opened and Marie stuck
her head in. "Hannah, are you up? You missed Edward's
departure this morning. That wasn't very wise of you."

"Oh, don't scold me, Marie! How could I have faced
him after last night? What must he think of me now?" Tears
welled up in her eyes.

Marie rushed across the room and draped a comforting arm around her friend's shoulder. "There, there,
don't you worry. Edward may be a hard man on the outside, but he's also very forgiving and even sentimental,
especially when it comes to family. If you only knew the
troubles Henry caused their father and now saw the way
Edward treats Henry as if they had always been close, like
he and Lewis have been, you'd understand."

Hannah thought for a moment, then straightened
herself in the chair and asked, "Marie, would you help me

with something this morning? I want you to go with me when I take Luke to see Mister Anderson."

"Oh, Hannah, you're not going to apprentice him out today, are you? Edward arranged for him to have another chance at school."

"No, I won't apprentice him today, but I want him to see what it would be like, for Mister Anderson to explain to him what being an apprentice to a blacksmith entails."

"But, Hannah, the forge isn't anyplace for us! I'm sure Mister Anderson would come here and do all that."

"No, it wouldn't have the same effect as Luke seeing the conditions. We don't need to go into the loft where the apprentices have their pallets, but Luke should. I feel I'm running out of chances to save him from going the way of his father and if I don't try, well, I just have to try, that's all there is to it."

Luke's eyes widened when his mother told him he'd have no time for breakfast as he had a stop to make before school. When he asked where, she told him and he turned pale, a scared look in his eyes. He knew the old Colonel would do it in a heartbeat, but never did he suspect his mother would go along with apprenticing him out. That had been his last hope, that no matter what the Colonel threatened, his mother wouldn't allow it. Now he saw he may have been wrong about how far he could push her.

Philip had wisely kept very quiet during the discussion, keeping his eyes glued to his plate and eating slowly, as if he were the only one in the room, yet hearing everything. He had tried to tell Luke earlier in the day yesterday not to go to the horse races. Edward was a man of his word and if he knew Luke was skipping class to gamble, he just might be apprenticed. Luke had just laughed off his warning, saying the old man couldn't do anything to him, his mother wouldn't allow it.

The two women followed right behind Luke as they walked the short distance from the Dandridge house to the Anderson house, behind which Mister Anderson had a large forge and blacksmithing operation. Mister Anderson saw them coming and intercepted them just inside the gate, not wishing to expose the ladies to the harsh world of the forge.

After Hannah explained her purpose, Mister Anderson got a wry smile on his face and said, if the women would just wait there, he'd be glad to show Luke what an apprenticeship with him entailed. Clamping a strong hand on Luke's shoulder, the stout blacksmith roughly guided the boy into the forge and out of sight.

"It really does smell awful, doesn't it, Hannah? Could you really put Luke here?"

"It's not a decision I'd relish, but I made up my mind this morning. He must either start mending his ways or I'll have no choice. Edward was right last night. He must either succeed through education or apprenticeship. I can't let him just continue in the ways of his father."

They were gone about half an hour and, when Mister Anderson returned, Luke had a scared, almost dazed, look on his face.

"I've explained to the boy that I'm in need of apprentices, so whenever you're ready to sign him over, ma'am, I've a place for him. I even had him pick out which of the empty pallets he'd like me to set aside for him," Mister Anderson said with a broad smile.

Marie and Hannah then marched Luke to school where Hannah had a short discussion with his tutor, trying to determine just how far behind Luke was with his studies and what he needed to do to make them up. Satisfied, they returned to Missus Dandridge's house.

That evening, as he was preparing for bed, Philip had a visit from his mother.

"You know, you really could help Luke out by being a good influence on him. You're older than he is and you could help show him how to behave better," Marie said.

"Mother, he doesn't listen to me, he thinks I'm stupid because I try to follow the rules."

"Philip, is that any way to talk about your best friend? What's gotten into you?"

"Mother, Miss Hannah is your best friend, but Luke isn't mine," he said, maybe a little too emphatically considering who he was talking to.

After fixing a hard look on him, Marie stood to leave, "Fine, don't help out. Just don't ask anyone to help you. Your Uncle Edward is trying to help, I thought the least you could do would be to help your Uncle Edward. But if you don't want to get involved..." she waved her hand and stormed out.

Philip sat alone in the room thinking how he hadn't handled that very well, not well at all. He was still sitting there, considering what he should do to sooth things over with his mother when Luke came in and flopped down on his bed across the room.

Still shaken from his experience that morning, he was also angry. "Why must that old uncle of yours meddle into my life?" he asked Philip, almost as if trying to pick a fight.

"I'm sure I have no idea. I wasn't here when you arrived in Williamsburg, when he arranged for you to go to school, so I really don't know what went on. All I do know is that he's not one to trifle with."

"Ah, he's just a tired old man. I'm not afraid of him."

"Well, maybe you should be. There are a lot of Shawnee who weren't afraid of him who will never make it back to the Ohio as a result."

"Those were just tall tales meant to amuse the women. He didn't really do all those things."

Philip fixed a hard stare on Luke before proceeding. "You've never really lived on the frontier, have you?" Luke shook his head. "Then maybe you should listen instead of talking. I can tell you that Uncle Edward did all those things, and more, and if he hasn't fully recovered from that running fight with the Shawnee, a fight that covered near fifty miles, don't let it lull you into thinking he's gone soft. He can be hard as stone when it's called for. Do you know what the Shawnee call him? No? They call him 'Great Bear.' Think about it." With that, Philip turned over to face the wall.

Luke swallowed hard before he, too, turned and tried to go to sleep.

⊗ Chapter 47 ⊗

The minister at the Timber Ridge church posted the bans announcing the marriages of Esther Jewett to Mark Agner and Rebecca Thompson to Captain Jeremiah Lewis, the date set during the Twelve Night celebrations at the Jewett fort. Lewis and Henry rode to Greenville to collect Charles and bring Ronald, Margaret, and Elam Samuel back for the ceremonies. They were joined in Greenville by Colonel Lewis and his large escort. On the way back, they stopped by Timber Ridge to add the minister to the entourage.

When they arrived at the Jewett fort, Margaret had a big grin on her face. Having the riding chair allowed her to travel some and she was really enjoying it. She had thanked Lewis and Henry over and over on the trip down and now she started her visit by thanking Edward. Ronald had insisted on bringing his ancient musket along, just in case the Shawnee were about, and Margaret got a good laugh when Edward pronounced it broken beyond repair. Then, to her surprise and horror, Edward turned to Elam.

"Elam, you claim to be a judge of firelocks. What say you take your father into the blockhouse where you'll find we're well supplied with them. They're all racked and ready for use. Look them over and pick one out for your father." Turning back to Margaret, he added, "Don't worry, Aunt Margaret, I'll teach him how to be safe with it before you head home. No sense trusting that job to Elam."

After the very festive dual wedding, Edward announced Mister and Missus Agner would have full use of Robert's cabin until such time as the Shawnee situation permitted them to build a proper home for the new couple. Edward bunked in with Lewis to allow Rebecca and Jeremiah use of his cabin. Captain and Missus Lewis departed the next day for their new home in Staunton, Fort Lewis being far too dangerous for any but soldiers these days.

Throughout the winter, everyone was keeping a close eye on Edward, limiting his activities to allow him to regain his health. The trip to and from Williamsburg so soon after his running battle with the Shawnee had set his recovery back. About all they permitted him to do, aside from eat and sleep, was to take a daily ride on his stallion for exercise and to keep up his military correspondence. At the rate military post riders were arriving, they started to regret agreeing to this condition. By the end of February, he was near fully recovered and ready to head back to Williamsburg for the spring session of the House. And then he received something in the post.

"Lewis, Henry, Esther, this came for me in today's post. Lord Loudoun has been replaced by Major General Abercromby and the Duke of Cumberland replaced by General Sir John Ligonier. Sir John may have twenty years on me but he is still probably the best officer I ever served under. And then there's news that Robert Dinwiddie has left for England to recover his health. John Blair, President of the Council and a good friend, will be Acting Lieutenant Governor until another can arrive."

"And for you, Edward?" asked Henry. "Surely they've recognized your talents and given you an important assignment."

"Well, yes and no. I have a nice note here from the Prime Minister," this announcement having an effect on those gathered, "thanking me for my thoughts on defeating the Canadas and that it is totally in concert with his own ideas. And these orders, placing me on the staff of Major General Jeffery Amherst and his expedition against Fort Louisbourg. They are sending a frigate to take me to join General Amherst. I'm to meet it in Williamsburg just after the Burgess meets."

Henry was disappointed, having for uninformed reasons expected his older brother to be promoted and given some important command. He still thought of Edward as having been somehow the confidant of the King, despite Edward's protests to the contrary.

"So, no promotion?"

"Sorry, Henry, it's worse than that. Until his promotion to Major General, Jeffery Amherst was a Lieutenant Colonel and his second in command, Brigadier General James Wolfe, was a Major. Both served under me in the late war." Edward just shook his head as he tossed the paper on the table. He was trying hard not to let slights like this bother him, though it was becoming harder with each additional slight.

Two days later, he and Aaron departed for Williamsburg and Fort Louisbourg, neither knowing when they would be able to return home but knowing it would be no time soon. Lewis had wanted to go along to visit with Marie and Philip. Under the circumstances and with

Henry's strong protests about being left alone again, he reluctantly decided to remain.

When they arrived in the Capital, everyone was talking about the changes taking place in the war against France. Colonial officers were now to rank senior to all junior ranks regardless of whether the junior officers were Colonial or Regular, only being junior to Regular officers in the same grade. And the Prime Minister, instead of demanding the support of the Colonies, was treating them more like allies and offering subsidies and other benefits for Colonial help in the war.

On his first night in the city, Edward sought out George Washington, finding him at the King's Arms Tavern in the company of Colonel William Byrd.

"Ah, there you are, George. Congratulations on filling out your regiment, and to you, Colonel Byrd, for taking command of the Second Virginia Regiment. Two full regiments led by you will have a great effect on our security and the prestige of Virginia. Now we should be able to defend the Valley properly."

"Yes, yes, but," added Colonel Byrd. "If you are successful in taking Fort Louisbourg, it will do more to defend the Valley than our two regiments. It will cut the Ohio Indians off from French guns and powder and cool their ardor for war."

The three men enjoyed an evening catching up and discussing the turn of events fostered by the surrender and subsequent resignation of the Duke of Cumberland. They finally had hope the war would end and in their favor. Edward ended the evening with an impromptu invitation for George to join him for dinner at Missus Dandridge's the following day.

Edward spent the morning locked in with the Acting Governor, though he had left specific instructions with

Aaron concerning dinner. Edward did manage to arrive ahead of George, so he was able to introduce the young Colonel to the others, their hostess, the Widow Frances Jones Dandridge; her daughter, the Widow Martha Dandridge Custis; the Widow Hannah Faircloth Davies; and his sister-in-law, Missus Marie Jewett. The dinner went very well and Edward seemed to take a special effort to encourage Martha, who he called Patsy, to talk about herself to George. This was not lost on Marie. On the contrary, she found it delightful and aided her brother-in-law wherever possible without seeming to be pushing the two together.

The next day, while still politicking for support for the Virginia regiments as the Burgess entered the Capitol for the opening session of the House, George looked Edward up and pulled him aside.

"Edward, what do you know about that delightful creature you introduced me to yesterday?"

"You mean Patsy? Well, George, I've known the Dandridge family for several years, since we first came to Virginia. They have treated me and my family very kindly. I know Patsy was married to Daniel Parke Custis, who, I'm sure you must know, left her an estate far too large for her to manage on her own."

George looked thoughtful for a moment before continuing, "So she was married to Daniel Parke Custis," emitting a low whistle. "I must confess I found her very easy to talk with and yet she had a dignified manner about her that I much admire. So, tell me, are you looking to interest her, for I wouldn't want to make advances where I'm not welcome?"

"Not at all, George, though her mother would like nothing better. I have heard Charles Carter is greatly taken with her, though he is nearly my age and hasn't made any advances as of yet."

"You're sure my calling on her would cause you no trouble?"

"Why, George, I was rather counting on it, truth be told. She's more your age than mine, just the thing you need to complete your ascent to the top of Virginia society. You can't run Mount Vernon as a bachelor forever!"

George became a regular visitor to the Dandridge house after that. He was careful to mask it as though he were visiting Edward, even though he only managed to arrive after Patsy would come to visit her mother. As the House session neared its end, Marie managed to catch Edward alone in the passage one afternoon as he was looking over the recent military dispatches just delivered to him by courier.

"Edward, it looks to me like George is interested in Patsy. Are you sure you're fine with that?"

"More than fine, and I have it on good authority that they have come to an understanding. George will be busy campaigning but, when he returns, Patsy has agreed that they be wed."

Marie fairly trembled, "Oh, that is so exciting! I'm so happy for them!"

Marie looked for Hannah, finding her alone in the parlor. "You'll never believe what I just heard! George and Patsy have an understanding and will wed after the campaigns are over this year. Do you know what this means?" Marie was nearly ready to burst.

"Does this mean Edward isn't interested in Patsy after all? But I thought…"

"Oh, no, Edward set this whole thing up. Think about it, he brought George here for dinner that first day, and he made sure Patsy talked about herself all during that dinner. Now, think back, you'll see he continued to put them together every time George came to discuss business with Edward. Oh, he is so good!"

"So, what does this mean? Or, rather, what do you think this means?"

"Silly, it means Edward is still available! It means there is a good chance you can interest him in you! Don't you see? This is perfect! You are still interested in Edward, aren't you?"

"After how he handled Luke, I am more interested than ever. He is a strong, good man and I need that, I really need that."

"Good, so we will need to convince him tonight that you're the right one for him. If we don't, he'll be off to war and who knows when he'll return. Okay, so I'm going to go think about how to make this work. Oh, I'm so excited!" With that, Marie fairly danced her way out of the parlor and up the stairs.

Hannah wrapped her arms around herself as she turned to look out the window at the spring flowers in the garden. She smiled and hummed to herself as she thought about what a change it would make in her life to wed Edward Jewett. Yes, he was older than her, though not as much older as he was with Patsy, and it was quite common for older men to marry younger women. Beyond that, she really didn't see any issues. He was tall, well formed, well educated, well spoken, and strong in character. Even though they had no understanding, just being around him when he visited always made her feel safe and secure, like there was nothing he couldn't handle.

Her thoughts were interrupted by heavy steps entering the room. Turning, she found Luke standing just inside the room, glaring angrily at her. He had grown, was now taller than she was, and his size and anger could sometimes scare her, like he was doing now.

"I heard you, mother, talking with Miss Marie. You can't do it, mother, you can't marry the Colonel. You're married to father, you're his wife, and you can't marry another."

"Luke, no one said I'm marrying Edward, but if he asks me, I will say yes. Your father is dead and I need to remarry."

"Stop saying that! You keep saying father is dead. I don't believe you! I've never believed you when you've said he's dead! He's not dead! He's out there, somewhere, looking for us!" Tears started to run down Luke's cheeks but, instead of the tears softening his mood, he seemed to become angrier.

"Stop it, Luke, your father is dead, you know he's dead. And I will marry Edward if he asks me."

"Don't say that!" Luke shouted as he stomped across the room, drawing back his fist to strike Hannah.

Hannah had nowhere to run, she was trapped against the wall, so she raised her hands and dropped her face, bracing for the blow.

❦ Chapter 48 ❦

Missus Mark Agner was content with her life. As she sat by the fire on a cool spring evening after supper had been cleared and put away, an open book in her lap, she reviewed all that had happened to bring her into her first marriage at this late point in her life. She had to admit, she had spent very nearly her entire life feeling quite content. Having not married young, as was the custom, she had remained in her father's house helping Aunt Bess, her father's favorite aunt, care for him and his household, learning a tremendous amount from that dear woman.

Lewis would always think he was the closest to their father, and, for the sons, that was undoubtedly true. But living in his house, helping to take care of him, and, after Aunt Bess passed on, keeping his house, it was Esther who really was the closest to their father. And it was Esther who was the most devastated by his passing.

While he lived, she had purpose in her life. She was his caregiver, his housekeeper, in addition to being his daughter. When he passed, Lewis had Marie to take care of him, Henry had Jenny, and Edward, well he had his servants though he could also have his pick of any widow in the Colony. Oh, she could have moved in and taken care of Edward, but Marie had come right out and said Edward would likely be taking another wife before too awfully long, and she'd be just an extra burden then. Without Robert, she lost her purpose, her reason for living, and it nearly crushed her. It probably would have had Mister Agner, as she would probably always call him, never Mark, not been there to offer her solace.

As she thought back, it was true. She had been fond of him before that, in an odd sort of way. She took to teasing him much as she did her brothers long before she had any conscious thoughts of marrying him. And that teasing had further encouraged him that she did have some feelings toward him. That encouragement had inspired him to make some changes in his life that were absolutely necessary before he could even hope of asking to court her. Those changes caused Esther to notice him more, even if they did take away some of the sources of her teasing, until she finally could see them together.

As soon as she and Mister Agner announced to her brothers their intention to wed, her brothers did the unthinkable, they stopped teasing her. The change was so sudden and so out of character, she fretted over its meaning. Did they not approve? Did they think her foolish? Finally, she'd approached her usual chief antagonist, Henry, and asked him flat out what she had done to cause them to treat her so differently. Henry made that sly smile of his and feigned ignorance at first, finally relenting when he realized she was seriously disturbed by the lack of teasing.

Her brothers, who had teased her all of her life, had decided not to do any teasing leading up to the wedding for fear it would cause her pain and possibly to even have second thoughts about marrying Mister Agner. They were determined to do nothing that might be misinterpreted as not fully supporting her decision. Of course, not teasing her at all led her to the exact same conclusion they were trying to avoid. Those brothers of hers always meant well, but one thing they had in common was their total inability to understand women. At least their hearts were in the right place.

After Robert's death, Esther had been invited to join in on the planning and discussions held almost nightly in Edward's cabin. Before, she had been represented by Robert and now she had to look after her own interests. Mister Agner would not be invited as he was an in-law, or as Henry pronounced it "out-law," and thus not a full family member when it came to discussions on lands and money. One thing Edward was intent on, that she and her brothers, not Mister Agner, would manage her portion, a portion that would not exist on paper but one she knew Edward had promised Robert he'd provide.

Esther felt much closer now to Jenny, Henry's second wife. In the weeks leading up to the wedding, it was Jenny who sat and talked with her, answering her questions, quieting her fears, and letting her know what to expect upon taking a man into her house as a husband. These were not conversations her brothers could have helped her with, though, if she had asked, Edward and Lewis would have tried to help. Henry would have just turned red and then hid from her to avoid some of the questions. No, Jenny had done everything she could to prepare Esther for the wedding and, while she was still nervous, she was nowhere near as nervous as she would have been otherwise.

And it had brought her closer to Jenny than her other sister-in-law. Esther naturally knew Marie much better than Jenny. They had grown up in the same town, Marie just a few years younger than herself, and had seen each other nearly every day after Marie married Lewis. Marie, however, was in Williamsburg now, with Philip as he went to William and Mary, so Esther didn't have her to help her prepare for her wedding, or even attend it for that matter. Had Jenny not stepped into the role, Esther wasn't sure what she would have done.

Sitting there thinking about what she and Jenny talked about brought a rosy redness to Esther's cheeks. Just at that moment, the door to the cabin banged open and Mister Agner came in carrying a load of firewood. His arrival startled her. He put the wood into the wood box, turned, and stopped, looking right at her.

"Miss Esther," as he had continued to call her, "is something wrong with you? Your face is all red!"

Putting her hands to her cheeks, Esther responded, "Oh, goodness me, I sat too close to the fire is all. I'll be alright in a moment, Mister Agner."

"You should be more careful, Miss Esther." Then, after a short pause, "I think I'll go on to bed now," he added with a yawn.

"I'm just going to read a little more before I join you, Mister Agner. You go on ahead," Esther said, almost unable to control laughter as she realized how much they sounded like an old, married couple instead of two newlyweds.

Mister Agner stopped and patted her shoulder as he went by, she patting his hand in return. Then, without another word between them, Mark Agner went on to the back corner of the cabin where curtains partitioned off what had once been Robert's bed and now was theirs.

It didn't take long after the wedding for her brothers to resume their lifelong passion for teasing her. They behaved through the wedding feast and didn't even start when she saw them the next day. Trapped inside a small overcrowded fort on the frontier during Indian troubles wasn't an ideal way to spend the early days of a marriage. How she had envied Rebecca, Jenny's daughter, whose new husband whisked her away to their new house in Staunton the day after the ceremony. That following day, however, her brothers resumed the teasing and had plenty of new ammunition to use. And, like always, she basically walked right into situations that gave them the best opportunities to tease her. One would have thought she'd have learned by now.

Now, in her fourth month of married life, things had taken on a comfortable routine. Mister Agner was very attentive to her, a kind man who only seemed to want to make her happy and content. If he did have any of the rougher tendencies common in the frontier men, he knew to keep them well hidden for fear of her brothers. Not that her brothers were prone to violence, just the opposite, but, once provoked, they would move heaven and earth to right a wrong done to a member of their family. If Mister Agner had had any doubts, just hearing the lengths Edward had gone through to return Sarah and smite the Shawnee would have given him pause. Still, she was now totally convinced that it was his nature to be gentle with her, while still capable of being rather rough with customers at the mill, especially any who tried to take advantage of him.

And Mister Agner had taken no issue with Esther participating in the "high council" of their little settlement while he remained excluded. She suspected, although couldn't prove, that Edward had explained to Mister Agner how things would work and if he couldn't accept that, he could go elsewhere, leaving Esther behind naturally. Edward must have complied with her request that he not scare Mister Agner off, because Mister Agner not only stuck around for them to be married, here he remained over three months later. With that thought, Esther closed the book she had been pretending to read, stood up, banked the fire, and followed Mister Agner to bed.

"Good morning, Missus Agner," grinned Henry as she left the cabin the next morning to go help the other women prepare and set out the communal breakfast.

Just the way he said it made her retort, "Henry, stop it! Just call me Esther like you always have, would you please?"

"Why, whatever for, Missus Agner? There wouldn't be trouble in paradise, now would there, Missus Agner?"

Realizing he was just doing this to get a rise out of her, she let it go with a smile, a flip of her head, and a "Wouldn't you just like to know!" before continuing on her way.

"Oh, don't mind him, Esther," came Jenny's voice from her cabin door as Esther walked past. "He's just feeling especially harassing this morning, what with the baby keeping us up most of the night and all."

"Is the baby still not doing well?"

"No, and I haven't any idea what's wrong with him. Betty is looking at him now to see if she knows what might be wrong. I had just shooed Henry out of the house when you ran into him. Sorry about that."

"Don't give it a thought. I know my brother and there's little he could say that would really get under my skin. You do look tired, is there anything I can do?"

"Do you think you could find Melinda Rice and ask her to come look at the baby? She also has a good knowledge of such matters."

Esther did as asked and walked with Melinda back to Henry's cabin. She then stayed, standing with an arm around Jenny as the other two women examined and quietly discussed the less than three-month-old baby laid out on the table near the fireplace.

"Well, Miss Jenny," Melinda concluded with Betty nodding. "Your little boy definitely has colic. I've never known this to be too serious, except for the parents who can't get any sleep," she said with a smile and a wink. "I'll fix up some herb tea. I've found this usually helps calm them."

"You could also try something sweet for him to suck on, maybe putting some honey on your finger. That also works in some cases," added Betty.

Jenny thanked them all for their help and sat down to try the honey suggestion while Melinda went to gather her herbs to brew the tea. Esther offered to stay with her, but Jenny told her to go have her breakfast.

After breakfast, Esther brought a plate of food back for Jenny, who had been able to quiet the baby with a combination of the honey and Melinda's tea. She then took over holding the baby upright against her shoulder, the only position he seemed to like, while Jenny tiredly ate her meal. She then stayed, holding a now sleeping baby, while Jenny laid down to get some sleep. Mister Agner brought her the book she'd been reading, so she sat by the small fire, humming softly to the baby and reading her book until the baby woke and started crying again.

"I think he's just hungry this time," Jenny said as she rose from her bed to relieve Esther of the child. "It's about his normal feeding time. I do feel a lot better, so if you want to go do your chores, I'll be alright now."

Esther gave up the chair by the fireplace and, once Jenny was seated, passed the child back to her. "What do you say I take little Isaiah with me today, then you only need worry about your two babies."

"Two babies?"

"Why, yes, little Henry and big Henry." This sent both women to laughing as little Henry quieted down and started feeding.

As Esther led Isaiah out the cabin, there was big Henry, laid out on the bench outside the door, asleep. It was just too tempting for her to pass up. Bending way over to whisper in Isaiah's ear, he listened at first, then his face lit up and he smiled a big, three-year-old smile and nodded. Dashing across the little street to where Mattie was plucking a chicken for their dinner, Esther saw him ask Mattie a question, saw Mattie look over at her, saw the recognition on her face, then saw Mattie look back to Isaiah, nod, and hand him a big wing feather.

Esther stood aside as Isaiah came back, looked to her for the nod, and then started gently tickling Henry's nose with the feather. At first, Henry just wrinkled up his face, then he swatted at his nose with his hand, finally grabbing at whatever was tickling his nose so violently that he fell off the bench. Isaiah couldn't hold his laughter in at that point, giving away that Henry was being teased.

"Isaiah, what do you think…!? Oh, is your bad, old Aunt Esther giving you ideas again? Well, shame on her," he said laughingly.

Their laughter was cut short by the sound of the alarm from the blockhouse at the far end of the street where one of the soldiers was banging the hammer against the old shovel blade.

∽ Chapter 49 ∽

Luke Davies went to strike his mother with all the force he could muster as her scream blocked out all other sound. Yet instead of feeling his fist impacting on her, he felt himself being propelled backward, lifted off his feet before slamming heavily onto the floor, flat on his back, a heavy weight in the middle of his chest. He saw stars and was gasping for air that didn't seem to fill his lungs. As his eyes cleared, he found he was looking up into two savagely bright eyes, eyes that were filled with rage. Fear gripped him as he continued to struggle to fill his lungs and squirm out from the gaze of those horrifying eyes.

"Don't move!" commanded a harsh voice, nearly choked with loathing.

Luke stopped struggling for everything but air, fearing to do otherwise would result in his death. After just a moment of lying still, Edward removed his knee from the middle of Luke's chest and stood, dragging Luke to his feet by the front of his weskit. Luke felt helpless in the powerful grip and continued to be compliant as the fear gripped his belly. He was no sooner on his feet than Edward spun him around, grabbed him hard by the back of the neck, and propelled him out into the passage. Once in the passage, the grip on his neck forced him to one side and then back, sitting him hard onto the wooden chair next to the door.

"If you so much as move, I'll finish you here and now," came a voice that could only be described as a growl. Then Luke was free, sitting perfectly still, fearing to move other than to breathe and swallow.

It only took Edward a few steps to cross the room to where Hannah remained, face in her hands, crying. "Did he hurt you?" he demanded. When only sobs answered him, he took her gently by her shoulders, turned her toward him, and, in a soothing voice, asked again, "I need to know, did he harm you, Hannah?"

Hannah shook her head before raising her face from her hands and looking up at her rescuer. "I was so afraid, just so afraid…"

Edward pulled her to his chest, patted her on the back, and assured her, "I'll deal with him. Now, you sit here until I send someone to help you." Looking up, he saw a shocked Marie in the doorway. "Good, Marie, come here and comfort your friend while I deal with the boy," almost spitting the last word out of his mouth in his disgust for who it represented.

As Marie moved to Hannah and draped an arm around her, Edward strode back out the door. "Boy, come with me!" he growled so that to do otherwise was unthinkable to Luke.

Out the back door, Edward strode through the garden to the garden shed behind, holding the door open for Luke to enter first. Slamming the door behind them, Edward turned, grabbed Luke by the shoulder, and forced him onto a barrel near the middle of the little room. For his part, Luke was so afraid he couldn't command his faculties to do anything other than to follow Edward's growled orders. He fully expected he would be beaten senseless. While he was now bigger than his mother, he was dwarfed by the tall, angry man facing him and he knew resistance would only make matters worse. Tears now started streaming down his cheeks.

Edward just glared down at him, hands on his hips, feet braced apart. After a long silence, Edward's growl resumed. Luke had to listen closely, for the words were spoken so softly they barely reached him, yet there was no mistake, these were not words of comfort. "What were you thinking, boy? What gave you the idea that striking your mother, for any reason, would be tolerated?"

"I don't know..." came the weak response.

"Why would you ever consider striking your mother?" the question more demanding this time.

"Father said..."

"Enough!" Edward roared, causing Luke to nearly topple backward off his seat, a warm wetness now filling his lap.

"You know what this means, don't you?" Edward resumed, noticing the boy's distress but not allowing it to reduce his resolve.

"Yes, sir, it means I'll be apprenticed out to Mister Anderson," came the feeble answer.

"Oh, no, boy, that's far too good for you now. No, sir, there's a Royal Frigate at Queen's wharf," the horror in the boy's face telling Edward he had Luke's full and undivided attention, as if there had been any doubts. "I'm going to give you a choice. Either I will turn you over to her Captain as a common deck hand or," pausing for effect, "you can go with me as Aaron's boy where you'll follow army discipline and do everything you're told and where I'll give Aaron a free hand to discipline your transgressions as he deems necessary. Who knows, behave and you may only have to 'kiss the Gunner's daughter' once or twice."

Luke couldn't believe he was being offered a choice. Looking back into Edward's eyes, he could see no softening, making him realize Edward considered either choice to be punishment. He gulped as he tried to grasp what "kissing the Gunner's daughter" meant.

"Sir, I think I'd rather go with you, if it's alright."

Edward grabbed the front of Luke's weskit and drew him up until they were nose to nose. After pausing while he gauged the proper level of fear in Luke's eyes, he then said, "Then back to the house," and propelled the boy toward the door of the shed.

The entire household had gathered in the passage when the two returned. The length of Luke's weskit covered the wet stain in his breeches, though he felt like they all could see it. He kept his head down, not daring look at his mother who was standing in the parlor doorway, Marie supporting her.

"Boy, get your things packed. Aaron, see he packs what he'll need for a campaign." Adding, as Luke started to climb the stairs, "And be quick about it. Aaron, when he's done take him to the frigate and get him berthed. It leaves with the night tide."

This announcement sent a new round of fear through Luke. He hesitated only a moment but knew he dared not ask so he simply quickened his pace up the stairs, Aaron right behind him.

As soon as Luke was gone, Hannah pulled from Marie's comforting hold and flung herself into Edward's arms, burying her face in his chest. "Oh, Edward, I was so scared I didn't know what to do."

Edward comforted her by patting her back again before turning her over again to Marie. "Missus Dandridge, will supper be ready soon? Ah, good. While we wait, Philip, would you join me in the parlor?"

Edward closed the door to the room behind them, closing out prying and curious eyes. When he turned back toward Philip, the rage was gone and the look was of a doting uncle toward his favorite nephew. "Have a seat. We've some things to discuss before supper and I must leave."

Pulling from his pocket a heavy purse, he handed it to Philip. "I'm going to be gone a long time, Philip, and I need you to take care of things here while I'm gone. In that purse are sufficient funds to provide for you, your mother, Sarah, and Miss Hannah for some time. Use them wisely as I know you will. Should that run out before I return, or if you need advice, go to Mister Bat. He knows to provide you advice and extra funds from my accounts, should they be needed. Do you understand what I'm saying?"

Philip nodded, too overwhelmed at the trust his uncle was placing in his hands to speak. Uncle Edward was treating him as a man, giving him responsibilities as a man. And it wasn't just for a day. He was heading off to join the army off Fort Louisbourg, so his uncle was confident enough in him to leave him in charge for quite some time.

"You're a young man now, Philip, and I realized it was about time I started treating you as one. Still, I hate to see you grow up as it may mean you'll find you have no more need for your old uncle and I'll not have you around anymore. This winter back home was very hard on us, your father and me, not having you around. No, it's a sad place without your youthful exuberance. Write to your father often and keep up with your schooling. Your professors tell me you're a fine student getting top marks, so you must know how proud of you I am. Now, if you've no questions, we best get ready for supper. I'll have to leave right after."

Not wanting to miss this opportunity alone with his uncle, Philip rose and threw his arms around Edward, burying his face in Edward's shoulder as he said his silent, heartfelt goodbyes.

While Philip and Edward were in the parlor, Hannah pulled Marie under the stairs and whispered, "How much did Edward hear before he came in on Luke and me?"

"I was with him, Hannah, and he heard it all."

"Oh, dear me, he must now think quite low of me if he heard all that. I'm so grateful he came in when he did, but you warned me not to let him know of my interest in him for fear of driving him away. Now I have gone and done just that, I fear I have ruined everything and I'm once again lost."

"Don't think too much about it, Hannah, things will work out, I know they will!" Marie comforted her friend as the door to the parlor opened and Edward and Philip came into the passage, heading toward the dining room.

It was a subdued supper that evening. They had just seated themselves when they heard Aaron and Luke come down the stairs and exit the house, not a word passing between any of them and the now outcast boy. It struck them as sad that it had come to this. He had been warned and given every opportunity to mend his ways. In the Jewett family, he had now attempted the worst offense, the most unpardonable one, and had to be removed lest he try it again.

After supper, Edward excused himself to gather his remaining belongings before leaving for the frigate that would take him north to join the rest of the army now with the fleet heading toward Fort Louisbourg. He said goodbye to each in turn, lingering longest with Sarah and Philip, before turning and stepping through the door. As he went to pull it closed behind him, he met resistance, finding Hannah following him through the doorway.

"I just couldn't let it go like that, Edward. I'm so embarrassed about what happened today," then, looking down, "and about what you heard of my intentions toward you."

Edward put his finger under her chin and raised her head so he was looking into her face. "So, you think I didn't know what you and Marie were up to? Why, Marie has made her intentions quite apparent, and you weren't exactly playing coy yourself."

"Oh, I am so sorry. I had no intention of offending you…"

"I wasn't offended, Hannah, I was flattered. But have you thought of what you'd be getting in this bargain Marie has you in? A worn out old warhorse best describes me. You should think on that while I'm gone and who knows, you might just come to your senses and run back up to Boston."

Taking his hand under her chin in both of hers, she kissed it. "I know exactly what I'd be getting Colonel Jewett, so come back if you dare, for I'll be here, waiting."

"I just bet you will be at that," Edward said before raising her hands on his, kissing them, turning, and, with that erect stride of his, walking toward Queen's Wharf and his waiting Royal Frigate.

∽ Chapter 50 ∾

Lewis had been expecting the Cherokee ever since their spring shipment of supplies had arrived along with more gifts from the Governor for the Jewetts to distribute. The Cherokee were later arriving this year than they had been last year and he had started to become concerned that something was wrong.

Sam and Jubal again saw to repositioning the awning outside the little fort so it could be used for the ceremonies that always accompanied the exchange of gifts. This year, instead of Edward, Lewis, and Robert meeting them, it was just Lewis and he was feeling rather alone. Henry would remain in charge in the blockhouse with Miles and the Sergeant.

"I'll go with you, Mister Lewis, if you'd like some company out there."

"Why, thank you, Mister Agner. I'd appreciate it very much."

In the opening speech, the Cherokee headman expressed his regret over Robert's death, a fact he already knew, and the increased respect they had for Edward, having recovered the captives and dispatched so many

Shawnee in the process, the headman putting the number above twenty. The figure somewhat surprised Lewis in spite of the tales told by Jim Rice of the running fight. As he usually did, Edward had kept the number of Shawnee slain to himself, never taking pleasure when circumstances forced him to kill. The Cherokee also informed them the Huron, Delaware, and other northern tribes of the "pays d'en haut," as the French called the northern regions, were suffering from smallpox, though the disease hadn't been reported in the Shawnee or Cherokee camps as of yet.

After Lewis thanked the Cherokee for their condolences and for not joining the French against the English, he delivered up the gifts entrusted to his care. The Cherokee were grateful, even though there weren't as many gifts as there had been the year before. Then came the anticipated question of other goods the Jewetts might have for trade, asking for guns, lead, powder, and flints as well as blankets, pots, and other, less offensive, trade goods. This year they also asked if there might be grain as their crops had been poor and the Cherokee would be hungry soon.

Surprised by the request for grain, Mark Agner signaled Lewis to step to one side, out of hearing of the Cherokee. "I do have six barrels of cornmeal, each a hundred weight. We couldn't sell them this fall. They're surplus to our needs. Four are ours and then there's one each from the Bennett and Fisher farms. We could trade or even give it to them as we've no real use for it. Better they use it than it molds on us."

Lewis thought for a moment before responding, "It wouldn't be fair to the Bennetts and Fishers to give away their property. But if we could get a reasonable price for it, we could send them the proceeds. How good are you at pricing furs?"

"I'm a fair judge of furs and what we can get for them."

"Good, you take over this part of the negotiations. We want a fair price for all, no gouging, but don't let them cheat us, either," Lewis said as he signaled for Sam to approach.

Mark explained to Sam where to find the barrels he'd set aside as surplus and for Sam to have them brought to the awning. Before turning to bring them, Sam waited for and received a nod from Lewis.

Returning to the awning, Lewis told the Cherokee they did have some cornmeal, passing the negotiations over to Mark. When the barrels were brought to the awning, Mark opened them to show the Cherokee that they were all the same and explained how much was in each barrel. The Cherokee women, who had come up when the barrels had been brought out, appeared to marvel at the quality of the milling and spoke to the headman all at the same time and in a tongue neither Lewis nor Mark could understand. Turning to Mark, the Cherokee headman made his first offer for the barrels, indicating the large stack of furs beside him.

"Mister Lewis," Mark said after he'd looked over the furs. "He's just offered us way too much, nearly triple what the cornmeal's worth even after making a good profit on it. What do I do now?"

"Nearly triple, you say? How much would be reasonable?" Mark provided the figure and Lewis thought about it for a moment. "It might come better from me. Why don't you separate out from that stack what you think is a fair price for the lot and bring them over?" he asked before turning back to the Cherokee.

When Lewis shook his head, the Cherokee headman looked crestfallen. He had basically offered up all the furs he had to trade in order to get the cornmeal. Mark had moved to the stacks of furs and was removing a little less than one third of them, setting his selection between Lewis and the Cherokee headman before signaling he was finished to Lewis.

Indicating the furs, Lewis then said, "You offered us far too much, my friend, and I won't have you cheated. This," indicating the much reduced pile of furs at their feet, "is what we think a fair price and all we ask for the cornmeal. If you agree, take it and feed your children so they may grow strong."

At first, the Cherokee headman just looked at Lewis in disbelief. He then turned and said something to his entourage Lewis couldn't understand, something that caused them to let down their stoic faces for just a moment before regaining control. The women, however, made no attempt at stoicism and their delight was clearly visible to Lewis and Mark.

Mark knocked the lids back tight on the barrels. As two Cherokee moved in to remove the first barrel, they were surprised at the weight and indicated as much to the headman. Turning to Lewis, he asked, "Do I understand these few furs," indicating the pile still between them, "for all of this meal? The barrels are very heavy and there is much meal in them."

"We take no more from you than we do from our own. The cornmeal is yours, all of it, fairly traded."

All six barrels were removed quickly, before the white settlers could change their minds, and the two parties then sat down to trade for the other goods the Jewetts had brought in just for this purpose. While they continued their tradition of not selling guns, or powder beyond what the Governor had provided, they had brought in a thousand flints and forty pounds of lead, which were well received by the Cherokee. Once again, the meadow surrounding the little fort took on a festive air and most of the settlers penned up in the little fort came out to participate in the Cherokee games while Lewis and Mark, assisted by Sam and Jubal, finished up the trading.

At the end of the trading, the Cherokee headman turned and said something to one of his assistants, who immediately ran off toward where the Cherokee had set up their camps, returning a few minutes later leading two women.

Sam and Jubal's eyes got quite large when they saw two young black women being led into the awning. Lewis and Mark were also surprised and not a little confused by the change in the routine.

"We took these two women last fall off a band of Shawnee who will never again see the Ohio country. My warriors do not want them and, as you have dark warriors," he gestured toward Sam and Jubal, "we thought you might trade for them."

Lewis thought for a moment and then pulled Mark, Sam, and Jubal aside to hear what they had to say. Listening to each in turn, he then made up his mind, sending Sam back to the fort. They remained huddled until Sam returned, at which point Lewis returned to the negotiations.

"As the Cherokee know of us, we do not buy other humans." Pausing while his words were translated to the Cherokee observers standing nearby, he noted how these words had changed the looks of hope on the young women's faces to looks of despair. "I will, however, make you a gift to thank you for returning these women who were obviously taken from the English settlements." With that, he indicated for Sam to step forward. "Please take these two fine fowlers as a token of our thanks for the safe return of these women to us."

Lewis had been very specific to Sam on which of their abundant supply of arms he was to bring. The Cherokee looked approvingly at them, seeing two fine Wilson made trade guns, polished bright and in excellent condition. Surprised and pleased at being offered guns for the women, the Cherokee headman nodded to Lewis, signaled for the women to be handed over, and then thanked Lewis for his generous gift.

Just like during their last visit, the Cherokee had venison roasting and invited everyone to attend a festive evening in their camps. Many of the settler families attended, although not Henry and Jenny, remaining back in charge at the blockhouse and watching after the small children. Even though the celebrating lasted well into the night, the Cherokee were packed and moving at sunrise the next morning, Lewis and Mark going out to see them off.

Returning to the fort, Sam and Jubal met Lewis at the gate. "Mister Lewis, what's to become of the two women you bought off the Cherokee yesterday?"

"Well, Sam, what did you learn from them about where they came from and who they belong to? You know I didn't so much buy them as simply reward the Cherokee for releasing them to us."

"They told us their master and all his people, black as well as white, were killed in the raid that captured them, that they were the only ones not killed by the Shawnee."

"The Shawnee are partial to black women," added Jubal. "Even if the Cherokee aren't."

Thinking things over and wishing Robert or Edward was here to give him advice, Lewis made his decision. "Well, they may not have a master now, or they may. I'll send a letter around and, if someone claims them, and can prove their claim, we'll have to turn them over. Until then, they'll stay with us."

"And if they're right and no one has claim to them, what happens to them then?"

"If no one has legitimate claim to them, then they're free and we'll provide papers to that effect. For now, you need to find out just where the farm was so I know where to send my letter."

Sam and Jubal broke out in big grins at this news. Thanking Lewis quickly, they couldn't wait to return to their cabin to pass along the news to their wives and the two women now in their care.

"Are you sure it was wise to give away those fowlers in return for the women?" asked Henry who had been listening to the conversation with Sam and Jubal.

"Wise, maybe not, but it just might encourage the Cherokee to help recover others captured by the Shawnee. If it does, a few fowlers are a small price to pay. Besides, it gives me some good news to pass along to the Governor. The Cherokee may not have openly joined the English cause, but, by bringing in these two women recaptured from the Shawnee, I can make a case that they are helping our war effort in fact if not in principle."

"Yes, and when you tell the Governor, tell him he owes us two fine Wilson trade guns to replaced the ones you just gave away," Henry said, grinning at his brother. "I sure hope the Cherokee never get mad at us, those were fine shooting guns!"

Lewis sent several letters out, both to the militia commanders to the south where the raid had occurred and to the county clerk to post notice at the courthouse. After six weeks passed, he received a letter from one of the militia commanders confirming the raid and that the entire family, slaves and all, had indeed been slaughtered.

The county clerk told him the estate had been settled and all creditors satisfied.

Sam and Jubal thought this excellent news even when Lewis cautioned them it wasn't over yet. Knowing the family name, he now wrote to Charles County, Virginia, where the family had originated, asking the county clerk for his help in determining if there were any surviving family.

The whole time they waited, summer work progressed as normal. Sam and Jubal had set up a saw pit and the laborers began sawing the timbers they'd been cutting over the winters into boards for eventual use in building houses and barns. The two young women, both maidens in their late teens, worked hard alongside Rachael and Sally, preparing meals, hauling in hay, and mending clothes. Watching things, Lewis began to hope there were no claims on these women as a few of the other laborers were quite taken by them. If they were able to remain, Lewis thought, there might be a couple of weddings soon after they received their papers.

Charles finished his schooling at the Augusta Academy by mid-summer and Henry rode up to bring him home. Returning with the post, having relieved the post rider from making the trip so far south in these unsettled times, they brought with them a letter for Lewis from the Clerk of Charles County.

∽ Chapter 51 ∽

Edward stood on the frigate's quarterdeck, enjoying the warm spring air. He had spent their two weeks at sea studying the task he was to assist with, the capture of Fort Louisbourg, and of the forces available for that attack. At fourteen regular battalions, plus five companies of American rangers and a siege train of artillery, it was a formidable force raised to meet a formidable task.

"Colonel, excuse me for interrupting you, sir," said Captain Lawton. "I am but a Commander and, out of deference to your rank and seniority, sir, I have held my tongue. But, sir, I am Captain of one of His Majesty's Frigates and must maintain discipline on my ship."

A bit perplexed, Edward responded as best he could, "Of course, sir, and I am but a passenger on your ship. So, tell me, what have I done to cause you such agitation?"

"That Davies boy, he's been gambling with the cabin boys and powder monkeys. The Gunner caught them the first time and now the Master's Mate finds them at it again. Sir, I can't have that on my ship. It'll work to undermine discipline."

"Quite right you are, Captain. And what is the Navy's cure for gambling?"

"Well," Captain Lawton continued, somewhat caught off guard by how easy the Colonel had taken the news. "If he were a common deck hand, he'd be flogged. As he's not and, as the penalty for the other boys he's been caught with is less, I'd be asking your permission for him to join his mates in kissing the Gunner's daughter."

"Naturally, Captain, while we are guests on your ship, we must abide by your rules and regulations. Where we fail to do so, you are well within your rights to execute the punishment prescribed." Edward bowed slightly to Commander Lawton, indicating his acceptance of the Captain's proposed punishment.

Later that day, all hands were called to mid ship to witness punishment. Six young men, Luke Davies included, were lashed by their arms to the front wheels of a ship's gun and their ankles to the rear wheels, leaving their faces against the metal barrel and their posteriors prominently in the air. While stripped of their jackets, they otherwise retained their clothing. After the Ship's Master read the charges, the Master's Mate administered a dozen lashes with a knotted rope to each of the presented posteriors in turn. After receiving equal measures of pain and humiliation, the boys remained tied to the guns until the ship's company had been dismissed, at which time they were freed and ordered to resume their normal duties.

Edward wasn't sure Luke had taken the message to heart, so several days later, after a common deck hand was flogged for stealing, Edward sent for Luke. Seated in the main cabin Commander Lawton had vacated for his guest, Edward allowed Luke to remain standing when Aaron brought the boy in.

"I've asked to see you to impress upon you what will happen to you should there be any further issues with your behavior either on board this ship or while in my service. Tell me, what did you think of the flogging you witnessed this morning?"

"It was ghastly, sir," stammered Luke, still pale and trembling from witnessing his first flogging.

"Precisely. You realize, because of your age and that you have already had the pleasure of kissing the Gunner's daughter, should you be caught gambling again, or any other serious infraction of ship's discipline, you will be flogged, just like that man this morning." The fearful look in Luke's eyes told Edward he had made the impression he had hoped for. "I just wanted to be clear on how things stood."

The rest of the voyage proved uneventful as Luke seemed to have learned a lesson, at least for the time being. Joining the fleet, Edward transferred from the frigate, joining Major General Amherst and his staff on the ship-of-the-line he used as his headquarters.

"Colonel, it is good to see you again. It has been a long time since I served as your quartermaster. And I'm sure you remember Wolfe here. Wasn't he our commissary then?"

"General, it is good of you to remember me."

"Yes, well it is awkward, even if you're too polite to say so. And you realize our promotions are good in the Americas only, so were we to sail for England today, when we arrived, you would still be the senior Colonel in His Majesty's service and I would be but a Lieutenant Colonel," General Amherst spit out, not bothering to hide his feelings on having received a promotion so limited in scope.

Rather taken aback by the uncharacteristic outburst, Edward looked to Major, now Brigadier General James Wolfe, twenty-seven years his junior. General Wolfe gave a slight shake of his head, indicating for Edward to let matters drop, advice he readily took. After a few moments of silence while General Amherst seemed to compose his thoughts, the three continued.

"Colonel, I asked Lord Ligonier for your services as you've actually been to Cape Breton Island, helping to capture Fort Louisbourg once. What can you tell us about it?"

The next several hours were spent in discussions about what they faced. Actually, General Amherst asked questions and Edward provided what answers he could, always stating that a lot could have changed in the thirteen years since the English had last seized the island from the French. The General gave no indication to either Edward or General Wolfe what his plans were, concluding simply that they were both invited to join him, along with his other two Brigadiers, for dinner.

"I find him difficult," General Wolfe confided in Edward as he showed the Colonel to his quarters. "He tells me nothing, just asking question after question. I know he is formulating plans, but he won't communicate them to me. I find it frustrating."

"Be patient, General, for it is a virtue," advised Edward.

That afternoon, Edward met Brigadier Generals Lawrance and Whitmore, two young officers suddenly commanding several levels above any of their previous experience. With the exception of General Amherst, they were an amicable group and Edward was struck with the deference they showed him, more than they showed to the other Colonels who were, like Edward, previously senior to them.

As they approached the island, General Amherst gathered his Generals and announced his plan for landing in three groups along the southern shore and in a small cove, Gabarus Bay, to the west of the city. There was no room for discussion so Edward and the three Brigadiers simply looked over the plans, learning their responsibilities. The first ashore was to be General Wolfe, landing in Gabarus Bay and furthest from the fort. After securing their landing, they would turn east to support the landings by the other two groups.

"I'll go ashore with General Wolfe, then, where my previous experience might be of some use," Edward announced more than asked, receiving a nod from General Amherst.

Later, bobbing in their heavily loaded launch just beyond the surf line and watching the breakers beat against the shore, a shore clearly lined with French breastworks, General Wolfe was no longer feeling confident in his Commander's plan of attack and Edward was fighting off feelings of seasickness.

"Once we get into the surf, there's no turning back. To try to turn would cause us to capsize or swamp. This is ill-advised, Colonel, don't you agree?"

"My opinion hasn't been sought until this moment, General, but, now that it is, I must agree. There are better places to come ashore than here, in this surf and under fire."

"Good, I'm calling it off." Turning to his aide, General Wolfe had the word passed to return to the transports.

As their launch had fairly completed the turn, Edward grabbed General Wolfe's elbow and, pointing, said,

"General, we have a problem. One launch has gone forward and is now in the surf!"

Seeing the subject launch was already past the point of no return, General Wolfe stomped his foot and cursed before countermanding his order to return to the transports. He then had his launch turned back toward the beach and directed the Navy coxswain to steer a course toward the hapless launch now drawing fire from the shoreline.

They were helpless on their run through the surf. All of their muskets were empty, though that was of little import as the surf's spray would have rendered them useless had they been loaded. As soon as the bottom scraped against sand, General Wolfe was shouting for everyone to get out and form on the sand. His four battalions had barely formed when he ordered a "Charge Bayonets" to clear the nearest breastworks and secure the beach. The French proved all too accommodating and, rather than stand in their protected positions, they decamped quickly for the protection of the fort. Still, the British had suffered over a hundred casualties in the few minutes it took to reach the shoreline and form.

"We were fortunate, General, very fortunate the French didn't choose to make a stand here on this narrow beach."

"Yes, Colonel, we were most fortunate indeed. What was that you used to tell us junior officers, wasn't it something about how you'd rather be lucky than good?"

Edward chuckled, "Yes, that's it precisely. Maybe now you're starting to understand what I meant."

"I am at that, Colonel. I am at that!"

Once ashore, the classic siege warfare so common in Europe began. The English dug, and dug, and dug through the hard, rocky soil, moving ever slowly closer to the two landside bastions that were the key to the city's defense. Once they had moved close enough, they began to rain heated cannonballs down on the city and the French fleet completely blockaded in the harbor. In just one night, July 21st, after six weeks of siege warfare, three of the five French ships-of-the-line were destroyed by the bombardment, the final two falling to British sailors using the cover of fog on July 25th to enter the harbor and board them.

With just four working guns left, the French Governor sought terms of surrender, finally lowering his flag on July 28th. Edward found the terms given the French to be excessively harsh.

"General Amherst, I must protest. It is customary to grant favorable terms when the adversary has fought with such gallantry."

"Colonel, this is a new war, ever since the slaughter of our surrendered forces at Fort William Henry. I am simply complying with my orders. The garrison will be made prisoners of war and the civilians, both of Cape Breton and Saint Jean Islands, will be deported back to France. I have no option."

Edward nodded his assent, not trusting his tongue to be as subordinate as he needed it to be and not wanting his commanding General's censor. It was General Wolfe who came to his quarters later to soothe the old Colonel's feelings of honor. General Wolfe made it clear, however, that he had come not on his own, having been asked by General Amherst, who fully understood Edward's feelings, to come console the old warrior.

"I'm befuddled, gentlemen, and I don't mind admitting it," General Amherst stated the next day at his staff meeting. "We invested Fort Louisbourg for six weeks, six weeks, and the French sent no relief. They didn't even make an attempt! My question is why, why allow your most important fort, the one controlling your only line of supply from France to Quebec, to fall without attempting a relief?"

The gathered officers muttered but none really had any opinion to express, so the meeting just floated aimlessly for several minutes. All knew two convoys had been intercepted in European waters before the English had even arrived, something that added to the muttering. Edward wasn't muttering, he was looking at the map, a map that showed western Europe and the eastern Americas, looking and thinking. When the younger men noticed his studied look, they fell silent, waiting for Edward to speak. Finally noticing this, Edward cleared his throat.

"It is my humble opinion the French have decided to focus their resources on the Continent, leaving the Canadas to fend for themselves. We, on the other hand, have applied our efforts to the Canadas. We have caught them in a grand miscalculation."

Intrigued, General Amherst leaned forward, saying, "Go on, Colonel."

"Well, it is only my opinion, mind you, but, if I were the French, after having humiliated the Duke of Cumberland last fall, I'd fully expect the English to strike back at them in Europe, the scene of our humiliation. I would therefore need to husband my strength, keep it close, in Europe, and let the Canadas fend for themselves. They have, after all, done an admirable job of it thus far. I think the convoys intercepted this spring were the only ones intended for New France. No more will be sent."

General Amherst thought several minutes before stating his opinion, which was nothing more than an agreement with Edward's. Amending this to his announcement on the taking of Fort Louisbourg, General Amherst then dispatched his brother, Captain William Amherst, to take word of their victory back to London while he set about the job of transferring his prisoners to England and the civilians to France.

Late July and early August in these northern reaches marked the end of the military campaigning season, so Edward went about the task of quartering the British troops for winter, lying in adequate supplies, and repairing the fort against any French attempt, no matter how unlikely, to regain possession. He was ready to return home, only he didn't dare ask for leave until offered by his commanding general. When he considered how much time he'd been able to spend with his family while still drawing active pay, he knew he had been most fortunate already.

A summons in late October amid city bells ringing and the fleet firing salutes brought the senior staff together in General Amherst's quarters.

"Gentlemen, it is with pleasure I announce General Bradstreet's success in taking Fort Frontenac at the other end of the Saint Lawrence, on Lake Ontario. We now hold both ends of this vital waterway and can starve the good Marquis's army!"

After the cheers had died down, General Amherst made the second announcement. He had been promoted to command all British forces in the Americas, replacing Major General Abercromby who had failed before General the Marquis de Montcalm that summer.

As the celebrating continued, Edward found himself standing next to General Amherst. "Edward, I'm rather surprised you haven't yet petitioned me for leave." Edward just shrugged and nodded. "There's really nothing more for you to do here. Why don't you take one of the next ships heading south and go see your family? I'll call for you in Williamsburg in time for next year's campaign."

∞ Chapter 52 ∞

Philip sat huddled under a too small rock ledge near the top of Indian Trail Gap as the summer thunderstorm roared all around him. Remembering his experience on this same trail five years earlier, he had wisely chosen to take shelter and wait out the storm rather than risk being swept off the trail again. He had spent the previous night with Mister Gladstone, who had been most gracious once he realized who the young man was standing at his door. Mister Gladstone had hired out some of his slaves as laborers to the Jewett family, laborers Philip's uncle had eventually purchased and freed.

The rain was a warm rain, the kind that got you wet but didn't cool you off on a hot summer's day. It had come up quickly from the southeast and was not letting up. Shrugging under his oiled cape, Philip decided he would remain where he was for the night and start again early the next morning. Trying to calculate his distance from home, he thought he could make the little fort late the next day if he got an early start and the storm didn't wash out the trail too badly.

Having made his decision, he pulled his hat down tight and ventured out into the downpour to unsaddle his horse and bring the rest of his gear into his small shelter. He left the horse tied and hobbled just outside his little shelter even though there wasn't too much fodder. When the rain let up, he promised himself, he'd give the horse some grain to tide him over until morning. What Philip didn't want was for the horse to wander and cause them to get a late start while he searched the mountainside for him.

He must have dozed off sometime during the storm. Something woke him with a start only he wasn't sure what it was. He could hear his horse stamping and moving nervously nearby but it was too dark to see anything, even though the rain had stopped. He sat still, listening to the horse and trying to hear beyond these immediate sounds to determine what was making the horse so nervous. As he listened, he wiped the damp powder out of the pan of his gun and poured fresh in its place, all by feel as Uncle Edward had taught them to do what now seemed a life-time ago. He only hoped the dampness hadn't extended into his main powder charge for, if it had, his gun would be no better than a club.

Hearing Philip moving about had comforted his horse and it settled down, still nervous but now standing quietly. That allowed Philip to better hear what was going on around him. That's when he heard horses' hooves on the trail moving toward him. He listened hard, trying to make out anything else that would tell him why someone would be out on the trail in the dark. He could tell when they made the switchback because one of the horses slipped and the rider cursed.

"Mose, are you sure that kid is worth this? I can hardly see the trail," the voice came to Philip from close by.

"You saw how he was dressed. Traveling alone like that, if he doesn't have a fat purse on him, why, I'll eat my hat, I will. Now, press on. There are some large rock ledges just up a piece. I'll venture we'll see his fire at the mouth of one of them."

Philip prayed his horse stayed quiet as the sounds from the trail started to pull further away. There were more sounds of hooves on stone and snapping branches as they first moved off far enough to be almost out of hearing and then started moving back toward Philip, only higher up this time as they worked past the next switchback. Reaching into his pocket, Philip took out the green apple he'd picked that morning and held it out toward where he knew his horse to be. The animal sniffed the familiar fruit, then took it and noisily chomped it. As noisy as it sounded to Philip, he also knew his horse was now calmer and standing still, reducing the chance he'd be discovered.

Settling back against the rock, he started thinking. Now what? There were two men between him and home, looking to relieve him of the fat purse he didn't have, not that he could convince them of that. And there wasn't but one way to travel and that was this trail through the gap. If he got off the trail, there were steep drops that neither he nor his horse could traverse. No, he'd have to keep to the trail and either go forward, into their waiting arms, or turn back down the trail, maybe returning to Mister Gladstone's. And then what? He didn't know. What he did know was he'd better get some sleep for tomorrow was likely to be a difficult day.

When he next woke, the clouds had cleared off to reveal a nice moon that allowed him to see a short distance. Feeling sufficiently rested, he quietly saddled his horse, gathered up his gear, and mounted. Heading up the trail, he kept his gun ready while giving his horse his head.

Although going very slowly, the horse was picking his own way and making very little noise in the process. Up the first switchback, there was more noise than Philip had hoped for, so he paused and allowed the woods to return to their peaceful slumber. He hoped someone listening would think it no more than a deer in the woods.

He continued on, moving, stopping, waiting, listening, and making very slow progress. With each step his horse took, however, he knew he was closer to facing the two men looking to do him harm. As he rode, he looked as far ahead as the moonlight allowed, continuously sniffed the air, and listened to the night sounds of the woods for anything unusual.

Starting the descent, Philip's horse stopped suddenly, pricking its ears and sniffing the air. Now Philip used all his concentration as he tried to detect whatever it was his horse sensed. At first, he could detect nothing, but, as they sat there, he finally caught the faintest whiff of wood smoke. Nothing distinct, just one whiff and it was gone. There was still no sign of the coming dawn, so Philip urged his horse to move on. Every few steps, he'd halt and strain his senses to determine where his adversaries were. He smelled the wood smoke more frequently now, telling him he was approaching where they had made camp and where they likely would still be.

Rounding a bend, Philip's horse stopped and shied. Philip could make out the very dim glow of a campfire off the trail ahead, ever so faintly illuminating the underside of a rock ledge. Taking careful stock of the situation, he realized it was still too dark to even think about cutting directly down the mountain and the camp was at the next switchback, meaning he would have to slow to change direction right in front of the men he was trying to avoid.

Having made up his mind, Philip slung his gun across his back before urging his horse forward again. Moving slowly, cautiously, and quietly, he made it all the way to the switchback without being challenged. As his horse turned to descend the switchback, when they presented their full flank toward the camp, there came a shout from under the rock ledge and Philip spurred his horse. Just as the animal leaped forward, a shot rang out from the camp, followed quickly by a second.

Philip felt the second ball pass close, too close, as he struggled to keep his horse under control. The next turn in the trail wasn't a true switchback, turning to continue on down the slope rather than cutting back almost on itself. Even though the turn wasn't as sharp, Philip's horse slipped as he negotiated the turn, nearly spilling them both down the trail.

As they went down, a third shot rang out, the ball lifting the hat off Philip's head. As quick as that, the horse regained its feet and they went charging down the trail. After a few more twists and turns, Philip felt confident enough to ease their gait a bit and proceed at a hurried, not breakneck, pace.

Now with some time to think about what just happened, a cold sweat trickled down Philip's back. Had his horse not slipped, the ball that took off his hat would have been right through is head. That was just too close. No, when his father asked where his hat was, he'd tell the truth, that he had lost it getting away from the two would be robbers, only he'd leave out the part about how the ball had contributed to its loss.

He put as much distance between him and the robbers as he could before he needed to ease back and give his horse a rest. Now walking and leading his horse, he kept listening to his back trail for any sign of a pursuit.

He thought he'd be fine as they would need to saddle up before starting after him. As soon as he felt the horse had recovered sufficiently, he remounted and continued on at a brisk pace, heading for the ford across the North River and home.

The trail on this side of the Blue Ridge was dry, the Ridge having held the rain back to the eastern slope and summit. That gave Philip an idea. When he reached the cutoff to their ford, he instead continued on toward the South River ford and the Virginia Road beyond. Then, once in the South River, he turned and followed it south before climbing its banks and making his way through the woods bordering the South and then North Rivers. He hoped this ruse would have his would be robbers thinking he was heading toward the Virginia Road and throw them off his trail.

Where the North River passed closest to the trail, he pulled up short behind some laurels, hearing riders coming fast on the trail. As he hoped, they continued along toward the South River ford. Waiting for them to pass, he moved out onto the trail again and rode hard to the cutoff, turning toward the North River ford and the trail home.

His horse fairly spent, he was walking as he cleared the rise and the little fort he called home came into view. The sound of the alarm carried to him and he saw people scurrying around, heading inside the gates that were soon shut tight. He waved both his hands over his head as a signal, knowing there were now many eyes on him. How he missed the feelings of danger while safe in school in Williamsburg. It was exhilarating.

When he finally made it to the gate, his father was there to greet him with a big hug before the questions began.

"What are you doing here, Philip? Has something happened to your mother or Uncle Edward?" Lewis asked as he tried to reason why his son had made the long trip, alone. Surely it indicated something dire had happened.

"Nothing like that, father. I missed you is all. You didn't come with Uncle Edward in the spring so I decided I'd come to you when school let out."

Lewis looked at his son in disbelief. "You mean you hazarded this trip alone just because you were homesick? Have you lost your mind? And why did your mother agree to it?"

"Mother, agree? Oh, well, you see, I didn't exactly ask. I did leave her a note, and would have asked had she been up when I left, but you know how she tends to sleep in when no one gets her up. So, as she wasn't up, I decided to get an early start anyway."

Realizing how Philip had essentially run away from his mother and made a hazardous trip the entire width of the Colony, Lewis began to feel his anger rising. Luckily for Philip, Esther chose this time to make her appearance and her greeting, followed by that of the other members of the little community, forestalling Lewis acting on his anger.

Philip learned how their neighbors remained basically living at the little fort, going to their homesteads only in groups to plant or tend crops now that all the livestock had been moved close to the fort. While he knew of his aunt's marriage, he had missed the ceremony and now found seeing her with Mark Agner a bit odd, almost too much for him to understand. Charles was also home from Augusta Academy and shared with Philip some stories about the Samuels and how they were faring. And Philip had a fair share of questions to answer himself, as his family and friends satisfied their curiosity over his sudden arrival.

Henry looked hard at Lewis when Philip told of his encounter with the two would be robbers on the trail. He wondered if they should send a patrol out to pick those two up. Lewis seemed to understand what he was thinking, however, and gave a quick shake of his head.

Lewis stayed to one side during all of this, remaining close but not interfering as he listened to everyone. Finally Philip's questions of the family and their questions of him started to die down and Lewis inserted himself into one of the pauses.

"Now that you've said your hellos to everyone, I think it's time we had a little talk, in private."

⌒ Chapter 53 ⌒

Edward was not especially enjoying his trip south. True, Major General Amherst had offered for him to accompany him as the General moved his command from Fort Louisbourg to New York. And he had even invited him to share the great cabin on the ship-of-the-line, the best accommodations on the ship. General Amherst also treated Edward far better than he did the other Colonels accompanying him south. At least he talked to Edward instead of ignoring him. He seemed almost intimidated by the older men, like he feared showing any weakness now that he had been promoted ahead of them. Still, the General was difficult, even more so since receiving the top command in the Americas, and that did not make for an easy voyage.

"Relax, Colonel, I'm sure Brigadier Wolfe will be successful in gaining you a promotion. You served with Lord Ligonier in the late war and I'm sure he'll remember you fondly."

"General, you misunderstand. I serve the King at his pleasure and General Wolfe's intent to seek a promotion for me is his own idea, not at my request."

After an awkward pause, General Amherst continued. "Well, yes, I see what you mean. Actually, I believe you would have received a promotion long before now had you not been a Colonial," he said the word as if it were somehow an insult to be a Colonial. "Pity, for you really are quite good. Had you commanded instead of General Braddock, I daresay things would have worked out quite differently."

"Thank you, General, for your confidence in my abilities." After pausing to choose his words carefully, Edward continued. "If you could see Philadelphia, General, I think you would begin to understand the resourcefulness of us Colonials and that we aren't without merit."

"Why do you recommend Philadelphia and not Williamsburg in your own Colony, or Boston, or New York?"

"It is little known in England or within the army but Philadelphia is second only to London in size in the whole Empire. It only lacks the age and the stone palaces and cathedrals, being made mostly of brick and frame for the lack of suitable quarries, to rival London's grandeur."

"So I take it you've visited Philadelphia."

"Yes, I have an acquaintance, Doctor Benjamin Franklin, who is one of that city's leading citizens."

"I have heard of this Benjamin Franklin. Let me see," the General ruffled through some papers in his field desk. "Yes, here it is, a pamphlet titled 'The Way to Wealth.' I found it quaint and humorous, though hardly intellectual."

"Yes, quaint is a good description of Doctor Franklin. It is his way of putting one at ease. But don't be fooled, he has a quick mind, one of the finest I've found, and a match for any I met in London. Can you honestly say some of the sayings Doctor Franklin used to illustrate his points haven't stuck in your mind?"

General Amherst would not concede the point, naturally, so, to end the awkward silence that followed, Edward asked, "Would it inconvenience you if we made for Boston? My young aide has family there. I would then find my own way to Williamsburg."

"Yes, Brigadier Whitmore mentioned your junior aide to me. I'll ask the Captain to make for Boston. But once you make it home, don't stray too far from Williamsburg, Colonel. I'm not sure when I'll need to send for you, though I can't imagine I'll have the time to go looking all over the Colonies for you."

Edward, Aaron, and Luke spent barely a day and a night in Boston before Edward had them on their way again. Captain Faircloth offered Edward use of one of his ships and Edward was most pleased to learn he would once again travel with his old family friend, Captain Cole. They first stopped in New York, again for just a day and a night, before proceeding on to Williamsburg.

"You know, Colonel, I've been ferrying these Regulars around through two wars now and I must tell you, this new crop is a far cry from those of fifteen years ago. Why, they have absolutely no respect for anyone not born in England or Scotland."

"I've felt that sting more than once lately, Captain Cole. There is a contempt there that I'm not comfortable with. I think they are selling our kind short."

"I know they are, Colonel, and mark my words, it can only lead to trouble."

Edward nodded, thinking about how the senior officers differed so much from those he was accustomed to in the late war. Confidence was one thing, arrogance another altogether.

Making Williamsburg's Capitol Landing, Edward thanked his friend before heading into town. Even Williamsburg had changed during the course of the war. His friend, Robert Dinwiddie, had worn out his health leading the Colony through the dark days of the war and now was gone. John Blair was the acting Governor in the spring when Edward was last there before joining the Louisbourg expedition. Now there was another at the Governor's Palace, Francis Fauquier, Lieutenant Governor under Lord Loudoun. Lord Loudoun, Edward suspected, would follow the tradition of most appointed Governors and never set foot in Virginia himself, leaving that to their Lieutenants. No, things had surely changed.

Not yet feeling ready to introduce himself to the new Lieutenant Governor and start the process of getting to know him, Edward continued on past where the Palace Green crossed the Duke of Gloucester Street. Passing through a gate, he was surprised at the sight before him.

"Imagine my surprise to find my whole family here waiting for me," Edward said coming up behind the little group.

Lewis, Henry, Esther, Sarah, Philip, and Charles at first stared, not believing their eyes, before they all gathered around the old warrior, hugging him and asking questions one on top of another.

"Please, please, remember where you are. First allow me to pay my respects to Aunt Bess. We can get caught up after that."

They all turned back toward the small grave with simple gravestone, locked arm in arm, heads bowed, as they remembered this special woman.

After leaving the Presbyterian Cemetery, Lewis was the first to break the respectful silence. "We were afraid our letter wouldn't reach you in time, let alone give you the opportunity to make it back. How ever did you do it?"

"It's magic," Edward responded, a sparkle in his eye and a pause for his words to take effect before he continued. "You see, your letter didn't reach me and I have no idea what has befallen our home to drive all of you back here."

Sarah, who was at Edward's side and had not let go of his arm since he joined them, blushed before telling him, "The worst of all tragedies, uncle. I am to be married to Bat in three days time."

Edward stopped, a broad grin on his face, as he turned and congratulated his niece. Her blush deepened as he kissed her cheek and commented on how he hoped Bat deserved such a fine prize. "I must speak to him first thing and let him know what will befall him should he ever so much as think of treating you badly."

"Ah, yes, that would be your famous Jewett warning to all suitors! Now, don't be scaring off Bat Dandridge or Sarah might end up waiting as long as I had to before marrying!" joked Esther.

"And where is that new brother-in-law of mine? Don't tell me you've run him off with your poker already!" he asked, laughing.

"Oh, he's back minding the fort with Miles. Besides, he's afraid if he runs off, you'll come hunt him down, so I think he's going to stick," Esther retorted, joining into the general laughter.

Edward looked around before asking his next question. "Is it wise for all of us to be away from the fort?"

"Haven't you heard?" asked Lewis. "Well, I guess you haven't! The Pennsylvania Quakers have concluded a peace treaty with Ohio Indians, led by the Delaware Chief, Teedyuscung, back in August. They've abandoned their alliance with France and made a separate peace with us!

We're still on guard, but our neighbors have moved home and things are looking much more normal in our district."

"That is good news!"

"Yes," added Henry. "And the whipsaw has been working day and night as we turn out lumber to start building regular houses once you return."

"I wish I could be there to see it," mused Sarah distractedly.

"What, and give up your plantation here?" laughed Philip, finally finding a way to get into the conversation. "I doubt that very much!"

Marie and Hannah met the happy group in front of Missus Dandridge's house on the Duke of Gloucester Street. Marie thought she saw Edward walk past the house earlier, only doubted herself, not for once thinking he'd actually be able to make the wedding. Yet here he was.

Dinner was just being put on the table when they entered the house. It was a lively meal, lots of laughter as they caught each other up on events.

"Philip did what!? What were you thinking, riding all that way, alone?" asked Edward, turning from Lewis to Philip.

"I know, I know. Believe me, I've heard it from father and then, when I returned here to start the next term, I heard about it again from mother. Don't get that started again, now that they seem to have forgotten!" Philip said only half jokingly.

As the meal ended, Edward turned to Hannah and asked her to join him in the garden. Hannah's heart leaped at the invitation. Although the trees were bare and flowers long gone, the boxwoods remained green and fragrant on this sunny, mild December day.

"Hannah, I asked you out here to speak with you in private, about Luke."

"I dared not ask when he didn't return with you," she said, tears starting to well up in her eyes. It was not the subject she was hoping for, instead being the one she dreaded. "I have been tormented fearing he would come to harm and it would be my fault." Squaring her shoulders and dropping her face, she continued, "I'm ready, how did it happen?"

"Oh, no, that isn't it at all. Luke is fine, or was fine last I saw him, and he sent you this letter." Edward took the sealed letter from his pocket and handed it to Hannah. "He learned some hard lessons, it's true, but learn them he did. He actually came to like the army. That's what his letter will tell you. At his request, I found him a position as an assistant clerk for one of the Brigades."

"Then he's not…"

"Oh, no, he's fine. What's more, I stopped in Boston and spoke with your father, about Luke, to get his blessing for Luke to serve with the army. He agreed immediately. I don't think they will ever be close, though I think your son made a favorable impression on Captain Faircloth on this visit."

"You took him to see father?" Hannah asked, surprise and worry both showing on her face.

"Yes, then I stopped in New York and put him on a supply ship bound back to Fort Louisbourg. He will remain with the Brigade of Brigadier General Whitmore and move with that unit when the campaign opens in the spring."

"So, as a clerk, he won't be in any danger?"

"He won't be in the front lines, if that's what you're asking. As for danger, he'll be in as much as he makes for himself. I know General Whitmore well, he is a stern taskmaster and Luke will learn a lot from this experience. But he will also be well looked after, as a personal favor to me. He has learned your father and I weren't just being overly harsh with him, that perhaps his father had set some false impressions on him, and that his behavior can work to his advantage, or not. He's changed a lot these eight months."

Hannah looked first at the letter in her hands, then up at Edward, placing one hand on his arm. "Thank you, Edward, thank you for everything." And then Edward was gone, leaving her alone with the letter.

⬟ Chapter 54 ⬟

It was a mild December day, a perfect day for a wedding. Patsy Custis had offered to host the wedding in the parlor of her Williamsburg house, locally known as "Six Chimneys," and Bat and Sarah had gladly accepted. It was just family and, on Bat's side, a few good friends in attendance. The Jewett family was there in force, the new patriarch Edward, Lewis and Marie, proud father Henry and stepmother Jenny, Esther, Philip, and Charles. Lewis stood to one side, looking at the gathering and thinking how pleased Robert would have been to see the whole family gathered for this occasion. Even though it meant a long trip, it would have been something he would have insisted on. His eyes misted as he thought to himself that Robert and Aunt Bess were here, how he clearly felt their presence.

Sarah was radiant as a bride should be and Bat looked suitably impressed when she made her entrance. Edward had held his tongue when informed it would be a Church of England ceremony. He would have preferred a simple Presbyterian wedding but knew the Dandridges belonged to the Established Church, as did most of the eastern planters. By law they had to, or at least appear to, support and belong. They enjoyed more freedom on the frontier where the Presbyterian Church predominated and one could ride all day and not find a member of the Established Church, only Dissenters, as the law referred to Presbyterians.

The newlyweds spent their first night at Six Chimneys and enjoyed another festive round of meals and receiving guests who were not at the wedding the following day. Then they were off to the Dandridge plantation to start their married life together out of view of the prying city eyes.

After the young couple left the city, Edward made his way to the Governor's Palace to present himself to the new Lieutenant Governor, Francis Fauquier. He had been expected and was shown into the parlor to the right of the entry hall where he waited. It wasn't long before the Governor's secretary came and ushered him upstairs to the Governor's private study immediately above the entry hall. Edward had spent many hours in this room, working with the previous Lieutenant Governor, his friend Robert Dinwiddie. The room hardly looked the same without the familiar furnishings.

As first meetings go, this was better than most. Governor Fauquier had met with Robert Dinwiddie when the two found themselves in London, one arriving and the other leaving, and evidently Robert Dinwiddie had highly recommended Edward to the new Governor as someone he could count on.

Their discussions were interrupted by a commotion on the Palace Green. As they looked out and saw a crowd forming around a rider, the Governor's secretary appeared and announced a message had arrived from General Forbes. Eager to learn the news but also fearing it could be bad news, the two men hesitated before opening the dispatch case.

"Colonel, you read it to me, if you will, and explain any of those military terms I find quite tiresome."

Edward looked the document over first, before saying, "I'm afraid there won't be any tiresome military terms today, Governor. The French have abandoned Fort Duquesne, blown up the works, and we are now in full control of the Forks of the Ohio!"

The crowd on the street had grown and started to celebrate news of the victory, firing off guns, shouting "Huzzah," and congratulating each other as if they had had a hand in the victory. Edward penned a short note to General Ligonier to append to the dispatch and the Governor wrote a more full account to the Prime Minister. Edward then took his leave and made his way through the crowd and back to the Dandridge house.

"Uncle Edward, isn't it wonderful?" Philip and Charles shouted before he was fully in the door. The boys were very excited and home early as the tutors at the College realized they could not compete with a victory over the French.

As they all sat down at Fanny Dandridge's table for dinner, they discussed what the family should do next.

"Well, I think you can all go home," offered Edward. "Save for the boys who must remain to finish their schooling and me, who General Amherst warned to remain 'available' to him." Looking to the back of the room, he added, "Even Aaron should go and see Betty. I can fend for myself here in the city." This brought a broad grin to Aaron's face.

"And we can start building real houses now, and stop living in the close confines of the fort," said a very excited Henry.

"While I doubt we've seen the last Indian raid, I think we will be sufficiently safe to do just that, Henry," Edward agreed.

Marie and Hannah had become rather quiet when Edward failed to include Marie in those to remain in Williamsburg. Turning to Lewis, she now asked her question plainly, "And should I go back as well?"

"Naturally," was Lewis's only response, not really answering Marie's unstated question but cutting off any further questions from her as he turned back to his brothers, who were busy talking of houses and locations for them.

The next day was spent gathering and preparing for the two week journey, probably longer with the women along. Finding Hannah sitting alone in the parlor, Edward joined her.

"So, you're not going along?"

"Ah, no, maybe after they have houses built and are better able to accommodate an unattached widow. I feel awkward staying here with Fanny, though the thought of returning to Boston is worse yet."

"I'm sure Fanny will appreciate the help. After all, there are still the boys to see to…"

A loud knocking at the front door interrupted their conversation and Edward went to find George Washington, still covered in mud and dust from the trail.

"Edward, I heard you were here and came right over to congratulate you on your victory at Fort Louisbourg."

"It was hardly my victory as much as Major General Amherst's and Brigadier General Wolfe's. But you're one to talk! You've taken Fort Duquesne!"

"Much like you, it was hardly my victory. You've heard of my election to the House?" Edward nodded. "I have come to resign my command, marry Martha, and remove to White House until I can make Mount Vernon ready for its new mistress."

Somewhat surprised at the eager agenda, Edward responded with a simple, "My, my, to do all that!"

After his family departed, the Twelve Night celebrations followed by George and Martha's wedding kept Edward occupied and not wanting for company. Just the opposite, it seemed he was in much demand with dinners or parties most every night. He escorted Fanny and Hannah to White House for the wedding, greatly disappointing Philip, who also wanted to attend but was left behind with Charles, who was indifferent.

Waiting for Edward at White House was a radiant Sarah Jewett Dandridge.

"Well, Missus Dandridge, it is so good to see you," Edward said, bowing deeply to his niece before sweeping her up into his arms. "You look as if marriage agrees with you. Are you truly happy?"

"Uncle Edward, I could hardly wait for you to arrive. I'm so glad you came. And, yes, I am happy, very happy with Bat." Sarah then took Edward's arm and throughout the ceremony, dinner, and ball, was constantly at his side, as Bat was at hers. While her marriage was a good one, she did so miss her family. Since her grandfather's death, she felt even closer to Edward. Not only had he saved her from the Shawnee, he was always ready with sound advice, just like her grandfather had been.

All too soon it was time for Edward to escort Fanny and Hannah back to Williamsburg. As Sarah rose up on her toes to kiss his cheek, Edward felt the wetness of her tears in spite of her smile. Truth be told, he missed her just as much. Like his father, family was what he valued most and he would have much preferred to have Sarah nearby. He sighed as he took his seat in the carriage, missing Sarah already.

To Hannah, Edward remained pleasant, friendly, yet at the same time distant. Rarely could she catch a private moment with him and when she did, he turned the discussion to the boys or the latest letter from Lewis before one thing or another interrupted. She saw her hopes of a better life with him fade more with each passing day until she gave up the hope all together. Even Marie's encouraging reply when Hannah shared this in a letter did nothing to restore her hopes. Now, resigned to a lonely widowhood, she started thinking of what she should do, where she should go, and came up with no answers.

Letter writing to his brothers occupied Edward when he was not keeping up on military news with the Governor or reading the Virginia Gazette as soon as it came off the presses. It was while sitting in the Raleigh Tavern just before the House of Burgesses was to convene, reading a still damp Gazette, that he was interrupted.

"Colonel, Colonel Jewett, I thought that was you when I was walking by. I'm Doctor Walker, Thomas Walker. You stopped by for some advice on your way to the Valley in, what was that, fifty-two?"

"Doctor Walker, it has been a while. Won't you join me?"

Thomas Walker had been a bit of an outcast since the death of Peter Jefferson nearly a year-and-a-half earlier. Many claimed it was Doctor Walker's doctoring of his friend and neighbor that caused the man's death. The Randolph family, one of the leading families in the Colony, had fairly shunned him after the death of their kinsman.

"I was hoping I'd run into you today. I want to interest you in a project of mine. Now, no need for you to make any commitments to me today, I just want you to hear me out and then think about what I'm saying before we meet at some later date to discuss particulars."

Doctor Walker then proceeded to explain to Edward how he had found the Warrior's Path through the mountains into a lush land beyond the Indians called "Kentucky." He had hoped to apply for a patent for a large tract of land there and sell off shares to families. Only, the war and trouble with the Shawnee had interrupted his plans. Now with the war all but won, he wanted to restart his little venture. Edward's reputation for having kept his portion of the Valley secure, even taking the fight to the Shawnee, made him the perfect partner, in Doctor Walker's estimation.

Edward promised he would give the plan some thought. When he returned to his rooms adjacent to the Dandridge house, he found a message asking him to call upon the Governor at his earliest convenience. Walking briskly to the Palace, he was led immediately up to the Governor's study where Governor Fauquier was sitting with more dispatches from England.

"Ah, there you are Edward. I'm afraid some news has come that concerns you. Sit and," handing over to Edward two sealed letters, "read these. I know the contents of the one, having been sent a copy by the Prime Minister."

The first one Edward opened was a letter labeled as being from "Major" General Wolfe. In it, the General advised Edward of Wolfe's selection to head an independent command to take Quebec and how the King had promoted him to Major General as a result. He then went on to say how the King had been reluctant to promote him and it had taken all of his and the Prime Minister's influence to manage it. Edward already anticipated what was to follow. The General went on to say how the King had refused to promote any Colonial officers to General in the

Regular Army, even one with such an outstanding record of Regular Army service as Edward's. General Wolfe went on to lament this would not allow him to place Edward as his second in command. It didn't come as a surprise nor was it a disappointment as he hadn't anticipated General Wolfe's efforts would succeed, no matter how much the General had assured him of success before they parted in Louisbourg.

The second letter did surprise Edward. It was from Lord Ligonier and advised Edward the King had placed him back on the retired list, expressed appreciation for his continued good service, and wished him well. While Edward did not expect a promotion, he also didn't expect to be summarily cast aside like this, just as another campaign was about to begin. He didn't know how to take this news, didn't know if it meant he had done something wrong in the eyes of the King.

"Edward, I see that second letter hit you pretty hard. That's why I wanted you here when you read it and didn't have it sent to you. I have a companion letter to that one, here, from the Prime Minister and in his own hand. After telling me of the King's decision to return you to the retired list, the King didn't want you to think your services had been unappreciated in any way. Here, look, the King authorized me to transfer to you fifty thousand acres of land in the Ohio country free from any restrictions. He's also sent along a gift of £5,000 sterling, a most generous gift."

The Governor rambled on a while longer, trying to ease Edward's mind and having only a mild effect. He even suggested Edward might want to look up Doctor Walker, participate in his Kentucky adventure, the Governor stating his own intention of investing. They then went on to review other military news and discuss strategy for the

House session about to begin. Edward left the Governor still reeling, feeling he had just been cashiered in spite of the King's generous gifts.

Meeting with the Burgesses while they were in session occupied Edward, as did the flurry of instructions he sent to Lewis and Henry concerning expanding farming on their Grant, building houses, and housing his indentured servants. After the House of Burgesses recessed, Edward remained busy, buying additional horses for his stables, occasionally visiting the Washingtons at Mount Vernon, and generally keeping his mind occupied. Try as he might to outwardly display a calm demeanor, those in the Dandridge house saw how hard the forced retirement was on him, the bitterness they saw in his unguarded moments, and they all tried to cheer him. One day, he learned Doctor Walker was back in the Capital, so he looked him up, finding him at the Raleigh Tavern.

"Doctor Walker, I've given your proposal some thought. I don't know if you realize it, but I have an interest in fifty thousand acres of the Ohio Country, which the Governor assures me includes your Kentucky should I choose to locate it there. I think I should like to help you with your venture, when you're ready to resume."

Doctor Walker became very excited about the prospect of not only having Edward's help, but now knowing there was a large piece of land already granted. All he needed to do was to somehow gain additional lands for himself and his other investors.

In late spring, at dinner one afternoon, Edward told Fanny Dandridge of his intention of remaining in Williamsburg only until Philip and Charles finished school for the session and then escorting them, along with the growing number of horses he currently had housed in her stables, back across the mountains where he likely would remain.

That evening, Hannah found Edward deep in thought in the garden behind the Dandridge house.

"Excuse me for intruding on your thoughts, Edward," she said hesitantly. "When you return home, what is to become of me?"

"Why, I'm sure I don't know what you mean, Missus Davies."

"Well, it's just that," pausing, not knowing whether or not to proceed, she continued with a sigh. "I don't really have a place in this world any longer. It would feel awkward remaining with Fanny after you leave, especially knowing I'm only here now because of your charity, although she has said she'd welcome the company. And I could hardly go with you and the boys, an unmarried widow and all. I just don't know what is to become of me." She turned toward Edward, her turmoil showing plainly on her upturned face.

Moving a step closer to her and taking both her hands in his, Edward cleared his throat. "Missus Davies, would you do me the honor…"

THE END

❧ About the Author ❧

Kenneth Jewett is a Colonel, recently retired from the US Air Force, and a lifelong student of history. He lives in rural Virginia.